SAND
CREEK

For David & Carol,

God bless you.

D.W.

Lindy

SAND CREEK

D. W. LINDEN

Intrigue Press | Madison

Published by Intrigue Press
923 Williamson St.
Madison, WI 53703

Published 2006

This is a work of fiction. Any similarities to people or places, living or dead, is purely coincidental.

ISBN 1-890768-68-5
Library of Congress Control Number: 2006921920

Jacket design: Peter Streicher
Cover photograph: Peter Streicher

Printed in the United States of America

First Printing

*To James O'Shea Wade for believing in me
and opening the essential doors.*

*To my wife Loretta, for believing in me
and pushing me through those doors.*

*To my daughter Jessica
for being an amazing person despite me.*

*To my family and friends for telling me
that I should be a writer
all those years I was being something else.*

*To my dog Hamlet
for being my little, hairy angel.*

*And to the people of southeast Colorado
for hanging tough with such warm hearts.*

CHAPTER 1

Sweat dripped from the end of his nose and added more stains to the leather glove on his left hand. It was October, but summer hadn't let up yet in Arizona. He was only half-aware of the announcer drawling his name from the tinny speakers. "Now folks, the 1990 Original Coors Rodeo Showdown has got a real treat for you—a real, live, Wild West deputy sheriff, John Hart . . ."

"Johnny! Johnny!"

Johnny looked up at the cowboy leaning down from the fence. The cowboy had a worried look on his face. Pointing down at Johnny's gloved hand, he said, "You've got that rope pretty snug. I've rode this bull before and, believe me, you don't want to stay on him one second longer than you have to."

"I know, Cody," Johnny nodded. "Dang this heat! My grip doesn't feel too strong today, that's all. It's all right." He wished his feelings matched his words.

Beneath him, the bull shifted and stretched its neck. Fear was natural, he told himself. Anyone who climbed astride a couple of thousand pounds of muscle and mean and wasn't afraid was just plain crazy. But it was worse tonight, he had to admit. It wasn't just the heat that made him sweat this way. In fact, there was an odd, icy chill in his knotted stomach.

Cody eased back off the rail, the frown still on his face. "You watch this ole bull, Johnny. He's a rank one. I've known him to twist and buck with the worst of 'em."

Johnny nodded, his gaze fixed once again on the mottled gray back of the bull.

The announcer was still talking to the crowd. "The Original Coors Rodeo Showdown is pleased to welcome this Colorado Cowboy to Scottsdale. Johnny's been a national finalist eight times and is having a real good year again. In chute number six, on Western Rodeo's White Lightning, from Eads, Colorado, Deputy John Hart!"

Johnny nodded at the gate man, who hollered "Outside!" as he slammed the latch back. Suddenly, the world receded. The noise of the crowd faded to a muffled murmur, and the only sound he was aware of was the breathing—his own and the bull's.

Concentrate, John, concentrate, he told himself. But from the very first jump, he knew something was wrong. The bull was mad as a hornet and focused on unseating the unwelcome human on his back. I can't get his rhythm, Johnny thought. I'm reacting too slowly. I'm sitting too far back and there's too much daylight between me and this damn bull.

White Lightning's front hooves slammed into the dirt of the arena like incoming mortar rounds, followed by a twist to the right that shook Johnny like a rat in a dog's mouth. With wide-eyed wonder, he felt himself flying off the left side of the bull. But instead of landing in the dirt, there was a sickening pop as his left shoulder dislocated. Only the heels of his boots dragged in the dirt. His left hand was still tightly wrapped in the rope.

"He's hung up!" the announcer exclaimed. The tourists in the stands jumped to their feet, horrified. The bull was now completely enraged by this cowboy who wouldn't leave but continued to flap against his side like a bird's broken wing.

Through a haze of pain, Johnny could see the bullfighters closing in, trying to distract the bull. To no avail. His body beat against the muscled side of the bull like a rag doll. Finally, there was a flash of color as one of the bullfighting clowns, long hair flying, leaped onto the back of the bull, balancing like a gymnast. He grappled with the rope. There was a shout of triumph from the spectators as the rope came free and Johnny slid into the dirt.

The clowns were slapping at the bull's face with their hats, but the animal would not be deterred. The taste of dust and pain gagged Johnny. Kneeling in the dust like a penitent, he watched in helpless wonder as the massive head lunged toward him. There was a roaring in his ears like thunder, then a heavy blanket of blackness covered all his senses.

⌃⌃⌃

Johnny was awake now, breathing heavily, beads of sweat along his upper lip. With a groan, he sat up and swung his feet over the edge of the bed. Reflexively, his hand went to his stomach, feeling the long scar. The produce crate that served as a bedside table held a clock radio that hissed with the sound of dead air. "It must be late," he mumbled. The Lamar radio station was off the air already. The light that was supposed to illuminate the clock had burned out a long time ago, so he peered closely at the numbers—2:32.

"Hope I can get back to sleep," he muttered. "I'm on duty early tomorrow." Light flickered through the plastic curtains at the window, followed later by the murmur of distant thunder.

Johnny reached for the bottle on the crate and upended it against his mouth. Only a few drops wet his lips.

Getting up from the bed, he padded barefoot across the worn rug onto the cool, cracked linoleum of the kitchen. Flicking the switch, he winced as the fluorescent light blinked and fluttered to life. The open cupboard revealed a jar of peanut butter, a half-empty box of cereal, and a dead cockroach, its legs in the air.

The refrigerator proved more rewarding. He pulled a can of beer from its cardboard container, popped the top, and took three swallows in a single fluid motion. Leaning back against the counter, he pressed the cold metal against his temple, closed his eyes, and sighed.

Three quick, hard knocks beat against the front door. "Must be the sheriff," he sighed. "Damn phone must be out again." Tiredly he crossed the tiny, darkened living room, swung the door open, and turned on the bare bulb of the front porch light.

"Hey, Cuz," said a deep voice. "Did I interrupt your breakfast?"

Johnny just stared. Smiling back at him stood a tall, handsome man, with long black hair tied back in a ponytail, and a stained, brown cowboy hat pulled down nearly to his eyebrows. The light glinted from his bronze face, and the beginnings of a smile moved at the corner of his mouth.

"It's good to see you too, Johnny." The visitor scuffed his cowboy boot against the doorsill and shook his head wryly. "That's one of the things I always admired about you. You don't talk too much, which is not what people always say about me."

"Char!" Johnny finally managed to say. "What the hell are you doing here?"

"Well, right now, I'm waiting to be invited in." Char looked over Hart's shoulder. "Unless, of course, you've got company or something."

"No, come on in." Johnny stood back and waved the visitor in with his beer can. "Can I get you one of these?"

Char had to take his hat off to fit through the doorway. "No, I quit drinking. Thanks, though." He dropped a canvas duffel bag on the floor by the door and followed Johnny into the kitchen. "But I am hungry. You got anything to eat?"

Johnny sank down onto the plastic cushion of the kitchen chair. "I don't think so." He took another couple of swallows and banged the empty can back down on the table. "You're welcome to eat whatever you can find." He didn't look at his visitor, but stared glumly at the floor. As Char opened the refrigerator door, Johnny said, "Toss me another beer."

Char stood in front of the open refrigerator. "Well, I see a carton of milk that I can smell from here. Some bread that looks like a piece of sod, it's so green. You trying to discover a new strain of penicillin or something? A bottle of Tabasco sauce! Things are looking up. And some potatoes," he reached forward to touch them, "that seem to be all right." Pulling four potatoes out, he looked toward the stove. "That thing work?"

Johnny shrugged, "I guess."

Char pulled a skillet out of the oven and found a knife in a drawer. Soon he was slicing potatoes into the sizzling shortening. After a long silence, he said, "I've got to tell you Johnny, you look like you've been rode hard and put up wet. Is the pain still bad?"

"Pain?" Johnny took a long swallow. "What pain?"

Char frowned, saying nothing as he stirred the frying food.

"That don't smell half bad," Johnny admitted.

"I made enough for the both of us." Char set the skillet down on a dishcloth on the table. Handing a fork to Johnny, he said, "I didn't see so much as a paper plate in here, so we're gonna have to cowboy it." Sitting down across from Johnny, Char splashed Tabasco sauce liberally across the food.

"Easy, there!" Johnny complained. "Too much of that'll give you an ulcer."

"Everybody's got to die from something," Char said, munching contentedly.

Johnny took a few bites and washed them down with beer, finally settling on the beer alone as Char ate.

"So, what are you doing here, Char?" Johnny asked, not sounding too interested.

"Oh, just gettin' on down the road."

"Ah," Johnny nodded. "Rodeo."

Char frowned. "Off and on. I'm not working as much the last few months. I've been trying to slow it down a little bit."

Johnny gave a bitter laugh. "Yeah, me too." He finished the can and leaned back to grab another from the refrigerator.

Char stared absently at the frying pan. "I must be getting old," he said quietly. "I've been doing a lot of thinking lately." He shifted his gaze to look intently at Hart. "You and me, we've been down a lot of roads, with nothing much to show for it, except some belt buckles and hospital bills. But it's not like we've changed the world or made much of a difference to anything. What do you think?"

Johnny's head rested on his chest, his legs stretched out in front of him. "What do I think?" He yawned. "At three in the morning, I think I'd better get some sleep. I'm on duty pretty early tomorrow—today, I guess it is."

Char blinked in momentary disappointment, but his smile returned quickly. "Yeah, you're right. I guess it is pretty late."

"You're welcome to bunk out on the couch, but I've got to warn you, with those old springs, the floor's likely more comfortable." He stood and stretched carefully, a small wince of pain crossing his face. "I'll try not to wake you when I get up."

"Thanks, Johnny. I'll see you in the morning."

Johnny nodded and shuffled back down the darkened hall to his bedroom. Tired as he was, he still didn't fall right to sleep. He lay for some time, staring up at the ceiling. "I ought to be gladder to see Char," he said to himself. Outside, he could hear the ceaseless drone of crickets. Distant thunder rumbled once again to the north.

The ringing of the phone woke him. Gray light filled the room. The clock read 5:30.

"Johnny?" a woman's voice said. "This is Kate."

"Yeah, Kate," he rubbed his hand over his face. "Good thing you called. I was about to oversleep."

"We had a call last night," Kate explained. "Sheriff said to let you go out on it this morning first thing, instead of coming in to the office."

Johnny sat up. "What's up?"

"You know where the L-S Ranch is, up north of Brandon?"

"The Cross place? Yeah, I know it."

"Well, they called last night and said that somebody's been driving around out there after dark. Some fences have been cut. Could be just kids out sparking, but, then, it could be rustlers too."

"Hamburger helpers," Johnny yawned. "Okay, Kate, I'll go check it out. See you later."

Putting on his boots, Johnny quietly opened the door of his bedroom. Tucking his uniform shirt into his jeans, he was surprised to find no one in the living room. A movement through the grimy front window caught his eye. Char was standing out in front of the house with his head thrown back and his arms opened wide. Dawn light shone on his prominent cheekbones.

The squeak of the front door caused him to drop his arms and turn quickly around. "Hey, Johnny."

Johnny looked puzzled. "What are you doing out here?"

Char gave a brief, embarrassed smile, looking away toward the rising sun. "I was praying," he said softly.

Ordinarily, Johnny would have laughed and said something crude, but something about Char's expression made him simply nod. "Look, Char, I've got to go out on a call. I guess there're some more potatoes if you're hungry."

"If it's all right, why don't I ride along with you?" Char suggested, walking back toward the house. "It'd be my chance to see a real-live, Wild West deputy sheriff in action."

"Very funny." Johnny didn't really want him along, but he said, "I guess it wouldn't hurt."

As they walked across the weedy front yard, Char looked at the house. "I guess they don't pay their lawmen much around here, huh? I've seen nicer places on reservations."

Johnny climbed in and slammed the door of his pickup, scowling at Char. "You just say whatever the hell is on your mind, don't you?" He started the truck and gunned the engine a couple of times. Glancing past Char to the house, he had to admit it was a dump—clapboard and peeling paint and a roof that should have been replaced years ago. "There's not that many places to rent in a town this small," he explained. "Besides, I've got child support to pay."

"Have you seen Barb and the kids lately?"

"No, not lately." He put the truck in gear and pulled away faster than necessary.

"The Sheriff's Department doesn't give you an official police car?" Char asked, shifting the debris of old paper coffee cups and fast food wrappers off the worn vinyl truck seat.

"Sometimes," Johnny said as he rolled down his window. "The Department's pretty strapped, though, so they give me a radio, a bubble light and thirty cents a mile to use my own vehicle. It's cheaper for them than buying a whole new car."

Highway 96 stretched directly into the rising sun. The two men pulled their hats low to shade their eyes. There was almost no other traffic on the road. There never was. Kiowa County, Colorado, was home to far more cows than people. Crows and hawks were busy cleaning up the nightly roadkills, barely stirring themselves as the pickup sped by. The police band radio crackled with occasional bursts of static and desultory reports.

Johnny was more awake now, and inclined to be more sociable. "How did you get here, Char? I didn't see a car or a truck or anything."

Char was fiddling with the truck's radio. Landing on a country song, he leaned back. "Somebody stole my truck a while back in Denver, and I haven't had much money lately to replace it. So I hitched a ride with a trucker hauling cows."

"Probably stolen, too," Johnny snorted. "Where did you say you were heading?"

Char grinned. "To see you," he said, casting a sidelong glance to see Johnny's reaction.

"Me?" Johnny took his eyes off the road to frown at Char. "What did you want to see me about?"

"Well, that's kind of a long story," Char said.

"Everything's a long story with you."

Char nodded. "That's true. But like I said last night, I've been doing a lot of thinking lately and needed to talk to somebody."

"Why me?"

"Well, 'cause we've put in a lot of miles together, you and me," Char explained. "Besides," he laughed, "we're kin."

"So you say." The town of Chivington came and went in less than a minute. "Just because I've got relatives in Oklahoma, doesn't make us kin."

"Tahlequah, Oklahoma," Char specified. "It's not that big a place. Yes, sir, you're an Indian, all right. You just aren't ready to admit it yet, that's all."

Johnny sighed and shook his head. "So, what was it you wanted to talk about?"

Char turned in his seat to look more directly at Johnny. "I guess being Indian is part of what I wanted to talk to you about. What does that mean really, to anybody but a redneck or an anthropologist? Shoot, forget the Indian part, what does it mean to be a human being?"

"Aren't you a little old for this identity crisis stuff?" Johnny asked. "I mean, you're a cowboy, for Christ's sake, who happens to be an Indian."

Char shook his head, unsatisfied. "No, Johnny, there's more to it than that, and you know it." He turned back straight on the seat, resting his elbow on the windowsill. "I just thought, with all that time you spent in the hospital, maybe you might have gotten some insights."

"Insights?" Johnny laughed. "All I got out of that hospital was a bunch of stitches and a humongous bill that I'm still fighting my insurance company over."

He slowed, but not much, to turn off the highway at Brandon. The metal bars of the cattle guard hummed as they headed north onto the unpaved road. The sun was fully risen and the air beginning to warm. Meadowlarks twittered and flashed in the golden grasses that stretched away on either side of the road.

"This sure is pretty country," Char observed. "It makes you feel small and large all at the same time."

They drove in silence for a few miles, the dust plume rising and falling behind them like a squirrel's tail.

"Look, Char," Johnny's tone was softer. "I don't mean to make light of what you're thinking about. It's just that right now, my life is not what you'd call real together. You know what I mean?"

Char nodded and smiled. "It's all right. It's just me. Like they say, 'Too soon old, too late smart.'" He punched Johnny lightly on the shoulder. "It's good to see you again though, hoss."

Johnny smiled. "Yeah." For the first time, he felt glad to see Char as well.

Two old wagon wheels and a faded sign framed the entrance to the L-S Ranch. Another cattle guard led to another, rougher, dirt road. The ridge in the middle was so high that only a full-sized truck could avoid scraping it. Johnny drove more slowly as they topped a small rise. A hundred yards ahead lay a cluster of cottonwood trees, looking cool and spring green. Beneath their shade stood the house. Part rock, part adobe, and part wood, it looked like a collection of orphaned rooms that had been abandoned by other homes and now huddled together for support. A splintered barn and corral stood at one end of the yard and a mechanical graveyard cluttered the other.

A pair of skinny legs clad in blue jeans and worn boots dangled from the open hood of a twenty year old Ford pickup truck. Johnny pulled his truck to a stop and stepped out into the morning stillness. The only sound was the ticking of his cooling engine and a stream of muffled curses rising from the gaping maw of the old truck. An Australian blue heeler cattle dog watched him warily with one blue and one brown eye from the shade of the truck.

Johnny walked toward the vehicle. "Mr. Cross?"

"Dad-blasted, spavin-gaited, no-good rust breeder!" A thin weathered face rose up from the engine, a battered cowboy hat pushed to the back of his head. "Who the hell are you?" The old man fixed a cold, blue eye on Hart. "Easy, Lady," he added, glancing quickly at the dog. Lady returned the look, shook her brown and black fur, and settled back onto the ground, tongue lolling.

Johnny tugged at his hat brim, feeling like a kid caught in some mischief. "I'm Deputy Hart. You reported some trouble here last night?"

"Last night is right!" The old man turned to face Johnny, wiping his hands on a flowered red bandanna. "And here you come, it's full sun morning! Damn good thing we wasn't bein' murdered out here!"

Johnny pushed his hat back on his head and glanced toward Char, lifting an eyebrow, before looking back at Mr. Cross. "Well, the dispatcher only just called me on it thirty minutes ago."

Mr. Cross snorted. "That figures! I guess they felt you needed your beauty sleep." Looking Johnny up and down, he added, "It appears they woke you up too early for that. You look like forty miles of bad road!"

Johnny sighed and pulled a small spiral note pad and a pen from his shirt pocket. "What was the trouble, Mr. Cross?"

Mr. Cross was not to be distracted. "Trouble? What the hell could you do about it? You don't even have a gun on you!" He shook his head in disgust. "Guts and gunpowder's what built this country and here you come, a deputy sheriff armed with nothing more than a pen and some paper. I swear!" He didn't, though. He just shook his head and said sadly to himself, "Helluva thing!"

"You making this visitor welcome, Grandpa?" Johnny turned to see a young woman leading a horse out of the shadows of the barn.

"Welcome." Mr. Cross said flatly. "Sure. This here lawman's the Lone Ranger." He waved his hand at Johnny dismissively.

"I'm Sandy Cross." She led the horse over to Johnny, smiled, and stuck out her hand. Johnny shook it, surprised at how small and how callused it was.

"Deputy John Hart." He gave a tug on his hat brim.

The smile faded quickly from her face. "Oh," she said. "You're the deputy who rodeos, huh?"

"Yes, ma'am." Johnny usually felt gratified when people recognized him, but he could tell that the woman was not pleased. In fact, she seemed positively disappointed.

Sandy Cross couldn't have been more than five feet tall on a good day. She had her grandfather's pale blue eyes set in a smooth, sunburned face. Long blonde hair, sunbleached to the color of straw, streamed from beneath her battered cowboy hat and was tied back in a ponytail. Scuffed old boots, faded jeans, and a man's frayed work shirt would never fool anyone into thinking that the wearer was not a woman.

Rubbing the horse's forelock, she asked, "Do you know anything about horses, Deputy Hart?"

Johnny smiled and tried to brag. "Just broncs, ma'am."

Sandy shook her head in faintly concealed disgust. "Well, come on in," she said, leading the horse past Johnny, who had to back out of the way to keep from getting stepped on.

He stood for a moment, confused by her open hostility, then shrugged, glanced at Mr. Cross, who was glaring back at him, and followed the horse.

As Sandy went by the window of Johnny's truck, she was startled by Char's deep voice. "Thrush," he said.

"What? Oh, I didn't see that there was somebody with you, Deputy." She squinted in the sunlight as Char opened the truck door, stepped out, and towered over her.

"This is a friend of mine," Johnny introduced, "Char—Charles Sixkiller."

Char touched the brim of his hat in greeting. "Thrush," he repeated. "You must have a boggy spot in the barn from the wet winter we had. Your horse is favoring her left hind foot. Most likely it's thrush."

Sandy shaded her eyes to see Char better. "Well, Mr. Sixkiller, you do seem to know more about horses than your friend here. Yes, I agree. I think it is thrush. I was just going to turn Feather out on dry ground for a while."

Char shook his head. "It'll take more than that, I'm afraid. She at least needs to be reshod."

Sandy smiled. "Are you a farrier as well as a veterinarian? I am impressed. I'd offer you a job, if I had any money, but I can at least offer you a cup of coffee too."

"Well, if Johnny here's not in a hurry, I'll be glad to shoe her while he makes out his report or whatever he does."

Sandy looked surprised. "That's real nice of you. I admit I'm not really handy when it comes to shoeing horses. Deputy?" she turned to Johnny.

Johnny looked uncomfortable. "How long will it take, Char?" He wanted to be gone as quickly as possible. The Cross family did not appear to be fans of Johnny Hart.

"Not too long," Char shrugged. "I should clean and trim the hoof. Fifteen, twenty minutes."

"Sure," Johnny nodded. "That's fine."

"Grandpa," Sandy said, "why don't you show Mr. Sixkiller where the tools are." With a winning smile, she handed the halter rope to Char.

Mr. Cross frowned and cocked his head, signaling Char to follow him. "Used to be I could shoe a dozen horses before breakfast. Course, that was before the damned arthritis set in on me." He wobbled stiffly across the pebbly yard of hard packed bare earth toward the barn as Char and Feather followed quietly.

"I like your friend, Deputy." She headed toward the house without waiting for a response from Johnny. "Is he an Indian?" she asked over her shoulder.

"Yeah," he answered. "Cherokee or something."

"An anthropologist as well as a cowboy! Wonders never cease!" she said sarcastically as she opened the door and gestured for Johnny to enter.

Johnny stepped inside and turned to face Sandy, finally allowing his annoyance to show. "Look, Miss Cross, I don't know what I did to rub you the wrong way. You called in some kind of disturbance last night. I just came out to take a report. Now, I'll do that as quickly as I can and get out of here."

Sandy's lips compressed into a straight line. She nodded. "I'm sorry. I have been rude. I just have very little patience for grown men who only spend eight seconds in the saddle and call themselves cowboys. Please, sit down." She waved toward the straight-backed wooden chairs that surrounded a scarred old kitchen table.

Johnny sat down, placing his pad and pen on the table. Sandy took down two stained porcelain cups from the cupboard with one hand and, using a dishtowel, grabbed a metal coffee pot from the back burner of the stove. Clunking the cups down on the table, she filled both and carried one over to the sink where she stood, leaning her hip on the counter's edge.

Johnny nodded his thanks, picked up his cup and nearly choked on the strong black liquid.

Sandy took a sip and smiled sweetly. "Most people use way too much water to make coffee, don't you think?"

"I'll just let it cool off a bit," Johnny said. Taking his hat off, he placed it upside down on the chair next to him. "Now, about last night's disturbance."

"Last night was the first time I called." Sandy's cup clattered as she placed it on the counter too hard. "There've been other incidents."

"Exactly what kind of disturbance are we talking about, Miss Cross?"

She paused a moment to consider her response. "In the last week, I've found signs of trespassers nearly every day—gates left open, fences cut, that sort of thing. But last night I was riding in from fixing a stretch of fence and saw this." Sandy opened the cupboard and pulled an object from beneath the sink. She placed it on the table. "It was sitting in the middle of the road on the ridge up there." She gestured toward the rise over which they had entered. "Right in the middle, like someone wanted to be sure I saw it."

Johnny studied the object. It was the white painted skull of an animal with two horns. "Why?" he asked, looking up.

She only shrugged.

"Was there anything else with it, a note, anything?" he asked.

"No," she answered. "Nothing. Just this, sitting there."

"Did you or your grandpa hear anything? A car or a truck?"

Sandy shook her head. "No. I was at least a mile south of here working on the fence, and Grandpa was moving some cows to a new range closer to the creek. He doesn't hear so well anymore, anyway."

Johnny took a handkerchief from his pocket to pick up the skull and study it. "Did anybody besides you handle this thing?" he asked.

A surprised look came to her face. "Oh! Fingerprints, huh?" She shook her head. "No, just me. I didn't even tell Grandpa about it. It's a little too weird."

"It appears to be white paint on it," Johnny mused. "No telling how old it is. Couldn't have just fallen off somebody's truck?"

She gave him a pitying look. "This is not the kind of thing most folks carry around with them, unless they're Georgia O'Keeffe. Besides, that was sitting there in the middle of the road, like somebody put it there. We don't get many visitors anyway."

"Well," Johnny shook his head, perplexed. "I'll take it with me and see if the Sheriff wants to dust it and send the prints off to the CBI for a match-up. I'll be honest with you, though," he said looking embarrassed. "He may not want to go to the time and expense, just for a simple trespassing, what with budget restrictions and everything."

"You do what you have to, Deputy," Sandy said coldly. "I'm not given to hysteria. But I don't like trespassers. I have a rifle, which I know how to use, and I know my rights. If the Sheriff's Department can't help us, we'll do it ourselves. I'm used to that."

Her bitter tone surprised Johnny. "We'll do what we can, Miss Cross. I'll talk to the Sheriff and see if we can't increase the patrols out here for the next few days."

Her expression softened to a smile. "Thanks, Deputy." Pointing at his cup, she asked, "More coffee?"

"No, thank you." He placed his hand over the cup. "This should be cool enough to drink now."

ᐱᐱᐱ

The barn was cool and dark, with the clean, sharp smell of alfalfa and manure. Swallows darted among the shadowed rafters and three other horses watched curiously from their stalls as Mr. Cross led Char and Feather to the workbench set up to the left of the entrance.

"The tools should all be there," Mr. Cross waved toward the bench. "Course, you might have to look for them. I haven't touched 'em in a long time."

Char tied Feather to a ring screwed into the wall and began rummaging through the things piled on and under the old wooden bench. "It's been a while since I've done any shoeing myself," he said. "But I always kind of enjoyed tending to stock. Except when you get an ornery jughead that wants to kick your head off." Tools in hand, he stepped up to Feather and scratched her jaw. "But you don't look like a jughead to me. No, you're going to be a real lady, aren't you?" In response, Feather stretched her neck to invite more attention.

Mr. Cross gave a wheezy little laugh. "Ol Feather there, she's real easy. Sandy's had her since she was a foal. Must be twelve, fifteen years ago." He shook his head in wonder at the passage of time. "Her daddy gave her to her for her eighteenth birthday."

Char leaned his shoulder against Feather's hindquarter and picked up her foot. Cleaning the mud out, he used the hammer and cutters to cut the clinches. "Her folks aren't around today?" he asked.

Mr. Cross turned away as if to study something across the yard. "No. My boy and his wife—Sandy's parents—they were killed in a car accident that same year."

"I'm sorry." Char glanced at the old man's back as if to see his feelings. "That must have been hard on her—on both of you."

"Yup, well," Mr. Cross turned back and took his hat off to wipe his face with his sleeve, although the morning was cool. "Life's hard, period. Billy—that was my boy's name, Bill—he was kind of a damn fool anyway. Never did want to grow up. But it was a damn shame he had to get that pretty little wife of his killed, too. Sandy—her name was Sandy, too—she was just the sweetest thing! I always hoped she'd drain some of the wild out of my boy. She tried, bless her heart, but he still kept chasin' them belt buckles. 'Got to be gettin' on down the road' he'd say." An old anger crept into his voice.

"He rodeoed?" Char asked, pausing in his work of pulling off the shoe.

"Rodeo!" the old man spat. "As if we didn't have enough cows and horses right here!"

Char wrinkled his nose, looking away from the hoof. "Whew, it's thrush, all right! It's got the smell and that black stuff oozing out." He pointed toward the hoof, as much to change the subject as to prove his theory.

Mr. Cross came over and squinted at the hoof. "Yep, thrush." He looked at Char, studying him. "You seem to know a thing or two about horses. You Mexican? Mexicans all seem to got a way with horses."

Char put the hoof down and straightened up. "No," he answered, "Indian." He walked off down the barn, looking into the stalls.

"Indian, huh?" Mr. Cross considered the information. "Don't get many Indians around here."

"These stalls all need to be mucked out," Char called from the back of the barn. "That's what causes the thrush—wet straw, old manure."

"I know that," Mr. Cross said, slightly annoyed. "But it's just me and Sandy working this place these days. Me, I got my arthritis cripplin' me up half the time and she's just a bitty little thing tryin' to do the work of a whole crew."

Char walked back down the barn, took his hat off and scratched his head. "If I had the time, I'd help out here, but I'm just hitching a ride with Johnny—I mean, the deputy." He thought for a minute then shrugged. "Well, let me get the rest of those shoes off. Feather's going to need to have her hooves trimmed first thing, before any new shoes go back on."

Char was working, Mr. Cross was talking, and the dog, Lady, was trying to sleep when Johnny and Sandy returned. "You about done, Char?" Johnny asked.

"Just now," Char answered, placing the hoof down and patting Feather's flank.

Sandy moved to the horse's head and kissed her nose. "New shoes, Feather!" she said. "Every woman feels better with new shoes."

Char adjusted his hat and looked down the length of the barn. "Lot of work needs doing around here, ma'am."

"I know," Sandy acknowledged quietly. "All we can do is do all we can," she shrugged. "And maybe the good Lord will keep sending nice people like you to help out from time to time."

"Well," Johnny said, clearing his throat. "We've got to get going, Char."

"Sure thing, Johnny." Char tugged the brim of this hat toward Sandy. Nodding to Mr. Cross, he said, "You take care now, Mr. Cross."

"I'm too old to care," Mr. Cross grumped, "and all I can do is take it."

Johnny and Char walked to the truck. Climbing in the passenger side, Char asked, "What ya got here, hoss? Looks like an antelope skull somebody painted!" He picked it up from the front seat to examine it more closely.

"Don't touch it!" Johnny snapped, too late.

Carefully, Char put the skull down. "Sorry, Johnny," he said sheepishly. "Evidence, huh?"

"Maybe." Johnny slammed the truck door closed. He sat for a moment staring through the dirty windshield. "Oh, the hell with it," he sighed, starting up the truck. He spun the tires in the dusty yard as he sped away.

They rode together in silence, bouncing on the rutted ranch road. Turning onto the smoother county road, Char asked, "So, is there any kind of a problem back there?" He jerked his thumb back in the direction they had just come.

"No, not really. Probably just some kids pulling pranks."

There was more silence in the truck while the tires growled on the dirt road outside. When they reached the pavement, Char said, "She is pretty," and cast a sidelong glance at Johnny.

"Hmph," Johnny responded. "Pretty ornery, if you ask me."

Char turned in the seat. "She didn't half care for you, now, did she?"

Johnny scowled back at him. "Not that I care, but she seems to have something against rodeo."

"Oh," Char nodded. "Her granddad was telling me, her father used to rodeo. He and her mom got killed in a car accident going down that road."

Johnny nodded. "That might explain it."

The radio crackled. "Unit Seven, this is base. Acknowledge. Over."

Johnny picked up the microphone and pushed the button. "This is Unit Seven. Go ahead, base."

"What is your 10-20, Unit Seven? Over."

"I've just left the L-S and I'm now about a mile west of Chivington. Over."

"Johnny, Sheriff Carter wants you to come on in. Over."

"Okay, Kate. I'm on my way. Unit Seven, out." To Char, he said, "I'd better drop you off at the house. I'm not supposed to be giving tours to civilians."

"No problem. I could use a couple more hours of sleep, anyway." Char yawned.

"I hear that," Johnny agreed, rubbing his eyes. With a smile at Char, he said, "Little Miss Cross didn't much care for me, but she sure seemed to shine for you."

"Well, of course," Char explained, poker faced. "I'm twice the man you are, hoss."

Johnny laughed. "I ought to make you walk, then see how much of a man you are after fifteen miles in cowboy boots."

"No problem," Char replied. "With my good looks, some pretty lady would stop to give me a ride before I walked a hundred yards."

"Shoot, Char, you'd stand a better chance if you put your clown makeup on first." They both laughed.

Pulling up at his house, Johnny said, "I didn't lock the door. Go ahead and make yourself at home. I'll see you later."

Char climbed out and gave Johnny a wave as he pulled away. As he drove, Johnny reached over and fumbled in the glove compartment, eventually finding a comb and a pack of chewing gum. Pulling up in front of the sheriff's office, he quickly brought some order to his hair and popped the stick of gum in his mouth.

A middle-aged woman with an elaborate, bleached-blonde hairdo and a too-tight uniform winked at him as he walked past the dispatcher's switchboard.

"Go ahead in, Johnny," she said.

"Thanks, Kate." Johnny knocked on the open door anyway before walking in and slumping into a rickety wooden chair in front of a battered desk. Johnny was always impressed at how neat and organized the sheriff's desk was. Sheriff B. J. Carter was impressive in many ways. A career military man, he'd run for sheriff after retiring from the Army.

Sheriff Carter was seated behind the desk, the phone to his ear. He was a big man, well over six feet tall and built like a professional linebacker. His hair was mostly gray and still kept as short as a new recruit. His uniform shirt was ironed and tucked with the precision that pleases boot camp drill instructors. He exuded energy like the sizzle on a frying hamburger.

"All right then, I'll get back with you." He hung up the phone and aimed his gray eyes at Johnny. "Deputy Hart, this county cannot afford to protect the people of this county the way we used to, but neither can we afford to let the people think that we can't protect them like we used to, if you understand my meaning."

Johnny sat up a little straighter in the chair.

"Now, I had a call from Miss Cross after you left, saying that you showed up unarmed and hung over." He held up his hand to forestall any comment. "She didn't call to complain. Actually, I've been somewhat concerned about your performance lately, so I asked a few questions about your conduct on this morning's call. She simply told the truth." Carter studied Johnny dispassionately for a moment. "I see you are still without your weapon and in need of a shave."

In spite of himself, Johnny blushed, feeling like a schoolboy who'd forgotten his homework.

"Miss Cross was hoping to get your home telephone number. It seems she would like to get in touch with a friend of yours. I explained to her that it is the policy of this department not to give out such information." The sheriff leaned back in his chair with a sigh. "It's not my place to pry into your personal life, Deputy, but your professional life is my concern. Frankly, I am very concerned." He paused to give Johnny a chance to say something.

Johnny was quiet for a long time. In fact, he couldn't think of anything to say. He knew he was a mess, but he really didn't care. With the sheriff staring at him, though, he felt like he ought to say something. "I'm working things out, Sheriff. It won't be a problem."

Sheriff Carter looked slightly disappointed, but nodded and said, "Good."

Leaning forward he picked up a couple of sheets of paper and placed them on the desk in front of Johnny. "I need you to drive a prisoner over to La Junta today. They've got a warrant and we've got the suspect. He's got a date in court over there tomorrow."

Johnny picked up the forms and scanned them. "What's the charge on this guy?"

"We've got him for burglary. It appears to be a career choice, so I assume that's what Otero County wants him for, too," Carter explained.

Johnny nodded. "Am I bringing anything back from La Junta? Or anybody?"

"No, but make sure that Sheriff Franklin signs that second sheet. They need to pay for this trip, not us." Sheriff Carter pulled a yellow notepad toward him. "So, what did you find out at the Cross place?"

"Cut fences, tire tracks, headlights after dark, that sort of thing. No cattle missing, yet. And Sandy Cross found this." He reached into the paper bag at his feet and, with a handkerchief, lifted the white skull out and placed it on the desk. "It appears to be an antelope skull. It was just sitting square in the middle of their road yesterday. She thinks someone wanted her to find it, but she doesn't know why or who?"

Carter frowned at it. "Anything else with it?"

"Nope."

"Well, stick it in the evidence locker. I suppose if anything more serious happens out there, we could always dust it for prints." Carter reached for the phone and began to dial, dismissing Johnny with, "You can use Unit Three, and be sure to get a receipt if you buy lunch over there. Otero County's paying for that too."

Johnny stood and let himself out.

"Sheriff chewed your butt a little, eh, cowboy?" Kate asked in a low voice.

"I wouldn't call it chewing," Johnny clarified. "Just nibbled a little."

Kate looked up from her dispatcher's seat and smiled. "You do look like hell warmed over, Johnny," she said matter-of-factly. "What you need is to let some good woman straighten your life out. And I," she arched her eyebrows suggestively, "am good, if you know what I mean."

Johnny walked slowly over to her desk and leaned forward intimately. "Now, Kate, I'm sure you're just too much woman for me," he whispered. "Everybody knows there's some broncs can't be rode."

Kate squealed with delighted laughter, slapping his hand on the desk. "Get out of here, Deputy! We both have work to do."

Johnny smiled. "Give me the keys to car three, okay?" She took them from a pegboard and handed them to him. "Is the tank full?"

"Full and ready," she said, adding with a wink, "like me."

Johnny laughed as he headed down the hall to the holding cells. The jailer signed custody over to him and accompanied the prisoner out to the parking lot as Johnny placed him into the back of the patrol car.

As Johnny slid in behind the steering wheel and started the engine, the prisoner, a sharp featured little man with long, greasy hair, leaned forward. "You're that rodeo cowboy, ain't ya?" he asked through the wire mesh. Without waiting for an answer, he went on. "I saw you a couple years back in Pueblo at the State Fair. You had some good rides. I'll bet you won a bunch of money, huh?"

Johnny shook his head, muttering to himself, "I finally meet a fan!" He glanced at the clipboard on the seat beside him to read the prisoner's name. "Cecil, do me a favor. If you don't talk to me, I promise not to beat you senseless on the drive over. Do we have a deal?"

Cecil sat back in the seat with a scowl.

"I'll take that for a yes," Johnny said, putting the car in gear.

CHAPTER 2

"J ohn! Good to see you." Sheriff Tom Franklin strode forward and shook Hart's hand, a broad smile spread beneath his bushy mustache. Johnny couldn't remember ever seeing Franklin without his cowboy hat on, indoors or out.

"Tom," Johnny nodded. "How's business?"

"Good enough that I'll probably get reelected," Franklin laughed, slapping Johnny on his bad shoulder.

Johnny signed the prisoner over to Joe Potts, the jailer. Joe had been a deputy since the Depression, when southeast Colorado had had more than its share of bank robbers and desperadoes. Joe had lost his left hand to a shotgun in a shootout and had been assigned to feeding and keeping the prisoners ever since. He always dressed in full uniform, with a white cowboy hat on his bald head and a black glove on his wooden hand.

"He's all yours, Joe," Johnny said. "Nice talking to you, Cecil."

Cecil cast a dark look at Johnny as he was led away.

"Did you have lunch yet, John?" the sheriff asked.

"Are you buying?" Johnny asked. "Sheriff Carter was real specific about that."

Franklin laughed. "He would be. Actually, I'm supposed to meet the mayor over at the Capri to talk politics. I'll get him to pay for the both of us."

Johnny drove the few blocks over to the Capri, a motel and restaurant on the east end of town. After the morning stillness, spring breezes were starting to blow grit around the parking lot as he pulled in next to the mayor's huge old Cadillac.

Johnny ducked into the men's room to clean up before entering the dining room. Spotting the sheriff and mayor, he started across the room but stopped halfway and turned at the sound of a woman's laugh. Seated at a table near him were an Anglo man, sporting a coat and tie, and a Hispanic woman nicely dressed in a business suit. The man was leaning forward, his smooth, clean-shaven face smiling at the woman, his hand resting on the sleeve of her coat. The woman had a napkin to her lips as if to suppress her amusement at his comments.

Johnny paused for a moment of indecision, then stepped over to the table. "Hey, Barb. How are you?"

"Johnny!" A succession of emotions flitted across her face. "What . . . ? Fine!" Her expression finally settled on slightly annoyed. "What are you doing in La Junta?"

Johnny fidgeted with the brim of the hat in his hands. "I had to deliver a prisoner." He didn't know what more to say. "You look real good, Barb."

"You don't." She frowned at him. "I guess I shouldn't ask."

The man at the table stood to his feet, smiled, and offered his hand. "Hi, I'm Alex Morgan."

Johnny seemed startled by the man's presence, but shook his hand, mumbling, "John Hart."

"I'm sorry," Barbara said, flustered. "Alex, this is Deputy John Hart, my husband. I mean, my ex-husband. Johnny, this is Alex Morgan. He's an assistant district attorney here." She paused. "We work together."

Morgan waved to an empty chair, his smile still firmly in place. "Why don't you join us? Bar and I tend to talk shop too much when it's just us. We could use some diversion."

Johnny suddenly had a pounding headache. "Ah, no," he stammered. "The sheriff—" he waved toward the booth where Franklin and the mayor were watching him curiously. "Maybe . . ." He looked at Barbara, feeling foolish. "I've got to go."

Abruptly, he turned away, walking stiffly past the sheriff and mayor and out of the restaurant.

He sat in the patrol car, his hands tightly gripping the steering wheel, staring at nothing through the dirty windshield. After a moment, he pounded the dashboard once with his fist. "Dammit!" He pulled away with a spray of gravel, not looking in the rearview mirror, not seeing the woman standing in the entrance of the Capri.

Barbara stood behind the glass doors and watched as Johnny pulled out of the parking lot. She'd resisted the urge to step outside and wave before he left. Now he was gone and her hand was tightly gripping the door's metal handle.

"Everything all right, Mrs. Hart?"

Barbara turned, startled. "Sheriff Franklin! Yes, I'm fine, thank you." With a brief smile, she started back toward the dining room.

"He doesn't look so good these days, does he?" Franklin asked, looking past her toward the parking lot.

She stopped. "No, he doesn't," Barbara agreed.

"Yes, sir," Franklin sighed, rubbing his chin. "Since you left him, it looks like he just can't find his feet." He shook his head sadly.

Barbara's eyes flashed. "Not that it's any of your business Tom, but Johnny was never really there for me to leave him." She stepped closer, hand on hip. "I had kids to raise and he had bulls to ride. End of story." She turned away, but stopped at the entry to the restaurant to add, "You're the one that fired him from your department."

Franklin frowned. "Now, Barbara, Johnny had a better offer from Kiowa County, that's all."

Barbara gave a short laugh. "If Johnny could have quit the bulls and the broncs, he'd have been the sheriff of this county and you know it Tom. When he was a national finalist you used that to help get yourself elected, but once he started finishing out of the money, you got rid of him."

"Some folks say the same about you, Barbara." There was ice in the sheriff's voice. "A man needs his woman to stand by him when the times are hard."

"And what about his friends?" Barbara snapped. Stiffly, she walked back into the dining room. Alex stood as she came to the table, holding her chair as she sat.

"Are you okay, Bar?" he asked.

"Fine," she nodded, picking at her salad as if the lettuce might conceal a snake.

"So that was your ex!" Alex leaned back in his chair, fingering his suspenders. "I can see why you dumped him. He's barely housebroken, from the looks of things."

Barbara laid her fork down. "Johnny just got out of the hospital a couple of months ago. He almost died," she stated quietly.

"Oh," Alex said in a more subdued tone, eyeing her curiously but saying no more.

She folded her napkin on the table. "We'd better get back to the office. I've got a motion in limine this afternoon and I need to go over the file."

"Sure, Bar, sure," Morgan said in a soothing voice. "I'll just go take care of the check." He rose and left.

Barbara sat frowning at the table for a minute before rising and leaving.

ᴧᴧᴧ

Heading east on Highway 50, Johnny hadn't gone far when he saw the electric sign blinking from above the doorway of Pedro's along the access road. He pulled off into the dirt parking lot and stopped next to a half-full cattle truck.

The noonday sky was a bright blue enamel, but the bar's interior was midnight dark, only dimly illuminated by the beer signs and the jukebox. Johnny sat on a stool near the end of the bar and leaned his head against the palms of his hands.

"John?" a Mexican accented voice asked. "It has been much time since I have seen you."

"How are you, Pedro?" Johnny greeted, shaking hands with the bartender. "Do me a favor, though, Pedro, and don't tell me how bad I look. I've heard. I need a beer."

"Sure, John, sure!" Pedro said, placing a glass beneath the tap.

"So how's business?" Johnny asked, surveying the nearly empty room. A dozen tiny tables, a small dance floor and a bandstand behind a chicken wire screen was all there was to Pedro's Cantina. A map of Mexico decorated one wall, flanked by a cheap serape and an embroidered sombrero; otherwise, the room was merely unpainted wood floor and walls. Two men sat at one table in the corner, their hands resting on the dewy necks of their beer bottles, their dark eyes covertly examining the lawman slumped at the bar.

Pedro shrugged. "Not so bad, at night. I have a band that comes in on the weekend. They play Tejano music."

"That's good, that's good," Johnny said, absently frowning at his glass.

Pedro gave a couple of unnecessary wipes to the bar. "I heard about your accident down in Arizona," he said, not looking at Johnny. "You are doing all right now, huh?"

"Oh yeah, I'm in great shape, Pedro." Johnny gave a sickly smile. "Say, you wouldn't have anything to eat around here, would you? I just walked out on a free lunch and I can't remember when I last ate."

Pedro smiled and leaned closer. "Usually we just have the salsa and chips, but," his voice lowered conspiratorially, "my Juana made some *chile colorado* that is so good . . . !" He threw the towel down and headed toward a door in the back. "You wait, John. I'll bring you a bowl." The door swung shut on Pedro's voice calling, "*Oyes, Juanita! Recuerdes el* John Hart?"

Johnny sipped at the beer with little interest. Shifting on the stool, he leaned an elbow on the bar and looked around. He'd seen it all before many times and nothing seemed to change, but he noticed that his gaze was making the two men at the corner table nervous. They exchanged looks and glanced toward the dirty window by the door. Johnny did not recognize the men, but did not find that too surprising. La Junta was a natural magnet for migrant field workers. But it was still kind of early in the day for them to be in Pedro's.

"You're going to like this," Pedro announced as the door flapped open. He carried the steaming bowl wrapped in a towel, gingerly on his fingertips. Behind Pedro, a short, round woman followed with a plate in her hands. Pedro placed the bowl before Hart. "You remember my wife, Juana?"

"*Por supuesto,*" Johnny said, touching the brim of his hat. "*Como está Usted, Señora?*" he asked with a passable accent.

Juana smiled and placed the plate of warm tortillas beside the bowl. "Homemade!" Pedro pointed out, beaming proudly at his wife's skill.

"Now this is exactly what my stomach had in mind," Johnny announced.

Chairs scraped as the two men stood up. Silently they each lay two dollars on the bar, nodding to Pedro and studiously not looking at Johnny. The door squeaked and sunlight crowded in. They stepped outside and quickly closed the door behind them. It took a moment for eyes to readjust to the gloom inside.

"Know them?" Johnny asked, eating contentedly.

Pedro frowned and shrugged. "They've been coming in off and on for a week or so. They don't say much."

There was a roar as a truck engine fired to life.

Johnny stood and walked to the window. He watched as the truck released its brakes and slowly started to roll. He fished the notebook and pen from his shirt pocket and noted the license plate, before returning to his bowl of chile.

Juana watched intently as Johnny ate, pleased at the deputy's appreciation of her art. When he pushed the empty bowl back, she picked it up, asking, "*Más?*"

"No, thank you, ma'am," Johnny patted his stomach. "*Gracias,*" he smiled. "*Muy sabroso,*" he added, much to her delight.

"John," Pedro leaned against the bar. "Are you coming back to La Junta?"

Johnny finished the last of his beer and shook his head. "I doubt it Pedro. There isn't much for me here anymore."

"How are your children?" Pedro asked, a look of concern on his face.

Johnny stood up, fishing in his pocket for money. "I don't see much of them, Pedro. I guess J. D.—Jack—had a pretty good basketball season this year. He'll be a senior this next year. And Gordy—uh, I guess she prefers Gloria these days—she's going to be starting high school this fall, too."

Pedro walked over to the corner where the men had been, picked up the empty bottles, and wiped the table. "I see your wife once in a while at the store." He didn't look at Johnny as he talked. "That's a pretty good job she has now, I guess, over at the District Attorney's." He glanced at Johnny. "She looks good."

Johnny nodded, laying a five-dollar bill on the bar. "She always looks good," he agreed, quietly.

Pedro pushed the money back toward Hart. "It's good to see you, my old friend. You come again soon, and maybe then I'll let you pay."

Johnny didn't look at Pedro as he picked up the bill. "Thanks, Pedro." He touched his fingers to his hat brim. "*Señora.*" His boot heels drummed loudly on the wooden floor as he left.

He blinked in the sunlight and sighed as he slid behind the wheel of the warm patrol car. With one hand he fished his notebook from his pocket while his other picked up the radio microphone. "Unit Three to base, come in base. Over."

"Base to Unit Three," came Kate's staticky voice. "Did you get Cecil there all right, Johnny?"

"Signed, sealed, and delivered," he drawled. "Listen, Kate, I want you to get hold of the Otero, Bent, and Prowers county sheriffs' dispatchers. There was a cattle truck, Peterbilt tractor, hauling an only half-full trailer of beeves. That struck me as a little odd. No feedlot or packer's going to waste his money paying to ship a half-load, and it's not the season for any rancher to be culling his herd. Have somebody stop them and check some of those brands." Reading from his notebook, he said, "It's a Texas commercial plate, 2YDF392, heading east on Highway 50. Must be about five miles east of La Junta by now. Over."

"I roger that, Johnny," Kate acknowledged.

"Unit Three out." Johnny snapped the microphone back on the dashboard. He sat, staring through the windshield for some time. Cottonwoods, bright and green, marked the course of the Arkansas River as it headed east. Tawny bluffs rose beyond the green to the north and, above it all, the sky stretched off to the ends of the imagination.

Johnny saw movement at the cantina's window. Pedro, a worried look on his face, was peeking past the neon Dos Equis sign at the patrol car. Johnny started the car, waved to Pedro, and pulled away.

Back on the highway, he settled in at a comfortable seventy miles per hour, heading east.

The house Johnny rented had no real driveway, just an area of dirt more hard packed from use than the rest of the dusty yard. As he turned off the engine of his truck, he saw Char walk out of the shed in back. As usual, a smile was spread across his face. Johnny felt strangely warmed by the fact that he'd come home to someone glad to see him.

"Hey, Cuz!" Char greeted, wiping his hands on an oily rag. "How are the bad guys doing today?"

The door of the pickup complained as Johnny opened it. "Better than the rest of us," he responded.

"I hope you don't mind," Char cocked his thumb back toward the shed. "I was kind of poking around being nosey and found that old Indian motorcycle back there." He shook his head. "Man, that is fine!"

Johnny walked beside Char toward the shed. "Yeah," he agreed. "An old man died a couple of houses down about a year ago, so I bought it from the estate real cheap. I was going to give it to Jack—my boy—for his sixteenth birthday, but when I was kind of fishing around just to see how he'd like it, it turned out he'd rather have a Miata or some fool thing. Didn't have any use for motorcycles." He looked directly at Char. "Can you imagine that? A flesh-and-blood American boy who'd rather have a toy car from Japan than a '47 Indian bike!"

Char laughed. "It's the end of civilization as we know it, hoss."

"I'm serious, Char!" Johnny looked indignant.

"So am I," Char grinned.

They stood looking down at the machine as it leaned on its kickstand. "I kind of got to tinkering with it. Looks like you've got all the parts."

Johnny nodded. "They should all be there. The old guy hadn't ridden it in years. He just couldn't bring himself to part with it." He ran his hand along the gas tank. "I didn't feel much like messing with it after Jack turned it down. Fact is, I missed his birthday altogether, being in the hospital."

"Well, if you don't mind, I'll go ahead and keep working on it," Char said. "Maybe by tomorrow, I'll have it fired up."

"No, go on ahead," Johnny urged. "I shouldn't have let it just set. Course, that's true of a lot of things in my life."

Char tossed the rag down next to the bike. "I walked over to the store earlier and got a few things. If you're hungry, I made some beans and fry bread." They headed for the back door.

"Mmm!" Johnny said, smiling. "Sounds good. Just what the doctor warned me against—fried foods."

"Hey," Char said, looking slightly offended. "All I know how to cook is poor folk food."

Johnny held the screen door open to let Char go in first. "Don't get touchy, Char. I've been on a mainly liquid diet for quite a while now, if you know what I mean, and, believe me, the doctor doesn't approve of that either."

Sitting at the table, hunched over the paper plates, they ate in silence. A single moth fluttered against the weak fluorescent light above them. Laying his fork down, Johnny leaned back in his chair, tilting it to reach the refrigerator and a can of beer from within.

Char frowned slightly at the pop top's hiss. "There's a pot of coffee on, if you want some." He picked up his plate and headed toward the sink.

Johnny watched him pour himself a cup and come back to the table. He lifted the beer can in a toast toward Char. "Let me have this one, anyway," he said quietly.

Char nodded, looking out the window where night was starting to fall.

"I saw Barb today." Johnny's finger rubbed the damp side of the can.

"How's she doing?" Char asked.

Johnny nodded before speaking. "She looked good." He took a swallow and was silent for a long time. "She was with some guy in a suit—a lawyer she works with." Another swallow followed by another silence. "I made an ass of myself." He smiled wryly.

Char smiled back. "What did you do, punch the guy out?"

"Nah, nothing as Hollywood as that. I just got all tongue-tied and staggered away like I'd just been kicked by a bronc. Felt that way, too." He took a bigger swallow.

Char laughed. "Sounds like me most of the time. You know, my best comeback line is 'Oh, yeah?'"

They both laughed, Johnny choking slightly on the beer.

"That's right," he nodded. "I remember that time in Rapid City, we were standing at the bar—the Crystal, or the Bronco or Jim's, I forget which one—and that big ol boy came up and started mouthing off. You didn't start the fight, but you sure as hell finished it."

They shook their heads ruefully, remembering. "You're a hard man to provoke," Johnny said, finishing his beer. "How'd we ever live long enough to get this old?"

Char stood up, stretching. "We're not that old yet. Just old enough to know better."

Johnny shook his head. "I'm forty years old, divorced, stove up so bad I'll probably never rodeo again, and a near washout as a lawman. I owe more than I make and I live in a shack on the edge of a town that's on the edge of nowhere." His voice had turned bitter. "You tell me what I now know that'll do me one lick of good tomorrow."

Char didn't answer immediately, looking at the frustration in his friend's face. "I know we're still alive, and I've got to believe there's a reason. And I know it's not over till we quit or die." Char shrugged. "I'm gonna go for a run."

"A what?" Johnny blinked.

Char went into the living room. "I'm gonna go run a mile or two before turning in." He came back into the kitchen and sat down, changing his boots for running shoes.

Johnny could think of nothing to say.

Char stood up and smiled again as he headed out the door. "See ya," was all he said.

The kitchen was silent except for the persistent ticking of the moth against the light. Outside, Johnny heard the flutter of a diesel engine as a truck down shifted for the turn in the road at the railroad underpass. He stood and walked to the stove, pouring himself a cup of coffee. At the sink, he looked out the window seeing only his own dark reflection in the glass. He sipped the coffee, made a face, and poured it down the drain. Opening the refrigerator, he grabbed another beer before heading off to his bedroom.

The next morning, Johnny sat at his desk leafing idly through the bulletins and memos. Kate sat at her dispatch radio, reading the newspaper.

"I swear I don't know what this world is coming to!" She glanced over at Johnny. "Did you read the paper this morning?"

After a pause, Johnny looked up to see that Kate really expected an answer. "No, Kate, I didn't. I don't read the paper much. I expect it says the world's going to hell in a hurry and that's not really news anymore."

Kate ignored his philosophy and squinted down at the newsprint. "It says that the Tribal Police on the Pine Ridge Indian Reservation have called in the FBI after discovering the body of a woman at the site of the Wounded Knee Memorial. The remains appeared to be those of a Caucasian female, probably in her twenties. It also says," Kate looked again at Johnny before continuing, "the body showed signs of mutilation." She savored the word. "Authorities are withholding details. A spokesman said that the woman had not yet been identified, but that she appeared to have been dead for at least several weeks before she was discovered by a group of German tourists." She shook her head. "That is just so sick!"

Johnny nodded. "I certainly want to thank you for sharing that with me, Kate."

She threw an annoyed look at him just as the intercom buzzed. "Miss Sorenson, please send Deputy Hart in," came Sheriff Carter's tinny voice.

"I heard," Johnny said, rising slowly and heading resignedly toward the door.

"Come in, deputy," Carter directed. "Have a seat." The sheriff laid down the papers he had been reading and sat up straight. "I wanted to let you know that you were right in your suspicions yesterday."

Johnny looked puzzled, so the Sheriff explained. "That cattle truck. They stopped it before it even got out of Otero County and it looks like those were stolen cows. No invoices or bills of sale . . . several different brands all mixed together. And the drivers were a couple of undocumented aliens who haven't said much so far. They're being held down in La Junta." The sheriff studied him in silence until Johnny began to feel uncomfortable. "You know, Hart," he finally said, "you really do have the makings of a first-rate lawman, if only . . ." He let the sentence hang, unfinished, then gave a sigh and picked up a pink telephone message slip. "I don't know if there's a connection, but Miss Cross phoned in again to say that she thinks those people came back. This time there are some cows missing." He handed the message across to Johnny, with the barest hint of a smile. "She asked for you." He glanced at his watch. "I guess you were just about to go out on patrol anyway. Start out there at the L-S."

It was breezy. On the high plains, where blizzards are the normal forecast for winter and tornadoes are a familiar sight, anything above freezing and below forty miles per hour is a breeze. Johnny judged it to be very breezy. The windmill on the stock tank behind the barn was spinning like a cropduster's propeller.

Sandy Cross walked toward Johnny's pickup truck clutching her hat. Her shirttails flapped and danced. Johnny, too, anchored his hat firmly as he stepped from the cab. "Pretty early in the day to be so breezy," she said. "Must be a storm coming."

Johnny nodded, giving a brief scan of the cloudless horizon. He followed her into the kitchen of the house. It was still inside and quiet except for the moaning of the wind at the eaves. He removed his hat and placed it upside down on the table.

"You look better today," Sandy said with a friendly smile.

"I guess that's a compliment," he said. "I feel better, too."

"Good." Sandy looked out the window as if embarrassed. "Want some coffee?"

"No, thanks," Johnny responded quickly.

"Look, Deputy," she paused, still not looking at him. "I was kind of rude yesterday. I'm really sorry." Her blue eyes stared at him a moment then looked away again.

Johnny shrugged. "No problem." He suddenly felt like he was with his daughter, which confused him. To break the awkward silence, he stuck out his hand. "Friends?"

She smiled again and shook his hand. "Friends," she agreed.

He pulled out his notepad and pen. "So, you got hit by rustlers last night?"

Sandy nodded, waving him to a chair at the table. Just then the door opened and the wind rushed in to scurry around the room, followed by Mr. Cross. He closed the door with a bang.

"Well, if it ain't deputy what's-his-name, packin' his pen and paper. Hope you brought a gun with you this time. The pen may be mightier than the sword, but it's no match for a .44 Colt, I'll tell you." Mr. Cross glared at Johnny. "Rustlers, by God! As if we ain't havin' a hard enough time, the bastards are stealing our beeves." He went to the stove and poured himself a cup of the always hot coffee. "Helluva thing!"

"Now, Grandpa," Sandy soothed. "They only got a couple head or so. The deputy's here to help us."

Johnny pushed his note pad across the table to Sandy. "Could you draw me a picture of your brand? I'm sure it's in the register, but I'm no artist."

Sandy quickly sketched the L-S brand on the page and handed it back to Hart. "There might be a problem, though," she said, wincing. "We hadn't gotten all the calves branded yet this spring, so probably only a couple of the mama cows have got brands."

Johnny sighed and rubbed the back of his neck. "That might be a proof problem, but, if the calves aren't weaned yet, I guess we could ID them as yours just by the mother cow they ran to."

Sandy brightened. "That's pretty good for a rodeo cowboy."

"I guess that's a compliment, too," he smiled. "Or, I'll take it as one. So, if you could show me where they cut fence . . ."

They got into Johnny's truck and drove south down the county road until Sandy directed him to turn into a side road. They hummed across the cattle guard and along the washboard surface for about a half mile. "Stop here," she said.

They climbed out and walked across a swath of sand lilies and paintbrush to the place where the fence had been cut and only partially repaired.

Johnny walked around slowly, studying the ground, crouching down and fingering the soil in spots. He then stepped over the barbed wire strand and continued to wander. A group of Hereford cows eyed him warily from a safe distance, the calves hiding behind their mothers and peeking out.

He nodded his head and walked back to where Sandy waited. "It looks like they came in first with a four wheel drive, cut the fence, and pulled out the post. Probably a Jeep," he pointed to the ground, "you can see where it turned, there, that it had a pretty short wheel base. Must have had a winch to get that post. Then," he pointed at another set of tire tracks, "they pulled a big rig on in, did a big, wide turn," his arm waved out over the pasture, "then faced the truck out. After that, they just drove the cows up the ramp." Again, he pointed to two cuts in the ground, where the end of the ramp had rested.

"I think from the looks of that scat over there," he pointed, "that they must have used at least one dog to do the herding. I don't know why they didn't take them all, unless they got spooked by something." He frowned.

"Maybe the truck was already full," Sandy suggested.

"Maybe," Johnny nodded. With a smile, he added, "Not bad for a cowgirl." He then headed back to the truck to radio in.

On the drive back to the ranch house, Johnny ventured, "It's none of my business, but it looks like a lot of work is not getting done on your place."

Sandy looked unhappy. "I know," she agreed. "We used to have a hired man, but he had some kind of family troubles and went back to Sonora right after the spring calving." She sighed. "Fact is, we can't afford to hire anybody else, so it's just me and Grandpa."

Johnny nodded, started to say something, but reconsidered. They drove for another mile in silence. As they turned into the ranch entrance, Sandy asked, "Is your friend, Mr. Sixkiller, still around?"

Johnny glanced at Sandy and was sure he saw a blush before she looked away. "Yeah, Char's still here. He's working on an old motorcycle at my place."

"He seems like a nice man," she said, half questioning.

Johnny smiled as he pulled the truck to a stop by the kitchen door. "Char is a pretty easygoing guy, I guess."

"Have you known him long?" she asked, showing frank interest now.

"Long?" Johnny seemed surprised to consider it. "I guess so. Probably the better part of fifteen years, at least. Maybe more."

"Where did you meet him? I mean, him being . . . are you part Indian or something too?" she asked, embarrassed.

"Char seems to think so," Johnny smiled. "You're not gonna like this, but he and I are both a couple of rodeo bums."

"Oh." She did seem disappointed. "He's another bronc rider, I suppose?"

"No, Char's a bullfighter," Johnny explained. "And a damn good one."

"A bullfighter? You mean a clown?" She shook her head and sat for a moment looking out the window at nothing as she considered the information. "Well, he still seems like a pretty nice guy."

Johnny thought for a moment before answering. "To be honest with you, I don't know a whole lot about Char. We spent a lot of time traveling and drinking and raising hell over the years, but he really doesn't talk about himself much. Either that or I don't listen much. But you know, bullfighters have a code they recite while they're putting their clown makeup on. It says 'You put on the greasepaint, you take what's due. If there's a hookin' to be done, it's done on you.'" He nodded. "I do know this, and this is God's honest truth," he looked at Sandy seriously, "if I'm gonna be out there on some rank bull that wants to stomp me, I'd feel a whole lot better knowing that Char's out there in the arena looking out for me."

Sandy smiled and nodded, satisfied with the answer. She got out of the truck and slammed the door. "I sure hope you can find our cows."

"I'll sure try." Johnny waved, turned the truck, and drove off.

CHAPTER 3

It's looking pretty good." Johnny stood in the doorway of the shed, beer in hand, looking down. Char lay on the ground reaching up into the underside of the motorcycle's engine. He gave a last few tugs on his wrench before standing up. "I think it's about ready," Char said. "I'll siphon some gas out of your truck later and try to fire it up tomorrow."

"You been working on it all day?" Johnny asked.

"Just about," Char nodded. He wiped his hands as they headed back toward the house. "Beans again," Char said, waving toward the stove.

"No complaints," Johnny said, draining his beer. "I ran into a friend of yours today," he said, pulling another can out of the refrigerator.

Char looked up from placing the pot on the table. "Who's that?" There was a worried look on his face.

"Relax, Char. It's not a jealous husband or a bill collector." He sat down and opened the beer. "Sandy Cross had all kinds of questions about you."

"Oh." The cloud passed from Char's face. "Well, of course she did," he smiled broadly. "Don't I keep telling you what a fascinating human being I really am?"

"You, and only you, do keep telling me," Johnny nodded, sipping. "She seemed a little put off that you're rodeo, but not enough to really change her mind."

"Maybe I should call on the lovely Miss Cross, one of these days. What do you think?" Char asked, spooning beans onto his plate.

"I think she's a little young for the likes of you and me," Johnny said, taking the spoon from Char.

"Speak for yourself, old timer."

"No, I'm serious," Johnny continued. "It was the strangest thing. I mean there's no question but that she's one fine-looking woman but, today, I really felt more like tucking her into bed than getting in there with her."

Char chewed without comment, swallowed, and said, "I don't think that means you're growing old. Maybe just growing up. Besides, she seems like a nice girl. Not like some of those bright and shiny rodeo groupies."

"Yeah, maybe that's it," Johnny agreed. "She could sure use some help out there though. Her grandpa's too old and rheumy to help much anymore and the place is just kind of falling down around their ears."

"I know," Char nodded. "Maybe I should call on her and see if I can help out."

"She can't afford to hire anybody, you know?"

Char seemed surprised. "I'm not looking to hire on, just be neighborly! Maybe there'll be a payday down the line someplace." He took a few more bites of food, pushed back the plate, and headed for the coffee pot. "Want some?" he asked Johnny as he poured.

"No." Hart lifted his beer can. "I'm covered."

"I was gonna ask you," Char sipped his coffee. "If I get that Indian bike running, would you sell it to me?"

"Sell it?" Johnny cocked his head considering. "I hadn't thought about that. Huh! Well, shoot, I was gonna give it to Jack, but since he's not interested, I might as well give it to you."

"Gosh, thanks Dad!" Char laughed. "Are you serious?"

"Yeah, why not," Johnny shrugged. "I doubt you've got any real money anyway and I've got no use for blankets or beads."

Char laughed again. "Pale face be speaking with no tongue if he keeps it up." He smiled. "Thanks, Johnny. I appreciate that."

⌃⌃⌃

"This is Unit Seven. I'm about a mile west of Towner on 96. There's a red pickup on the side of the road. Nobody's in or around it. Probably out of gas or something. I'm gonna stop and check it out," Johnny reported.

"Roger, Unit Seven. Base out," Kate responded.

Johnny clipped the microphone back to the dashboard and pulled onto the sloping gravel shoulder behind the red truck. He shut off the engine of his truck and stepped out into the bright, noon sunlight. There was very little breeze today and the air was warm. A few clouds were beginning to build up to the west, which might mean a thunderstorm by evening.

The red truck was a beat-up '75 Ford. The windshield had a long crack that stretched from either side of a rock-starred hole. Johnny laid his hand on the hood. It was still warm, but not hot. Looking in the open driver's window, he saw a cracked and peeling black vinyl dash, some fast food litter on the floor, and a nylon bag, such as people pack clothes in for a gym workout. A PRCA sticker with its stylized bronc rider was on the back window.

Looking down the highway in both directions, Johnny could see no one. The shadow of a hawk glided over the dull surface of the truck. Johnny shaded his eyes to see it against the sun, hovering over some potential prey that was trying to be invisible in the roadside grasses. In the distance, low against the horizon, was the cluster of buildings that made up Towner. In every other direction there was only space, an immensity of undulating land beneath an infinity of azure sky.

The radio in Johnny's truck crackled. "Base to Unit Seven."

Johnny's boots sounded loud as they scrunched across the pebbly dirt of the highway's shoulder. He reached in through the open window to pluck the microphone. "This is Unit Seven. Go ahead base."

"Johnny," Kate said, "we've got a report of a possible break-in at the Stewart place in Sheridan Lake. Sheriff wants you to go check it out."

Johnny frowned. "Somebody broke in, in the middle of the day?" he asked.

"Probably last night," Kate explained. "Mrs. Stewart only just got around to putting her glasses on. She says she doesn't wear them when she does her needlepoint. They hurt her eyes. But when she went to fix lunch for her grandkids, she noticed a broken window in the shed out back."

A truck that had been growing out of the west blew past Johnny, causing his pickup to shudder and sway. "Was anything taken?" he asked, after the noise of the diesel engine had faded away.

"She's not sure. She said her son stores some tools and chemicals and stuff back there. He'd know what's missing," Kate said.

Johnny sighed. "That means somebody will have to go back out later when Ben gets off work. All right, Kate, I'll go take a report. Unit Seven out." He started to clip the microphone back inside but changed his mind and pushed the transmit button. "Unit Seven to base. Come back, Kate."

"This is base. What'd you forget, cowboy?"

"Kate, I'd like you to run the plate on this truck. I guess we don't get enough traffic of any kind to just ignore an out-of-state vehicle on the side of the road."

"Go ahead with it, Johnny."

"It's a Montana plate," Johnny said, giving the number.

Kate read the number back to him. "Got it. I'll let you know," she said. "Base out."

Johnny climbed back into his truck and started the engine. After a quick glance in his side mirror, he made a U-turn and headed east. As he got up to speed, he saw a vehicle at a distance in his rear-view mirror, coming from Towner. Johnny slowed down. He could see a black Jeep pull over onto the north side of the road opposite the red truck. Johnny pulled over also and watched, his engine idling.

A tall man wearing a brown cowboy hat climbed out of the passenger side of the Jeep and walked around the front. He held a gas can in his hand. Johnny was about to start off again, but as he put the truck in gear he noticed that the man seemed familiar. Long black hair pulled back in a pony tail flowed from beneath the hat. As he poured gasoline into the truck's tank, the man waved at the driver of the Jeep, who pulled back onto the road and continued westward.

Johnny waited. As the Jeep came alongside, he could see that it was well equipped, with KC lights on the roll bar, a tan canvas bikini top, and a winch mounted on the front bumper. The driver, a blond man with a black Stetson, glanced through the passenger window at Johnny, smiled, nodded, and drove on.

As he pulled out to follow, Johnny grabbed the microphone. "Unit Seven to base."

"This is base. Go ahead Unit Seven."

"I've got another plate for you to run, Kate."

Kate chuckled. "Traffic's heavy out there today, Johnny, or are you just bored?"

"It's Texas and it appears to have mud spattered on the first few numbers, but the last couple are 2-R, as in Robert. It's a late model Jeep Wrangler, black. I've got to pull off in Sheridan Lake, but why don't you have the other units keep their eyes open and see if they spot it. Maybe they can make the rest of the numbers off the tag . . . at least see where it goes."

"Why, Johnny? What's he up to?" Kate asked.

"He's a good-looking blond feller, Kate," Johnny drawled. "Maybe I'm just jealous and figure he's after you."

"You are so bad, cowboy!" Kate laughed. "Base out."

"Unit Seven out."

The Jeep was opening more distance between itself and Johnny, but not enough to stop it for speeding. "I'd sure like to compare his tires to the tracks out on the Cross place," he muttered to himself.

"Base to Unit Seven."

"This is Unit Seven, go ahead Kate."

"We've got that Montana plate for you Johnny."

"Great. Go ahead, base."

"It's not reported stolen," Kate said. "It's registered out of Lame Deer, Montana, to somebody named Sixkiller . . . Charles Sixkiller."

Johnny looked in his rear-view mirror, but all he could see was an empty highway.

ᴧᴧᴧ

It was after five o'clock that day when Mr. Cross pulled up to the barn in his pickup. "Where'n hell did this here motor machine come from?" he demanded, limping stiffly into the barn.

"Oh, hi, Grandpa. That's Char's," Sandy waved toward the last stall where a large and very dirty man emerged pushing a wheelbarrow full of damp straw and manure.

"Hey, Mr. Cross, how're you today?" he greeted, as he rolled out of the barn and around the side where the refuse was dumped and raked out to dry.

Mr. Cross stared at Char until he was out of sight, then at Sandy who came to meet him.

"He showed up to visit and stayed to help," she explained.

"Who'n the hell is he?" Mr. Cross asked frowning.

"Don't you remember?" Sandy said. "He came out the other day with Deputy Hart. He shoed Feather."

"The Indian?" Mr. Cross exclaimed. "Well, I'll be . . . I wouldn't have recognized my own reflection under all that horse shit." He took a second look at Sandy. "You look like you've been rollin' in it yourself, little girl."

"The stalls are all clean and dry now, Grandpa," she said happily. "Come see."

She coaxed him in to view a couple of the stalls, now spread with clean, dry, sweet smelling straw.

"Well, it's a damn sight better than it was," Mr. Cross agreed. He lifted his hat and scratched his bald head. In a whisper he asked, "He ain't expecting no wages, is he?"

"No," Char said, looming up behind them. "I'm just strange enough to where I do this sort of thing for fun."

Mr. Cross studied him warily to see if he was joking. Deciding he was serious, he nodded. "Well, I'm obliged, Mister. It's mighty white of ya."

"Grandpa!" Sandy gasped.

"What?" Mr. Cross looked puzzled.

Char laughed. "It's just crazy enough, you're probably right," he said, shaking his head. "Well," he looked at Sandy. "It's been fun, but I'd better get cleaned up and get out of here."

"Oh," she looked disappointed. "Don't you want to stay for dinner?"

Char smiled. "Thanks. But I'd better get back and check on Johnny."

"Dinner," Mr. Cross brightened. "There's a good idea. My belt buckle's rubbin' against my backbone."

"You go ahead in, Grandpa," Sandy said. "I'll clean up some at the stock tank then be right in."

"What do you mean, 'check on Johnny'?" Sandy asked as they walked beneath the cottonwood to the stock tank behind the barn.

Char considered his answer. "He's had some problems lately and I'm not sure he's really handling them too well," he finally explained.

"It's obvious that he drinks too much, if that's what you mean," Sandy said, dipping her hands down into the water of the tank. The bottom of the tank was green with slime. Tadpoles could be seen darting along the bottom, but the water was cool and clean.

"Drinking's only part of it," Char explained. "It's like everything in his life came unglued at about the same time." He washed his face and ran his wet hands through his hair. "Man, I am a mess!" he noted, looking at his muddy hands. "Would you mind if I took my shirt off, so I can really get wet?"

"No, I don't mind," she said, surprised. "And thank you for asking."

Char seemed self-conscious as he unbuttoned his shirt and draped it over the wooden corral fence rail.

Sandy nearly gasped. Although streaked with dirt, he was as muscled as a body builder and as scarred as an old boot.

Char saw her wide-eyed expression and looked embarrassed. "I'm kind of a mess, huh?"

"What happened, Char?" Sandy asked, concerned. "You're all beat up."

"Kind of an occupational hazard," he shrugged. "But that's a long story." He continued to talk, seeking to change the subject. "I don't know where it started, with Johnny. He started finishing out of the money, then he started drinking more, which didn't help his rodeo standings any. Then Barbara, his wife, filed for divorce." Char dunked his entire head under the water and scrubbed his scalp. When he surfaced, his long hair was dripping and he shook his head, sputtering. "Man, that's cold!" He laughed, squeezing the water back away from his forehead as rivulets coursed down his grimy upper body.

Sandy loosened her hair and combed her fingers through it. "Lots of people get divorced," she said, frowning. "That's no reason to let it destroy you."

Char looked at her curiously. "You're divorced?" he asked quietly.

She let her hair fall forward hiding her face as she continued to comb with her fingers. "Yes," she admitted. "It wasn't much of a marriage anyway." This time, she changed the subject as if she didn't want to talk about herself. "Deputy Hart had been married a long time though, huh?"

Char nodded. "Nearly twenty years, I think. But that was only part of it." He dipped his shirt into the water, working the mud loose. "He was put on suspension over in Otero County. He was a deputy over there. Some kind of a shooting thing, where a kid got killed. He took it pretty hard." He wrung the shirt out and draped it over a crosspiece on the stock tank's windmill tower. "But then there was the accident last year." He shook his head and leaned back against the tank, his arms folded across his chest. "That was bad."

Sandy leaned her hip against the tank, her hands in the pockets of her jeans. "There was a little article in the paper about it, not much, though. What happened?"

Char sighed and described Johnny's accident. "We got him loose, but he was real tore up and couldn't get up. The bull turned on him and gored him real bad. Ripped him open, actually. Lost his spleen, lacerated his liver, broke his ribs, torn rotator cuff, lost a lot of blood." Char was quiet for a moment, remembering. "I rode with him to the hospital. He nearly died."

Sandy reached out and laid her hand on Char's arm. "You really care for him, don't you?"

She thought he wasn't going to answer. Looking down with a frown, he seemed to be staring at his muddy boots. His voice was so soft she could barely hear his words. "Most white people, when they look at me, they see a big Indian. Even people I've known for years! But Johnny was always different." He shrugged. "He just saw me."

There was a darkness on his features that she hadn't seen before, but like a cloud's shadow on the land it passed. He heaved a sigh and smiled. "Anyway, right now, I'm kind of worried. He seems about as lost and low as I've ever seen. I don't know what I can do but, hey, friends have to be good for something, right?"

"A friend loveth at all times, and a brother is born for adversity," Sandy quoted softly.

Char looked surprised. "Yeah," he agreed. "That's nice."

"Proverbs," she explained.

"Oh, the Bible?" he asked.

She nodded.

They stood quietly, the evening light shining coolly on the green leaves and shimmering off the still water of the tank. In the west, clouds were piling up, their tops tinged with pink from the setting sun. Thunder rumbled in the distance.

"Well, I'd better be going," Char said, getting his shirt from the rail. He winced at the cold, wet cloth as he put it on. "I don't even know if the headlight works on that bike."

They walked back to the front of the barn. Char straddled the machine.

"Thanks for your help," Sandy said. Awkwardly, she stuck out her hand.

He smiled and shook her hand. "Thanks for letting me be useful." He looked around the yard. "If you've no objection, I'll come back and do some other chores. It's kind of nice to be back on a working ranch again. Keeps me from getting bored."

"You're always welcome," Sandy said, shrugging her shoulders. "We've got enough work here to just entertain you to death."

Char nodded. He opened the fuel line, set the spark, and kicked the starter. The engine immediately burst into raucous life. He smiled. "Purrs like a kitten," he yelled above the din. "See ya!" Smoothly, he let out the clutch and roared away across the yard and up the road, looking back and waving as he passed over the ridge and out of sight.

⋀⋀⋀

Johnny sat in the gathering gloom of the kitchen, his boots propped on the opposite chair, a beer can in his hand. Several empty cans lined the table. He heard the motorcycle roar into the shed and fall silent. Char's boots crunched across the yard and drummed up the wooden kitchen steps. The screen door yawned and banged as he came into the house.

"Evening, Char," Johnny greeted.

Startled, Char wheeled and crouched to face the voice, his right hand back in a fist and his left hand out flat before him. His expression was grim and emotionless.

"Easy there, hoss," Johnny urged, dropping his feet off the chair and sitting up. "It's a six pack, not a six gun," he said, pointing to his can of beer.

Char blinked, then uncoiled into a relaxed stance. Smiling, embarrassed, he said, "Shoot, Johnny, I didn't expect anybody to be sitting here in the dark."

Johnny gave a nervous laugh. "Hell, I don't need a lot of light to drink. I'm real talented that way."

"Yeah, well . . ." Char switched on the light and looked around the kitchen. "I'm gonna take a shower, if you don't mind. I did some honest work today."

"I wouldn't know about that," Johnny drained the can. "I don't run into too many honest folks in my job."

"Bad day?" Char asked, heading for the living room.

"Nah, just kind of interesting."

"How's that?" Char came back with clean clothes draped over his arm.

"Well, I have a feeling I saw one of our rustlers today," Johnny said.

"Well, that's good."

Johnny nodded. "I also saw your truck today." He watched closely to see Char's reaction.

Char became very still. "What do you mean?"

"I mean I saw a red Ford pickup with a cracked windshield, a PRCA sticker, and Montana plates. Appeared to be heading for Kansas with an Indian at the wheel." Johnny paused. "Seemed like kind of a coincidence so I called in the plate and darned if it didn't come back registered to Charles Sixkiller, Lame Deer, Montana. Didn't you report it stolen?"

Char pursed his lips and ran his hand through his hair. "Well, no, not exactly. You see, the truck has practically no blue book value and no insurance, so what was the point of reporting it?"

Johnny nodded. "Kind of a coincidence, though, don't you think? The guy that steals it is also an Indian?"

Char shrugged. "You know us Indians, natural born thieves! If it's not horses, it's pickups!" There was an unfamiliar, bitter tinge to his voice.

"Some white guy in a black jeep with Texas plates was helping him fill up from a gas can when I first spotted it." Johnny looked at the empty beer can in his hand. "You don't have some kind of trouble, do you?" He looked up, concern on his face. "Maybe I could help."

Char studied Johnny's face for a moment then smiled. "Nah, just broke and out of work. But I've still got my health, my good looks and," he nodded at Johnny, "my friends."

Johnny was embarrassed. "Well, go ahead and shower. That sweat may be honest, but it still smells like horse shit. I'll try my hand at burning the beans tonight."

When Char left, Johnny stood at the sink and stared out the kitchen window frowning. Char was holding something back, he was sure of it. That familiar feeling of fear began to twist in his stomach the way it did right before the chute gate swung open.

⋀⋀⋀

Otero County has one building that contains virtually all of its government departments, including the county supervisors, the courtrooms and the district attorney's office. When it was new, there was room for everything. It was at least twenty years past new, and now it was crowded. At least, it felt crowded from Barbara's cluttered corner in the D.A.'s office. She was fishing around in a stack of files piled under the desk when she noticed scuffed cowboy boots arrive at the front of her desk. Someone cleared his throat.

She rolled back her chair and looked up. "Johnny!"

He stood smiling, cowboy hat in hand. "In the flesh, what's left of it."

She was annoyed to realize that she was glad to see him. "What are you doing here?" She waved at the place where he stood.

Johnny frowned. "I thought you wanted me here." He fumbled in his shirt pocket and pulled out a piece of paper. Unfolding it, he lay it on the desk in front of her. "If I'm not mistaken, that is a subpoena to appear as a witness. I guess you're going to arraign those two hombres driving the stolen cattle, and I'm your 'probable cause' witness."

Barbara put her hand to her forehead. "Holy cow!" she looked at the subpoena. "I'd completely forgotten." She scraped papers back from the calendar on her desk and checked the date. "It's at one-thirty." She looked at her watch and relief flooded over her features. "It's only one. Thank God! That's all I need is to blow off a court appearance."

Johnny slumped into a chair at the front of her desk and looked at the confusion of paperwork spread everywhere. "You're usually the most organized person I know. What happened here?"

Barbara disappeared under the desk again, searching for another file. "We've just been swamped lately, and I can't seem to stay on top of it." Her voice was muffled by the desk.

"The county having some kind of a crime wave I didn't hear about?" he asked. "I really ought to read the papers once in a while."

She resurfaced with two manila files in hand, shaking her head. "I don't know. It's a little bit of everything. Drugs, assaults, thefts, domestic violence." She pointed to different stacks of files. "And the county's cut back on staff. When people retire, they don't replace them. So our caseloads just keep increasing." She opened the files she had retrieved, scanning them briefly. "Do you need any memory refreshing before we go and do these guys—Jesus Rocha and Manuel Garza."

He shook his head, "Nah, I remember them. I looked at my notes again just a little while ago."

"Well, let's go ahead upstairs," she said, rising and stuffing the files into her briefcase.

In the hall, her high heels clicked loudly as she took two steps to every one of his. At the door to the courtroom they stopped and tried the door. "Locked," she said. "I guess the clerk's not back from lunch yet."

Johnny leaned back comfortably against the wall and crossed his arms. "Time to kill, huh?"

Barbara looked at her watch. "Yeah, I guess so."

Other people were starting to fill up the hall outside the court-rooms. Some were talking, some were silent and grim. Most checked the list of cases on the afternoon's calendar posted on clipboards beside the courtroom doors.

"Hey, cowboy, how's it going?" A smiling Otero County deputy lightly punched Johnny's shoulder.

"Hey, Bob." Hart shook hands with the man. "So you got bailiff duty today, huh?"

The deputy nodded. "Yep, it beats driving around." He tugged the brim of his cowboy hat toward Barbara. "Ma'am." He arched an inquisitive eyebrow toward Johnny.

"You know Barbara, don't you, Bob?" Johnny asked. "I'm her witness today."

"That's right, them rustlers," Bob nodded. "Well, I got to tend to some business 'fore court convenes. Good to see you again, John. Ma'am."

The deputy walked down the hall and disappeared into the men's restroom. As he entered, a big man came out of the same door. The scowl on his face caught Johnny's attention. The man scanned the people in the hall, his gaze locking on a short woman across the hall from Johnny and Barbara. He was so intent that Johnny felt himself tensing.

"Earth to Johnny, come in, deputy!" Barbara called.

"What's that, honey?" Johnny said, still focused on the man.

Barbara looked annoyed. "I said that the kids would like to see you once in a while. It's not like Eads is a thousand miles away or anything!"

Johnny didn't look at her. "I know, I know," he muttered, distracted. The man had his hand in the pocket of his coat and had almost reached the woman. Her back was turned.

"You're just totally ignoring me. I can't believe this!" Barbara sputtered.

"Bitch!" the man yelled. Johnny started moving. "You're not going to steal my kids! They're mine! They're my babies, too!" His hand was coming out of his pocket, leveling the pistol at her head when Johnny reached him.

He knocked the man's arm up into the air just as the gun went off. People screamed. Some scattered down the hall away from the danger while others cowered on the floor. The woman who had been the target of the man's wrath said simply, "Oh, Carl," and stood frozen, her hands to her mouth.

Johnny was reaching for his gun with one hand while hanging onto Carl's gun hand with the other. This left Carl with the only free hand. A left punch sent Johnny reeling against the wall, but he kept a tight grip on the man's gun.

"Backup!" Johnny yelled. "Bob?" He had to block another punch.

Carl was as strong as he was big. He scored another punch, and Johnny could feel the gun hand being forced down despite his best efforts. With the heel of his cowboy boot, Johnny stomped against the man's foot, then his knee, then his foot again until Carl cried out in pain. Johnny then took the opportunity to get a knuckle punch into Carl's solar plexus and finally he could feel some of the fight slackening in the big man.

Johnny was about to get another body blow in when something hit him in the back of the head, knocking his hat off over his eyes.

"You're hurting him!" the ex-wife screamed, smashing Johnny's head again with her heavy purse.

"Dammit, Bob!" Johnny yelled. "I need backup!"

"Hey, lady!" Barbara rushed across the hallway, shoving the woman away from Johnny and against the wall.

The two women were struggling and Johnny was banging Carl's gun hand against the wall when Bob finally appeared, running down the hall, drawing his gun as he came. "What the hell . . . ?"

"Get him behind the knees," Johnny instructed, loudly. "No, don't shoot him! Kick him!"

Bob did as directed and Carl finally collapsed. Before he could recover, Bob's gun muzzle was resting in plain sight, inches from the tip of his nose. "Drop the gun and roll over on your stomach!" Bob yelled. Carl did. As Bob was putting handcuffs on Carl, Johnny dropped a bear hug on the wife from behind.

"Calm down, lady, it's all right now," he soothed. The woman soon stopped struggling and started to cry.

Other deputies came trotting down the hall to assist, called by a court clerk, and Johnny released the woman to their care.

Barbara stood panting, her hair disheveled and one shoe missing.

"You okay, Barb?" Johnny asked, brushing some hair back from her eyes.

"Damn you, Johnny Hart!" she hissed, slapping at his hand. "No matter what, I spend all my time being scared for you! I'm not even living in the same county with you anymore and still I'm scared. Don't touch me!" She found her shoe and retrieved her briefcase. "Let's do this arraignment and then get away from me!" She stomped into the courtroom, leaving Johnny in the hall.

"She's a good little fighter, John," Bob observed, appreciatively.

Johnny nodded. "Always has been. But, hey, where in the hell were you while I was doing the two-step with old Carl?" Carl was being hustled down the hall, handcuffed, with deputies on either side.

Bob looked sheepish. "Gee, Johnny, I must've flushed just when the gun went off. I didn't hear a thing till I came out and saw you stomping on him." He shook his head. "Man, these family court things sure can get ugly."

"Tell me about it." Johnny combed his fingers through his hair. "Well, guess I'd better do what I came here for." He headed for the courtroom door.

"John?" Bob detained him with a hand on his arm. "Thanks for being here. We'd have had a murder without you."

"We almost had one with me." Johnny tucked his shirt in. "Oh, and Bob."

"Yeah, John?"

"Your fly's still open." Johnny nodded at the deputy, then went into the courtroom.

CHAPTER 4

The evening still was rattled by the noise of the Indian bike growling into the shed like a lion returning to its den. After it quit, there was a brief quiet before Char's boots crunched across the yard and paused on the kitchen steps. The door was ajar. Warily Char opened the screen door and pushed the door wide.

Johnny sat, beer cans before him, his hat still on, his head sunk onto his chest. Char thought that he was asleep, but Johnny's voice rasped, "You know, Char, you've been here for a couple of weeks already and we haven't gone on a hoot yet. What do you say? Wanna party some tonight?"

Char looked annoyed. "Nah, Johnny, I'm pretty tired, and, since I quit drinking, I quit going to bars. Besides, don't you have to work tomorrow?"

"Nope!" Johnny stood up and stretched awkwardly. "I got myself a one-week vacation. Sheriff calls it a suspension, but it's the same thing. For some reason Sheriff Carter objects to his deputies driving under the influence." He grinned at Char. "Come on, buddy. I'm bored. You can be the designated driver and I'll be the designated drinker. You can have coffee or whatever, but me, I feel like getting drunker than Cooder Brown."

"You know, that's really not good for you, after all that internal damage last fall," Char cautioned.

"Dammit, Char," Johnny snapped. "You're not my father and you're sure as hell not pretty enough to be my wife. Now I'm heading out tonight with you or without you." He frowned and softened his tone. "Come on, Char. Like old times!"

Char sighed. "Okay, Johnny. But not real late, all right? I really am tired."

Highway 50 crosses to the south side of the river at Lamar, pauses in town for a couple of traffic lights, then resumes its course due east toward Kansas. On the eastern edge of town is a good-sized bar with a parking lot filled primarily with pickup trucks.

Every head turned as the Indian bike, sounding like a jackhammer on wheels, rolled into the parking lot. Johnny climbed stiffly off the back as Char pulled the motorcycle onto its kickstand.

"Runs pretty good, huh?" Char asked proudly.

Johnny adjusted his hat over his windblown hair. "If I didn't before, I sure need a drink now, just to wash the bugs out of my teeth," he growled.

Char laughed. "I told you not to smile."

"That wasn't a smile, Char. That was tooth-chattering terror at the way you drive. Didn't you hear me screaming?"

"Was that you?" Char exclaimed in feigned surprise. "I thought it was the wind."

Two surly bouncers in tight black T-shirts and wide-brimmed hats studied them as they entered the cavernous honkytonk. The only light seemed to come from the neon beer advertisements on the wall. Country music, like a fist, pounded them as they walked to a small table near the dance floor. The gaudily dressed band made up in volume what they lacked in talent. Several couples danced to the music with grim expressions, as if determined to get the steps but avoid the fun. It was a weeknight, so the place was only half-full.

Johnny grinned broadly, taking in the surroundings. "No place like home, eh cowboy?" He had to yell to be heard above the noise.

Char's response, unseen by Johnny, was a brief, wintry smile.

A waitress in a skirt short enough to be a belt came to their table. "So what are you drinking?" she asked brusquely.

Johnny rubbed his hands together. "Bring us a couple of Coors."

Char leaned forward toward Johnny. "I'm not drinking, remember?"

"They're both for me, Char," Johnny explained. "You order what you like. I'm buying."

"All right, I'll just have a Doctor Pepper," Char told the waitress.

With weary patience, the waitress explained, "We don't have no soft drinks. This is a bar." Her foot began to tap.

"Oh, well, how about a cup of coffee?" Char asked. "Got any of that on tap?"

She rolled her eyes. "Two Coors and a coffee. That's six dollars. Pay first, no tabs."

The band ended its torment and announced a break. A dazed silence settled momentarily over the room. Coins clattered and the juke box boomed into the void.

"Six dollars!" Johnny dug into his jeans. "Better make that coffee last," he said with a wink at Char. "Here's ten dollars, darling. Keep the change and don't get too far away. I'm a fast drinker."

Johnny looked around with the bright expectancy of a child on Christmas Eve.

"You really love this, don't you?" Char said in amazement.

Johnny nodded, his fingers drumming to the beat of the music. "Sure! When I was a kid, we went to Disneyland one time. Except that my Dad got drunk and he and my Mom got into a fight, I loved that too. Same thing." He waved his hand to take in the room. "Make believe, colored lights, a little bit of excitement in the air."

"Is that what that is?" Char said sarcastically, rubbing his stinging eyes against the cigarette smoke.

"Shoot, Char, you've got to use your imagination," the drinks arrived, "or this," he said, lifting the sweating bottle, "to get the right perspective on it."

"That's just it, Johnny," Char said earnestly. "It is make believe. It's phony. Mechanics, bank tellers, and farmers, dressing up like cowboys and cowgirls then turning down the lights so you can't see the truth."

"The truth is a whole lot easier to swallow when you wash it down with one of these." Johnny upended the bottle then clunked it noisily down on the table. "More than one is better," he added, reaching for the other bottle.

"I'm serious, man," Char said, leaning back in disgust.

"So am I, Char." Johnny leaned closer. "What the hell is so good about the truth?" His voice was clipped and angry. "True or false, it all leads to the same thing: you're dead, gone, and forgotten. It all means nothing no matter how you slice it. Nothing plus nothing still equals nothing, so why are we all working so hard for nothing?" He slumped back in his chair again. "Just relax. Have a beer." He took a long pull on the bottle.

"You really believe that?" Char asked, incredulously. "There's no meaning? Good and bad, right and wrong, true or false are just words? Then why are you a cop?"

Johnny shrugged. "Beats me. Seems to be a real puzzler for Sheriff Carter, too." He laughed.

"All right," Char tried a different approach. "What about your kids? Whether they were born or not, whether they live or die, it's nothing, it doesn't matter?"

Johnny frowned, and it appeared as if he wasn't going to answer. He sat contemplating the empty bandstand for a moment. Finally, looking irritated, he turned and leaned toward Char. "Well, it might matter to me, but that's just 'cause they're my flesh and blood. Beyond the borders of my brain," he tapped his forehead, "it really doesn't matter."

"I'm not talking about your brain, I'm talking about your heart. If everything is a meaningless accident, where does love figure in? Isn't love real?"

"Oh, for Christ's sake, Char!" Johnny snapped. "Do we really have to unravel the mysteries of the universe right now? If you really think there's anything to save us from or save us for, you came to the wrong place." He waved his hand at the surroundings, which the waitress took as a signal to come back. "This is a bar, not a revival meeting. We came here to hoot and holler and have a good time. Yes, ma'am," he turned his full attention to the waitress. "Beer just isn't doing the trick tonight, darling. How much for Jack Daniels?"

"Three dollars a shot." She looked at Johnny skeptically as if challenging him to come up with the money.

"Well, then," Johnny pulled out his wallet. "Here's ten dollars. That's three dollars each for three shots and one dollar for you for looking so fine tonight."

The waitress took the bill and gave Johnny a small, charitable smile. Turning to Char, she asked, "More coffee?"

"Oh, no thanks," Char replied. "I have to drive tonight."

Johnny laughed, but the waitress just rolled her eyes and headed for the bar.

The band was regrouping behind their instruments for another assault.

Char leaned forward toward Johnny. "Look, Johnny, you're killing yourself," he pleaded. "And for what? Because you never made the top money in rodeo? Because your wife divorced you?"

Johnny waved his hand at Char as if he were a fly. "Leave it, Char. Just leave it. It doesn't matter anyway."

The band began to blare once again, just as the drinks arrived. Johnny downed all three drinks in as many gulps, lurched to his feet, and announced, "It's time to dance." The waitress was within reach. Johnny took her tray and set it down on the table.

"Hey, I gotta make a living!" she protested as Johnny led her onto the dance floor. The two bouncers quickly arrived on either side of him and tapped him on the shoulder.

"Let her go, cowboy. She ain't paid to dance."

"Is that right?" Johnny seemed surprised. He gave her hand a quick kiss and put his hand over his heart. "So long, darling. It could've been beautiful."

The waitress quickly retrieved her tray, glancing back at Johnny as if he were crazy.

Johnny looked at the two bouncers, who were watching him and scanning the room at the same time. "I don't suppose either of you wants to dance?"

"Sit down, cowboy, or you're outta here."

Johnny shrugged and stumbled back to the table. "Damn, Char, everybody else in here is as serious as you!" He didn't sit down. Scowling, he turned toward the band and yelled, "Can't you play something besides that whining hillbilly music? How about some Texas music? Delbert McClintock, Joe Ely? Texans gotta be good for something, anyway!" Johnny looked around belligerently as if hunting for Texans.

Char shook his head and sat up at the table. "Come on, Johnny, sit down and take it easy."

The band began to play "Amarillo by Morning," and Johnny smiled. "That's better." Turning to Char, he said loudly enough to be heard across the room, "Welcome to Lamar, old buddy." He threw his arms wide and staggered a little. "Lamar, where men are men and calves are nervous." He laughed.

A few men left their dates at the bar and started walking toward Johnny.

"What are you trying to do, Johnny?" Char whispered urgently.

Johnny turned to face the approaching group. "Oh, look, Char! It's cowboys! Now's your chance to play cowboys and Indians, but, this time, the Indians can win!"

The two bouncers joined the men who formed a ring around Johnny and Char.

Char stood up slowly, muttering, "Don't do this, Johnny."

The band fell silent.

Johnny wheeled toward Char. "What's that you said, old buddy? Why, I'll just bet you're right!" He turned back toward the grim faced men and smiled broadly. "Boys, my friend here is a full blooded Indian, and he just told me that he could kick your lily white asses any day of the week. And you know what? I'm part Indian myself, so maybe I'll just help him!"

The bigger of the bouncers stepped forward. "You're out of here, asshole." The man's fist cocked back and shot forward but, before it could reach Johnny's face, it smacked into the palm of Char's hand and stopped. A look of surprise passed over the man's face, quickly replaced by a grimace of pain as Char's hand closed tightly on his.

"We really don't want any trouble," Char pleaded, tossing the man back into the circle of frowning cowboys. The bouncer nursed his hand under his arm.

"That's it," the other bouncer yelled. "You guys are dog meat!" He pulled a wooden nightstick from his belt and swung it at Char's head as the other men closed in.

Char ducked the blow and allowed the bouncer's momentum to carry him off balance, guiding him crashing into two others who were moving in on Johnny.

"Yes!" Johnny yelled gleefully, laughing as he kicked another would-be assailant in the groin.

His face expressionless, Char whirled like a dancer, low to the ground, sweeping the feet out from under another man. Before that one hit the ground, Char, with the same fluid movement, brought his elbow into the face of the first bouncer who had imprudently stepped into the fray once again.

Johnny stepped back and crossed his arms, smiling contentedly as Char quickly and efficiently incapacitated the half dozen men. Standing above the carnage, Char swept the room with a fierce glare as if to warn off all others.

Johnny shook his head, marveling. "I'd forgotten just how good you are, hoss! Man, that was beautiful . . ." His words were cut short by Char's right hand grabbing him by the back of the neck like a puppy and dragging him toward the door.

Once outside, Johnny stumbled and fell to the ground.

"What is wrong with you, *veho*!?!" Char shouted. The finger he pointed toward Johnny was shaking with adrenaline and rage. "Were you hoping I'd kill somebody or did you just hope we'd get the living shit kicked out of us by some local yahoos?"

Johnny propped himself up against the back wheel of a parked Jeep and watched as Char paced in a tight circle, his fist beating against his leg. "Come on, Char! Just a little harmless fun. You got some exercise and they learned a little respect. What's the big deal?"

Johnny's words seemed to make Char angrier. He stopped and stared at Johnny in astonishment. "You don't get it, do you?" He closed his eyes and took a deep breath. "Everybody else exists just to suit your fancy? I'm just the clown who's supposed to save your sorry butt and be entertaining while I'm at it!"

Char bent forward until his tight face was only inches from Johnny's. "You play the cards you're dealt, Johnny! That's all there is to it. That's life! You're no different than anybody else. But you seem to feel that unless you're holding a royal flush, you just won't play at all." Char stood upright. From Johnny's perspective, he looked like a giant.

"You know, Johnny, you've pissed away more than most men could ever hope to have. It's high time you made a stand before you lose it all."

Johnny scowled and shifted his back to a more comfortable position. "Christ, Char, you're not my father!" he muttered.

"No, I'm not," Char said, his voice now calm and sad. "And I guess I'm not your friend, either." He gave Johnny one last withering look, then turned and walked away. In a moment the Indian bike roared. Johnny watched as Char flashed beneath the streetlight and disappeared into the night.

Johnny closed his eyes and rested his head against the tire.

"You know, deputy, them old boys inside are starting to get up off of the floor," drawled a man's voice.

Johnny saw silver tipped black cowboy boots standing about three feet away. A nice pair of women's legs in fishnet stockings and cowboy boots stood beside them. Johnny tilted his head back to see better, but the man's face was in shadow. Only his silhouette was haloed against the neon lights.

"Yeah, well, I wasn't having all that much fun here anyway." Johnny struggled to his feet and stood swaying.

"I expect those sirens I hear have something to do with you, too," the stranger noted.

Johnny cocked his head to listen. There was indeed the sound of sirens approaching. He laughed softly. "Ain't that a kicker!" He looked back at the man. "I'm sure you had other plans," he glanced at the woman clinging to the stranger, "but could I trouble you for a quick ride out of town?"

The man laughed and Johnny saw the flash of even white teeth. "Sure, climb on in. This is my Jeep."

"I appreciate it." Johnny struggled into the small back seat as the couple piled in to the front. The woman giggled as if enjoying some private joke.

"What direction are you heading?" the man asked. As he turned on the engine, Clint Black's voice blasted Johnny from two speakers on either side of his seat.

"North would be nice," Johnny yelled above the music, "but I'm not too particular just now."

"Good point!" the man agreed. Blinking red and blue lights could be seen rounding the corner from Main Street.

The Jeep, with Johnny slumped in back, bounced out of the parking lot just as the patrol car pulled in. In five minutes they were across the river and around the curve where the lights of the radio tower blinked at a quarter moon. Across from the feedlot, the man pulled over.

"This should do," the driver said, climbing out and flipping the seat forward so Johnny could exit. "You can probably thumb a ride from a cattle truck up ahead," he said, pointing toward the feedlot entrance.

Johnny took a deep breath. The air was heavy with the pungent smell of cattle. "I sure thank you," Johnny said, shaking the man's hand.

"No problem," the stranger said, touching the brim of his black Stetson and getting back behind the wheel. He smiled, nodded, and pulled away, making a U-turn back toward town.

Johnny's stomach lurched as he suddenly recognized his rescuer. He strained his eyes in the darkness and could just make out the Jeep's license plate—Texas with most of the numbers covered except for a 2 and an R—the same plate he had called in along with Char's red pickup.

CHAPTER 5

The summer sun was just rising as Sandy stepped out of the house. It had been a warm, humid night and promised to be a hot, hazy day. She wasn't looking forward to it. The crunch of her boots seemed particularly loud in the still air. Even the usual morning celebration of birdsong in the trees sounded subdued and halfhearted.

The barn was still nearly dark. "Come on, Feather," Sandy said entering the horse's stall. "We've got work to do, as usual."

"It's gonna be a hot one for sure today!" a deep voice announced from the stall across the way.

Sandy turned, wide-eyed, her hands to her mouth.

Char stepped out of the stall, brushing straw from his hair and clothes.

"My God!" Sandy gasped. "You scared me half to death."

"'Scare myself sometimes," Char said in mock seriousness.

"Smart aleck!" She punched him playfully on the arm. "How did you get here and where have you been? I haven't seen you in two weeks." Sandy shook her head and turned back into Feather's stall. Taking the halter off its hook on the wall, she slipped the bit easily into the horse's mouth.

Char walked next to her as she led the horse to the barn's entrance. "I had to go down to Arizona to work a rodeo. I haven't won the lottery yet, so I still have to get a paycheck now and then."

"You could have told me you were leaving." Sandy tried not to sound too petulant. She hadn't wanted to admit how disappointed she had been when he disappeared, but she felt foolish and adolescently glad to see him now.

"I had to leave in kind of a hurry," Char said.

Sandy threw a padded saddle blanket across Feather's back. She struggled with the saddle a little, but managed to get it in place before Char could help.

"Did you sleep here last night or something?" she asked.

"I rolled in around three o'clock this morning and got a couple hours sleep in the stall."

"I didn't hear a thing." She looked accusingly at the dog, Lady, who simply raised her face, grinning innocently.

"Well, I didn't want to wake anybody, so I shut off the engine and pushed the bike in the last mile," Char said.

Finishing with the cinch, Sandy leaned against Feather's side. Bluntly, she asked, "So why are you here? I thought you were staying with Deputy Hart?"

Char frowned. "I remembered there being a lot of work to do around here, so here I am—ready, willing and cheap. Like I told you, I'll work for chow and a place to sleep."

Sandy searched Char's face as if to discover some other reason that he wasn't willing to say. She nodded, "I sure could use your help, that's the truth. But I'll have to ask Grandpa how he feels about it."

"Here's your chance." Char nodded toward the house where the screen door squealed and banged as Mr. Cross stepped out. He walked stiffly, with short, painful steps. He lifted his hat and ran his hand across the few hairs left on his head, revealing the line where suntan met hatband.

Arriving at the barn, he stared hard at Char, nodding a curt greeting. "You just drop in out of the sky?"

"No, sir," Char smiled. "I came in by land."

"Char here just offered to work for us,—with us really,—if we give him a place to sleep and feed him."

Mr. Cross squinted at Char. "Three squares and a bunk?" He looked at Sandy, then back at Char. "I know you can shoe horses, but can you ride 'em? We got a lot of country to cover out here."

Char nodded. "Yes, sir. I've been afoot a lot lately, but I was riding almost before I could walk as a kid."

Mr. Cross looked away across the range to the west. He adjusted his hat again, considering. He scuffed his boot in the dirt, glanced again at Sandy, then stuck his hand out to shake Char's. "Well, cowboy, I believe we got a job for you." Turning to Sandy, he said, "There ought to be some biscuits and bacon left from breakfast. Why don't you go heat something up and we'll give this hand his first paycheck."

Sandy looked pleased. "Come on, Char," she said.

"You go on ahead, girl," Mr. Cross suggested. "I want a word with the new man first."

Sandy nodded, handed Feather's reins to Char, and went into the house.

Mr. Cross studied Char for a while before speaking. "Times aren't so hard that any man has to work for just beans and a bunk anymore. I'm old, but I ain't stupid. I suspect your being here has a lot to do with the fact that my grandbaby is mighty easy on the eyes." He held up his hand to forestall anything Char might have to say. "I'm too old for most everything now, especially wasting breath, so I'll tell you straight out, mister, that you being an Indian don't bother me near as much as the fact that you're a man I don't know nothin' about. Now, Sandy there, she's been hurt before, badly, by a jackass on two legs. She seems to like you and thinks you're pretty square. I hope she's right. But I'm tellin' you, if you do anything to hurt that girl, I'll kill you. I can't say it no plainer than that. She's good people and deserves to be treated right." Mr. Cross stared hard at Char. "You hear me?"

Char nodded. "I hear you." He glanced at the house, then back to the old man. "Sandy is pretty, Mr. Cross. No denying that. And I like her. I'm not here to hurt her or anyone else."

The two men measured each other in silence, each with his own thoughts. Finally Mr. Cross seemed satisfied. "Well, get on in and eat somethin'. I'll cut you out a horse. You'll have to saddle him yourself, though. My arthritis is actin' up somethin' fierce today. It's too much humidity. Probably rain come sundown."

⌃⌃⌃

"I don't know why I even read the paper!" Kate exclaimed, crumpling it down so she could look at Johnny. "Did you read yesterday's paper, Johnny? The section on Denver and the West?" Without waiting for a response, she read, "Authorities in Graham County, Arizona, are investigating a possible homicide. Teenagers on dirt bikes yesterday came upon the remains of a body near the Aravaipa Creek, several miles east of Fort Grant. A spokesperson for the Sheriff's Department said that the body appeared to be that of a woman. Because of either animal depredations or mutilation, identification is expected to take some time. The coroner has been able to identify a gunshot wound as the possible cause of death. The woman had been dead for approximately one week when the body was discovered.'"

Kate slapped the newspaper down onto her desk. "Now is that just too sick, or what?"

Johnny's head was pounding. His face was in his hands, apparently hunched over a report, but in fact, his eyes were closed. He could feel Kate's stare on him and her question, though rhetorical, seemed to be hanging, waiting for his response. With a sigh, he pushed back in his chair. "Why do you even read the paper, Kate?" He waved at the clutter of reports on his desk. "I mean, we have enough car accidents, shootings, bar fights, and runaway kids to satisfy anybody, I should think."

Kate sniffed, offended, and turned back to her dispatch board. "Some of us just like to keep informed, that's all." Her intercom buzzed.

"Send Deputy Hart in please, Miss Sorenson," the sheriff said.

Kate jerked her thumb toward the sheriff's door.

"No offense, Kate," Johnny mumbled, rising.

He stood before the desk. Sheriff Carter hadn't invited him to sit since he returned from his suspension.

"Deputy Hart, I want you to head out to the Flying V Ranch to check on another possible theft of livestock." He handed Johnny a note with a man's name on it. "The foreman out there is Al Weston. He called in the report. You know where the Flying V is?"

"Yes, sir," Johnny acknowledged.

"Very well, radio in once you've talked to him. I'm getting pretty tired of rustlers."

Johnny nodded, turned, and left.

⌃⌃⌃

The phone rang. She picked it up and answered, her attention still on the arresting officer's report on her desk. "This is Barbara Gutierrez."

There was a long pause. "Barb?" Johnny asked tentatively.

Barbara stopped reading. "Johnny?"

"You started using your maiden name again, huh?" he noted quietly.

She felt irritated and guilty at the same time. "Just around here, but let's not make a big deal about it, okay?"

"No, no, that's fine. The Hart name doesn't exactly shine around there anymore. That's my doing, not yours." Johnny sighed.

"Ay, Johnny, *burro!*" Barbara said, exasperated. "If you must know, I use Gutierrez because I want people to know that I'm Mexican-American, even on the phone."

"Oh." Johnny paused again. "Why?"

Barbara leaned forward and rested her forehead on her hand, eyes closed. "I have several reasons. Do you really want to know? Is that why you called?"

"No, that's not why I called but, yes, I would kind of like to know."

"Well, partly I do it to put other Latinos at ease when they call. *Gringo* authority figures kind of make us nervous, you know." They both laughed. She felt oddly glad to be talking to Johnny. "And I also use Gutierrez because, frankly, it bothers some of the redneck types around here."

Johnny laughed. "I hear that. *Viva la raza!* And all that."

"Exactly," she nodded, smiling. "And there's another reason." Her voice grew softer so that Johnny had to strain to hear her. "Now don't take this wrong, Johnny, but all those years of being married to you, I kind of lost any sense of who I was. When people looked at me—when I looked at myself—I was always Mrs. John Hart, the wife of the rodeo star, or Mrs. Deputy Hart, the lawman's wife, or Mrs. Hart the mother of Jack and Gloria. Everything that defined me came from outside me." She fell silent.

"I never thought about that," Johnny said. "But what else is new?"

"No, Johnny," Barbara said. "It's not something you did to me, it's something I allowed to happen to me. I was proud to be your wife. I'm proud to be the kids' mother. It's good to be a part of something bigger than ourselves, but I have to be something in and of myself too, for my sake. And Barbara Gutierrez is the woman who put herself through law school and now works as an assistant district attorney."

"I'm impressed," Johnny said. "I always have been, though I guess I never mentioned it."

There was a long silence on the line.

"What did you call about, Johnny?" Barbara asked.

"Oh, it's those two guys you've got over there, the ones that were driving the stolen cattle. Have they told you anything useful?"

"No, not really. Of course, the public defender doesn't give me much of a chance to talk to them directly. But the P.D. has to use a translator and I don't," she chuckled, "so I've managed to slip by him from time to time. They're undocumented, to no one's surprise, but it seems like whoever they're working for has promised to keep sending their wages back home even if they do jail time, as long as they keep their mouths shut."

"They haven't said anything about where they were taking the cows?" Johnny asked.

"No, but in talking about the man they work for, they usually just refer to him as *el Patron*, but once I heard them call him *el Tejano* and another time as *el Rubio*."

Johnny smiled. "The Texan! The blond guy! I think I know just who they were talking about."

"You do?" Barbara sat up in interest. "That's great! Do you have a name?"

"No, not yet. But they confirmed a hunch I had. I plan on getting a name, though, and the Texan and the Jeep he rode in on. Thanks, Barb."

"Take care of yourself, Johnny," Barbara said. She added, quietly, "It was nice talking to you."

"Yeah," Johnny agreed, softly. "Bye, Barb."

⌃⌃⌃

Sunset stained the gathering clouds a rich and bloody color as Sandy and Char headed home. The soft rhythm of their horses' hooves was echoed by the distant rumble of thunder. Sandy reined Feather to a stop and pointed toward a bend in the creek bed.

"Look, Char." A small family of antelope was grazing along the opposite bank.

A smile creased Char's dusty face. "That sure is pretty." A crow cawed noisily from the branches of a cottonwood and caused the antelope to look up warily in the direction of the two humans. After a moment, most of the animals returned to their grazing but one male continued to watch warily, his short tail switching nervously. When Char's horse shifted, shaking its head at a bothersome fly, that was enough for the male. Spinning, he bounded away from the direction of the people, drawing the other animals with him like birds taking flight. Like water over a rock, they leaped smoothly in single file across a fence and quickly bounded out of sight.

"Spooky critters, aren't they?" Char observed.

"That's the way they protect themselves," Sandy said. "Better to run from imagined danger than be caught by the real thing."

Char glanced sidelong at Sandy, a quizzical expression on his face. "Kind of a sad way to live, don't you think? Always running away?"

Sandy just shrugged, starting Feather into a walk again. "It's a cliché but true. Better safe than sorry."

Walking his horse beside hers, Char waved his hand back toward where the antelope had been. "You've got that whole section around the creek fenced in. Why is that? It looks like pretty good grazing."

"Grandpa did that years ago. He said he didn't much like the idea of cattle tromping across there. Too disrespectful."

Char reined his horse to a stop. "Of what?" he asked.

Sandy looked back at the creek bank, now dappled in evening shadows. "The people who died there," she said simply. "That's where the Sand Creek Massacre happened."

Char leaned forward on the saddle until his elbow rested on the pommel. "So that's it," he said flatly. "I knew it was around here someplace."

Sandy looked at his expression, which was unreadable. "What kind of Indian are you, Char?"

He gave her a half-smile and winked. "Well, I'm still alive, so I guess not a very good one."

She flushed and shook her head, laughing in spite of her embarrassment. "You are such a wise guy! I meant, what tribe are you?"

He looked back at the creek bend. "I know what you meant," he said softly. He was quiet for what seemed a long time to Sandy. Feather shifted her weight, impatient to get home.

The light was fading and the creek bed was completely in shadow. To the west, black mountains topped by clouds of purple and gold stretched low along the horizon. With a sigh, Char finally straightened up. Stretching his back and neck, he winced slightly at some old pain. Turning his horse back into a walk toward the house, he said, "Man, I'm hurting today. I haven't done this much work in the saddle in a long, long time."

Sandy and Feather fell in alongside him. "We got a lot done today," she nodded. "Do you mind me asking about you, Char? You always seem to change the subject when I ask anything at all personal about you. I mean, I know it's none of my business and all, but . . ." Sandy realized that her loneliness had caused her to ask too few questions of this man.

Char laughed at Sandy's discomfiture. "But you're curious anyway," he finished her thought. "No, it's all right. You've got a right to wonder about a total stranger who drops in out of the blue and then sticks around as long as I have. I can't promise to tell all," he said. "This saddle would make a pretty uncomfortable psychiatrist's couch, but what would you like to know about me?"

She considered for a moment. "Well, Deputy Hart thought you might be Cherokee. Is that true?"

"As usual, Johnny only got it half right," he said with a hint of bitterness. "My father was Cherokee."

"And your mother?" she pressed.

"Cheyenne," he said.

"Oh!" Sandy glanced back at the massacre site, now completely dark. "Then you know about Sand Creek."

"I sure do," he said simply.

It was difficult for Sandy to read his expression in the twilight. Hesitantly, she asked, "So, did you—your family, I mean—lose anybody there?" She pointed back toward the creek.

"The Cheyenne aren't that big a nation, so, sure, everybody lost somebody at Sand Creek," he explained.

"Now, the Cheyenne are up north aren't they? Montana, I think. But I thought the Cherokee were from Oklahoma or back east. Where did you grow up?" Sandy asked.

"Some might wonder if I ever did grow up," he winked at her. They reached a fence and Char climbed down to open the gate. He waited until he was back in the saddle before answering.

"I was born in California. Oakland. During the war,—the Second World War—and after, a lot of Indian people were relocated from reservations into cities. Part of the government's attempt to throw us into the melting pot. It turned out to be more like out of the frying pan, into the fire. But that's how my parents met. My mom was from Montana and my dad was from Oklahoma. They worked in the ship- yards when they first went out there.

"I don't remember much about Oakland. I was born when my father was in the army over in Korea. My brother was born when he came back, but they didn't stay together long after that. My dad went back to Oklahoma and my mom took us back to my grandparents on the reservation."

"Montana?" Sandy clarified.

Char nodded. "Lame Deer."

They were in sight of the house now. It was nearly full dark and the only lights were at the kitchen window and the blue bug light over the barn's entrance.

"So why do you say you grew up all over if you went back to Lame Deer?" Sandy asked.

"Mom couldn't stay. She'd get into a fight with my grandparents, or hear about work someplace or just get restless and, bang, there we go, we're hitching a ride with somebody or on the bus or, once in a while, she had her own car." He laughed. "She was the worst driver and we always had lousy cars." He shook his head at the memory. "But we traveled a lot. I've picked fruit and crops and gone to school in at least eight states."

They dismounted in the yard and led their horses into the barn. Removing the saddles, they draped them over saw horses set against the wall. Char took the bridles, bits, and blankets off, while Sandy filled the trough with grain. While the horses ate, they brushed and combed them.

"You said you have a brother?" Sandy asked, returning to the subject.

"I had a brother," Char corrected. It seemed to Sandy that he brushed a little harder. "Dwight, his name was. He got killed though."

Sandy paused in her brushing. "I'm sorry. How did that happen?"

"Vietnam," he said simply. He gave one last brush to his horse, then returned the brush and comb to the workbench. He leaned back against the bench and shoved his hands down into his pockets.

"Dwight had no business being in the army, but all his buddies were going in and the recruiters were taking anybody they could get." He studied an invisible spot on the ground, a troubled look on his face. "But it was my fault really." He took a deep breath and fell silent.

Sandy came and set her brushes on the bench. "You don't have to talk about it if you don't want to."

He didn't seem to hear her. "Dwight always wanted to come along and do whatever I was doing. I was in the army already. As soon as he hit eighteen, he signed up too. I tried to get them to turn him loose. He wasn't . . . right. Fetal Alcohol Effects, they call it now." Char tapped his finger on his temple. "But they took him anyway."

Char's jaw tightened and his voice became a little louder. "This is what is so stupid. Dwight wasn't killed by the Cong. He drowned." He shook his head at the memory. "His patrol was down in the Mekong Delta region. They were wading across a stream, and he was the last one in the line. They were under orders to keep quiet, right? Well, I guess he slipped or something, went under with that heavy pack, and drowned. Nobody was looking out for him. They were a full klick down the trail before they noticed he was gone." He grew quiet. "Dwight never could learn to swim."

Sandy rested her hand on Char's arm. "Why would you say that it's your fault? It was just a terrible accident."

Char stepped away from her to stand in the barn doorway. A half moon was rising from the eastern ridge, large and yellow and bright. "I worked in army recruiting," he said. "In high school, I was kind of a hot shot bronc rider, at least on the Indian rodeo circuit. When I graduated from high school, I went down to the recruiter like most of the other guys and the recruiter said, 'You're a celebrity, boy. You can work with us.' Joining the army was what you did when you turned eighteen on the reservation, but I wasn't really all that hot on the idea of going to Vietnam, so I said, sure, let 'er buck!"

He turned back toward Sandy. "It seemed so easy." His voice pleaded for understanding. "A group of us would go around the country to all these reservation rodeos and powwows. We'd ride our different events as an exhibition, then stand up in our dress uniforms and talk about all the benefits of joining the army. See the world, get an education, be a man!" His hand waved at an invisible banner, then dropped to his side like a bird shot in mid flight. "I did that for almost two years, until Dwight died, then I couldn't do it anymore." He shoved his hands back into his pockets and stood silent and sad.

Sandy could think of nothing to say that would penetrate Char's sense of guilt. For several minutes, the only sound came from the puffing and grinding of the horses intent on their grain.

The silence was finally broken by the bang of the screen door on the house. Mr. Cross marched across the pebbly yard to the barn. "You two plannin' on standing here all night jawin' or are we gonna eat some supper? If I have to keep addin' water to them beans, you're gonna have to eat 'em with a straw."

⋀⋀⋀

A blizzard of moths fluttered and danced in the lights of the arena. It was dark by now, the slow summer evening having finally faded through the spectrum from crimson and gold to silver and black. The air was cool and dusty. The bleachers were beginning to empty, but the arena was still ringed by pickup trucks. The people who had arrived early for the rodeo had backed their trucks up to the fence so that they could watch the events from the comfort of lawn chairs set up in the truck beds, ice chests and picnic baskets close at hand. Those people for the most part continued to visit and laugh even after the last animal had been ridden.

Johnny had to admit that he liked these little jackpot rodeos. The mood was relaxed and friendly as farm and ranch families came together, more to enjoy one another's company than to watch their sons and daughters compete.

Johnny had accepted the invitation to be a judge at this rodeo in Las Animas only because he needed the little bit of money they offered. It was risky though. If the PRCA found out he was working non-sanctioned rodeos, he could be fined or suspended. Not that suspension mattered, he thought. He hadn't been able to enter a single rodeo, official or otherwise, all year.

As he walked to his truck, he was occasionally greeted by people who recognized him, so that he was feeling pretty good as he fished in his pocket for his keys. He was also feeling pretty good from the case of beer he had split with the other judges. His attention was caught, though, by a raised voice coming from a truck about fifteen feet away.

"Screw your mom, girl, we're gonna party!"

"Don't talk about my mother like that," came a girl's voice, rising in anger. "Now you take me home, Jeff, right now!"

Johnny put his keys back in his jeans and walked toward the argument.

"Screw you too, Gloria!" the young man's voice grew louder. "You're nothing but a damned little tease, coming over here with me, and all, then not putting out."

Johnny stood at the window of the truck. A tall teenage boy in a cowboy hat was turned away from him, yelling at the girl in the passenger seat. "You want to introduce me to your friend, Gordy?" Johnny asked calmly.

The boy jerked his head around, his face tight with anger, his breath heavy with beer. "Take a hike, mister, this don't concern you none!" he sputtered.

Casually, Johnny reached in through the window and laid his hand with apparent gentleness on the back of the boy's neck. In a reasonable tone, he asked, "Now how can I explain how wrong you are, so that even a pea-brained pissant like you can understand?"

Jeff's eyes widened and his shoulders hunched in pain as Johnny's grip tightened.

"Why don't you climb on out of there, Gordy," Johnny suggested, looking beyond the boy at his daughter who huddled against the passenger door.

"Don't hurt him, Daddy," Gloria pleaded as she opened the truck's door. "He's just kind of drunk."

"I recognize the symptoms, Gordy. He's also kind of a jerk." He punctuated his last word by sending the boy sprawling on the truck seat.

"Damn, dude!" Jeff complained, rearranging his hat and his attitude. "I didn't do anything. We were just talking, that's all," he whined.

"If that's just talking, son, you'd better learn a second language," Johnny snapped. Turning to his daughter, he demanded, "And what are you doing out here with a cow pie like this?"

"Oh, Daddy!" she exclaimed, exasperated. "I'm not a little girl any more." With that she turned and stomped away.

Watching her walk away in her tight jeans, her long, dark hair flowing from beneath a cowboy hat, he had to admit she didn't look like the chubby little girl who had earned the nickname Gordy, short for the Spanish "Gordita." But Johnny wasn't ready to concede the point. "Wait a minute there, missy. I may have lost a few brain cells over the years, but I can still count. There were only fourteen candles on your last birthday cake."

Gloria ignored him and kept walking.

"She's only fourteen?" Jeff marveled, looking after her as he rubbed his aching neck. "No shit?"

"Shut your damn mouth, boy," Johnny ordered before setting off after her.

Gloria walked to the far end of the arena fence, beyond the parked vehicles. She stood, hands on hips and watched, without seeing it, as a livestock truck backed up to the pens where the rodeo stock was kept.

Johnny walked around in front of her in order to make her look at him. "You look just like your mom when she's mad." That was not what he had intended to say. "'Course that's about the only expression I've seen on her for years."

Gloria took a deep breath and shoved her hands into her pockets. "You didn't have to come on like such a cop, Dad. I can take care of myself."

Johnny lifted his hat and ran his fingers through his hair. "Well, from where I was standing, it didn't look like you had too many good options. You could either drive on down the road with a kid who's three sheets to the wind and likely to end up wrecked in a borrow ditch, or you could park someplace with the pimply faced little pervert and let him play grab-ass half the night. Which would you choose?"

Gloria kept silent. She swept her long hair back behind her shoulder and folded her arms across her chest. The toe of her cowboy boot began to tap. Maintaining her serious expression, she announced in her best Jack Benny impersonation, "I'm thinking," then burst into laughter.

Johnny hadn't expected that. He looked at her in surprise, then shook his head as a smile spread across his face in spite of himself. Opening his arms, he said, "Come here, little girl."

"Hi, Daddy," she said, as she hugged him.

Johnny took off her hat and kissed the top of his daughter's head. "It's good to see you, baby."

Gloria leaned back and wrinkled her nose at her father. "You smell like beer, too," she said.

"It's my aftershave," he replied, but his attention had suddenly shifted to a black Jeep with KC lights pulling out of the dusty arena parking lot. "What'd you say, Gordy?"

"I said can you give me a ride home?"

"Yeah, of course I can." The Jeep was turning toward town. "Let's hurry, though." He grabbed Gloria's hand and started walking quickly toward his truck. "I've got to get to my radio." He broke into a trot, almost dragging his daughter after him.

"What is it, Daddy?" She had to use her free hand to keep her hat on.

"I just spotted somebody I've been looking for." He fished his keys out just as he got to his truck. Flinging the door open, he snatched the microphone off the dashboard. "Unit Seven to base, come in." Silence. "Unit Seven to base, come in." Silence. Gloria tapped on the window of the still locked passenger door.

Johnny leaned over and flipped the button up. "This is Unit Seven. Where the hell is the damn dispatcher? Over!"

As Gloria climbed onto the seat and slammed the door, the staticky voice of Sheriff Carter came over the speaker. "This is base to Unit Seven. The dispatcher is in the can. Go ahead, Unit Seven, but remember the FCC still has rules about profanity on these frequencies. Over."

Johnny rolled his eyes. "Sorry, Sheriff. I'm at the rodeo arena in Las Animas and I just spotted our Texas Jeep leaving here and heading back in toward town. I thought maybe we should alert the Las Animas PD and the Bent County Sheriff's Department and see if we can't grab this sumbitch."

"Language, Deputy Hart, language! But, yes, we'll contact them immediately." There was a hiss as the transmission ended, then almost immediately another click. "Good work, Deputy. Base out."

"Unit Seven, out." Johnny returned the microphone to the dashboard and started the truck. As he pulled out, Gloria asked, "Was that a bad guy you spotted?"

"We think he's a rustler. Probably the boss of a couple of hombres your mother's prosecuting," he explained.

Gloria half turned on the bench seat. She looked more like a little girl again. "You and Mom have been talking more lately, huh?"

Johnny glanced at his daughter, then back at the road. "Mostly business," he shrugged. "Besides, she's got herself a new admirer now, doesn't she?"

"Who, Mom?" she asked, puzzled.

"Yeah, that guy in her office. What is it, Al . . . Allen?"

"Alex?" Gloria asked, amazed. "Are you joking? The guy's totally retentive!"

"Retentive, huh?" He pondered that. "Still, he seems kind of interested, doesn't he? And, I mean, he's white collar and all. A lawyer?" He hoped his probing wasn't as clumsy as it felt.

"Well, Mom calls him a *mosca.* You know, one of those horseflies always buzzing around your face."

Up ahead, Johnny saw the Jeep pulling out of a gas station. He could be heading back toward Lamar on Highway 50, he thought, and sped up.

Gloria realized that her father's attention had shifted again. "Is that the perp, Dad?"

"The what?" Johnny glanced at her.

"The perp, you know, perpetrator. That's how the cops on TV talk."

"Perp, huh? Now isn't that cute!" He smiled at his daughter. "But, yeah, that's our bad guy." He looked around. "I don't see any local white hats on him, though."

He picked up the microphone again. "Unit Seven to base, come in."

"Go ahead, Unit Seven."

"Freddy, I called in a black Jeep for the Bent County folks a little while ago. Did you get hold of anybody yet?"

"Sure did, Johnny, but they got some kind of big beer party— bunch of bikers or something—that turned into a fight over at the John Martin Reservoir, so nobody's in the area right now."

Johnny sighed. "Saturday night!" he shook his head. Clicking the microphone, he said, "Well, all right. I got the suspect spotted, so I'll birddog him for a while, but I'm off duty and I've got a civilian with me, so see if you can't keep on 'em to get a unit out here."

"I sure will, Johnny."

"Unit Seven out." He put the microphone back on the dashboard.

Ahead, the Jeep crossed the Arkansas River and turned west on route 194 instead of continuing east on Highway 50.

"Now where are you off to, Tex?" Johnny muttered. "Off to do a little shopping for beef?"

"Do you have your gun with you, Dad?" Gloria interrupted his reverie.

"I suppose it's around here someplace. Why? Do you need it?"

"No," Gloria said with infinite patience, "but you might."

"Shoot, I hope not," Johnny said. "I don't much like guns."

The pickup and the Jeep were just about the only two vehicles on the road at that hour. The moon was dark and the night seemed particularly black. Houses were few and set back so far that their lights gave no illumination to the road. The taillights of the Jeep were like red eyes staring back at those who followed. From his open window, Johnny could hear the hum of tires matching the steady drone of insects from the fields.

They drove on for another ten minutes, due west. Gloria found the La Junta radio station and turned it up loud. Johnny immediately lowered the volume and picked up his microphone. "Unit Seven to base. Come in."

"This is base. Go ahead, Unit Seven."

"Yeah, Freddy. We're still by ourselves out here. Won't be long before we hit the county line. Why don't you call Otero County and see if they can send a car out this way to meet this guy. Over."

"I'll do that Johnny. Base out."

As soon as Johnny clicked off the microphone, the Jeep began to pull away from his truck. He could hear the whine as the driver down-shifted and accelerated.

"I'll be damned," Johnny muttered as he pushed down on the gas pedal. "He must have a police band scanner in there and finally tuned us in." Reaching onto the floor of the truck, he picked up the flashing bubble light, clicked it on, and, reaching out the window, stuck it on the top of the truck's cab. "Put your seat belt on, Gordy. Daddy's got to go to work now."

The flashing light spurred the Jeep on faster. The whining descended as he shifted into fifth gear. The truck's speedometer quivered at 80 and the fence posts became a blur on the edge of the headlights.

Johnny was keeping up, but wishing he'd had two or three fewer beers back at the rodeo. "Hell of a way to spend my day off," he said to himself. The wind whistling past his side mirror made it difficult for Gloria to hear him. All she could see by the dashboard's light was her father frowning in concentration.

"Wonder if he knows about that bend in the road up here by Horse Creek?" he wondered out loud. Through the open window came the screeching of brakes and the Jeep's taillights wavered in a cloud of dust as the driver spun to the left. With his high beams on, Johnny could see the Jeep sway over onto the right two wheels and nearly roll, before heading off in the new direction with a spray of gravel from the shoulder of the two-lane road.

"Hang on, baby," Johnny called to his daughter, who was already hanging on. He pulled the wheel hard to the left before reaching the curve and let the truck drift sideways for twenty feet until the tires finally got traction and launched them off in their new direction.

"Yeah!" Gloria yelled, laughing in excitement. "Too cool, Dad!"

Gripping tightly with one hand on the wheel, Johnny grabbed his microphone. "Unit Seven to base. Come in."

"Go ahead, Unit Seven."

"Freddy, we've got us a by-God chase going on here now. Did you raise anybody over in Otero County?"

"Their nearest unit is out in Cheraw, but he's on his way."

"Well, he'd better hurry or he'll miss this party. Unit Seven out."

Jeep and truck skidded through a sharp right turn and hurtled on through the night like train cars in a tunnel. As they crossed into Otero County, the road angled more toward the southwest. The truck's windshield became a killing field for nocturnal insects. The eyes of a coyote sparkled briefly in the headlights as it crouched by the side of the road, waiting for the speeding vehicles to pass.

A sign announcing Bent's Old Fort, 1 mile, came and went by the side of the road. A faint glow in the distance marked where the town of La Junta lay. Suddenly, the Jeep's taillights disappeared. Johnny's first reaction was to slow down, his eyes straining ahead into the darkness. Within a few seconds, a thin cloud of dust drifted across the high beams of his headlights. He braked, skidding to stop.

"He pulled off!" he grumbled, as he threw the truck into reverse. Fifty feet back, he could see the dust drifting out past the sign announcing the entrance to the Bent's Old Fort National Historic Site. Johnny turned left and entered. The parking lot was to the right.

"It sure is dark tonight," Gloria noted. "I can't see anybody."

"Me either," Johnny agreed. He leaned out his window to get a clearer view than his bug-spattered windshield could provide.

The parking lot was laid out in a horseshoe. As he slowly circled back on the curving side of the lot, he noticed that one of the concrete bumpers was knocked askew in its parking space. He turned his truck so that the lights illuminated it directly. There was a black streak on the gray concrete, as if a tire had struck it.

Johnny put the truck in park and stopped the engine. The flashing bubble light continued to blink on the roof of the cab. Stepping out, he strained to listen. All he could hear was the chanting of crickets and the ticking of his truck's overheated engine as it cooled.

"It looks like he busted out into the field beyond there someplace. He must be sitting quiet and holding his breath," Johnny said in a hushed tone to his daughter. "I want you to stay here, Gordy. Roll up the windows and lock these doors. You know how to work the radio. I'm gonna take a look around."

Without a word, Gloria nodded, wide-eyed and nervous. As he walked away, Johnny could hear the click of the locks and the squeak of the window being rolled up.

The parking lot lay about a quarter mile from the walls of the restored old adobe fort. In order to give visitors a more authentic experience, a berm of earth had been thrown up along the south side of the parking lot to hide it from the view of those within the fort. In his flashlight beam, Johnny could plainly see where the Jeep had slammed over the concrete bumper and spun its wheels as it scrambled furiously up the embankment of earth.

Johnny followed the tire tracks, his boots sounding loudly in the stillness of the night. Once he crested the edge of the berm, the open field stretched out through the gloom toward the denser mass of the old trading post. The Jeep had only gone about fifty yards before stopping.

Johnny approached the vehicle carefully, holding the flashlight as far to the side of his body as he could reach, just in case the Jeep's owner had a gun. He could detect no movement from the vehicle.

From ten feet away, his light explored the windows and open driver's door. There was no movement. Faintly, in the distance, he could hear the howl of a siren that he hoped was coming his way. After a few seconds, he stepped up to the open door to check the interior.

The windshield was shattered from at least two impacts, one on the driver's side and the other on the passenger's. Johnny sucked his breath in as his light caught the shape of something dark on the floor of the passenger side. The flashlight revealed a dog, a Doberman by the looks of it, crumpled on the floor in front of the passenger's seat. One hind leg was still caught up on the center console. The animal's mouth was open in a bloody grimace, and its eyes were half-open and lifeless. Johnny assumed that the dog must be responsible for at least half of the shattered windshield.

He flashed the light back on the dog's hind paw. Just about the right size for that paw print he had seen out at the Cross place. Leaning back out of the Jeep he glanced around. "Now where did . . . ?" The answer struck him with almost physical force before he could even complete the question. "Oh, God!" he exclaimed as he turned and ran back toward the parking lot where he'd left his truck and his daughter.

As soon as her father disappeared from the truck's headlights, Gloria began searching the interior of the truck. In the glove compartment, beneath a crumpled map and a half-eaten fruit pie, she found her father's gun. It was an old-fashioned Colt .44 caliber revolver, strapped into a leather holster. Johnny had taught both of his children how to use and respect the danger of that weapon, so Gloria quickly determined that the chamber and all the cylinders were empty.

"Oh, Daddy!" she muttered to herself in frustration. A further search revealed a box of ammunition in the seat cover pocket. It had been a long time since she'd handled the pistol. That, and her nervousness, made her fumble as she started to load it.

From the corner of her eye, she saw a dark shape move through the headlights of the truck. "Daddy?" she looked up.

A face, grim and blood-streaked, stared at her through the driver's side window. A bloody hand pressed against the glass. "Open it! Open the door!" the man hissed at her, rattling the door handle.

Gloria shrank back in horror against the passenger's side door. "No," she whispered, shaking her head furiously. She wanted to scream but couldn't find enough breath.

"Open it!" the man demanded one more time, more loudly.

Gloria could only shake her head, sobbing in fear.

The man stepped back, and she could see a tire iron lifted, then smashed against the driver's side window.

As glass showered across the truck's interior, Gloria finally found her voice. "No!" she screamed.

Just as the man reached in to lift the lock on the door, Johnny reached him. Using his flashlight like a nightstick, he swung at the man's head. He delivered a glancing blow as he himself was knocked to the ground. There was a pain in his thigh like a hot knife.

"Get him, Eva! Kill him!" the man yelled, urging the dog on.

The Doberman needed little encouragement. With a throaty snarl, the dog again lunged at Johnny's leg as he lay on the ground, but Johnny managed to land one good blow with the flashlight on the dog's nose, making her yelp and retreat momentarily.

Gloria saw the man turn his attention on Johnny. He was kicking at Johnny and trying to get a solid hit with his tire iron. Galvanized by the appearance of her father, she quickly finished loading the pistol and snapped the chamber closed. Jerking her door open, she rushed out and around the tail of the truck.

Men, girl, and beast were all so absorbed in their desperate struggle that none of them noticed as the Otero County Sheriff's Patrol car screamed into the parking lot, lights flashing. Skidding to a stop, the headlights flooded across the scene, revealing a man on the ground, one arm raised to fend off a blow from a man with a tire iron while a large black dog attacked his leg. A woman raised a gun and pointed it in the direction of the prostrate man. There was an explosion, and her gun spat fire.

Deputy Bob Evans leaped from the patrol car. Jerking his own gun from its holster, he leveled it across the top of the open car door. "Drop the gun! Do it now!" he commanded in a voice even louder than he'd intended.

Johnny looked at the dog, now dead at his side, at his attacker frozen in the headlights, the tire iron still raised, his face toward the patrol car, and at his daughter, a bewildered, stunned look on her face as she turned, gun in hand, toward the voice.

"Drop it, lady!"

"No!" Johnny lurched to his feet, straining toward his daughter. From the corner of his right eye, he saw the flash of the muzzle a split second before the sound of the shot. Johnny kept going until he stood, his daughter wrapped in his arms, his back to the patrol car. "Wait! Don't shoot! It's all right!" he yelled into the night sky.

The confusion suddenly ceased and silence, like the dust, settled on the scene.

"John? Are you okay?" Deputy Evans asked, anxiously.

Johnny held his daughter at arm's length and studied her. She was weeping quietly, the gun held limply in her hand. Beside them, the man lay groaning on the ground.

Johnny knelt quickly to check. "You shot him, Bob! You'd better call for an ambulance."

"Well, hell, I was aiming at the gal with the gun!" Deputy Evans called back, annoyed.

Johnny stood up. "That's my daughter, Bob. She just shot the dog that was chewing on me." Gently, he took the gun from her hand and put his arm around Gloria's shoulder. Kissing the top of her head, he whispered, "Thank you, baby."

Bob walked over to them, pushed his cowboy hat back, and let out a frustrated puff of breath. "Well, then, who did I just plug?" he asked.

"You did good, Bob. He was trying to bust my head in with that tire iron."

Bob shook his head. "After the last time I saw you, I got booted out of that nice, easy bailiff's job in the courthouse to driving around in the middle of the night. Now, after this," he waved at the dead dog, wounded man and weeping girl, "I don't know where I'm gonna wind up. You know, I'm really not all that glad to see you anymore, John."

Johnny patted him on the shoulder. "I know just how you feel, Bob. But listen, you'd better get that ambulance now, before this fellow bleeds to death."

⋀⋀⋀

Johnny sat on the uncomfortable vinyl couch with his arm around his daughter. Bob stood at the other end of the emergency room listening as a Pakistani doctor talked to Sheriff Franklin.

The automatic doors wheezed open as Barbara and Jack hurried in. Johnny was surprised to see how his son towered over his mother. It has been a long time since he had seen him.

"Ay, mija!" Barbara rushed to her daughter. "Are you okay?"

Gloria sat up, smiling sleepily at her mother. "Hi, Mom."

"They gave her a sedative of some kind," Johnny explained, "so she's kind of out of it. But otherwise, she's all right."

"No thanks to you!" Barbara's eyes flashed as she turned toward Hart. "Que clase de padre eres tu?" she sputtered. "What do you mean taking your own daughter out on a chase? You might have killed her, you ... you ..." In frustration at her inability to express her anger properly, she slapped Johnny on the shoulder. "Idiot!"

"Now wait just a dang minute, Barb," Johnny stood up, pushing his hat back belligerently, his own anger flushing in his face. "What do you mean letting her go off to a rodeo in Las Animas with some drunken yahoo?"

Barbara looked both angry and baffled. "What are you talking about? Gordy said she was going over to Linda's house."

"Well, we seem to have some kind of communication problem here," Johnny said sarcastically. "Unless Linda lives in Las Animas and is trying to grow a mustache!"

Jack folded his arms across his chest. "You're in some deep shit now, Gordy," he observed smugly.

"*Callate*, Jack," Barbara snapped. Turning to her daughter she demanded, "What's going on, Gloria? Tell the truth!"

Gloria continued to smile dreamily, her eyelids drooping. "Hi, Mom! Daddy's home!"

Barbara looked at Johnny, who shrugged. "That shot they gave her, I guess."

"Well, she's got some serious explaining to do tomorrow. Come on, let's get her home," Barbara said, taking her daughter by the arm to lift her from the couch. "Help me, Jack. Get her other arm."

They guided Gloria to her feet, where she sagged against her brother. For the first time, Barbara noticed the blood on Johnny's pant leg. The white of the bandage showed through the ripped jeans. "Johnny," she pointed, "what happened? Are you okay? Did you get shot?" She frowned in concern.

"No," he assured her, pleased at her attention. "It's a dog bite, that's all. Like I was a damn mailman or something." He smiled ruefully.

"Still," she said. "You probably shouldn't drive. You can come stay over at the house." She glanced at her son, who avoided her eyes.

"Well, thanks, Barb," Johnny said quietly. "I'd like that." He rubbed his hand on the back of his neck. "Do you have anything to drink at the house?" he asked, laughing. "This has been a hell of a night!"

Barbara's expression turned to stone. "No, Johnny, I don't have anything to drink in the house anymore."

"Oh, well," Johnny looked uncomfortable. "I'd probably better talk to Tom and give him some kind of report." He waved toward Sheriff Franklin, who was saying something to a very downcast Deputy Evans. "I'll be along in about an hour."

"No, Johnny." Barbara said in a tightly controlled voice. "You are welcome to come now, right now, with me and your son and your daughter. Not later. Not after you've put away a six pack." She waited for Johnny to respond, but he just sighed and looked down at his boots.

"Come on, kids," she said quietly. "Let's go home."

Johnny didn't look up to watch them leave. He only heard the thump of the automatic doors as they closed behind his family.

CHAPTER 6

As Sandy drove into the yard, she was glad to see Char emerge from the barn and smile at her. Lady stood at his heel, tongue lolling, tail wagging. She stopped the truck, but the cloud of dust that had followed her drifted past, covering man, dog, and barn before settling. The truck itself chugged and clattered for another minute before sputtering into silence.

"Boy, that thing's dieseling like a son of a gun, isn't it?" Char observed as he walked toward the driver's-side door. "I'm not that great a mechanic, but I'd better take a look under the hood before it shakes itself to death."

"You'd better check with Grandpa first before you fix it. Battling this truck is practically his whole reason for living these days. If you actually fixed it, I don't know what he'd do." Sandy stepped out of the truck. "It's good to see you back, Char."

Char gave a low whistle of appreciation as he half circled around Sandy. "My, my, my! Don't you look fine today, Miss Cross! What's the occasion?"

She cocked her head, embarrassed and pleased. "It's Sunday. I went on in to church."

Char shook his head admiringly. "To see you in a dress, yes sir, I'm convinced there is a God." He leaned against the truck bed, smiling.

Sandy closed the truck's door. "You should come with me sometime. You might like it."

He spread his arms wide, looking up at the sky with his eyes closed, a contented look on his face. "This is all the church I need, thank you."

"You don't come for the building, silly. You come to learn something about God—to meet with him," Sandy said in a soft voice, giving Char a quizzical, sidelong look.

"Oh, we've met," Char said, his tone more serious. He looked out at the horizon, away from Sandy.

"So tell me about him," Sandy said in a teasing voice. "Describe God for me."

Char looked back at her, a puzzled look on his face. "What do you mean? God is a spirit. It's not like he's short or tall, fat or thin, or anything."

Sandy nodded. "I know that. No, what I mean is like, if you know somebody, you can describe their nature, their character. I've known you for a little while now, and I'd say you're a pretty nice guy. You're real thoughtful and hard-working, and you're real gentle with the animals. If I were to describe you that way to somebody else who knew you, I think they'd recognize you. So how would you describe God?" She arched her eyebrows, a hint of a smile on her lips.

Char looked uncomfortable. "I don't know." He folded his arms and lowered his chin to his chest, thinking. "I don't know," he repeated. "When I was a kid, I guess I thought God was distant and powerful and kind of scary. But now," he looked at Sandy to judge how she would react, "now, I get the feeling he likes me. Strange as that sounds."

Sandy smiled. "That doesn't sound strange. That sounds like the same God I know. But what makes you think so?"

His expression turned more serious and he looked squarely at Sandy. "He saved my life."

"How?" she asked, equally serious.

Char sighed. "You sure you want to hear all this? This is getting pretty heavy."

She laid her hand on his arm. "Yes, Char, I really do want to know, unless it bothers you to talk about it."

Char nodded, turned around and leaned his forearms on the wall of the truck bed. Lady lay down in the shade of the truck, her chin resting on her paws. "I'm sure you know all the stereotypes about drunken Indians. Man, I hate that! My mother was an alcoholic. Anyway, I swore I wasn't going to be another drunken Indian. But hanging around with my friends and then, later on, with the rodeo, it seems like that's all everybody does is drink and party.

"So I just kind of rolled with the flow, thinking I had it all under control. I'd tell myself I could handle it, that it wasn't doing anybody any harm.

"But then, last year . . ." He paused, glancing at Sandy, who nodded for him to continue.

"Down in Scottsdale, I was working the rodeo. That's when Johnny got hung up on that rank bull. Right then, I felt like I was moving through molasses. Everything I did was just a little too slow, just a second too late. I saw that bull turn back on Johnny when he was down, and I knew he was aiming to gore him. I've seen it a hundred times! But I couldn't move until it was too late. It's like my feet were lead and my brain was mush and I just watched as that bull ripped him wide open."

Char closed his eyes and rubbed his hand across his face as if to wipe away the memory. "I could've saved him! I knew what was going to happen. But I was so hung over and out of shape, that I was just too slow and too late."

He shook his head. "I rode with him to the hospital." He gave a short, dry laugh. "Johnny's for sure part Indian now. Turned out we're the same blood type, so they used me to give him a transfusion.

"Anyway, after that, I went on a real tear. I quit rodeoing and just drank my way north from Arizona. I guess I thought I was heading home to Montana. I wound up in Denver." He looked again at Sandy. "You ought to get a kick out of this, Church Lady. It was Christmas Eve, and colder than a witch's . . . well it was plenty cold. Just a little bit of snow and plenty of wind. Well, there's old Char Sixkiller, the man who hated all the stereotypes, drunk and sick and freezing, and leaning against the wall of a liquor store on Colfax Avenue with a couple of guys, arguing about who gets to take the last swallow from the bottle."

Char took a large gulp of air and let it out slowly. "It was like one of those cartoons where the light bulb goes off over the character's head. Only this was a flashbulb, showing me a snap shot of myself as every drunken Indian I ever looked down on while I said, it won't happen to me."

He was quiet for a long time, seemingly studying the tips of his dusty boots. "I sure am taking a long time to get to the point, aren't I?" he asked, embarrassed. "Anyway, I walked away from there and tried to dry myself out, wandering around trying to keep warm, doing a little panhandling, trying to decide if I should buy a bottle or a gun, when I ran into this Arikara bronc rider I knew from the Indian rodeo days, and he's looking pretty good. Real healthy.

"He sized me up real quick and handed me a business card. Seems there's an Alcoholics Anonymous group in Denver, made up of Indian men. I kind of tried to shine him on, telling him I was cool, I didn't have a problem, but he could see what was happening.

"So he packs me into his truck, drives me out, buys me a meal, and takes me to the meeting. I listened for about thirty minutes and realized that push had come to shove."

Char gave a weak smile, embarrassed at having revealed so much about himself. "The point of all this is, that, part of the program is to realize that you can't get yourself together. You have to call on a power greater than yourself to pull you up. Well, I did, half expecting the line to be busy or to find that scary, indifferent power I imagined as a kid. But, I just said, 'Grandfather—Wise One Above—whether I live or die, it's in your hands. Help me.'"

He shook his head, unaware that a tear had rolled from the corner of his left eye and was making its way slowly across his cheek. In a whisper, he said, "And he did. There weren't any flashing lights and rolling thunder. It was more like somebody came up behind me and put his arms around me, you know, just to let me know that he was there. And he's been there every day since then." Char fell silent.

"I've seen you praying in the morning," Sandy said quietly, blinking back her own tears. "I'm glad. I think we're kind of praying to the same God."

"Whew!" Char gave a little laugh, standing up straight and clearing his throat. "Could we change the subject a little, I feel like we're on Oprah or something."

Sandy laughed. "What do you say we eat something? Then I'll step into a phone booth someplace and change back into super-cowgirl again."

Char nodded.

"So how was your trip?" Sandy asked as they headed toward the house. "Where was it this time, New Mexico?"

"Yeah," Char said. "We can get a couple days work done, but then I'll have to head on down to Texas."

ʌʌʌ

"Have a seat, Deputy." Sheriff Carter pointed toward the stiff backed chair in front of his desk. The slight twitch at the corners of his mouth was what passed for a friendly smile. "How's the leg healing?"

"Fine, fine," Johnny said, taking the seat. "I've been hurt worse bumping into barstools." He immediately regretted his feeble attempt at humor.

The already faint smile disappeared from the sheriff's face. "I'm sure you have," he said, turning his attention to the yellow note pad on his desk where it was his custom to organize his thoughts into days and his days into the administration of the department. "Well, we have some work for you. I've just gotten off the phone with Deputy District Attorney Gutierrez, in La Junta. I believe that you are acquainted with her?" The twitch reappeared on the sheriff's lips. "She's been doing a lot of work on the case against our rustler."

"Oh? Anything new?" Johnny inquired.

"As a matter of fact, yes," the Sheriff replied. "She ran the license plates on that cattle truck the two Mexicans were driving and found out it had been rented by somebody in Amarillo—somebody who fits the description of our man in the Jeep. He gave a false name and used a phony driver's license in the name of Vick Eden. They got back the identification on his fingerprints, though, and it seems his real name is William James King of San Angelo, Texas."

"San Angelo, huh!" Johnny mused. "I've been through there plenty of times, rodeoing." He paused, then laughed and shook his head. "Vick Eden? Vick and Eden are two little towns southeast of San Angelo. I don't know where he got the license, but I'll bet that's where he got the name."

Carter nodded. "That's very interesting, Deputy. So is where he gets his real name, King. It seems his father is a rather prominent cattle buyer down in that part of the country. San Angelo police think the father is probably legitimate, but they wouldn't be a bit surprised if young Billy wasn't using his father's good name to peddle those stolen beeves, no questions asked. It seems they have a bit of a sheet on young King going back to juvenile court. So he steals them up here in Colorado and sells them down there in Texas where he can cash in on his father's reputation."

"Would you call that, 'cattle laundering'?" Hart asked, smiling.

"I suppose so," the sheriff said, unamused. "Now here's where we have a little bit of a proof problem, according to your wife—Ms. Gutierrez," he corrected. "With the exception of those cattle we seized with the truck, we've got no proof, at least as long as those two Mexicans continue to keep quiet."

"Past evidence is all Big Macs by now, huh?" Johnny observed.

"Yes, Deputy," the sheriff agreed wearily. "It seems the strongest charge we have on him is stealing that cattle truck in Amarillo. He used false identification, only paid for one week, used a stolen credit card to post bond for it, and never did turn it back in. That, of course, is all down in Texas. But then, why should the hard-pressed taxpayers of Colorado have to go to the expense of prosecuting this individual, then housing him in Canon City for the next several years? Why not send him back home to Texas and let them foot the bill? They gave him to us, so we'll just give him back again."

"Makes sense to me," Johnny nodded.

"I'm glad you think so, Deputy Hart, because returning this prodigal son is going to be your assignment." The sheriff reached into his in basket and picked up a packet bound with rubber bands. Laying it before Johnny, he explained. "That's the extradition order from the judge, along with a travel voucher from the Potter County sheriff down there. You can use one of our vehicles—a car with a cage, not your truck—and transport young Billy the Kid back to Amarillo. You pick him up in La Junta. We've notified all the law enforcement agencies between here and Amarillo. Keep good track of every mile and meal from the moment you leave here. It should be just one day down, one night stay over, and one day back. You leave first thing tomorrow morning. Any questions?"

Just thinking about the long drive made Johnny tired. "Is our boy, Billy, up to travel already?"

The sheriff nodded. "He lost some blood, but it wasn't that serious a wound. A few years back you'd have been flying him down first class, but nobody's got those kinds of budgets anymore."

Johnny sighed. "I guess I should be glad they didn't send me a bus ticket and have him sit on my lap the whole way." He picked up the paperwork. "Anything else, Sheriff?"

"No." Carter frowned and cleared his throat. "You did a good job on this case, Deputy Hart. It was your investigation, your hunches, your legwork, and your luck. Now I hope I don't need to say this, but stick to water and coffee on this trip. Do you hear me?"

Johnny stood up, his face flushing slightly. "I hear you, Sheriff." He nodded. "I'll see you in a couple of days."

⌃⌃⌃

Char turned to face the approaching horse. "Morning, Mr. Cross."

The arthritic old man who seemed ancient afoot, seemed twenty years younger sitting ramrod straight in the saddle. He didn't try to dismount, though, in deference to his painful knees.

Reining his horse to a halt, he leaned forward, resting his forearms on the pommel. "You're a pretty early riser, young feller," Mr. Cross said, squinting across the dry creek bed. The tops of the trees were just beginning to glow in the light of the rising sun. "Thought I might find you out here." He looked at Char, who stood, reins in hand, next to his horse. "Sandy told me you were Cheyenne."

Char nodded. "What made you decide to fence this in, Mr. Cross?" The wave of his arm encompassed the site of the Sand Creek Massacre. "No offense, but you strike me as a whole lot more cowboy than Indian."

Mr. Cross gave a brief, wheezy laugh. "Used to be an old cowboy song. I can't sing a lick, but the words were, 'Oh, the Indians and the Cowboys, they used to live in peace, till the goddamned dryland farmers come driftin' in from the East.' Maybe cowboys and Indians aren't all that different after all. We both kinda liked things better the way they were."

"Still, these weren't your people," Char said.

"Nope, no they weren't," he nodded. "But maybe that's a part of it too. I don't even know my people."

Char looked up quizzically. "How's that?"

Mr. Cross straightened up, stretching his back. He loosened the reins to allow his horse to crop a mouthful of grass. "Well, I was an orphan who came west on the orphan train back in 1919. I was luckier than most, I guess. Five years old, I landed with a family working a little piece of land outside of Guyman, Oklahoma. They were trying to make a go of it raisin' broomcorn, and later, wheat. They were named Cross. I don't even know what my real mother and father were called. Well, I just barely got there, it seems, and Mr. Cross up and died from the influenza. That was a bad winter. Lots of folks died down there."

He shook his head at the old memory. "Mrs. Cross lost the farm and we moved on over to Boise City where she did some work as a seamstress and laundry woman. Business wasn't too bad among all the roughnecks out there workin' the oil rigs. Year or two later and she managed to marry again. A man named Grover. He was a tough old buzzard. He'd already worked one wife to death. He ran a few cows up along the Cimarron. He didn't much care for me, but I did get my first real experience cowboyin' on his place.

"Mrs. Cross, God rest her, she up and died of the diphtheria along about '27. By then, me and old man Grover had about had our fill of each other, so I drifted on." Mr. Cross scratched his chin. "Listen to me, now, blowin' on like an old man about times gone by."

"No, I'm interested," Char assured him. "What happened next?"
Mr. Cross laughed. "I became a bootlegger. I made good money at
that, but I moved on. Just started cowboyin' from one spread to
another. Drifted north to this country and kinda liked it." He smiled.
"What I really liked was Sandy's grandma. Her folks had been home-
steaders down near Two Buttes, just scratchin' out a living. After the
First World War, the price of almost every crop just dropped like a
rock, so they'd gone up to Lamar and her daddy tried to make a go of
it as a mechanic.

"Eleanor hadn't much cared for farming, but she didn't like bein' in
town neither. Well, we met at a dance and once I fell in love, I got
downright ambitious.

"I'd worked as a hand on this place," he waved his hand at the
surrounding land, "and liked it. The man that owned it, never had no
kids of his own, so he finally decided to quit fightin' and he let me take
over the mortgage as long as we'd let him stay on until he died. Eleanor
agreed with me that that was about as good a deal as we'd ever get, not
havin' a nickel of real money between us. So I got the ranch and a good
wife and I've been here ever since." Mr. Cross gave a contented sigh.

"What about this place, though?" Char asked, swinging up into the
saddle.

The two men started their horses back toward the house. "That's
right, I kinda got off the subject, didn't I? Well, it was the old man told
me about this place," Mr. Cross continued. "He called it The Battlefield.
He'd pick up souvenirs like old shell casings and arrowheads. Used to
even brag that he was related to old Colonel Chivington. It wasn't till
later on that I learned what really happened here.

"Eleanor, my wife, had gotten more schoolin' than I did, and she
used to love to read. Got me started too. Many's the long winter
evening when we'd set and read after Billy was in bed. Not sayin' a
word, just content to be together." He rubbed his eyes.

"I got to readin' history, I guess 'cause I don't have no personal history myself. But the more I read about what really happened, the more it bothered me. I took the old man's souvenirs and buried them back out there by the Creek bed. Then I got to thinkin' about them cows grazin' on this piece. Believe me, I've been a cowboy too long to have any romantic notions about cows. They're dumb and dirty, and that's the truth. After Eleanor died, I got to thinkin' how I'd feel with cows trompin' all over her grave and that's when I decided to fence off that area."

Char nodded. "The old people would talk about it sometimes. How the people were moving closer to the army for protection so they wouldn't be mistaken for hostiles. The federals ordered them to stay here and not come any closer. Then Chivington and his Colorado Volunteers rode out and butchered them—women, children, old people. Chief White Antelope died beneath the American flag he'd raised to protect the people. The old ones remembered that—the sound of that flag snapping and popping in the cold wind as they ran up the creekbed and scattered out across the snow to escape." Char's face was hard, and his voice was too.

"You know your history," Mr. Cross said quietly.

Char turned in the saddle, intense. "My history, that's right! My personal history. I've got names for the relatives who died here. I can even tell you stories about some of them and the way they lived, what made them laugh or cry, the foods they liked, and the way they died."

They rode the rest of the way in silence. As they dismounted before the barn, Sandy came from the house smiling. "So where did you two disappear to?"

Char didn't answer as he uncinched and removed the saddle. Without a word, he walked with it into the barn.

Sandy turned to her grandfather, who simply raised his hand and shook his head to forestall any questions.

When Char emerged from the barn, he was rolling his motorcycle. "I've got to take off," he stated flatly.

"Texas?" Sandy asked. "How long will you be gone?"

Char shook his head, frowning. "I don't know." He pointed at his horse, which was standing unattended. "Grab his halter, Sandy. I don't want him to spook when I start this."

Sandy did as instructed. Both horses jerked their heads and shied back as the motorcycle roared. Char looked briefly at Mr. Cross and then at Sandy, his expression unreadable. Nodding, he said, "See ya," then rolled away from them up the dirt road and over the ridge without pausing or looking back.

"What happened, Grandpa?" she asked. "Why was Char so upset?"

Mr. Cross shook his head. "We were out there by the massacre site. He goes out there almost every mornin' before sunrise lately. We got to talkin' about what happened there—the massacre and all—and he just changed." He shook his head again, looking up the road where the dust of Sixkiller's passing was settling. "I like that feller, Sandy, I truly do. But something is gnawing away at him."

Turning again to look at Sandy, he said, "If he comes back, you watch yourself, hear!" He took the reins from Sandy and led the horses into the barn.

Sandy hugged herself, looking at the empty ridge. "If he comes back?"

⌃⌃⌃

Johnny pushed open the glass door of the Sheriff's Department relieved to get out of the Amarillo heat. It had been hot all night and the noisy air conditioner in his Grand Street motel room had not been very effective.

He'd arrived late the night before. The trip had been long and uneventful. Billy King, the prisoner, had slept the whole way due to the medication he was still taking for his gunshot wound. Johnny had tried to amuse himself by tuning in local radio stations along the way, but so many had taped, automated formats that they all sounded alike. The result was that he'd had long hours of silence in which to do nothing but drive and think. By the time he reached Amarillo he was thoroughly depressed. He'd handed the prisoner over to the jailer but, since the Sheriff wasn't in, he was not able to get the travel voucher signed. He'd gone back to the motel with a bag from Taco Bell and a six-pack of Lone Star and killed a couple of hours channel-surfing on the motel's cable TV. The novelty of that had worn off quickly. Between the air-conditioner and the traffic on Interstate 40, he had not slept well.

Now he was back at the stucco-coated office on South Pierce, travel voucher in hand, looking for the Sheriff so that he could start the long return trip to Colorado. The office seemed very busy, but he thought that might just be the difference between Amarillo and Eads. Johnny approached the woman deputy on duty at the front counter. Touching his fingers to his hat brim, he explained his reason for being there.

"Well," she frowned, "you're just gonna have to take a seat for a spell. Sheriff's mighty busy, right now, mighty busy! He's in with a couple of fellers from the FBI." She pursed her lips and nodded her head to underline the magnitude of the occasion.

Feeling like he was dealing with Kate's sister, Johnny voiced the expected question. "Something big going on?"

"I'll say!" she leaned forward conspiratorially. "Murder!" She nodded her head for emphasis. "And not just any old murder, mind you, but a serial killer." She pronounced the last two words very carefully.

In spite of himself, Johnny was a little curious. "Oh, yeah?" He lifted his eyebrows to give the deputy her cue to continue.

"You bet," she continued. "Happened just south of here in Randall County. They found a body this morning by the road outside Palo

Duro Canyon State Park." She looked around at the few people who were paying no attention to what she was saying, then dropped her voice to a theatrical whisper. "It was a woman, all mutilated! FBI thinks some Indian did it. One of our deputies even thinks he saw the guy ride through here last night on a motorcycle." She nodded, satisfied now that she had imparted most of what she knew. Before she could give any further embellishment, the phone on her desk rang.

"Yes, sir, right away." Hanging up, she gathered a stack of files and headed down the hall. "I'll tell Sheriff you're here," she called back over her shoulder.

Johnny took a seat on a molded plastic and aluminum chair and settled in for a long wait. He felt an uneasy knot beginning to form in his stomach after hearing "Indian" and "motorcycle."

But the deputy hurried back down the hall and waved to Johnny. "Sheriff will see you now."

At the end of the hall, she opened a door. A tall, rangy looking man in uniform stood behind a desk. Across from him stood a man in a business suit talking on the phone. On the other side of the office another younger man in a suit was talking on a different phone while two uniformed Texas Rangers stood conferring at a large wall map.

"Sheriff, this here's that deputy from Colorado that brought a prisoner down last night," the woman explained before leaving the office.

The sheriff extended his hand. "Tim Craig, Deputy. Welcome to Texas."

Johnny shook the hand. "John Hart. I guess I picked kind of a bad time." He waved at the crowded office.

The sheriff nodded. "We got us a bad one out there, all right."

The man in the suit hung up, and the sheriff made the introduction. "This is Special Agent Adam Sutton, with the FBI—their Denver office, in fact, up in your country. Agent Sutton, this is Deputy—I'm sorry, I just forgot your name in all this confusion."

"Hart. John Hart, Kiowa County Colorado Sheriff's Department," Johnny said, extending his hand. The agent gave it one quick shake as if that was all he could spare the time for. "Hart," he nodded curtly.

Sheriff Craig gave Johnny a second look. "John Hart, the bull rider?" he asked.

"Well, I used to be . . ." Johnny began.

"Why hell, I saw you last year out here at the Fairgrounds." Turning to the agent, he explained, "Deputy Hart here is a rodeo cowboy. Can ride most anything with hair on it, I'll allow!"

"I'm sure he can," Agent Sutton said, uninterested. "Sheriff, I want to get together a press release for those reporters down in the briefing room before they start reporting rumors. And how soon before your lab can give us some dental info so we can ID the victim?"

Sheriff Craig held up his hand. "Just a second, Mr. Sutton. Let me take care of Deputy Hart here real quick and I'll get on it."

"I just need you to approve and sign these travel vouchers," Johnny said, handing them to the sheriff.

Special Agent Sutton stood impatiently as the sheriff read through the mileage report and receipts. The man on the second phone raised his voice to make himself heard better by whomever was on the receiving end. "That's right. Six foot two, two hundred pounds, long black hair, dark complexion. American Indian. Goes by the name Charles Sixkiller. Yes, Six—like the number—Sixkiller."

"I said, here's your papers," the sheriff said, calling Johnny's attention back.

"Excuse me, Sheriff, but what do they want Sixkiller for?" Johnny asked.

"Do you know Charles Sixkiller?" Sutton asked as if only just noticing Hart.

"I know a man named Char . . . Charles Sixkiller. Rodeo clown. I've known him for years. What's going on?"

Agent Sutton and the other FBI man, now off the phone, exchanged looks. "Have a seat, Deputy Hart."

Johnny sat.

"When did you last see Sixkiller?"

Johnny hesitated, his mind racing. "Last year, October, at a rodeo in Arizona." He wasn't at all sure why he lied.

The agents looked less interested. "You should check your bulletins more often, Deputy. Our Behavioral Science Unit put out a Serial Killer Alert a week ago, after we were called into the case. It took time to figure out that there might be a connection between all these murders."

"I've been off duty for a few days," Johnny explained. "A Serial Killer Alert on Char Sixkiller?! What's he been doing, swatting too many flies? Even that would surprise me."

"You're very funny, Deputy," Sutton said, his face expressionless. "We have four or five, maybe more, murdered women who aren't laughing though. How well do you know Sixkiller?"

"We go way back in rodeo. This is crazy!"

"That's the word for it, Deputy," Sutton's partner deadpanned. "Is Sixkiller likely to contact you, do you think?"

"Well," Johnny's mind worked furiously, "yeah, it's possible he might." He wanted more information.

The agents exchanged looks again and Sutton nodded slightly.

"All right," the partner said crisply, "let me fill you in. First, tell me what you know about Sixkiller."

"He's probably the best bullfighter clown in rodeo," Johnny began. From their impatient looks, he knew that wasn't the information they wanted. "He was in the Army. Went to 'Nam."

Sutton nodded. "Special Forces."

"He's Cherokee, I think. Has some relatives in Oklahoma, maybe."

Sutton gave a sour look. "You really ought to get to know your friends a little better, Hart. Okay, here's the profile. Charles Sixkiller, born 1951, Oakland, California, to a Cherokee father and a Cheyenne mother. They weren't legally married. After the birth of a second child, the father went back to Oklahoma, where he did marry another woman. A white woman in fact. Sixkiller tried to visit his father once in 1976. The father wouldn't talk to him. The new wife called the cops to run him off the property. Note that, Deputy. That was a seed being planted.

"Earlier, Sixkiller's younger brother comes home from Vietnam in a box and Sixkiller whacks out. He's in Army recruiting at the time, winds up assaulting an officer. They give him a choice. He can go to Leavenworth or he can go to Vietnam. Our boy is on his way to 'Nam by way of the Special Forces school in Georgia.

"Once in-country, Sixkiller turns out to be a natural born killer. He gets all the spook missions, infiltration, assassination, demolition, you name it. He's real good with his hands and with a knife.

"Sixkiller is supposed to be on one of the last choppers out of Saigon. He misses it, but makes it back anyway. All right, he's back here maybe six months and his mother dies. She's drunk, her car breaks down, she freezes. This is Montana, February 1976. Another seed is planted."

Sutton's partner picked up the narrative while Sutton took a phone call. "Sixkiller starts working the rodeo circuit about then. He also begins making contact with certain radical elements in Indian country. 1978, Sixkiller's involved in what they called 'the Long Walk' . . . bunch of Indians walking across country to draw attention to their grievances."

Johnny actually remembered that. It was one of the few times Char had visited in his home. When the Walk came through La Junta, he and Barbara had let Char and a few other walkers spend the night. He hadn't thought much of it at the time. He'd done the same many times for other rodeo people passing through.

"Sixkiller has a way of getting around," the agent continued. "Over the years, he turns up when a bunch of radical Mohawks seize some land in upstate New York. When there's trouble in Arizona between the Navajo and Hopi, he shows up at some demonstrations. There's protests in Minneapolis, Sixkiller's there. Back in Arizona, the Fort McDowell Reservation gets all riled up 'cause they take their slot machines away. Sixkiller's on the scene again."

Agent Sutton rejoined them. "Meanwhile, Sixkiller's personal life is coming apart. His mother's dead, his brother's dead, his Cheyenne grandparents die within a year of each other, and his father's side still wants nothing to do with him. And our boy's getting himself a real drinking problem.

"Then this past winter, he bottoms out. He falls in with a bunch of other Indians in Denver who are into spiritual healing and other weird stuff, and now all those seeds are rooted, watered and grown. Pow!" He slapped his hands together. "It's harvest time. Sixkiller snaps. He focuses on white people as the source of his problems—white women in particular. Remember that woman who married his father?

"Now, what I'm about to tell you is strictly confidential. This is part of his MO, and we don't want this leaking out so we can have a dozen copycat wackos starting up. His targets are white women, generally blonde—the wicked stepmother was a blonde—and he doesn't just kill them. The killing is usually done with a gun, but afterward he carves them up. Probably some sick sexual thing according to the Behavioral Science people. But then he takes the body and dumps it someplace near a site where he thinks some injustice has been done to Indians in the past. We've got a historian working on that angle."

Agent Sutton opened a three ring binder to consult some notes. "We've got bodies now at the Wounded Knee battle site in South Dakota last winter, near Fort Grant in Arizona in the spring, outside Fort Sumner in New Mexico, and again along the Mimbres River outside Silver City, New Mexico, both this summer. And now we've got one by the Palo Duro Canyon here in Texas. Our historian says that all these places would mean something to somebody pretty familiar with Indian history."

Johnny felt numb. "So Char's had a rough life. How does that make him a suspect in all this, anymore than any other Indian?"

Sutton's partner smiled. "That's where we got lucky. Last month, after the Silver City killing, we found his truck broken down and abandoned in Las Cruces. Red Ford pick-up with Montana plates registered to none other than Charles Sixkiller, with an address in Lame Deer on the Cheyenne Reservation. And the tire treads match the tracks found near the body outside Silver City. And, to ice it, there's blood in the back of the truck that matches the victim."

Johnny almost blurted out that Sixkiller had said the truck was stolen, but realized that would reveal that he'd seen Char recently.

"Now, there's another kink in this guy's chain," Sutton continued, obviously enjoying performing before these unsophisticated cowboy cops. "He likes to leave little mementoes behind with the body, like clues to his little charade. Our historian had a real ball with these. In South Dakota we found a size fourteen tennis shoe next to the body. Big thing, obviously not the victim's. But it seems that the leader of the Indians in that battle back in 1890 was a Sioux Chief named Big Foot. By the body outside Silver City there was a red shirt." Sutton consulted his binder again. "In 1863, there was a Mimbres Apache chief named Mangas Coloradas—Spanish for Red Sleeves—who was killed by soldiers near there.

"The Fort Sumner body had a .32 caliber bullet in its mouth, unfired. It seems that the army kept a big part of the Navajo tribe penned up near there in the 1860s. The Navajo leader was a guy named Manuelito but the soldiers had a nickname for him—Pistol Bullet. This guy, Sixkiller, must really think he's cute.

"The Arizona body, the one by Fort Grant? Now that one nearly stumped our historian. Next to what was left of the body is a chalk line, you know, the kind carpenters use? Well, they had to work on that. In 1871, a band of Aravaipa Apache were just about wiped out by a bunch of Papago Indians and Mexicans out of Tucson. Not the Army, for a change. The leader of the Apaches was called Eskiminzin. Well it turns out, that was just a mispronunciation of his real name, Hash-ki-ban-zin, which means Angry Men Stand in Line for Him. Get it? 'In line'?"

Sutton shook his head, an odd half smile on his face. "Now this morning's body is a little simpler. They found one of those little wolf dolls like you can buy at Yellowstone or Yosemite. I just got off the phone with our historian. In 1874, the Cavalry surprised a bunch of Comanche and Kiowa hostiles in the Palo Duro Canyon. They drove off most of them then burned their food supplies and shot their horse herd so that the Indians would have to surrender before winter. The Kiowa Chief was named Lone Wolf." Sutton nodded. "This is one sick puppy we're dealing with."

Johnny could feel a vein throbbing in his neck, and there was a pain pounding against the back of his eyes in time with his heartbeat.

Sutton snapped his binder shut with a flourish. "If Sixkiller contacts you, I guess I don't have to tell you, we want to know about it, Deputy."

"Sure, sure," Johnny's voice made a tinny, echoing sound in his own ears and he felt like he might fall as he struggled to his feet. "I'd better get on down the road," he said, shaking hands again with Sheriff Craig. "Colorado's a long ways off." He nodded at the FBI agents and walked stiffly out of the office, crumpling the travel voucher into a wad.

Johnny walked past the talkative deputy at the counter without acknowledging her good-bye. He almost made it to his patrol car before he doubled over and vomited into the parking lot's gutter. The Texas sun burned hotly on his sweat-soaked shirt. He closed his eyes and steadied himself with one hand on the bumper of a parked pickup truck. His other hand clutched his stomach. He heard footsteps as someone approached, slowed, then passed him by, pretending not to notice.

With slow, deliberate breaths, he straightened up and stumbled the rest of the way to his car. The vehicle's interior was stifling and the steering wheel burned his hands, but he quickly started the engine, backed out of the parking space and left.

ʌʌʌ

"Deputy Hart, we haven't seen you out here in quite a while." Sandy held open the screen door, inviting Johnny to step into the kitchen. "Have you eaten yet? We were just about to have supper." Two plates and three pots were laid out on the kitchen table.

Johnny removed his hat. "Gee, I'm sorry to interrupt. It's kind of important, though."

Sandy smiled. "Well, I knew you guys weren't supposed to drink on duty, but does that include eating too?"

Johnny shook his head. "I'm not really on duty. I'm also not too hungry." He glanced toward the door leading to the rest of the house. "Is Char here, by any chance?"

"No," Sandy said, the beginnings of concern forming on her features. "Is something wrong?"

Johnny gave a long sigh. "Yeah, I'd say something's very wrong."

Mr. Cross paused in the doorway, nodded to Johnny, then sat down at the table. Lifting the lid to the largest pot, he asked, "You gonna set and eat with us, Deputy? Looks like macaroni and cheese."

Johnny twisted the brim of his hat in his hands. "Char's been spending a lot of time out here lately, hasn't he?"

Mr. Cross frowned up at Johnny. "He's a durn good hand," he said. "No law against that, is there?"

Sandy gripped the back of her chair. "You're starting to scare me, Deputy. What's going on?"

Johnny pointed at the chair. "You'd probably better sit down." When Sandy was seated, he briefly told them what the FBI suspected about Char.

"Oh, dear God!" Sandy gasped. "You don't believe them do you?" she asked staring hard at Johnny.

"No, I don't," Johnny said, hesitantly, "most of the time. But then a little voice goes off inside my head asking, 'what if?' What if his truck wasn't stolen? What if that was really him I saw in the truck? What if I really don't know Char? Or, what if he has a partner and they're both out there killing people?"

"No!" Sandy vehemently shook her head. "Char couldn't do that."

"What about Vietnam?" Johnny asked. "I mean, I knew Char was hell in a bar fight, but . . ." He shook his head.

Mr. Cross had been silent, staring at a spot on the table. Now he said, "Man is the most dangerous critter on earth. There's no way of knowin' for sure what any of us might do, given the wrong set of circumstances." He held up his hand to forestall another protest from Sandy. "I ain't saying he is the one doing the killin'. I thought he seemed like a pretty decent feller, myself. But I always did wonder what he was doing here."

"He just wanted to help out," Sandy insisted. "And I think he liked it here." She blushed slightly. She didn't want to admit that she had been more interested in the fact that Char was there than why.

Mr. Cross pushed his chair back from the table. "I'll tell you the truth, I thought myself, at first, that he was just a tomcat prowlin' around my granddaughter. I even asked him about it one time."

"Oh, Grandpa!" Sandy groaned.

"But he said that, much as he liked little Sandy," Mr. Cross continued, "she wasn't the only reason he was here. Then there was the other day when him and I was riding back from the massacre site and Char got all"—he paused, searching for the right word—"intense. Then he just up and rode on out of here."

Johnny leaned forward. "You said massacre site?"

"That's right," Mr. Cross said. "I forget you're still kind of new to this county." He pointed toward the west. "Out yonder there, along the creek, the Big Sandy Creek—that's why this place is called the L-S Ranch, Little Sandy—anyway, right here on this ranch is where the Sand Creek Massacre took place back in November of 18 and 64."

Sandy sat back in her chair, one hand over her mouth, eyes wide and unhappy. Johnny noticed, and asked, "I think I can guess, but tell me about it."

"Well," Mr. Cross explained, "back during the Civil War, there weren't that many regular army personnel out West here. Most of the regular army was back east killin' each other. The Indians thought the army leavin' meant that they'd won and driven the blue-coats away. Some of 'em started to get a little bold, and that's all the excuse some of those greedy Denver politicians needed. They screamed that it was a full scale uprisin' and sent out the Colorado Volunteers under Colonel Chivington to drive out or wipe out all the Indians in Colorado Territory. You see, a big chunk of this part of the state was supposed to be a Cheyenne Reservation. Well them big bellied boys in Denver couldn't stand the thought of all that river water and grass land goin' to waste on a bunch of Indians when they could be makin' money off it.

"One group of Cheyenne—yeah, Cheyenne, Char's folks—they wanted to live in peace, so they asked the army if they could come on down to the Arkansas River and live near the troops at Fort Lyons so nobody would mistake them for hostiles. They was on their way when the army ordered them to stop here and not come any closer.

"It was the end of November, and it snowed that night. Next morning, the Cheyenne woke up to see Colonel Chivington and his Volunteers all around 'em. Well, it didn't take much of an excuse. The soldiers started shootin' and burnin' teepees. And it wasn't warriors they was shootin' at. Women, little kids, old people. Them people that wasn't killed in the first volley, started running up the creekbed with bluecoats like hornets on their trail. Some of the younger men dug caves and trenches into the sides of the creek with their bare hands in order to protect the little ones from the soldiers' gunfire pourin' down on 'em from the banks above. The few that survived had to run off half naked and bleedin' onto the frozen plains headin' back toward the other Cheyenne away off in the Smoky Hills over in Kansas.

"One of the troopers brought a little boy, probably no more'n five or six years old, brings him up to Colonel Chivington and says, 'Colonel, what about this little boy?' And old Chivington, just as cold as ice, just looks down on him and says, 'Nits breed lice. Kill him.'

"And the women! Lord, what those men did! Carvin' out their private parts to use as tobacco pouches and cuttin'... well, I ain't gonna go on, with Sandy here and all." He shook his head in disgust.

"And Char knew about this massacre?" Johnny asked.

"Hell, yes!" Mr. Cross snorted. "He could put names on his kinfolk that died out there."

They sat in silence for a long moment around the table. Sunset began to stain the kitchen curtains pink.

Quietly, Johnny asked, "And where was Char headin' when he left here?"

"Texas," Sandy replied.

Johnny's shoulders sagged and his eyes closed.

"What is it, Deputy?" she asked.

"Those FBI agents I was talkin' to. It was down in Texas. They'd just found the body of another woman south of Amarillo and somebody said they'd seen an Indian on a motorcycle."

"This is crazy!" Sandy nearly screamed. "Char would not do that! He couldn't! And you ought to know that, Deputy Hart. He's your friend. He really cares about you. Don't you care about him? You've got to help him!" There were tears in her eyes. "You've got to believe in him!"

Mr. Cross shook his head. "I just don't know," he muttered.

Johnny stood slowly to his feet. "I'd better be going." He walked with heavy steps toward the back door, pausing with his hand on the doorknob. "If Char shows up back here, have him call me. I'm real confused right now, but I know there's a whole country full of lawmen looking for him right now and he's in real danger. Please have him call me."

He put his hat on and started out. "Oh, one more thing," he stopped, the door open, one foot on the step. "What was the name of the chief of the Cheyenne that were killed here?"

Mr. Cross answered. "Feller named White Antelope. They killed him too."

CHAPTER 7

"Hello?"

"Jack? Hey! It's me." Johnny was pouring the friendly act on pretty thick. "So how's everything?"

"Fine." Jack leaned against the kitchen wall, phone to his ear, looking out the window into the night, seeing nothing.

"Summer's almost over. Did you do basketball camp this year?" Johnny asked, trying to spark some kind of conversation with his son.

"Nah, I had to work."

"Oh, yeah? Where did you get a job?"

"I've been doing stock and delivery over at the Factory Outlet." Jack crossed his arms, frowning. "Did you want to talk to Mom or something?"

Johnny sighed. "Sure. Yeah, I would like to talk to her."

Jack let the receiver drop, dangling and spinning below the wall phone. "Mom," he called. He walked from the kitchen into the living room where Barbara sat reading. "Your ex-husband is on the phone," he said curtly, jerking his thumb back toward the kitchen. Without looking back, he continued on to his room, slamming the door closed.

"Hello?"

"Hi, Barb," Johnny said wearily. "How are you?"

Barbara frowned at the phone, puzzled. "I'm fine."

"How's Gordy doing? Is she recovered from our little joyride?"

"Aside from the fact that she's grounded for the next ten years, she's doing all right." Barbara paused. "Did you just call to talk, Johnny?"

Johnny sat back on his bed, his back against the wall. The only light came through his window from the house next door. "Kind of," he answered. "I just got back yesterday from transporting our rustler to Texas."

Barbara turned off the kitchen light and sat down at the table. The only light came from the reading lamp in the living room. "Did everything go okay? No problems with the prisoner?"

"We didn't talk much on the drive down. He was still pretty doped up. About all I found out from him was that the dog that bit me was named Eva and the one that got killed in the Jeep was named Adolf. Pretty sick sense of humor, huh?" Johnny drummed his fingers on the bedside. "There was quite a bit of excitement going on down in Amarillo when I got there, though. Seems they found the body of a murder victim at some State Park south of town. Had a couple of FBI agents down from Denver and everything."

"FBI?" Barbara mused. "Some interstate angle involved?"

"Oh, yeah!" Johnny gave a humorless laugh. "They think they have a serial killer on the loose." He closed his eyes and took a deep breath. "Barb," he said in a near whisper, "they think it's Char."

"Johnny, you can't be serious!" Barbara leaned forward, elbows on the table, her hand pressed against her forehead. "Char Sixkiller? I mean I haven't seen that much of him in the last few years, but he always seemed like such a sweet, gentle guy."

"They have some theory," Johnny explained. "You know, their Behavioral Science Unit did some kind of a psychological profile that they say fits Char." He shook his head. "They told me a bunch of stuff about Char I never knew. Seems his father abandoned them, married a white woman, and refused to have anything to do with him. His brother died in Vietnam. Hell, I didn't even know he had a brother. Then his mother dies. They say he's tied in with a bunch of radical Red Power types."

"I remember Char could get to talking a lot about almost anything," Barbara said. "But I really don't remember him talking much about himself. Still, I can't believe there was anything that awful inside him the whole time." She stood up, walked to the window, and watched as a police car cruised slowly down the street. "What is there that connects him to the murders?"

"Well, they're pretty sure it's an Indian, 'cause all the bodies have been left at the scene of different massacres and stuff that happened to Indians. They think it's Char because all the victims have been blonde, white women, just like the gal that married his father. Then they found Char's truck abandoned, and can tie some bloodstains and the tire tread pattern to one of the bodies in New Mexico. They spotted somebody that matched Char's description in Amarillo the day before they found that body."

Johnny ran his hand through his hair. "The fact is they've got a pretty strong circumstantial case. It seems Char wasn't just in the Army. He was a highly trained assassin, a Green Beret. Good at it too, apparently—not like the rest of us grunts, just trying to stay alive long enough to make it back to the world."

Barbara nodded, remembering. "That was the longest twelve months of my life. I hated to watch the news, but I couldn't help myself. I was always afraid I'd see you being loaded into a body bag between commercials for laundry powder and deodorants." She closed her eyes. "I was what, fifteen, sixteen years old? I've spent nearly my whole life being afraid for you, Johnny. What kind of life is that?"

The question hung in the air, like static on the line, unanswered.

"It gets worse, Barb," Johnny continued. "Char's been spending a lot of time up here in Kiowa County, the last couple of months. He's been working—and living—at the L-S Ranch which just happens to have a blonde woman as one of the owners—Sandy Cross—and, on the ranch, is the site of the Sand Creek Massacre. You ever hear of that?"

"Yes, I have," Barbara answered.

"Oh," Johnny was surprised. "How did you hear about that?"

"I stayed home and helped the kids with their homework, that's how."

Johnny winced at the criticism implicit in that statement. "Anyway, if Char is a killer, maybe he's just waiting for the right time to kill Sandy. The only other person out there is her grandfather and he's pretty old and stove up."

"So you think maybe Char is the killer?" Barbara asked.

Johnny paused, eyes closed. "Could a person change that much?"

"People do change over time, Johnny," Barbara said.

"Did I change, Barb? Is that what happened?"

Barbara gave a dry, short laugh. "No, Johnny. I think the problem is that you're the only one in the world who hasn't changed over time."

They sat in uncomfortable silence for a long moment.

"You know, Johnny, whether Char's the killer or not, that Sandy Cross is still in danger. She fits the profile for the victims and she's right there at the massacre site."

"I know," Johnny said. "I've thought about that, too. I'm gonna have to spend a lot more time out that way."

"If I had a dollar for every time I've said this to you, I'd be a rich woman, but be careful, Johnny, okay?"

Johnny smiled, wearily. "That does have a familiar sound to it. Thanks, Barb. And thanks for talking with me."

Barbara sighed. "We should have done more talking over the years. It might have helped."

"I know," Johnny nodded. "'Night, Barb."

"*Adios*, Johnny."

ᴧᴧᴧ

The next morning, Sandy was in the kitchen when she heard the motorcycle chattering over the ridge.

"Shoot!" she exclaimed, looking out the window. Sandy hadn't wanted to be alone when Char returned. She'd come back to the house to get some lunch, while Grandpa had gone in to the supply store to get some cattle vaccine. He probably wouldn't return for an hour . . . maybe more, if the truck wouldn't start up again.

The Indian bike growled into the shed against the barn and fell quiet. A few moments later, Sandy heard the crunch of boots across the gravelly yard, approaching the house.

"Well, hello, Feather," she heard Char address her horse, still tethered by the kitchen door. There came the sound of Feather groaning in appreciation as Char scratched her neck. Sandy stood at the sink, her coffee cup clenched tightly in her hands.

The bootheels drummed on the wooden steps, the screen door creaked open, then Char stood, filling the kitchen door. His eyes were hidden behind his aviator sunglasses so that Sandy wasn't sure if he saw her.

A smile slowly appeared on his lips. Taking off the glasses, he rubbed his eyes. "Hey, Sandy," he said affably. "Got another cup? I sure could use some of your industrial strength coffee right now."

She cleared her throat. "Sure." She turned so quickly to the cabinet, that some of her coffee sloshed out on the counter.

Char closed the door. He took a few steps around the kitchen table, stretching his back and neck. "I think I pushed it a little too long on the bike without a break. I'm stiff and creaky as an old tailgate."

Sandy handed him the cup of coffee, suddenly conscious of how big he was and how small the kitchen was.

"Grandpa's not around?" Char inquired, sipping from the steaming cup.

Sandy cleared her tight throat again. "No, he had to go get some medicine."

Char frowned. "He's not sick, is he?"

"No, it's for the cattle. We've got some wormy calves."

Char looked closely at her over his coffee cup. "You've got the look of a deer in the headlights, Sandy. What's wrong?"

Sandy took a deep breath. "We've got to talk, Char. Why don't you sit down."

Sixkiller's frown deepened. "I'd just as soon stand, if you don't mind. I've got too many miles on the seat of my jeans, if you know what I mean." He put his cup down on the table and folded his arms across his chest. "Now, what's the matter?"

Sandy also put her cup down and folded her arms in unconscious imitation. "Johnny came out yesterday. He said the FBI is looking for you." Her voice tightened and she sobbed. "They think you're some kind of a serial killer." She stuck her fist against her lips in an effort to control her emotions.

Char swayed on his feet as if struck. "I think I will sit down," he said.

He sat staring at the backs of his hands, palms down on the table before him. "What did Johnny say? Does he think the FBI is right?"

Sandy shook her head, struggling to control the emotions that were shaking her. "I don't think so. I don't know," she whispered.

Char sat back as if to focus better on Sandy. Quietly, he asked, "What do you think? Are they right?"

Sandy could no longer contain the tears. Her body trembled as if in a cold freezer rather than a hot kitchen. "Oh, Char, I'm so scared!"

Char stood up so quickly, the chair fell back with a crash. "Scared of me?" he asked, hoarsely.

Her long hair flew in a blur as she shook her head back and forth. "No, no, no! They're wrong, Char! But what's going on? What's going to happen?" she sobbed, her face hidden in her hands.

Char took two short, stiff steps toward her. His hands reached forward, but he quickly pulled them back to his side like dogs on tight leashes. His face was twisted as if in pain. "Don't, Sandy. Please, don't cry! Shh, don't cry."

Blindly, Sandy stumbled forward to bury her face against his chest, her shoulders heaving.

Slowly, Char's arms came up and wrapped themselves around her. "It's all right, Sandy! It's okay, really!" His hand gently stroked her hair. "Shh. It'll be okay."

Gradually, her trembling stopped. She took a deep breath and pushed herself back from his embrace. She stood again at the kitchen window, her back to him. "Oh, man!" she gasped, taking another deep breath. "I've been wound up tighter than a fence wire ever since . . ." Sandy turned back to face Char, drying her tears on her shirtsleeve. "Now, I'm embarrassed. I thought I was tougher than that."

Char smiled. "You're as tough as you need to be, Sandy. But you don't need to be all the time."

Sandy nodded. "This is serious, though, Char. Deputy Hart said to have you call him as soon as you got back. He thinks it's dangerous for you what with the FBI putting a nationwide alert out, and all."

"You don't think Johnny just wants to be the one to make the arrest? That might win him a few points with the sheriff?"

Sandy frowned. "No, Char. I think he really is worried that somebody might hurt you." She studied his face. "Why do they think you killed all those women?"

Char started to say something, then stopped, shook his head, and shrugged. "I don't know. Maybe it's because we all look alike to the white guys in the FBI."

Sandy was surprised at the bitterness in his voice. "How did you know it was an Indian? Do you know who the killer is, Char? Is it somebody you know?"

"I can't answer that, Sandy." Char turned away to look out the window of the door.

Sandy stepped forward, tightly gripping the back of the chair. "If you know who's doing this, Char, you've got to tell somebody so they can stop him! He might kill somebody else!"

"I know that!" he snapped, then deliberately calmed himself. More quietly, he repeated, "I know that. I've tried . . ." He held up a hand and shook his head. "I can't turn him in."

"Oh my God, you do know the killer!" Sandy said, horrified. "Char, how can you not do whatever you can to stop him?"

"Look, Sandy," Char's voice rose in anger and frustration, "I just can't, okay? But I won't let anything happen to you. I promise I won't let him hurt you."

They stood, silently staring at each other for a long moment. Sandy shook her head. "It's not right, Char. Not if you know who did it. You have to tell somebody so they can stop him!"

Char started to speak, but stopped himself. Shaking his head, he turned, opened the door, and stepped outside.

"Char?" Sandy followed. He was striding purposefully across the yard toward the barn. "Char?" she repeated, trying to catch up. "Char!" her voice broke. "Don't leave me!"

He walked slowly back to where she stood. Without a word, his arms went around her shoulders. He pulled her carefully into his embrace. Sandy's arms went around his waist and she clung tightly to him, her cheek pressed against his chest, her eyes closed.

"Hey!" he said softly. When she looked up, he laid his hand gently on her cheek. "I'll be back. I have to go talk to Johnny, but I'll be back, and then I won't leave anymore. I'll be here to protect you, I promise."

"Be careful, Char," she whispered.

He simply nodded, smiling, and let his thumb lightly touch her lips. "See you later."

Walking into the dark shed, he emerged with a roar, waving as he sped off on the dirt road.

⋀⋀⋀

Johnny parked his truck and walked wearily across the barren yard to the kitchen door of his house. The screen door complained and banged shut behind him as he stepped from the evening light into the shadowy room.

Johnny started as a voice greeted him. "Hey, Cuz!"

Char sat at the kitchen table, a coffee cup hidden in his large hands. "I made a pot, if you want some."

"It's good to see you," Johnny said, removing his hat and combing his fingers through his hair.

"Is it?" Char asked.

Johnny walked over to the refrigerator, grabbed a beer, and took a long pull before settling into a chair across the table from Char. "You've talked to Sandy?"

Char nodded. "That's why I'm here."

Johnny sighed. "We've got some serious troubles, old buddy. Real serious!"

Sixkiller stared at his coffee. "Do you think I'm a killer, Johnny?"

"I know you're a killer, Char. I heard about your 'Nam experiences. Hell," he took another swallow, "I'm a killer too. Shot a kid just last year. But do I think you're a murderer out hunting for blonde women?" He put his beer can down and leaned forward, looking directly at Char.

"No, I don't believe you're the one. But," he held up his hand, pointing his finger at Char, "I think you know something. I think you know who the killer is. That's why you keep showing near the crime scenes." He paused. When Char didn't respond, he asked, "Am I right?"

Char took a deep breath and leaned back in his chair. "Yes."

"Well, tell me so we can put the Feds on the right trail," Johnny urged. "Otherwise, they're out hunting for you. Somebody could get trigger-happy and take you out before we could explain anything. So who is it? What's his name?"

Char pushed back from the table and stood up. He began pacing the room tensely. "I can't tell you that."

Johnny stared in disbelief. "Why in the hell not? Why would you want to protect this slimeball?"

Char stopped pacing, one hand forward and open, pleading. "You don't understand. From the beginning, the white man has played divide and conquer with us. One tribe against another. Indian scouts leading white troops. Assimilationists against Traditionals. Five hundred years and it's still going on. I can't be the one to turn another Indian in. I can't!"

"Char!" Johnny also stood and took a step toward Sixkiller. "This guy is not an Indian. At this point, I wouldn't even say he's human. He's a monster! Do you know what he does to these women? He doesn't just kill them, he butchers them!"

"Just like the cavalry did to us!" Char snapped.

"Oh, give me a break!" Johnny said hotly. "Is this supposed to be some kind of justice? These aren't symbols he's destroying. These are individuals—somebody's wives, sisters, daughters—real people!"

Char spun suddenly and slammed his fist against the kitchen door. It splintered and trembled. "I know, God damn it, I know!" he shouted. "Do you think this is easy for me? I've been tracking this guy myself, trying to figure out where he's going to be next, so I can stop him myself! But I'm always either guessing wrong or I'm a little too late!" He rubbed his face with both hands and took a deep, shuddering breath, trying to control his frustration. "The other day, in Texas, I must have been less than an hour too late. I found the body of that poor woman and she was still warm. I had to get out of there before the sun came up and somebody spotted me."

Johnny sat back down and took a drink from his beer. "Somebody did spot you in Amarillo. They know you ride a motorcycle, and the fact that you were there makes them that much more certain you're the killer." He leaned forward and asked quietly, "What about Sandy? You know about the massacre site on their ranch, so you know she's a target."

Char slumped wearily back into his chair. "I know. Why else do you think I'm working for free out there? I can't find him to stop him, so I'll just stay with Sandy and make sure he doesn't get her."

"Meanwhile, how many other women is this sicko gonna kill, Char?" Johnny asked angrily.

"Hey, man," Char's voice rose, "you're the cop. You find him!"

Johnny waved his hand in disgust. "I'm not a cop. I'm a burned-out rodeo bum with a badge."

Char leaned forward. "Well, maybe it's time you became a cop, Johnny. There's a whole lot more riding on this than a belt buckle and some prize money."

They sat in silence for several minutes, each man wrapped in his own blanket of thoughts. Finally, Johnny asked, "So you won't help me out and give me a name?"

Char shook his head. "I can't, Cuz." He gave a short, weary chuckle. "Out there in the arena, I took my job pretty seriously. I always felt I could save everybody from harm. Well, it turned out I couldn't save my brother, or my mother, or you. I found out I couldn't even save myself. Right now I'm just pretty damn tired. I'll see what I can do to protect Sandy and Mr. Cross, but the rest of the world is gonna have to be somebody else's responsibility."

Johnny looked down at his empty beer can. "You did save me, Char," he said quietly.

Char also looked at Johnny's empty beer can. "Did I? We'll see." He stood up slowly. "I'd better get back out to the Cross place."

"You know, Char, the FBI isn't stupid," Johnny said, rising also. "They've got a historian who's already figured out the killer's pattern. Sooner or later they're going to check out Sand Creek."

Char nodded. "I'll worry about that when it happens."

Johnny frowned. "Help me out with something, Char. Where is this guy likely to be next?"

"I honestly don't know, Johnny," Char said. "You might want to do a little reading—brush up on your history. The thing is it could be anywhere. This country is soaked in Indian blood." Char stepped to the screen door. "Sorry about your door," he said, fingering the splintered wood.

"Ah," Johnny shrugged. "The landlord probably won't even notice. This place was trashed already."

The two men stood staring at each other.

Johnny stuck out his hand. "You watch yourself, cowboy. You drew a rank one this time, for sure."

Char shook Johnny's hand. "I'm praying for you, Cuz," he said, then turned and left.

Johnny stood at the door, watching the night fall long after the sound of the motorcycle faded into the darkness.

ᴧᴧᴧ

As Johnny pulled into the shady parking lot at the Sheriff's Department a week later, he noticed the white car with U.S. Government license plates. He wasn't surprised, or pleased, to see through the open door that the two FBI agents were seated in the sheriff's office.

"Deputy Hart," the sheriff called. "Come in here, please."

Kate rolled her eyes and shook her head as Johnny walked past her desk.

"I believe you've already met Special Agent Sutton and Agent DiRosa, Deputy." Sheriff Carter's expression was serious and unreadable.

Johnny nodded to the two agents who did not offer to shake hands.

"I think you have some explaining to do, Deputy," Agent Sutton said. He pointed to a plastic bag on Sheriff Carter's desk that contained the white antelope skull from the L-S Ranch. "You sent some prints in last week that you apparently lifted off that thing. Well, the lab identified them and logged them into the computer. We had already flagged the name, so the information landed on my desk."

He picked up the bag and pretended to study it. "Now isn't that an interesting coincidence? We fill you in on our investigation down in Amarillo and a couple of days later you lift some prints belonging to your old buddy Charles Sixkiller. The same guy you said you haven't seen in a year." He returned the bag to the desk.

"Here we have Sixkiller's prints on what can only be described as a white antelope skull coming to us out of Kiowa County, Colorado, the very county where a certain Cheyenne Indian Chief named White Antelope," he waved at the bag, "was killed back in the 1860s in a battle along Sand Creek, or Big Sandy Creek, or whatever."

Sutton looked hard at Johnny. "Don't you find that interesting, Deputy Hart?" Both Agent DiRosa and Sheriff Carter were also watching Johnny.

"You know, it's the darndest thing . . . ," Johnny started to say, but Sheriff Carter interrupted him.

"Deputy Hart," the sheriff said, frowning down at his desktop blotter, "since Special Agent Sutton didn't mention it, perhaps I should, before you say anything. These gentlemen came in here pretty hot under the collar, making all kinds of threats which I don't appreciate." He cast an icy glance at Sutton. "But among those threats were suggestions that perhaps you were guilty of obstructing a federal investigation or even aiding and abetting after the fact. Now, if they are serious," Sheriff Carter's steely gaze fastened on both agents now, "then perhaps they should be cautioning you that you have the right to remain silent, that anything you say can be used against you in a court of law, that you have the right to an attorney and, if you can't afford an attorney, one will be provided to you."

Carter turned to look at Johnny, one eyebrow arched. "You've Mirandized enough suspects yourself so you understand all that, don't you, Deputy Hart?"

"Yes, sir," Johnny said, grateful for the sheriff's not-so-subtle warning.

"Now, Sheriff," Agent DiRosa said soothingly, "we seem to have gotten off to a bad start here. We just want Deputy Hart's assistance in our investigation."

"Oh, so I understand you to be saying that you are not going to bring any charges against my deputy, is that right?" Sheriff Carter smiled like a man pleasantly surprised.

The two agents glanced at each other and Agent Sutton finally mumbled, "Yeah, that's right."

"My mistake," the sheriff said, leaning back in his chair. "You'll have to excuse a poor old country sheriff like myself. Blame it on my military background. I'm very literal-minded. I like things done by the book. Now," he turned to Johnny, "you were about to say something, Deputy Hart?"

Johnny cleared his throat. "About five months ago, Char Sixkiller was passing through. He stopped in to see me and he rode with me on a call out to the L-S Ranch where some nighttime trespassing had been reported. Miss Cross gave me that painted skull which she'd found on her entrance road. I placed it on the seat of my truck, where Sixkiller picked it up before I could warn him not to. That's how his prints came to be on that."

Agent Sutton scowled at Johnny. "I seem to recall you telling me you hadn't seen Sixkiller in a year?"

Johnny shrugged. "I forgot. It was a short visit. He was just passing through. He's rodeo, you know. We're always heading on down the road."

Agent DiRosa crossed his arms, frowning at Johnny. "Now that's another curious thing. Sixkiller used to work a lot of rodeos all over the country. We checked with the PRCA in Colorado Springs, though, and it seems he hasn't made more than a couple of sanctioned rodeos all year long. Could it be that he's pursuing some other line of work lately? Found other ways to pass the time?"

"Could be," Johnny nodded. "Like I said, I haven't seen him in a while."

"What did you two talk about the last time he was through here?" Sutton asked.

"Oh, the usual," Johnny smiled. "Women, old times, that sort of thing. I think he wanted to see how I was doing. I had an accident last year."

DiRosa nodded. "We know."

Sheriff Carter cleared his throat, frowning, then asked, "You have a file on Deputy Hart, then?"

DiRosa smiled. "Of course. Hart and Sixkiller go way back. We have information on everybody connected with the suspect."

"Did you boys drive all the way down from Denver just to rattle my cage?" Johnny asked. "You could have phoned. Saved the taxpayers some gas money."

"No, Deputy Hart," Sutton replied acidly, "Sand Creek is a part of our investigation. Your little memory lapse is just incidental. That antelope skull with Sixkiller's prints just moved Sand Creek further up the list of possible sites where he might kill somebody."

"You know," Johnny drawled, "I've been doing some research of my own. And if this killer is just looking for places where Indians might have a grievance, you might have to call out the army, the National Guard, and the Boy Scouts to cover all that territory. He could just as well choose any place in the country from New York, where George Washington's army burned out the Iroquois, to California, where they hunted Indians with dogs for sport."

DiRosa gave an odd smile. "You sound like you almost sympathize with Sixkiller, Deputy."

"No," Johnny waved his hand in disgust, "of course there's no justifying murder like this. All I'm saying is Sand Creek is just one out of a whole bunch of possible sites."

"True," Sutton agreed. "But he seems to be sticking to the West. And this," he pointed at the skull in the plastic bag, "would seem to indicate that Sand Creek is pretty high on his list. It seems a little odd that he would leave a clue before the crime is even committed but, as a Cheyenne, Sand Creek probably has a special significance for him."

"Actually, Sheriff," DiRosa said, turning to look at Carter, "we came down to ask for the cooperation of your department. We'd like to go out and check out the ranch where this Sand Creek battle site is located—talk to the family."

"That's William Cross and his granddaughter, Sandra," Sheriff Carter explained. "Why don't I assign Deputy Hart here to take you gentlemen out there. He is acquainted with the family."

Johnny frowned. "Maybe I should call ahead, you know, just to see if they're home. Being just the two of them, they spend a lot of time out with the cattle. And it's a mighty long drive to make for nothing."

"No," Agent Sutton shook his head. "That won't be necessary. If they're not home, we'll just look around and get an idea of the layout. Maybe talk to them another time."

Reluctantly, Johnny departed with the agents. In the parking lot, he suggested, "Maybe we should take your car. The three of us would be pretty cramped in my truck."

"No," Sutton assured him with a tight smile, "you're still on duty and need to stay in radio contact. Your truck will be fine."

There was little talk on the drive out. Agent DiRosa made a couple of attempts at conversation, but otherwise they rode in silence.

Johnny was sweating with nerves and hoping the agents didn't notice as he bounced the truck down the rutted entrance road to the yard of the L-S Ranch. No one was in sight as he shut the engine off.

"What a dump!" Agent DiRosa exclaimed, squinting at the faded house and barn as he wiped the dust from his sunglasses.

"Not exactly the Ponderosa, is it?" Agent Sutton agreed, opening the pickup's door.

Johnny stepped out of the truck as he saw Mr. Cross come walking stiffly out from the barn, wiping his hands on a blue bandanna.

"Deputy," Mr. Cross nodded to Johnny. He cast a suspicious scowl at the two agents in business suits.

"Mr. Cross," Johnny touched the brim of his hat. "This here is a couple of fellers from the FBI in Denver. Special Agents Sutton and DiRosa," he pointed to each.

"FBI, huh?" Mr. Cross grunted. "I don't recall seein' my picture on the Post Office wall. What brings you boys out here?"

"You're William Cross?" Sutton asked brusquely, studying the house, not looking at Mr. Cross.

"I am," Mr. Cross's frown deepened. "Nobody's called me William since my wife died. And that used to be only when she was mad at me."

"We'd like to ask you a few questions, Mr. Cross," Agent DiRosa said. "Is your granddaughter around?"

"No, sir, she's not. She's out doctorin' cows today. We keep pretty busy, bein' just the two of us to run the ranch. I'm trying to put my truck's carburetor back together, which is why I'm afoot today."

"Can we talk, Mr. Cross?" Agent Sutton asked.

"I thought that's what we been doin,'" Mr. Cross said. "If you're askin' can we set and socialize for a while, I gotta repeat myself. It's just the two of us, so we're both kind of busy. Why don't you just ask me what you want to know."

Johnny leaned back against the fender of his truck, pleased to note that Mr. Cross was ill-tempered with everybody, not just him.

Agent DiRosa sighed and pulled a notepad and pen out of his jacket's inside pocket. "We're investigating a murder, Mr. Cross. A whole string of murders, in fact. We think that an Indian named Charles Sixkiller is responsible for those murders. Are you familiar with the name Sixkiller?"

"Well, it sure ain't Smith or Jones, now, is it?" Mr. Cross said. "No, I reckon I'd remember a name like that."

Agent Sutton frowned. "We understood that Deputy Hart came out here on a call several months ago, and Sixkiller was with him. You don't remember that?"

"Did Deputy Hart tell you that?" Mr. Cross scowled at Johnny.

"Not right away," Agent Sutton smirked, "but yes, Deputy Hart told us he brought Sixkiller out here on a call having to do with tres- passers."

"Oh," Mr. Cross remarked, "that must've been that tall feller with the ponytail. I thought he was a Mexican." He grunted. "Indian, you say, named Sixshooter?"

"Sixkiller, Charles Sixkiller," DiRosa repeated patiently. "He hasn't been back here since? You haven't seen him around?"

Mr. Cross shook his head. "We don't get many visitors. We're pretty far out in the country here."

Agent Sutton took his sunglasses off to stare at Mr. Cross. "Sixkiller won't be making social calls, Mr. Cross. He's a serial murderer. We think you and your granddaughter could be in danger." His voice rose in irritation.

"Are you aware that there's an old Indian battle site on your ranch, Mr. Cross?" Agent DiRosa asked in a more soothing tone.

"Of course I am," Mr. Cross snapped. "I've lived here more'n sixty years."

Sutton started to say something but DiRosa restrained him with a hand on his arm. "The point is, Mr. Cross," DiRosa said patiently, "because this is a battle site—a Cheyenne battle site—and Sixkiller is Cheyenne, it seems very likely that he could try to kill someone here. That's his pattern."

"Huh," Mr. Cross grunted. "I caught your drift, but there's not a whole hell of a lot I can do about it. We'll keep our noses to the wind, but we've got a ranch to run. I suggest you boys find this Sixpack feller, pronto, so I can get back to work. In fact," he glanced at Johnny, "I'd like to get back to work right now. You boys know the trail out of here." With a dismissive wave, he turned and limped back into the barn.

Agent Sutton turned to Johnny, cocking a thumb back in the direction of the barn. "What the hell is his problem?"

"Problem?" Johnny sounded surprised. "I thought Mr. Cross had his company manners on today." He opened the door to his truck. "You guys were lucky. You should see him on one of his bad days."

"Jesus," DiRosa shook his head and walked to the truck's passenger door. "We'll let you deal with the locals from now on, Hart."

"Yeah," Sutton nodded, "but you'd better get on the team, cowboy. No more covering for this Sixkiller. Your old buddy is a stone killer, and that's a fact you'd better learn to deal with." He climbed into the truck after DiRosa and slammed the door. Pointing his finger at Johnny, he added, "You screw with us and we'll take you down with Sixkiller. You'll wish that bull had finished the job last year."

"Hmm," Johnny gave a humorless chuckle and squinted out at the horizon. "Many's the time I've wished just that."

The two agents gave him puzzled looks as he turned the key and spun the truck back toward the highway.

CHAPTER

"Come on, Char. Try it!" Sandy urged with a laugh.

Sixkiller looked doubtful, but he untied the lariat from the saddle and measured a loop out between his fingers. "I don't know. It's been an awful long time since I did any roping." He began to spin the lasso slowly above his head. The calf glanced back nervously at its mother but didn't move.

Char half-stood in the stirrups, leaned forward slightly, and let the loop float out across the twenty feet separating him from the calf. As it settled down around its neck, the calf started to turn and run, but Char quickly gave the rope a turn around the pommel. His horse, more experienced at this than its rider, began to back up pulling the calf off balance until it flopped onto its side.

"All right, Char!" Sandy whooped, leaping from her saddle to the ground. Lady ran between the calf and its mother, barking a warning at the cow to keep its distance.

Char quickly scrambled from his own saddle. "I'll be darned!" he marveled. He stopped, standing over the fallen and struggling calf. "What do I do now? I don't have a string!"

Sandy arrived at his side, hypodermic needle in hand. "I should have thought of that, but I didn't really expect you to actually rope him on the first toss. Just sit on him and hold him still while I stick him."

Char threw his weight on the bawling animal, while Sandy injected the antibiotic. The whole operation took only a few seconds. Char took his rope back as the calf struggled to its feet and ran, complaining, to his mother's side.

Standing side by side, Sandy lightly punched Char on the shoulder. "Dang, Char! That was good! I didn't know you could rope."

"Surprised me too," Char smiled. "I haven't touched a rope in years."

"So you used to do some roping?" she asked, returning to Feather, taking up her reins, and swinging easily up into the saddle.

Char also remounted. "Oh, yeah. My grandpa taught me when I was just a little kid. Me and my brother Dwight used to do some team roping in the Little Britches rodeos. We were pretty good, too."

Sandy spotted another animal in need of vaccine. As she turned Feather, she asked, "So why did you become a clown? Why not stick with roping?"

Char laughed. "I quit roping about the time I reached high school. I noticed that the girls were more impressed with bronc riders than with ropers, so a bronc rider is what I became."

Sandy shook her head. "You guys are all alike. But, okay, why not stick with bronc riding? Why get down in the dust with face paint and funny clothes as a clown?" She wrinkled her nose.

"You really want to know?" Char asked, looking at her closely.

"Well, yeah, I do," Sandy replied.

"It hasn't been all that long since Indians kept to our own rodeo circuit, blacks on theirs, and white cowboys in the spotlight with the PRCA. Even though probably the best bulldogger of all time was a black man, Bill Pickett, and the best bronc rider was an Indian named

Jackson Sundown. For that matter, Will Rogers, who most folks think of as an old-time movie actor and comedian, was actually one of the best ropers ever, and he was Cherokee. But being a clown was one way I could get into the main action. Then, once I started doing it, I found I really liked it."

"No offense, Char, but you seem like a pretty serious guy. Not at all what I think of when I think of a clown."

"Actually, in our Indian cultures, being a clown,—we call it a Contrary,—is a holy calling." Char smiled. "In rodeo though, the people in the stands think you're just there to make them laugh between rides, but my job is to keep cowboys from being hurt or killed. And I was pretty good at it until last year when I let that bull split Johnny open." He looked away from Sandy.

"Char," Sandy brought Feather alongside Char's horse. "You can't keep beating yourself up over that. From what I hear, you didn't do anything wrong. Johnny tied himself on too tight and that's why he got hung up."

Char shook his head. "It's not that. That happens all the time. It's after that, when he was kneeling there in the dust." His fist began to beat on his thigh. "I knew what that bull was going to do, and I knew what I had to do. But for some reason I waited too long."

His face was tight and pained as he stared at Sandy. "I knew what to do and I didn't do it, and my friend nearly died because of it . . . because of me."

"'If thou, Lord, shouldst mark iniquities, O Lord who shall stand?'" Sandy quoted quietly. "This is not just about Johnny, and I think you know it."

Char looked at her, his expression stony and unreadable.

"You can't protect everybody from all harm," she said earnestly. "God bless you for trying, or for even wanting to, but it's crazy to think you can save everybody. God himself can't save everybody if they don't want him to, and you're not God, Char." She took his hand in both of hers. "You're just a man Char, and from what I can see, a very good man. Certainly, after all you've been through, a far better man than anyone would have a right to expect."

Char closed his eyes and took a deep breath. Squeezing Sandy's hand, he said quietly, "You're good people, Sandy. Your ex-husband must have been a USDA prime jackass to let you go."

Sandy laughed and picked up her reins again. "He was that! But I wasn't so bright myself getting hooked up with him in the first place."

Char loosened his lasso once more. "Let me take another crack at this, just in case that last throw was pure luck."

They worked steadily throughout the hot, dusty afternoon. As they headed back toward the house in the slanting rays of evening sun, Lady was so tired and sore-footed that Char picked her up and carried her across the front of his saddle, where she lay with her head gratefully against his thigh.

"You know, I had a thought a while back I'd like you to think about," Char said. "You'll probably think I'm crazy, but hear me out." He glanced at Sandy who slumped wearily in the saddle, seeming too tired to pay attention to anything. "Buffalo!" he said.

She looked up at him, startled. "Did you say buffalo?"

"Yeah, let me explain my idea . . ." he began.

"No, that's too weird!" she said, wide eyed. "I was just riding along right now thinking about buffalo. But go ahead, what were you going to say?"

"Well, this is actually not a new idea with me but, you know we've been out here all day trying to doctor these cows because of some parasite they lack resistance to. But a buffalo! He's native to this country. Nothing bothers him."

"That's exactly what I was thinking!" Sandy marveled. "And I was thinking about the fact that summer's almost gone. Every winter it's such a battle to keep these cows alive. They freeze if it gets too cold or they starve if the snow's too deep. And we practically kill ourselves babysitting them all the time."

"Exactly!" Char said, enthusiastically. "Buffalo are totally self-sufficient. And have you ever tasted the meat?"

Sandy nodded, her fatigue evaporated. "I had some at The Fort, that restaurant outside Denver. Good taste, real lean but tender."

"And the price!" Char waved his hand as if he'd burned it. "The price of beef keeps going down, but buffalo is really getting popular and the price keeps going up. That means you'd do a whole lot better than break even raising buffalo instead of beef."

"This is unbelievable, Char," Sandy said. "I've actually thought about selling off our cattle and trying to start a herd of buffalo, but it just seemed kind of risky and somehow I don't think Grandpa would really go for the idea. He's an old-time cowman. I think he'd just think I was crazy."

"Well," Char observed, "it's not any crazier than keeping a bunch of cows on welfare, which is what it amounts to when it costs more to produce the beef than the market will pay for it."

"Let's try to work up some actual hard numbers on this, Char. Maybe we can convince Grandpa."

They'd arrived back at the house. Lady jumped down from Char's saddle and trotted toward the barn where Grandpa was emerging, wiping his hands.

Char swung down from the saddle. "Hey, Mr. Cross, did you get that carburetor rebuilt yet?"

"Just about. If my fingers weren't so stiff, I'd a been done a long time ago." Grandpa stood and waited until both Char and Sandy had led their horses to where he stood at the barn's entrance. "They're closin' in on you, son. Deputy Hart was out here earlier with a couple of FBI agents."

"Johnny brought the FBI out after me?" Char looked stunned.

"No, I think it was their idea. They sure had no idea you were livin' out here." Mr. Cross chuckled at the irony. "They're trying to protect us from you. We're trying to protect you from them. And you're trying to protect us from some other guy you won't tell them about." He shook his head. "If that makes sense to anyone then I guess I've lived too long after all."

"They'll be back," Sandy noted, worried.

Char nodded, rubbing the back of his neck. "Yeah, they will," he agreed. "Unless Johnny can find the real killer pretty soon."

"Hart?" Mr. Cross snorted. "You've got a lot more faith in him than I do. He looks to me to be nothin' more than a broke-down rodeo cowboy—what my son used to call a brush hand. And a drunk, to boot. If you can see a detective in him, you've got better eyes than me." He shook his head.

Char gave a weak smile. "Well, if Johnny is going to believe in me, the least I can do is believe in him. And frankly, he's the only one I have to believe in right now."

⋏⋏⋏

"Deputy Hart? I'm Jim Little Crow. You wanted to see me?"

Johnny shook hands with the man, noting the firm grip, clear eyes, and ravaged face all in one glance. "I appreciate your time," Johnny said.

Little Crow frowned. "Is this an official visit? Is there some kind of trouble?"

"Well, no and yes." Johnny looked around at the plump receptionist and the two other people sitting on vinyl chairs watching the television. "Could we talk somewhere more private?" he asked.

"Sure." Little Crow led the way down a blank hallway to a room filled by twenty or so folding metal chairs. "Nobody will be using this for another couple of hours. We can talk here." He waved at the empty chairs. "Have a seat."

"Plenty to choose from," Johnny noted, moving to a chair farthest from the doorway.

Little Crow pulled a chair out of the row and set it down facing Johnny. "So, Deputy, what's up?"

"I understand that you're the drug and alcohol counselor for the center," Johnny said.

"That's right."

"I think you may know a friend of mine," Johnny began. "Char Sixkiller?"

Little Crow's expression changed from friendly to stony. "The FBI's already been here." He stood up and walked behind his chair. "What? They think that I'll tell you something I didn't tell them, just because you say you're Sixkiller's friend?"

Johnny frowned. "FBI's been here, huh? Look, I don't blame you for not trusting me but, believe it or not, I'm not working for the FBI. And, believe it or not, I am a friend of Char's." He looked at the floor. "At least Char's always been a friend to me," he added quietly.

"Yeah, well," Little Crow folded his arms across his chest. "I'll tell you just what I told them, which happens to be the truth and all I do know." He pointed his finger at Johnny. "Sixkiller is not a murderer."

"I agree with you," Johnny said. The two men stared at each other for a long moment. Johnny stood to his feet. Taking a card from his shirt pocket, he handed it to Little Crow. "If you change your mind and want to talk with me, give me a call. I'm really just trying to help Char."

"Wait a minute." Little Crow read the card. "John Hart. Johnny Hart, the bull rider?"

"Used to be," Johnny nodded. "A bull rider, that is. I'm still John Hart."

Little Crow nodded, studying Johnny. "Sixkiller talked about you." He tapped Johnny's card against his lip several times, thinking. "Have a seat." He waved Johnny back to the chair.

"Okay, maybe you are trying to help Char, but to be honest with you, I really don't know how I can help. In my heart, though, I don't believe he's a murderer."

"I don't know how you can help either. I came to you simply because I was never a very good friend to Char. I don't know much about him—family, friends—outside the rodeo." Johnny leaned forward, elbows on knees. "I guess if we could just kind of talk, maybe something will pop up that I can grab hold of."

"All right," Little Crow shrugged.

"When did you first meet Char?" Johnny asked.

"Right after Christmas last year. Ernie Fox brought him in. He was pretty bad off." Little Crow shook his head. "Nobody drinks like an Indian. There's nothing social about it. It's just suck it down, as much and as fast as you can." He gave a pained, crooked smile. "I know. I wasted most of my youth and a lot of my health trying to commit liquid suicide."

"So what happens here?" Johnny looked around at the room. Cracked vinyl tile on the floor and broken acoustic tiles on the ceiling were unrelieved by block walls painted an institutional gray green color. A poster of Geronimo scowled across the room at a poster of Sitting Bull.

Little Crow leaned forward. "The truth happens here, Johnny. Is it okay to call you Johnny?"

"Sure," Johnny shrugged.

"Char used to talk about you quite a bit, so I feel like I know you."

"What kind of truth are you talking about?" Johnny asked.

"Well, let's see. How many kinds of truth are there?" Little Crow leaned back and stuck his hands in his pockets. "There's the statistical kind of truth, the facts that say that alcohol is destroying Indians as a people." He nodded bitterly. "Yeah, that's a fact. But fortunately, there's a truth that's more important than just facts. That truth is that we are not the highest power in the universe. This higher power is not only greater, it's better than we are."

Johnny looked doubtful. "I'm sure this all makes for some interesting discussions, but what does that have to do with drying out a bunch of drunks?"

"Let me put it as simply as I know how, Johnny," Little Crow said quietly. "There is a God, and you're not him." He nodded, smiling. "And I'm not him, and Sixkiller's not him, and all of us put together aren't him."

Johnny gave a dry laugh. "Yeah, Char started in on me with this God stuff. I see where he got it from."

Little Crow frowned. "Let me tell you about me, for a minute. I'm Lakota from Pine Ridge up in South Dakota. From high school I thought about going on to college, but this was back in the early sixties, and an Indian in college was still pretty weird. So I joined the army, went to Vietnam and hunted people who looked a lot more like me than the snot-nosed second lieutenant from Georgia who was ordering me to kill them."

Little Crow stood up and began to pace, one hand in the pocket of his jeans, the other waving as if to pluck memories from the air. "I'd done some drinking with my buddies back home. Shoot, what high school kid doesn't, right? But, man, Vietnam just blew me sideways! I couldn't deal with it! So I didn't. I got blasted instead. I drank, I smoked, I snorted, I popped . . . if it would get me high, and get me mentally out of there, I'd take it . . . as much as I could, as often as I could.

"When I came back here to the world, I was totally out of control, I mean to tell you! I got my discharge in California in 1968. To this day, I don't even remember 1969, that's how bad I was, man."

Johnny noticed that Little Crow seemed to be talking to himself more than to him.

"But then," he paused and looked at Johnny slyly out of the corner of his eye, "I went to this rally—meeting—whatever, over in Berkeley, and Richard Oaks was the speaker." He smiled and shook his head. "Yeah, Richard. He was Iroquois. He's the guy who led the takeover of Alcatraz." He laughed. "Yeah, Richard was something else." His smile faded. "He's dead now. But he set me off on my political phase. I fell in with the American Indian Movement—Russell Means, Dennis Banks, George Mitchell, the Bellecourts, Carter Camp—bunch of guys like me who just kind of said we're tired of drifting in the white man's world. It's time to take a stand. Push back for a change."

Little Crow sat down again and leaned forward, explaining intensely. "You see, we'd seen what happened when we tried to blend in, not threaten anybody, play the game by the rules. Well, hell, it was their game, their rules! And we were still losing! Losing land, losing culture, losing language, losing our young people, losing our souls!" His hands were fists.

He shook his head. "The Trail of Broken Treaties, Wounded Knee! It didn't work out the way we planned. It wasn't just us. There were other people coming into the movement, sowing some really evil seeds. They started poisoning everything, turning people against each other. Turned out later that they were working for the damn FBI."

He paused and stared at the floor in silence. Johnny shifted uncomfortably. Little Crow looked up, startled and smiled. "I'm sorry, Johnny. I didn't mean to talk on so much. This isn't what you came to hear."

"I don't know what I came to hear, Jim," Johnny said. "I've got to admit, this is all news to me. After I got back from 'Nam, I went to school, got married, had kids, rodeoed. I had no particular idea this other stuff was even going on. Was Char into all this, too?"

Little Crow nodded. "Some of it. By the time he got out of the army, Wounded Knee was over and things were starting to fall apart. By the time the '80s came along, most of America was tired of Indians and their problems. Some things got better, some got worse." He laughed. "I got worse. Boozing and drugs. Without the political stuff to make me feel like I was doing something worthwhile, I just fell down and couldn't get up.

"That's one of the points I wanted to make to you. You know that expression about pulling yourself up by your bootstraps? Try it sometime. You'll see how ridiculous it is. No matter how hard you pull, you can't lift yourself one inch off the ground. Why? Because we're human. We're made of the very same stuff as the ground. We're subject to physical and spiritual gravity. But inside us"—he tapped his chest with his fist—"there's an empty space that can only be filled by something spiritual. We humans try money, and power, and things, or sex, drugs and rock 'n roll. Whatever we try, ultimately, it won't work, because that space is shaped like God, and only he can fill it.

"I was just about dead from the booze when I ran into a couple of Bros from AIM. They brought me back up to South Dakota, over to Crow Dog's place on the Rosebud. He did a healing ceremony. I can't tell you much about it, since you're not one of the people." He smiled. "Nothing racist, Johnny. It's just that you don't talk about some things unless a person is ready to receive them.

"Anyway, I remember coming out of the sweat lodge feeling like I'd been run over by a train. But inside," he shook his head in wonder, "something had touched me. Something good and clean and powerful. And I wanted more of it. And that's when my healing began. When I began to have a greater thirst for that Grandfather Spirit—God—than I did for alcohol."

He frowned at Johnny. "Are you following me on this?"

Johnny sat still for a long time before replying. "I have to admit, Jim, you've given me plenty to think about." He stood up and took a couple of steps, his arms crossed, as if hugging himself. "This Spirit. It's always good?"

Little Crow started to nod, but stopped himself. "We run kind of a twelve-step program here. We ask people to reach out for their higher power. Because we come from different tribes and backgrounds, we try not to put labels or culture specific attributes on that Power. Most of the people, like Char, when they connect finally, yes, they agree, the Great Spirit is good."

"But," he ran his hand through his hair, troubled, "once in a while, for whatever reason, the people either don't make the connection or they connect with something darker."

"Wait a minute," Johnny laughed nervously. "We're not talking about *The Exorcist* or *Nightmare on Elm Street* kind of stuff, are we?"

Little Crow was serious. "I wouldn't laugh, Johnny. Evil is real. I guess maybe it depends on what's inside you. You grab hold of the thing you're reaching for."

Johnny straightened up and walked back to Little Crow. "When Char was here, was there anybody else here who maybe grabbed hold of this darker spirit you're talking about?"

Little Crow's expression grew guarded. "Maybe. That was a while back. It's hard to remember."

Johnny frowned, picking up on Little Crow's reticent response. He started to say something then reconsidered. "You say you have a twelve-step program here. Is that like Alcoholics Anonymous?"

"Basically," Little Crow nodded. "We've modified it a bit, to make it a little more relevant to Indians."

"For example?" Johnny prompted.

"Well, like the drum. We usually have a sing at least once a month. It strengthens the sense of community. Indians don't think of themselves as individuals the way you whites do. For us, the people are what's important. We don't have a meaningful identity apart from our place among the people. Believe me, the alcohol can really destroy that sense of belonging. We also have the sweat lodge for physical and spiritual purification. And, since a lot of the reason some Indians drink is low self-esteem, we get into a lot of teaching. History, traditions, that sort of thing. We try to instill some pride."

"With the history," Johnny noted. "I've been doing some history reading myself lately. Seems like that might just make people bitter and angry rather than proud."

Little Crow shrugged. "Yeah, sometimes it makes people angrier, but we try to channel that into constructive outlets." He smiled. "Even your Jesus said, 'The truth shall make you free.' I believe that."

"Some people I know would be pretty surprised to hear you call him 'my' Jesus." Johnny said. He tapped his finger against his temple. "I seem to recall that AA has some kind of a buddy system, don't they?"

"Kind of, yeah," Little Crow nodded. "I mean, we can't spend all our time in a group, so there needs to be somebody that you can call on when you're feeling weak. Somebody you can count on and be accountable to, so you're not just shucking and jiving in the meetings and going back to the old ways the rest of the time."

"Char had a buddy? A partner?" Johnny asked.

The guarded look returned to Little Crow's eyes. "Yeah, he did."

"What was his name?"

"I don't remember right now."

"Well, do you keep records or something?" Johnny asked, annoyed. "I mean you seem to remember Char real well. Why is it so hard to remember his buddy?"

"Look," Little Crow stood up, shoving both hands once again into his pockets. "You said you're here unofficially. I don't have to answer your questions."

Johnny stood up as well. "What the hell is going on here? You said you wanted to help Char! You know . . ." He stopped suddenly and turned away, staring at the Geronimo poster without seeing it. "That's it!" he muttered. Turning back to Little Crow he said, "Char had a partner here, didn't he? I'll even bet the guy looks a little like him."

Little Crow's eyes narrowed.

"Of course," Johnny began to pace. "Char would feel responsible for the guy, like he had to help him. Even lend him his truck to help out. And," he pointed at Little Crow, "I'll bet this partner is one of those who tapped into that darker power you were talking about. Yeah, you shake that all together with a few history lessons on how many Indians were killed for no worse crime than defending their homeland and you might just have a murderer on your hands."

Johnny turned back to Little Crow. "Do the guys talk about themselves? Personal stuff like old hurts, that sort of thing?"

"Yeah, we call it ventilating," Little Crow nodded. "It's usually a good idea to get the old garbage out."

"Oh, man!" Johnny put his palm to his forehead. "I'll bet this guy thinks he's doing Char some kind of favor killing off blonde white women!"

"You think . . . Char's partner is the murderer?"

"I sure as hell do!" Johnny answered. "And if you'll give me some basic information on him, we can find him, stop him, and get Char clear of this mess."

"You don't have a court order, so I can't give you that information," Little Crow said flatly.

"Why would you need a court order to give me the information? I'd think you'd want to! We're talking about a murderer?"

"We're talking about a brother Indian, somebody who's part of my counseling group." Little Crow's face was hard and angry.

"You're . . ." Johnny spluttered in frustration. He gave a complete turn as if appealing to the empty chairs. "I'm sorry, man, but you are so full of shit! Really! You've got the gall to sit there and give me this crock about how you've found God and everything and yet . . ." He slapped his hat on his leg, turned and headed for the entrance.

At the door, he stopped and pointed his finger back at Little Crow. "If you actually think that your God cares more about whether somebody is Indian, or white, or black or Chinese than he does whether they're guilty or innocent, then you're praying to some kind of celestial redneck. You can keep that brand of religion! I'm better off with my six-pack of beer than I would be in your church!" He paused as if to say more, but simply slapped the doorframe and walked out.

CHAPTER 9

"Ms. Gutierrez?"

Barbara looked up, frowning, from the papers on her desk. "Yes. May I help you?"

The man smiled and stepped into the office. "My name is Joe DiRosa . . . Agent DiRosa, FBI. Do you have a couple of minutes to talk? You look like you're completely absorbed in something there."

"Oh, yes," Barbara waved at the statement on her desk. "One of the problems of law enforcement in rural areas. The arresting officer often knows the suspect, might even be related to him, so he forgets to follow the full procedure. No problem, right? No problem until his lawyer steps in with a motion to dismiss or a motion to suppress evidence, then our case starts to melt like ice in a Chinook." She pushed her chair back away from her desk. "I'm sorry. I'm sure you're not here because our cops and robbers are buddies. Please, sit down."

DiRosa sat in the metal chair across from Barbara. He tugged sheepishly at his ear. "Well, to tell you the truth, that is kind of why I'm here."

Barbara looked skeptical. "You're kidding!"

DiRosa drummed his fingers nervously on his leg. "I'm down here from our Denver office . . ." he began. "You're Deputy John Hart's ex-wife, am I right?"

Barbara folded her arms defensively. "Yes," she acknowledged.

"Do you have much contact with him still?"

"We talk. He calls maybe once a week, sometimes more, sometimes less." Her eyes narrowed. "What is this all about?"

DiRosa cleared his throat, then looked around to be sure they were alone. "First of all, let me tell you that I'm not here officially. All right? I'm here because I do know what you're talking about when you say that the cops and robbers are buddies. I was a cop—NYPD. I grew up in Queens. So when I joined the department, they assigned me to precincts in Staten Island, the Bronx, Manhattan, away from my old neighborhood, just so I wouldn't have any divided loyalties or pressure to cut somebody a break, just because we came up together, you know?

"Anyway, I'm here today because I think your husband—your ex—is maybe cutting an old friend a break. I guess I'd like you to pass the word along. He doesn't know what he's dealing with here and it could destroy his career."

"This is about Char Sixkiller, isn't it?" Barbara asked. "What is it you think Johnny's doing?"

DiRosa shrugged. "I don't know. Maybe he knows something he's not sharing with us. Maybe he's actually in contact with Sixkiller and helping him avoid arrest. I don't know," he repeated. He avoided Barbara's eyes.

"Are you just trying to get some secondhand information out of me?" Barbara challenged. "You think maybe Johnny told me something and you can scare it out of me because I still care about him?"

DiRosa frowned. "No, I'm not that devious. The fact is, Hart seems like a nice guy, that's all." He looked around again, then leaned forward and nearly whispered. "The thing is, the special agent in charge, Adam Sutton, can be a real mean son of a bitch, if you'll excuse my language."

He sat back again shifting nervously. "I've only been out here at the Denver office a little less than a year. I've worked with Sutton on a couple of other things and he's pretty professional. Not a lot of laughs, you understand, but he does his job. But when this Sixkiller thing came up . . ." He shook his head. "I don't know, maybe it's the Indian angle! What do I know from Indians, right?" He pointed at himself. "I mean, come on, I'm from 21st Street, right? But, Sutton! I don't know, it's like he's driven. It's personal, you know?"

DiRosa abruptly stood up. "Anyway, this was all completely off the record. But, if you could pass the word along to Deputy Hart, I'd appreciate it. He does not want to be on the tracks when Sutton rolls through, okay?"

"Okay," Barbara nodded. She extended her hand. "Thank you."

DiRosa hesitated a moment, then shook her hand. "Maybe I should have stayed a cop," he smiled. "Life was simpler." With a nod, he turned and left.

ᴧᴧᴧ

Pedro leaned across the bar so that his lips were just a few inches from Hart's ear. Even so, he nearly had to shout to be heard over the norteño music booming from the jukebox. "John, I think maybe you had enough, yes? You got a long way to drive back to Eads."

Johnny continued to stare at his nearly empty glass of beer. "I'm not even close to being drunk yet, Pedro." He lifted his glass, frowning as he studied it by the light of the Corona sign. "I think you must be watering your beer, old buddy. I'm more likely to drown than get drunk." Notwithstanding, he swallowed the last of the glass's contents.

Pedro looked around nervously. It was a Friday night and his bar was crowded with men and women, farm and ranch hands, field workers, most from Mexico. Spanish was the only language heard. Everyone seemed to be relaxed and enjoying themselves but no one was standing too near the American at the bar.

"Still, you have to work tomorrow, I bet. It's better, I think, if you go home now," Pedro urged.

Johnny smiled. "I am home, Pedro," he said, too softly for Pedro to hear. He pointed at his glass. "Darned thing keeps running dry!" he said, louder.

Pedro sighed and took a long time to refill the glass. "So how come you're back in La Junta, John? It's a long way to come just for a drink, no?"

"Oh, maybe not," Johnny said, sampling the foam at the top of the glass. "I'm on my way back from Denver. My big investigation started today. Yep, started and ended all on the same day." He took a bigger swallow. "Why I'm every bit as good a detective as I was a bull rider." He shook his head. "End up flat on my face," he muttered.

Pedro glanced around the room at the faces of men studiously ignoring Johnny, or staring daggers at him. Pedro leaned close to Johnny's ear once again. "You are my friend, John. You are welcome in my house anytime. You are welcome in my cantina during the day. But you should know better than to come here at night."

"I'm just drinking a beer, minding my own business," Johnny pouted.

"These people," Pedro waved at the crowded room, "they work hard all day long doing work that most Americans would not do. They are surrounded by people of strange language and customs, people who do not treat them with dignity or even decency. And this is very confusing because they do work that must be done if people are to eat. What is the shame of honest work? Yet they are treated with contempt. They would not be here if there were some way to feed their families on the other side.

"But here, in my little cantina, they can relax and hear their own language and music and not be under the eyes of some American who does not like or trust them. Here they can see themselves as men and women of dignity, and they can see that in each other's eyes. They are not dogs and burros as the Americans see us." He put a hand on Johnny's arm. "I know you are not like that, John. But just as Americans do not see us clearly as human beings, these people—my people—they do not see too clearly either. So here you sit, reminding them of what they came in here to forget."

Johnny nodded. "I know Pedro. I didn't mean to cause trouble." He started to take another drink but stopped, the glass halfway to his lips, and pushed it away. "I wasn't gonna drink today. I said that when I left Denver. I said it in Springs and in Pueblo. I was even saying it when I came through Rocky Ford, but by the time I got to La Junta, my mouth was so dry, I just couldn't say it anymore."

Headlights briefly flashed across the window as a car entered the parking lot. Pedro glanced up and Johnny saw his eyes widen slightly in surprise. Patting Johnny on the arm again, he said, "Why don't you go home now, my friend. Get some rest."

Johnny nodded. "Yeah, I guess I'd better get out while I can still walk." He stood up, swaying on his feet. "If I can walk, that's a good sign . . . means I can probably drive." He shook hands with Pedro. "Adios, Pedro. It's always good to see you." He turned and walked stiffly toward the door.

Outside, the night air was cool and clean. The jukebox was audible but muffled.

Johnny walked slowly to his truck. He fumbled his keys from his pocket, dropping them onto the ground. Bending forward to pick them up, he lost his balance and landed on his knees, skinning the palm of his hand in the gravel.

"Johnny?"

He looked up in the direction of the voice, his vision blurred and tinted from the pulse pounding in his temple. He pushed himself up to one knee, leaning against his truck for support. "Barb?"

Barbara gave a long sigh. "Juanita called and said that you were sick and maybe needed to go to the hospital." She shook her head. "I guess she knew I wouldn't come if she just said you were drunk."

Johnny eased himself down to a sitting position, his back against the rear tire of his truck. His forehead was beaded with sweat. He looked up at Barbara, in T-shirt and jeans, her arms crossed, a sad expression on her face.

"I really didn't think I was this drunk," Johnny said, surprised.

Barbara frowned. She stepped forward and lay her hand on his face. "You've got a fever." She stood up, hands on hips. "The doctor told you that alcohol was bad for you, Johnny. You lost your spleen, your liver and kidneys were damaged. You're just killing yourself!"

Johnny didn't answer. He rested his forearms on his knees and hung his head, his eyes closed.

The jukebox in Pedro's switched to a slow, sad mariachi ballad. The muffled sound of weeping violins and trumpets drifted across the parking lot. A watchdog at the tractor dealer down the street barked at some imagined threat, and a night breeze rustled through the dry grass along the highway.

"I guess you can't drive," Barbara said. "Can you stand?" She bent forward and put a hand under Johnny's arm.

He struggled to his feet, swaying against Barbara and grabbing the side of the truck for support. Barbara brought his arm over her shoulder and guided him toward her car. By the time they reached it, the back of Johnny's shirt was soaked and the muscles of his jaw were bulging and clenched in pain.

"Ay, Johnny!" Barbara said, exasperated, as she leaned him against her car. "Tonto! Look what you've done to yourself! Maybe I should take you to the hospital."

"No," Johnny gasped. "I hate hospitals. I think I just need to lie down and sweat this out. I'll be fine in a while."

Barbara opened the car door and eased him into the back seat. Slamming the door shut behind, she hurried around and got behind the steering wheel. Starting the car, she looked at him in the rear-view mirror. "What am I doing here?" She shook her head. "We're divorced. You're not supposed to be my problem anymore."

"Sorry, Barb," Johnny gasped. "You may not be my wife, but you're still about the best friend I have." He closed his eyes and let his head fall back against the seat. "Yessir," he muttered. "You and Char are the two best friends I have, and I've let you both down."

Barbara pulled out of the parking lot and turned back toward town.

Smithland Avenue was quiet and calm beneath its canopy of trees. She pulled into the driveway. With her fingers, she wiped tears from her face as she walked around the car to help Johnny out.

"I think I can walk now," he said, swaying. Slowly, he moved to the front door, as Barbara hovered protectively behind. She unlocked the door and held it open for him.

In the living room, Gloria was curled up on the couch watching television. "Daddy?"

"Hey, little girl!" Johnny's smile was a grimace of pain.

Gloria looked inquisitively at her mother, who just held up a hand to forestall questions. Barbara took Johnny's arm and led him to her bedroom. After a few minutes, she came back, closing the door behind her.

"Mom?" Gloria arched her eyebrows. "What's going on? Is Daddy drunk again?"

Barbara dropped heavily into the armchair and closed her eyes. "He was drinking over at Pedro's. But he's mainly sick. The alcohol, it's like poison to him since that bull broke him all up inside."

"So why does he drink?" Gloria asked, indignantly. "That's so dumb!"

Barbara rested her forehead on the palm of her hand. Shaking her head, she said, "He won't admit it, but he's an alcoholic. I couldn't see it for years either. My father was an alcoholic, but your father wasn't like him, so I guess I didn't want to recognize the same sickness."

"What do you mean?"

Barbara looked wearily at Gloria. "You never really knew your *abuelo*. He died when you were still a baby. But he used to drink and get mean. He'd hit your grandmother and whip us kids." She nodded. "He would get really mean and ugly when he drank. But Johnny," she looked toward the closed bedroom door, "your father, was never like that. He never raised a hand against me. He's always been very gentle. But over time he just drank more and more. It was like a river, and he just floated further and further away from us . . . from me." She was crying softly.

Gloria got up from the couch, sat on the arm of her mother's chair, and put her arms around her.

The front door opened and Jack stepped into the living room, his basketball tucked familiarly under his arm. His affable expression turned into a frown at the sight of his mother's tears. "What's wrong?" he asked.

Barbara dabbed at her eyes. "Nothing's wrong, Jack."

"Dad's here," Gloria said, nodding toward the bedroom door.

"What?" Jack's expression clouded with anger. "You let that drunk back into this house? Into your bed?"

In one movement, Barbara sprang from her chair and slapped her son across the face. "*Callate, tu!*"

Jack just stood, astonished.

"You, who are all of sixteen years old," Barbara said, angrily, "you have no right to judge me or to judge that man in there," she pointed toward the bedroom. "He is still your father."

"I can smell the booze from here!" Jack retorted, indignantly. "You're not married to him anymore, so why are you playing nurse-maid?"

Barbara visibly restrained herself. "Because we're not married does not mean we don't . . . care for each other. Your father is sick."

Jack waved his hand in disgust. "Oh, come on, Mom! Don't make excuses for him! He just never wanted to grow up, that's all. What was that you used to say? He wanted to be good time Charlie forever."

Barbara glared at him. "And you are so smart? You know all about your father?" She pointed at the couch. "Sit down." When Jack hesitated, she repeated more sternly, "*Sientate!*"

Jack sat.

"Your father may have many faults, but he does not make excuses for himself. Do you know what it was like for him when he was growing up? No, of course not, because your father doesn't talk about it.

"His father was a prison guard at Folsom Prison in California. You knew that, but did you know that he was a hard man? Very hard. And he used to drink, much more and much worse than your father does. He'd come home from work and because of fear or stress or something, he'd drink and terrorize his own family. He'd slap his wife around and beat the kids, your father and his sister. When he got older, maybe ten, eleven years old, your father would try to protect his mother and sister and just get beaten that much worse.

"One day, when he was thirteen years old, he came home to find that his father had shot himself in the head and killed himself, right there in the kitchen. Johnny,—your father,—was the one who found him.

"After that, the family struggled. His mother worked nights as a waitress and Johnny worked odd jobs after school just to keep the family together. If the government found out that his mother couldn't afford the children, they'd have been put in foster homes. It was your father's hard work, when he was younger than you are now, that kept them together. He had no time for basketball like you.

"Then, from high school he got drafted and sent to Vietnam. He never told me much about what happened there, but I know it wasn't good."

Barbara ran her hand through her hair. In a calmer voice, she said. "My point is, Jack, that your father may not be your idea of a perfect father, but he tried, believe me he tried, to overcome all the garbage he had to deal with growing up. And then lately, there was that accident where that boy was shot, and then that rodeo accident . . ." She shook her head.

"For whatever reason, I think he's more disappointed in himself than you could ever be with him. Whatever he does that's good isn't good enough for him, and whatever he does that's bad just confirms what he believes about himself.

"But," she pointed at Jack, "he's never asked for pity, or made excuses for anything, or taken any of the anger and disappointment out on us. And that's important for you to remember. Unfortunately, he just distanced himself from us. What he needed, he seemed to be afraid to give himself. And we've all lost something important."

Barbara stood, arms folded, looking sadly at the closed bedroom door. Gloria, curled tightly in the armchair, had tears on her cheeks.

Jack, his hands dangling from their resting place on his knees, stared glumly at the floor, unaware of how much he resembled his father at that moment.

∧∧∧

The floorboard creaked, despite Johnny's best efforts to be quiet.

"Johnny?" Barbara raised her head from the pillow on the couch. She pushed the hair back from her eyes and peered through the predawn gloom of the living room.

"I forgot about that squeaky board," Johnny whispered. "I didn't mean to wake you."

Barbara sat up and rubbed her eyes. "Why are you up so early? How do you feel?"

Johnny sat at the end of the couch and pulled his boots on. "I'm supposed to be at work today by eight." He twisted his wrist to read his watch. "That gives me a couple of hours to get back, maybe shower and be on time." His fingers drummed on his knee and he looked sheepishly at the floor between his feet. "Sorry to put you out of your own bed last night."

"You didn't answer all of my question, but I guess you are feeling better." She turned on the couch to face him. "So what happened yesterday? What were you doing at Pedro's? You know better than that, Mr. Gringo."

Johnny sighed and slumped back in the couch. "Yeah, no excuses. Yesterday was kind of a bad day."

Barbara looked at him, waiting. "You're going to make me pull teeth, aren't you? Okay, what happened yesterday that made it so bad?"

Johnny frowned and considered a moment before answering. "Char won't tell me who the real killer is, but he asked me to help him anyway. It was my day off, so I thought I'd go up to Denver and see if I couldn't get a lead on something. Char was living there last winter and that's about the time these murders started. I figured there must be a connection in there somewhere."

Johnny stood up and went to the front window. Outside, the birds were starting to twitter and sing as the sunrise touched the tops of the trees. "I went by this Indian Center place where Char had been in an Alcoholics Anonymous type group."

Barbara resisted the urge to say something.

"I talked to the drug and alcohol counselor. He said that most of the guys, they're reaching out to some higher power to grab hold of and help them get their lives together. But once in a while, some of them grab on to something destructive or evil. Well, I had this theory that somebody in Char's group—they've got like a buddy system—that maybe his buddy was one of those who grabbed on to this dark power and thinks that white women are the root of all evil or something."

He turned back to face Barbara. "Sounds a little farfetched to me this morning, but it seemed like a decent lead to me yesterday. Anyway, this counselor wouldn't give me the name of Char's buddy. End of lead, end of super-sleuth John Hart's big investigation."

"Of course he wouldn't give you the name," Barbara yawned. "He's a counselor." She stood up and stretched. "I'm going to make some coffee, then I'll drive you over to your truck."

Johnny followed her into the kitchen. "What do you mean, 'of course'? I think he's just trying to protect this crazy simply because he's a fellow Indian."

"Well, that may be, but the fact is, legally anyway, there's a privilege, and he can't just hand over the name. Even if you were officially investigating, which you're not, and had a subpoena, he'd be in kind of a tight place and still might not give you the name."

Johnny leaned against the doorframe, watching her make the coffee. "Okay," he sighed. "You're the lawyer. Explain that to me in a way that even somebody who's landed on his head as often as I have can understand."

"You see," she pointed a spoon at him, "the law wants to encourage people who need help, to get help by going to a priest, pastor, counselor, somebody. But if everything they say or confess is going to be blabbed to the first person who asks about it, they're not going to seek the help. So that's what the law calls a privilege. The counselor can't be compelled to reveal information unless the person who confided in him gives him the green light, or"—she paused and looked at Johnny, eyebrows raised—"unless the counselor has a reasonable belief that someone else is in imminent danger and the information can prevent the harm." She shook her head. "That's a big if, though, particularly if this counselor doesn't want to undermine his credibility, his trust within the Indian community."

Johnny smiled.

"What?" Barbara asked, looking at him.

He shook his head, accepting the proffered cup of coffee. "I confess, when I first asked you out back in high school, it was because you were the prettiest girl I'd ever seen. And now," he sipped his coffee, "all these years later, it turns out you're the smartest too."

Barbara lifted the edge of her blanket and curtsied. "Thank you, kind sir. Now drink that, it's late. Let me wash my face and then we're out of here."

When they were in the car, Barbara said, "You've got to talk to Jack, Johnny. He's all twisted up inside, over our divorce, your drinking, everything. He's very angry."

Hart gave a short, humorless laugh. "I'm not sure what I can tell him. I'm not real thrilled about our divorce or my drinking either."

She frowned. "Come on, Johnny, don't blow this off. It's serious. He's still your son and you're going to lose him."

"I don't know what . . ." He stopped himself. "Yeah, you're right. I'll try."

"There's something else, Johnny." They pulled into the parking lot of Pedro's. One or two other vehicles had been left by drivers too drunk or amorous to drive. Barbara left the engine running. "I had a visit from an FBI agent. He wanted me to warn you about starting an investigation of these killings on your own. He said that the agent in charge would bury you."

"About time somebody did," Johnny grinned. "Dead bodies shouldn't be left above ground too long."

Barbara shook her head in exasperation. "Will you be serious, Johnny!"

"I am serious," he nodded. His grin faded. "I'm sorry about last night, Barb, I really am."

She sighed. "I know you are, Johnny. I know you always are."

"Yeah, well . . ." he hesitated in nervous silence. Softly he asked, "Could I kiss you, Barb? Just a good-bye peck?"

She turned her head away to look out her window. "No, Johnny," she said quietly. "I don't think that's a good idea."

He nodded. "Maybe you're right." He opened the passenger door and climbed out. "Thanks again." He closed the door and stood watching as she drove away, the sun beginning to warm his back.

ʌʌʌ

"Buffalo Bill and them fellers worked pretty hard to clear this country for cattle," Mr. Cross noted. "Now you want to bring the buffalo back, is that the idea?"

They sat in the kitchen, steaming cups of coffee before them on the table amidst the dinner dishes. The small radio on top of the refrigerator played quietly.

"Well, Char and I have been talking about it," Sandy explained. "It seems like a good business decision."

Mr. Cross turned to Char. "You're in on this too, eh? What's your thinkin'?"

Char cleared his throat. "The price of beef has been going down to where it's less than the cost of production. And that's not just on a bad year. That's a long-term trend."

"That's right," Sandy piped in again. "People are going to chicken and turkey and other things they think are healthier for them. The fact is buffalo meat has less fat than beef, and less cholesterol than chicken."

Char nodded. "And buffalo steaks are going for about $15.00 a pound. Buffalo would be easier to keep healthy on this land. They're native to it, unlike the cows, so they'd resist diseases and winter a whole lot better. That all makes them cheaper to raise."

Mr. Cross sipped his coffee. "So what would it cost to start up a herd of buffalo?"

Sandy exchanged a look with Char. "Well," she hesitated, "breeding stock runs about $1,300 to $1,500 a head."

Mr. Cross winced. "Kinda pricey, don't you think?" He looked first at Sandy, then at Char. "You'd have to sell off every cow we have to get enough to even start a herd of buffalo. Then it'd be a few years before you breed enough head to start marketing. What'll we do for beans and taxes in the meantime?"

Sandy pushed her chair back, stood up, and began to pace the small kitchen. "We talked about that. I could try to get a part time job in town to bring some money in. Char said that he could keep on rodeoing and keep a cash income. It'd just be a few years before the herd started paying. And," she stopped and shoved both hands into the pockets of her jeans, "we're losing money right now to where we'll have to start mortgaging the ranch just to eat pretty soon."

Mr. Cross shook his head. "Pretty sorry state when grown men playin' ball games are makin' millions and hard workin' people raisin' food can't make enough to eat."

All three were quiet. A slight breeze stirred the curtains above the sink.

"So, Char," Mr. Cross said. "How did you get roped into this plan? No offense, but your last name don't happen to be Cross." He looked at Sandy, who blushed. "You two worked out some kind of partnership without lettin' me in on it?"

Char glanced at Sandy, then back to Mr. Cross. "No, we haven't really talked about it. I'm not really looking to get anything out of it. I'd like to see you two doing well and I'd like to see buffalo back on this land." He shrugged. "That's all."

"That's what I figured." Mr. Cross scowled at Sandy. "You ought to be ashamed of yourself, little girl, takin' advantage of this man's good nature."

"I'm sorry, Grandpa, Char," Sandy stammered. "I didn't even think about it."

"Let me remind you that this ranch is still in my name. You're my heir, Sandy, but I ain't dead yet. So that means I've got a say in this." Mr. Cross drummed his fingers on the table. "I got this ranch for work and a promise, not cash. I worked hard and I kept my promise. I expect Char would too, but," he held up his hand in caution, "the FBI has other plans for you, son. What happens if they cart you off to the hoosegow for a long time? They don't pay all that much for makin' license plates.

"And have you thought about this," he continued. "Even if that deputy friend of yours manages to catch the real killer—and I'm not puttin' any money on that horse—what happens if the two of you," he pointed two fingers at Char and Sandy, "aren't gettin' along so well in a couple of years and you get yourself a girlfriend or some Prince

Charmin' rides on in here lookin' for Sandy?" He arched his eyebrows in silent question marks.

Sandy and Char looked at each other then looked away, embarrassed.

"I ain't no lawyer, I'm proud to say, but it seems like you two got some serious thinkin' and talkin' to do." He stood stiffly to his feet. "I still ain't sayin' I'm all for this buffalo thing in the first place, but I'll sure think on it." He stretched his back painfully. "Right now, though, I aim to sleep on it. Lord willin', I'll see you both come mornin.'" With a wave, he limped from the kitchen and down the hall.

Left alone, Sandy and Char were quiet. The radio was the only sound. Sandy leaned against the kitchen sink, her arms crossed. Char stretched his legs beneath the table, one hand wrapped around his coffee cup.

"So, what do you think?" Sandy asked.

He didn't look up. "It's your call, Sandy." He finished his coffee. "There's definitely got to be some cash coming in while the herd grows big enough to be commercial. And, grandpa's right. I wouldn't say you could rely on me to be out of jail or even alive six months from now, let alone for the next three or four years."

Sandy moved quickly behind Char's chair and placed her hands on his shoulders. "Don't say that, Char."

He reached up and patted her hand. "Let's deal with reality." He stood and moved across the room. Opening the back door, he stood at the screen looking out at the night. "Right now we're kind of in the eye of the storm. It seems peaceful, but the FBI isn't going to go away. Once they've looked everywhere else, they'll either figure out I'm here, or at least figure it's worth checking on again."

He turned back to face Sandy. "And I don't know if Johnny can do anything or not. Maybe I have faith in him because he's all I've got." He shook his head. "My faith doesn't make him all I need, though."

"What he needs," Sandy snapped, "is a little help from you. I don't know why you won't give him the name of the man you think is doing this. It makes no sense at all."

"No," Char frowned. "It probably doesn't. But what if I'm wrong?"

"If they don't have the evidence, he won't be convicted," Sandy reasoned.

"Oh, please!" Char waved his hand. "Time for a reality check, Sandy. They can't have any real evidence against me, and yet here I am hiding out from every lawman in the country. Larry Pelham has been in prison for the past fifteen years for two murders practically everybody, in Indian country at least, knows he didn't do." He shook his head. "When it comes to Indians, evidence doesn't have a whole hell of a lot to do with it." He turned back to the screen door, looking at the blackness outside.

Sandy paced the room a couple of times, looking unhappily at the linoleum floor. "I still think we can be partners in this ranch . . . this buffalo ranch. And I think we can make it work."

Char gave a short surprised laugh, and turned to look at her. "Do you have that much faith in the justice system? Or is your faith in old Johnny Hart?" He shook his head.

Sandy looked at him seriously. "You know where my faith is, Char."

They just looked at each other for a long moment. Char nodded. "Yeah, God can make this thing come out any way he wants." He picked up his coffee cup, took it to the sink, and rinsed it. "Why do you want me as a partner, Sandy? I mean, you really don't even know me."

She shoved her hands into the pocket of her jeans. "I think I know you. I've seen how hard you work. I know something of what you care about. And, I know we share a dream for what this ranch—maybe all this high plains country—could be. That pretty much covers it for me." She shrugged and smiled. "Besides, this used to be Cheyenne land. It seems only right that a Cheyenne have a stake in it again."

"Well, we'll see what tomorrow brings," Char said, then yawned. "I'd better go lie down before I fall down." He pushed back his chair and rose.

"You know, Char, you don't have to sleep in the barn. We've got a couple of spare bedrooms in the house here."

They exchanged a long look before Char gave a small smile. "Maybe I'll move my stuff in tomorrow. Good night." He closed the door on his way out.

ᴧᴧᴧ

"Yeah, hello." Johnny struggled to wake up. He'd gone to bed early, feeling virtuous for that, and for making it through the day without drinking anything stronger than coffee. His clock radio light was still burned out, so he had no idea what time it was or who was calling.

"Deputy Hart? I'm sorry to be calling so late. This is Jimmy Little Crow, from the Indian Center in Denver. I wanted to talk to you."

"Well, hi!" Johnny sat up, fully awake. "I'm glad you called."

"I've been doing a lot of thinking," Little Crow said. "I've prayed about it. I'd really like to help you. I'd like to help Char. But I'm kind of between a rock and a hard place on this."

"I know," Johnny said. "I'm really sorry I flamed off on you the other day. My wife—my ex-wife—is a lawyer. She explained to me about the counselor-patient privilege and all that."

"That is a big part of my problem," Little Crow agreed. "But it's more than that." He paused. "From the little bit the FBI told me, I understand that the killer doesn't just kill. He takes the body, travels with it, cuts it up, stuff like that, right?"

"Yeah, that seems to be his pattern."

"Well, let me just say, that doesn't sound like something Char would do, of course, but it doesn't sound like something this other man—his buddy—could be doing either."

"To tell you the truth," Johnny said, "it doesn't sound like something any sane person would be doing, but, I guess it goes without saying, that we're not dealing with a sane person here."

"But," Little Crow's voice was pained, "Char's buddy was a Navajo. The Navajo, more than almost any people I can think of, have this thing—this fear—about ghosts. Even just killing requires a healing, a cleansing ceremony. To kill, then mutilate, and carry the body around, and not just once but several times? A Navajo just couldn't do that!"

"You know, Jimmy," Johnny said patiently, "I don't believe we're all just the product of our culture. I mean when we're first born, and after all is said and done, we're all human. And it seems like we humans, all of us, have it in us to do tremendously evil things. Even sane people do bad things. You add a twist of loco to somebody, and I think probably even a Navajo could be doing this."

"Maybe you're right." Little Crow sounded weary. "Well, promise me you won't tell anybody where you got it, but I guess I'd better give you a name. If he is the killer, somebody had better stop him."

Johnny fumbled for the light switch, then got his pen and notebook from the pocket of his uniform shirt, which hung on the closet door. "I really appreciate this, Jimmy. Go ahead."

Little Crow sighed. "His name is Lee . . . Ross Lee."

"Lee, huh?" Johnny frowned. "Jeez. I wonder how many people named Lee there are in this country? Do you know where he is, this Ross Lee?"

"I'm afraid not," Little Crow admitted. "He hasn't been around in months."

"Great," Johnny groaned. "Any idea where he was from originally? I mean, I understand the Navajo are a pretty big tribe."

"I think he said his family was from around Tuba City, Arizona, someplace," Little Crow said. "He spent some time in Utah, too, I think. Provo, I think it was."

"Can you think of anything else?" Johnny asked. "Wife, girlfriend, job, anything like that?"

"Not really," Little Crow confessed. "He never did really open up much in meetings. He came into the program before Char, but he didn't seem to make any progress until Char came along. He really seemed to like Char. Looked up to him. He's several years younger than Sixkiller and seemed to need a father figure or a big brother or something."

"Okay. Listen, Jimmy, I appreciate this more than you know."

"Just make sure nobody knows I gave you the information," Little Crow urged. "I've been able to do a lot of good here. But if people think I'm liable to dime them to the cops or blab about some secret shame, I'm history. You understand that, Johnny?"

"I understand," he assured him.

"Let me know what's going on, if you can," Little Crow said. "And keep in touch. From what Char told me, maybe I can help you some."

"Me? I'm fine as frog's hair," Johnny said. "Thanks again."

ᴧᴧᴧ

It was still dark, but Sandy had practically grown up in that barn, so she had no difficulty finding the spot where Char lay sleeping. She dropped to her knees beside him, taking his shoulders in both her hands. "Char!"

In one motion, Char's eyes flickered open, and he grabbed Sandy by the back of the head, pulling her across and face down in the straw beside him. A second later his knee was in the small of her back and his hand was knotted in her hair.

"Char! Stop! It's me!" Sandy gasped, trying to catch her breath.

"Sandy?" Char let go and sprang to his feet. "What are you doing here? Are you okay? Did I hurt you?"

Sandy rolled over onto her back, her hands clasped across her stomach. Wide eyed, she nodded. "I'm fine! Fine! But Grandpa," she struggled to her feet, "I think he's having a heart attack or something. Come help me!"

They sprinted back into the house, where Mr. Cross was lying, half-propped against the wall of the hallway. "He was too heavy for me to pick up," Sandy said, her voice pinched with anxiety.

Char lifted Mr. Cross and carried him back into his room, laying him on the bed. Mr. Cross groaned in pain.

"What happened?" Char asked.

"I'm a pretty light sleeper," Sandy explained. "I heard Grandpa get up. I thought he was going to the bathroom, then I heard him collapse in the hall." She wrung her hands. "I couldn't move him. I couldn't help him!"

Char laid his head on Mr. Cross's chest. "Go call an ambulance. Wait! No. Call Johnny! Tell him to get an ambulance. We'll meet them on the way, it'll save time."

Char took hold of Mr. Cross's head and positioned the jaw so that he could give him artificial respiration. "Go, Sandy, go!"

Pinching the old man's nose, Char gave three quick breaths into his mouth, followed by three quick pumps to his chest. Sandy ran for the phone in the kitchen.

"Hello," Johnny's groggy voice responded.

"Johnny! It's Sandy Cross. My grandpa's having a heart attack, I think. Char's giving him CPR. He said to start an ambulance out this way. You know what our truck looks like? Tell them we'll meet them on the way."

"Got it," Johnny replied crisply. "I'm on my way too."

"Thank you." Sandy hung up the phone and hurried back down the hall.

Char straightened up as Sandy entered, nodding at the prostrate Mr. Cross. "He's breathing on his own now, but his pulse is still not good."

"Oh, God," Sandy bit her lip.

"You'd better get dressed," Char said, pointing at Sandy, who was barefoot, wearing only a thigh length Denver Broncos tee shirt. Her shivering was as much from fear as the chill of the late September night. "I'll stay here with your Grandpa. Honk when you get the truck started and I'll carry him out."

Sandy was sitting behind the wheel, gunning the engine and honking the horn in less than five minutes. The screen door banged open and Char hurried out with Mr. Cross in his arms. The dog, Lady, trotted and danced nervously beside him.

Barefoot and without a shirt, Char stepped up on the bumper and over the tailgate in one fluid motion, laying Mr. Cross on the bed of the truck, his head on his lap. "Go!" he yelled.

The truck fishtailed, spraying dirt as Sandy raced up the rutted road.

The eastern horizon glowed with the dull silver band of sunrise as they reached the highway and turned west. Pink fingers of light were streaking the sky by the time Sandy finally saw the ambulance approaching. She flashed her lights, pulling over onto the right-hand shoulder.

Siren screaming, the ambulance did a quick U-turn and pulled to a sliding stop directly behind the pickup. Char squinted into the headlights, kneeled, and lifted Mr. Cross. Nimbly, he stepped out and down, laying Mr. Cross onto the waiting gurney. A paramedic immediately put an oxygen mask over the old man's face.

As they loaded the gurney into the back of the ambulance, Johnny pulled up onto the opposite shoulder, his bubble light blinking. He hurried across the road.

Sandy stood beside Char, trembling slightly in the chilly morning air. "Do you want to ride in the ambulance? Johnny could probably bring you back later on."

Sandy looked at Johnny, who nodded. "Thank you," she muttered. Handing Char the keys to the truck, she patted his bare chest with distracted affection as she hurried back to the ambulance, climbing in before they shut the doors. The siren could be heard in the stillness, long after the taillights faded.

"How'd he look?" Johnny asked.

Char shook his head. "We got him breathing within a couple of minutes, I think, but who knows." He rubbed his hands on his bare arms to warm himself. "He's a tough old boy. If orneriness counts for anything, he'll pull through."

Looking at Johnny, he asked, "How about me, Cuz? Am I gonna make it? How's the investigation going?"

"Does the name Ross Lee sound familiar?" Johnny asked.

Char stood very still.

"Yeah, I thought so," Johnny nodded. "I know he's Navajo, from Arizona originally. Spent some time in Utah." He looked at Char. "Jump in anytime, if you'd like to add something," he continued ironically.

Char sighed deeply. "You're more of a cop than you give yourself credit for, Johnny." He gave a tired smile. "I can't tell you much more than that, myself, though. Ross didn't talk much." He shivered. "Do you mind if we sit in the truck? That was one of the coldest rides I've had in a while."

Once in the cab, Johnny said, "Somebody told me that because this Lee is Navajo, he'd have some kind of superstition about ghosts that would make it real unlikely he'd spend anytime in the company of dead women, even if he was the one that killed them in the first place."

"Well, Ross wasn't altogether raised Navajo, so it's possible some of these traditions aren't too deeply ingrained in him," Char said.

"How was he raised?"

"That's the Utah connection," Char explained. "Used to be, not too many years back, that Navajo parents could be persuaded that it was a good idea to let some of their children be placed in good Mormon homes where they'd get plenty to eat and a good white man's education. It was called the Indian Student Placement Program or something. If the parents were poor enough, they'd go along with it. Not too many generations back, it didn't matter if they agreed to it or not.

"Ross's family was in what they called the Joint Occupancy area of the reservation, which the Hopi and Navajo shared. In order to generate a little business and distract the tribes from getting together to protect their resources, a group of white lawyers decided that, after centuries of living side by side, it was just intolerable for Navajos to be living on land that was marked on the government's map as being Hopi and vice versa. So they had to draw more lines, build fences, file some lawsuits and bill it all back to the tribes for all this high-priced legal work. It was really all about the coal under Black Mesa that Peabody Coal Company wanted to get on the cheap. Some of the lawyers representing the tribes were working for Peabody at the same time." Char's voice was sarcastic and bitter.

"The Lee family was one of those that was supposed to be relocated. By then, Ross was already living with a white Mormon family in Provo. After he graduated from high school, he went back to the Rez and found that his family was destroyed. While they waited for their relocation home to be built, they'd camped out in a cardboard and plywood shack outside of Tuba City. They waited and waited. His brother started sniffing glue. His sister got pregnant and ran off to Phoenix. His father got drunk and died after getting run over by a truck that didn't see him lying in the road. Finally, his mother was placed in a crummy prefab house in Flagstaff that she got swindled out of less than a year later. Ross wasn't quite sure where she was. He thinks she may have gone down to Phoenix too."

The sun was up now and the air was beginning to warm. Though the windows were still rolled up, the sound of bird song was clear.

"Pretty rough," Johnny muttered.

"Pretty typical, I'm afraid," Char corrected. "Anyway, Ross went back to Utah. Got about a year of college, but started drinking himself. I think he got married. Married a white girl, too, I think, but he never really talked about it. And that," Char shrugged, "is about all I know about Ross Lee."

Johnny looked out the side window, thinking. A passing big rig made the truck sway. "What about this 'higher power' thing with AA? You talk about it like it's a wonderful, positive thing. Some other people do too. This Lee, though, what was his experience?"

Char gave Johnny a quizzical look. "Not bad, hoss. You're really pretty good at this cop thing." He nodded. "You're right. I don't really think Ross found a higher power. But he did find a purpose, a reason to quit drinking and live." He paused. "Hate."

"Hate?" Johnny repeated.

"Just that," Char nodded. "He hated white people for obvious reasons, but I think he hated Indians too, for surviving. He thought it would have been nobler or something if we'd all just died fighting." He arched his eyebrows. "Interesting theory, huh?"

"Stupid theory," Johnny snorted.

"We'll have to talk about it some time." Char turned the key and the truck shuddered reluctantly to life. "I'd better get back out of sight again. Can you give me a call if you get any news from the hospital?"

Johnny opened the door. "Sure thing."

"Oh, and Johnny," Char added, "don't use my name on the phone. Maybe I'm paranoid, but it wouldn't surprise me if the FBI hadn't bugged your phone. You did kind of piss them off, you know."

Johnny shook his head. "Is this a great country or what?" He stepped out. "I'll call."

Char extended his hand. "Thanks, Johnny."

Johnny shook the hand but didn't release it right away. "Why did you tell me all that about Lee? I thought you weren't going to help me on this."

Char smiled. "You were halfway there already, Cuz." The smile faded. "Seriously, though. I can't go to jail now. Sandy is depending on me, particularly now, with her grandpa in such bad shape."

Johnny smiled. "I've never heard you use the word serious in the same sentence with a woman's name before. Something changing?"

Char nodded. "Everything."

"See ya," Johnny said, closing the truck's door. He waited until the truck was out of sight, squinting into the sun, before crossing back to his truck and driving toward Eads.

CHAPTER 10

Barbara looked up from her desk. "Agent DiRosa!"

The FBI man smiled and bowed with mock formality from her office door. "Ms. Gutierrez. I was wondering if you were free for lunch?"

"Are you buying?" she asked, cocking her head.

"Well, Uncle Sam has given me a generous expense account that I hate to see go to waste," he replied.

"Sounds good," she nodded. "I may as well get some food in return for my tax dollars."

Once seated at the restaurant, DiRosa leaned forward and lowered his voice. "Did you pass along that warning to Deputy Hart?"

"Well, kind of," Barbara frowned. "I haven't talked to him in a while. He hasn't called, and I've been pretty busy."

DiRosa sighed. "I'm afraid he's been pretty busy, too." He looked intently at her. "This is strictly confidential, you understand?"

Barbara nodded, as a cold knot formed in her stomach.

"We've got a tap on Hart's phone. He's in contact with Sixkiller, despite what he's told us. And, to make things worse, it looks like he's trying to run his own private investigation." He shook his head. "He is way out of his league here. You've got to get him to back off or he's going down, too."

"What do you mean?" Barbara asked. "Are you saying that Johnny could be charged with aiding and abetting?"

DiRosa leaned forward even closer, frowning, his voice an intense whisper. "I'm saying that Special Agent in Charge Sutton is a wacko, to put it bluntly, and I think he hates Indians. He did a background check on your ex and found out that he's part Indian." He nodded. "Did you know that?"

"I don't think Johnny even knew that," Barbara shook her head. "But what does that have to do with anything?"

"Hart has some cousins or something in Oklahoma who are enrolled Cherokee Indians," DiRosa explained. "Sixkiller is half Cherokee. For Sutton, that's enough to push a conspiracy charge down on old Deputy Hart." He leaned back, nodding.

Barbara's mouth dropped open. "Conspiracy to murder?"

DiRosa continued nodding. "You got it, counselor. Maybe even the felony murder rule."

The waitress arrived with their plates.

"Why are you telling me all this?" Barbara demanded.

He took a bite of his enchilada and chewed thoughtfully before answering. "Because it's not right." His fork toyed with his beans. "I'm Italian, right? My father worked hard all his life—New York City Transit cop. He was a good man, you know, but all his life—all my life—we've had this Mafia thing hanging over us. It's like everybody looks at you or hears your name and think, 'Oh, okay, another guinea wise guy.'" He shook his head. "It's just not right. And neither is this."

ᴧᴧᴧ

The setting sun gave a soft, velvety appearance to the tawny grasses. The shadow of the pickup stretched out before them on the eastbound lane. Johnny was driving Sandy home from the hospital where her grandfather had been admitted.

"I like this time of day," Johnny said. "This and morning. It makes these plains seem a little friendlier . . . closer, kind of."

Sandy smiled. "I like them at any time of day, but I know what you mean about morning and evening." She looked over at Johnny. "I forget that you're not from around here."

Johnny nodded. "Nope. But I've been out here so long, this is pretty much home now. Even so," he pointed with his chin toward the distant horizon, "there's times when it's just so big, wide and lonesome, it's hard to feel like anybody really belongs here, you know?"

Sandy shook her head. "Not me. I'm like a bird who just can't get enough sky. I tried living up along the Front Range, in Boulder. It's pretty, with the mountains and all, but I was born here. This is definitely home."

"That was when you were married?" Johnny glanced at Sandy from the corner of his eye. "Up in Boulder, was it?"

She nodded. "I went up there to go to school at the University and wound up marrying a professor." She gave a dry chuckle. "Talk about a fish out of water!"

"Pretty bad, huh?" Johnny prompted.

"Pretty bad," Sandy agreed looking out her side window. "I went to school in the first place so I could learn how to run the ranch better. But when Gerry showed an interest in me, it just kind of threw me off balance. I was flattered that this important, intellectual of a professor would find me, a little country girl right out of the saddle, interesting or attractive. So I tried to fit in with his world and his friends." She paused. "Biggest mistake I ever made."

"I don't know," Johnny said. "You seem like a pretty intelligent woman to me. Seems like you could hold your own with about anybody."

Sandy shook her head. "Maybe that was the problem. They all claimed to be seeking the truth. And yet, they couldn't come to a conclusion." She laughed. "What's the point of seeking something if you refuse to recognize it when you find it? No guts! Just a lot of intellectual posturing! Truth is everything for them is based on feelings. How they felt about things was more important than how things really were. They were so open-minded their brains had fallen out. Fact is, most of them wouldn't have recognized the truth if reason and logic both slid up and bit them on the rump."

Johnny laughed. "My, my! You do get heated up over it, don't you?"

It was Sandy's turn to laugh, shaking her hair out. "Yeah, I guess I'm still trying to finish arguments that started a long time ago. But there was some good that came out of those years. It made me come to some conclusions myself about things I'd just been either fuzzy or lazy about."

Johnny gave her a look out of the corner of his eye. "Will I be very sorry if I ask what those things were?"

"You may be," Sandy smiled. "But to make a long story short, my conclusions led me back to the ranch and back to church."

"Another shitkicker for Christ!" Johnny said with a smile, looking to see how she'd react.

Sandy laughed. "And proud of it, mind you!"

He cleared his throat. "Changing the subject a little bit, have you reached any conclusions about Char Sixkiller?"

She blushed. "What do you mean?"

"I mean my old buddy, the bullfighter, seems to be thinking pretty serious thoughts about you lately and I was just wondering how you felt about being the object of affection for an accused serial killer?"

"What an awful way to put it." Sandy scowled at him.

Johnny nodded. "It's a pretty awful situation."

"Yeah, well," she frowned down at her hands, which she folded on her lap. "I'm not so sure I like how I feel about Char."

Johnny raised an eyebrow. "I had the impression you had kind of a soft spot for Char in that cowgirl heart of yours."

"'He that trusteth in his own heart is a fool,'" she muttered with a sigh. "That's kind of the problem."

"I can see plenty of problems for the two of you, but how you feel about each other isn't one of them." Johnny looked away from the road to try to read her face. "Is it because he's Indian and you're white?" he frowned.

"Oh, please!" She gave Johnny a pitying look. "Christ only recognizes one race . . . the human one. No," she shook her head, looking out the window at the fading light. "It's that Char isn't a Christian," she said softly.

"Oh, for Pete's sake," Johnny snorted. "You mean two people can't love each other unless they believe all the same things?"

"Of course they can love each other," Sandy retorted, "but I'm not so sure they can live together for any length of time. It's like two people starting from the same place and one goes northwest and the other goes northeast. The further they go, the farther apart they'll be. Love is only the starting point. If people don't share the same values, beliefs, goals, they're going to wind up apart sooner or later. I know. I've been there before."

Johnny frowned, looking straight ahead. He turned on the truck's headlights and nodded. "I've been there, too," he agreed quietly.

They drove in silence for a while. Turning north at Brandon, Johnny drove slowly through the moonless night. As they crested the ridge above the ranch house, the truck's radio hissed. "Base to Unit Seven, come in please."

Johnny picked up the microphone. "This is Unit Seven. Go ahead, base."

"Johnny," the dispatcher said, "Garrett just called in sick. Sheriff wants to know if you'd mind pulling another shift tonight? He'll give you some comp time down the line. Over?"

Johnny sighed. "Sure, Billy. It's not like I've got anything better to do. I'll be there in about twenty–thirty minutes. Over."

"Thanks, Johnny. Base out."

"Seven out."

The only light came from the kitchen window. "Well, say hey to Char for me," Johnny said to Sandy. "I'll see him sometime."

"Thanks for the ride, Johnny," Sandy said opening her door.

"Thanks for the conversation." He tugged the brim of his hat, nodding good-bye.

Sandy watched as the truck circled and headed up the road, its tail-lights disappearing over the ridge.

"How's your grandpa?"

Sandy gasped, spinning around. "Criminy, Char, you scared me half to death! I thought you were in the house." She punched him on the shoulder. "Don't do that!"

Char smiled. "Hmm. Red man move like leaf on wind," he said, crossing his arms and affecting a Hollywood Indian accent.

Sandy smiled and shook her head. "Pack it, Tonto! I'm starving." She turned and headed for the kitchen door. "Did you cook anything?"

Char fell in step beside her. "Beans and franks and some biscuits," he replied, holding the door for her to enter.

"Perfect!" She took a plate from the cabinet, loaded it at the stove, and sat.

Char poured a cup of coffee and stood at the sink watching her eat. "So how's he doing?"

Sandy nodded, chewing. "Much better. He was awake and stable and madder than a wet hen when they said they were keeping him for a few days of observation."

Char shook his head. "Those poor nurses don't know what they're in for."

"Isn't that the truth," Sandy agreed, pushing her empty plate back. "Did anything happen around here today?"

No," Char sipped his coffee. "I rode fence all day, but everything was quiet."

Sandy brought her plate over to the sink. "You seem kind of quiet, too. Is everything okay?"

Char studied his coffee for a while. "You don't expect any snakebite around here, do you?" He avoided looking at her.

She laughed, surprised. "What are you talking about?"

"I mean you don't have any liquor in the house." He looked at her miserably. "I know. I looked everywhere."

"Oh, Char!" Sandy took his hand in both hers. "What happened? Was it being alone all day?"

Char sighed. "I guess. I don't really know. I thought I was used to being alone. I came in around six and started looking for something to cook and before I knew it I was looking for something to drink. I went through every drawer and cabinet here in the kitchen. Then I looked in the medicine cabinet and under the sink in the bathroom. I'm afraid I even went through some of your drawers in your room." He shook his head. "I'm really sorry."

Sandy didn't know what to say. "Oh, Char!" she repeated. "I'm so sorry." She laid her forehead against his chest and wrapped her arms around his waist. "Are you all right, now?"

He nodded. "Yeah, I think so. I called a friend in Denver. A rehab counselor. We talked for a while. I think I'm okay now." While he spoke, his arms enfolded Sandy and drew her closer.

They stood that way, feeling the tension growing in each other's bodies. The only sound was the dripping of the kitchen faucet into the plate Sandy had placed in the sink.

The phone rang.

Reluctantly, Sandy pushed herself away from Char, one hand nervously rubbing her temple as she walked across the room to the wall phone.

"Hello." She listened. "Just a minute." She covered the mouthpiece and whispered, "Jimmy Little Crow?" Her expression asked if it was all right.

Char nodded. "He's the counselor." He walked over and took the phone. "Hello."

Sandy leaned against the wall, close to Char, her arms hugging herself.

"Yeah, I'm okay now, Jimmy. Thanks for calling. Oh, hey," Char frowned, "where are you calling from?" He nodded. "Okay, good. Yeah, I think a pay phone is safer. You take care, *kola*. Later." He hung up.

They stood almost touching. Char cleared his throat. "It's been a hell of a day. We'd better get some sleep." He took a step toward the back door.

Sandy detained him with a hand on his arm. "I don't want you to sleep in the barn, Char," she whispered.

His fingers brushed lightly across her cheekbone. She could feel the trembling in his hand. "I know." He pulled his hand back, opened the door, and left. She could hear the crunch of his boots on the pebbles of the yard until the barn swallowed the sound.

⋀⋀⋀

Johnny flicked the switch but the porch light didn't come on. He opened the door anyway.

"Barb?"

"Can I come in?" She pressed past him without waiting for his reply. "We've got to talk."

"Well, sure." He closed the door. "Is my phone out again? The kids are all right, aren't they?"

Barbara nodded. "The kids are fine." She looked around the living room with obvious distaste. "Nice place," she said, sarcastically.

Johnny shrugged. "It's a dump. I don't spend much time here, anyway." He waved toward the hallway. "Come on back in the kitchen. Want some coffee?"

"Coffee?" Barbara sounded surprised. "Good for you! Sure, I'll take a cup."

She sat down at the table, smiling stiffly when Johnny placed the steaming cup before her.

"It's good to see you," he said taking the seat across the table. "But what are you doing here?"

"You're in trouble, Johnny. Big trouble!" She laced her fingers around the cup, staring into the dark liquid as she spoke. "The FBI has tapped your phone. They know that you've been talking to Char and trying to investigate things on your own."

"Yeah, well . . ." he began, but she cut him off.

"They even did a background check on you," she continued. "And because some of your relatives in Oklahoma are Cherokee, they want to make you a co-conspirator with Char."

"Cherokee, huh? I'll be darned!" Johnny laughed. "Here I just thought we were Okies."

"This is serious, Johnny! Conspiracy to commit murder!" She slapped her hand on the table to emphasize the last word. "*Ay, Dios mio!*" She rested her forehead against her palm as if she had a headache.

Johnny frowned. "Well, what am I supposed to do? Not help Char? He's not a murderer."

"Johnny, all I'm saying is that you can't help Char from the next prison cell."

"Good point," he acknowledged. He drummed his fingers on the table, thinking. "How do you know all this about the FBI anyway, Barb?"

She avoided looking at him. "I can't tell you that, but believe me, it's true."

Johnny stood up. "If they've been listening in on my phone, they may have traced where Char is. I'd better warn him."

"Johnny!" Barbara stood also. "Weren't you listening to me? You can't help Char. All you can do is hurt yourself."

"Come on, Barb," Johnny pleaded. "I've got to try. He saved my life."

"I know, I know." She came around the table and clutched the front of his shirt. "Please, Johnny! For the sake of the kids, for me, back away from this. Don't make us watch you be hurt again!"

He hung his head. "What else can I do? I'm sorry, Barb."

She studied his face as if searching for a reason she could understand. A tear rolled down her cheek. She shook her head. "You're really quite a selfish man, aren't you?" she commented, with more sadness than anger. "Good-bye, Johnny." She walked quickly to the door.

"Barb?" Johnny called. Louder. "Barb?!" The door closed.

⋀⋀⋀

"Did you have a nice day off in La Junta?"

DiRosa looked up from his desk, startled by the voice. Special Agent Sutton stood in the doorway of the office, his tie loosened, his shirt sleeves rolled up, his arms crossed.

"I didn't know anybody was still here," DiRosa said. "It's pretty late."

Sutton shrugged. "You know me, Bureau to the bone. Sutton never sleeps, isn't that what they say about me?" He slumped into the chair across the desk from DiRosa. Sighing wearily, he asked, "What are you doing?"

DiRosa held up a handful of papers. With a weak smile, he explained, "You know me, Bureau to the bone. I just thought I'd see what came in today."

Sutton shook his head. "I'm not talking about being in the office at night after hours. I'm talking about trips to La Junta on your day off. I'm talking about lunch with a suspect's ex-wife." He leaned forward, propping his forearms on his knees. "I'm talking about a rookie agent who's maybe not one hundred percent on the team."

DiRosa simply stared at him.

Sutton leaned back. "Did you think nobody would notice or that I wouldn't find out?"

DiRosa frowned, laying the papers down on his desk. "Did that same somebody also notice that Deputy D.A. Gutierrez is a very good-looking woman?"

Sutton smiled. "Nice try, Joey. But I'm really not stupid. You didn't just happen to meet her. You looked her up. Besides, a young, single, good-looking guy doesn't have to drive three hours one way just to get a date for lunch."

When DiRosa remained silent, Sutton stood up and began to pace, his hands shoved into his pockets. "I know what you and some of the other touchy-feely types around here think. You think I'm a racist who hates Indians and wants to nail the first one that comes within reach." He paused and looked at DiRosa to see if he would react.

DiRosa just watched Sutton impassively.

Sutton shrugged and continued his pacing. "The fact is, I'm about as far from a racist as you can get. To me, it is totally irrelevant. And this constant hammering on the 'distinctive Indian cultures' and all that crap probably does Indians more harm than I ever could just doing my job.

"The history of the world is the history of different people wandering around the face of the earth colliding like so many cars in a demolition derby." Sutton stopped and placed his hands on the back of the chair. "That's not genocide, that's evolution."

He resumed his pacing. "It was no different here. Before the Europeans came, the different tribes were pushing and shoving each other all over the continent. Sometimes they'd come together to form new groups like the Iroquois. Sometimes they'd split apart like the Shoshone and Comanche. Or they'd swap tools or seeds or something. Hell, the Navajo got half their religion from the Hopi. It's natural. It's the way it's always been."

He pointed a finger at DiRosa. "What's unnatural is what a bunch of soft-headed romantics and church people did in locking up Indians on reservations like exhibits in a museum or animals in a zoo, so they could preserve what they imagined to be the 'noble savage.' They interfered with the natural order of things, that's what they did."

"My, my," DiRosa shook his head. "I never would have imagined you as a philosopher."

Sutton scowled, waving his hand dismissively. "I went to college too, though I have no use for most philosophers. But there was one bit of philosophy that you may know about. Hegel talked about thesis, antithesis, and synthesis. That, my friend, is history in a nutshell. But the romantics and professional victims want to stop that, so we never get to the synthesis."

Sutton sat down again. "Let's get back to our immediate concern, though, which is one Agent Joseph DiRosa, who is possibly leaking confidential information about our investigation to a suspect."

DiRosa leaned forward earnestly. "That's just it. Why are we so focused on Sixkiller? What about this Ross Lee that Hart turned up?"

"Oh, give me a break!" Sutton snorted. "That's just a name this Little Crow came up with. Little Crow is Sioux. Sixkiller's Cheyenne. They've been allies since before the Little Big Horn. Again, just check your history books. Why not divert our attention to a Navajo named Lee? The Navajo just happen to be the biggest damn tribe in the country, making that lead all the more difficult. And Lee? Not exactly an uncommon name, is it?" Sutton shook his head. "No, I know these AIM types like Little Crow and Sixkiller. Believe me, I know the type! A gang of thugs hiding behind their feathers and beads."

DiRosa frowned. "Sixkiller's a rodeo clown and Little Crow is a rehab counselor. What is this 'AIM type'?"

"Jeez, you're young!" Sutton stood up. "And from New York to boot! AIM . . . the American Indian Movement. One of those radical groups that made some trouble back in the '60s and '70s. Some serious trouble!" He closed his eyes and shook his head.

"Did you ever hear of a couple of agents named Willis and Colter? Ron Willis and Jack Colter?"

DiRosa frowned. "I've heard the names, but I couldn't tell you anything about them."

The phone rang. DiRosa picked it up. "DiRosa. Yeah, he's here." He held the receiver out toward Sutton.

"Sutton," he barked, taking the phone. He listened for a while. "You're sure of that?" He smiled. "I'll be right down."

Hanging up, he grinned at DiRosa. "We've found Sixkiller. An aerial photo recon over the Cross ranch got a picture of him out there on horseback." He shook his head. "Can you believe what fools some people can be? They're trying to hide the very man who plans to kill them!" He turned and headed for the door. "I'm going to the lab. Come on with me."

ᴧᴧᴧ

Johnny leaned against the wall frowning as the computer voice said, "We're sorry. Your call can not be completed as dialed. Please hang up and dial again." He hung up but did not dial again. He'd been trying for nearly an hour. He looked at his watch. "After midnight," he muttered. He debated whether to wait until morning. He was tired. But . . .

Grabbing his hat off the back of the kitchen chair, he headed out the back door. As he drove, he listened to his Sheriff's Department frequency, which was quiet except for the usual check-ins from the deputies on patrol.

Just before Chivington, though, he heard, "This is Unit Three. I'm now westbound out of Sheridan Lake. At Brandon, I guess I'll head north and check things out."

"Negative, Unit Three. Not tonight, Chris. We've got orders to keep away from there tonight."

"Orders? What are you talking about, Billy?"

"Base to Unit Three, this is Sheriff Carter. Something's come up, Deputy, which I can't explain on the air. I'll talk to you later. Just stay off that county road until we tell you otherwise. Do you read me, Unit Three?"

"I read you, Sheriff. Unit Three out."

Johnny pulled off the road in Chivington. Parking on the west side of an abandoned store, he shut off his lights and waited. In about ten minutes he saw the patrol car drive past westbound on Highway 56. He waited another couple of minutes, then turned on his headlights and sped off eastbound.

Johnny fishtailed turning north at Brandon. His truck bounced and rattled as he pushed it hard up the rough, unpaved road. A mile short of the ranch, a single flashlight pointed at him. He slowed. Soon his headlights illuminated a man in a dark windbreaker standing in the roadway, his hand lifted to signal a stop. Behind him were several parked cars blocking the way and a half dozen other men, also dressed in dark windbreakers. One of the men had his back to Johnny. The headlights picked out the yellow letters FBI emblazoned across the back.

Johnny came to a stop close enough for the man with the flashlight to touch the grill of his truck. Another man appeared at the driver's side window, an automatic pistol in his hand, and tapped on the glass. Johnny rolled it down.

"FBI. Step out of the truck, slowly, with your hands in plain sight."

"Well, shoot!" Johnny slurred, then his eyes went wide and his hands went up. "Just an expression, pardner!" he quickly clarified, looking at the pistol. "My wife threw me out for drinkin' again," he explained, feigning drunkenness. "I was just looking for a quiet place to sleep it off in the truck, but it looks kinda busy around here, so why don't I just turn this thing around and git?"

Emotionless, the agent repeated. "Just step out of the truck, slowly." He took hold of the door handle and tried, but it wouldn't open.

"Oh, that there's kind of tricky," Johnny said, turning sideways and reaching helpfully for the lock button. "Here, let me give it a crack." He pulled up, his fingers seemingly slipping off the button. Off balance, his right shoulder lurched against the steering wheel. The truck's horn blasted with shocking violence into the still night.

"What the hell?" The agent grabbed Johnny and shoved him sideways off the horn. Another agent appeared beside the first. "Can you make any more noise, Bill?!" he hissed.

"We got a drunken cowboy here," Bill whispered angrily in his own defense.

Snatching open the door, they dragged Johnny out and threw him roughly against the hood of his truck. Kicking his legs wide and forcing his face down onto the warm metal, they twisted his right arm back.

"He's got a gun in here!" the second agent announced, searching the truck's interior.

"Yeah, and a radio and a badge, if you look hard enough." DiRosa, also wearing a dark windbreaker and carrying an assault rifle, walked slowly into the light of the truck's headlights. "This is Deputy Sheriff John Hart, gentlemen. Kiowa County's finest." Leaning down, he whispered in Johnny's ear, "You just couldn't leave it alone, could you asshole?" To the other agents, he directed, "Cuff him and stick him in the back of a car. I'm going ahead to the ranch to see what damage he's done with that horn stunt."

ᴧᴧᴧ

Char opened his eyes. The barn was still dark. He lay still, listening to the night sounds, trying to figure out what had awakened him. Slowly he rose to a crouch and moved silently to the open barn door. He waited a minute, two minutes. He tensed. There was a movement under the cottonwood near the kitchen door. He was about to stand and move forward when he caught another movement out of the corner of his eye. Someone else was approaching the house from the far corner of the barn in the direction of the front door.

Char opened his mouth slightly to enhance his hearing. Almost imperceptibly, he could tell that the crickets had fallen silent near the corner of the house where Sandy's bedroom window was. Someone else must be there.

He frowned and moved further back into the darkness. Several people were sneaking up on the house. That could only mean that it was the police or FBI coming for him.

A slight crunch on the dry ground warned Char that someone was passing next to the barn, a few inches from where he crouched. As the figure crossed the opening of the barn, the faint light of the ultraviolet bug light over the entrance caused the letters FBI on the man's back to glow. He carried a weapon. From the way he carried it, Char assumed it was an automatic.

Char moved silently back farther into the darkness of the barn.

ᴧᴧᴧ

Sandy opened her eyes. Lady, who usually slept on the rug beside her bed, was on her feet, facing the window and growling softly. Sandy sat up in bed. "What is it, Lady?" she whispered.

Glancing at Sandy, Lady returned her attention to the window, her growl growing louder, the fur standing up on the back of her neck.

Sandy rolled away from the window to glance at the time on her clock radio. 1:07. Before Sandy could get up to get the rifle she kept in her closet, Lady barked. There was a crash of breaking glass, a deafening explosion, and a flash of bright light.

〰〰

DiRosa heard the command in his earpiece a moment before he saw the explosion. He was about fifty yards from the house. He heard the bang of the stun grenade, followed immediately by the crash of splintering wood as agents battered the front and kitchen doors open. "Go, go, go!" he heard as a dozen agents rushed into the house, guns at the ready.

In the darkness, DiRosa saw movement at the barn entrance as a large shape emerged. In a clatter of hooves, the horse bolted past the stock tank and disappeared into the darkness to the west. There was a single gunshot.

DiRosa jogged the remaining distance to the house. The lights were on, and the acrid smell of smoke burned his nose. Special Agent Sutton stood in the hallway, his windbreaker open to reveal his bulletproof vest, an automatic rifle in his right hand. With his left hand, he cupped the earpiece of his radio to listen to the reports.

"Damn it!" Sutton pounded the wall with his fist, causing a photo of a little girl on horseback to slip and sway. Spotting DiRosa, he exclaimed, "He's not here!"

"What was that shot?" DiRosa asked.

Together they moved down the hallway. In Sandy's room, the smoke was thick. Sandy was sprawled face down on the floor beside her bed. Her face was mostly covered by her hair, but DiRosa could see a trickle of blood at the corner of her mouth. She wasn't moving as a helmeted agent kneeled and checked the pulse at her throat.

"Casualties?" Sutton demanded.

The agent shook his head. "Just knocked out, I think."

"Still," Sutton said. "We'd better get an ambulance in here."

"Right," the agent nodded, stood, and left the room.

"What was that shot?" DiRosa asked the three remaining agents.

"That was me." An agent on the other side of the bed nodded at the floor. "Looks like this dog tried to pick up the grenade. I was just putting her out of her misery."

"I can't believe this!" Sutton muttered in frustration. "Get out and search the barn. Alert the perimeters in case we only just missed him."

"Looked like one of the horses bolted out of the barn when the grenade went off," DiRosa added.

"All right," Sutton sighed, disgusted. "Tell the perimeters not to be too trigger-happy. I don't want to have to pay for dead horses, too."

ᴧᴧᴧ

Barbara was putting her makeup on when the doorbell rang. She assumed it was one of the kids' friends stopping by to pick them up on the way to school.

"Mom!" Gloria called. "I think you'd better come here." There was something in her voice that made Barbara respond immediately.

The front door was open. In the doorway stood two La Junta police officers in uniform. Behind them, still in his FBI windbreaker, stood Agent DiRosa. Gloria clung nervously to the doorknob.

"Mrs. Hart," the officers politely removed their hats. "We have here a warrant to search your house." The older of the officers, somewhat embarrassed, proffered the folded paper.

"Hey, Mom! There's cops in the back yard!" Jack entered from the kitchen. He stopped when he saw the group at the front door.

There was an awkward pause as Barbara scanned the warrant.

Agent DiRosa stepped forward into the room. "Actually, Barbara, this was our doing. Their jurisdiction," he indicated the police, "but our idea. We're looking for Sixkiller."

"Here?" Barbara laughed.

DiRosa shrugged.

Barbara frowned. "Well, the house is a mess."

The policemen shifted uneasily.

"Well, go ahead," she laughed, embarrassed. "Andy, Dave," she nodded at the two officers. "Excuse the house." She stepped back, waving them into the house.

"Thanks, Mrs. Hart," Dave said, relieved. "We'll try not to disturb anything."

"Jack, Gloria, you'd better go or you'll be late." Both children looked reluctant to leave, but quickly gathered their books and headed out the door.

"So," Barbara turned to DiRosa, "what is going on?"

"Do you mind if we sit?" DiRosa asked. "It's been a very long and lousy night."

When they were seated, Barbara asked, "Why would Char be here?"

DiRosa sighed wearily. "Because he's not where we thought he would be. We spotted him yesterday out at the L-S Ranch—the Cross place, right?—but when we raided it last night, he managed to slip away. It seems he wasn't staying in the house, but in the barn." He shook his head. "Sutton was so sure that if the Crosses were protecting him, it must be because there was something romantic going on between Sixkiller and Sandy Cross. So we focused the assault on her bedroom. We managed to," he ticked off the points on his finger, "trash her room, break the doors, kill her dog, and send Sandy Cross to the hospital with busted eardrums and who knows what else."

Barbara shook her head. "Johnny told me Sandy was a real serious Christian, so it doesn't surprise me that they weren't sleeping together. But Char out in the barn? That seems a little more unfriendly than chastity requires."

"I think it was probably his idea," DiRosa said. "I think we've been underestimating Sixkiller's commando background." He laughed. "I have to admit, the guy's good. With a couple of dozen agents in and around, all over the place, he managed to ride on out of there bareback on a horse. I even saw the horse, but I sure didn't see him. He must have been hanging on the side like Spiderman." He chuckled again. "We found the horse tied to a speed limit sign on Highway 50 west of Lamar this morning. That's why we thought he might be coming this way."

"And what did Johnny have to say about all this?" Barbara asked.

"Not much, after we read him his rights."

Barbara sat up. "You arrested him?"

DiRosa nodded. "He showed up just as it was all going down and nearly blew the whole thing trying to warn Sixkiller. He's sitting in his own jail right now in Kiowa County. Believe me, Sutton wants to hang him high."

Barbara's hands gripped the arms of her chair. "Was he . . . is he okay? He wasn't hurt?"

DiRosa shook his head. "Why is it that the guys who have the most, and the best, appreciate it the least? Yeah, he's fine. Nobody laid a hand on him."

The police officers returned. "Everything checks out," Dave reported. "No sign of the suspect."

DiRosa pulled himself wearily up from the chair. "Well, Barbara, I hope you have a better day than I think I will." He paused at the open door. "Oh, just a word of caution. Sutton has decided to go very public on all this, in the hopes that somebody will spot Sixkiller and give us a lead. That probably means a media feeding frenzy.

Anybody with any connection to Sixkiller will be just chum in the water, so be prepared."

ᴧᴧᴧ

Char debated in his mind, but finally decided to risk it. He'd caught a ride from a group of migrants earlier. They hadn't spoken much English and originally mistook him for a fellow Mexican. Having stopped, though, they were still willing to give him a ride, but they were only going as far as Granada.

It had been in their sputtering old car that he'd heard his name on the radio. He was the only one in the car who had understood the newscast, which was fortunate, because the description of "Charles Sixkiller, dangerous serial killer" had been detailed and accurate.

But he still had a long way to go just to get out of Colorado. So, with his hair shoved up inside his hat, he stuck his thumb out at the approaching big rig. The brakes squealed and hissed as the truck slowed to a stop. The passenger side door swung open and high, nasal, hillbilly harmonies poured out onto the quiet, prairie roadside.

A big, red-faced man smiled down from the driver's seat. "If you ain't peddlin' nothin', then just you climb on up in here. I'd appreciate the company."

Char settled into the seat as the truck bounced and roared back up to speed again. "Where are you heading?" he asked.

"Heaven's my destination, thank you Jesus!" the driver laughed. "But not this trip. I got me a load of some kind of computer stuff which I need to get to Fort Smith, Arkansas. Then from there, I'm supposed to pick up some kind of paper products and roll on up to Knoxville, Tennessee, back home in God's country." The driver stuck his hand out. "Lester Campbell's the name."

Char shook the offered hand. "Ah . . . Hart," he stammered. Then, thinking better, in case Johnny's name had somehow also made the news, he continued, "Brave Heart. Charles Brave Heart."

"Indian, are ya?" Campbell asked. "My missus, Lord Bless her, she's part Injun herself. Shawnee, I think she said her granddaddy was. Me, I'm Scottish. Well, we're both just pure hillbilly by now. Smoky Mountain folks." He glanced sideways at Char.

"Is that the radio playing?" Char asked. He hadn't heard any announcers, and the music seemed to be country gospel.

"Lord have mercy, no!" Campbell laughed. "Ain't nothin' but bad news and worldly songs on the radio. I got me a tape deck and some almighty good speakers, so I just listen to praise music all the day long." Giving Char another sidelong look, he continued, "Which brings up an important point. If this here truck were to jackknife and kill us both, do you know where you'd wind up, son? I mean do you know Jesus as your personal savior?"

Char glanced out the window, smiling at the "Welcome to Kansas" sign they had just passed.

⋀⋀⋀

"Close the door, please, Deputy," Sheriff Carter said to the officer who had brought Johnny from the jail cell. Johnny couldn't recall ever seeing the sheriff's door closed.

"Sit down, John," the sheriff waved at the wooden chair across the desk. Johnny also couldn't recall the sheriff ever calling him John. There was something unsettling about it.

Carter studied him for a full minute in silence, his elbows resting on the desk, his fingers steepled before his face. Finally, he sighed and leaned back. "You could have been a fine lawman, John, if you could have disciplined yourself. Fact is, I'd once given some thought to suggesting that you run for sheriff when I retired."

"I guess getting arrested won't look so good on my campaign literature, huh?" Johnny said, forcing a smile.

Sheriff Carter frowned. "That's a smartass response, Hart. And that's the problem. You just don't seem to want to grow up, do you?"

Johnny looked down at his own hands, folded in his lap. "I just kind of say things when I can't think what to say."

"A bad habit, Deputy," Carter snapped. "You need to learn how to think before you do or say anything."

Johnny sat silently.

Sheriff Carter placed his hands together on the desktop, studying Johnny. "What exactly, if anything, were you thinking when you drove out there last night to warn a suspect wanted for multiple murders, when you interfered with a federal law enforcement operation, for that matter, when you started trying to investigate this on your own and aided and abetted the suspect for months?" He waited, crossing his arms across his chest. "That wasn't a rhetorical question, Hart. I really want to know what was going on in your mind."

Johnny looked at the sheriff, studying his face. "It's simple, really," he said. "I owe Char Sixkiller my life."

"That's too simple, John," Carter scoffed. "You're a loner, but you can't be so indifferent to everybody else that you'd help a bloody killer just to balance your own personal ledger."

"Well, no, of course not," Johnny frowned. He'd taken orders and endured lectures from Sheriff Carter, but this was something new. The sheriff really seemed to want to understand something.

"You were an officer in the army for a lot of years, weren't you, Sheriff?" Johnny asked.

Carter nodded. "Twenty years. Enlisted man before that."

"You've commanded a lot of men, then, if you add them all up. Am I right?"

"Right," Carter agreed.

"Would you consider yourself a pretty good judge of character?" Johnny asked.

Carter gave a humorless bark of laughter. "I thought I was," he said, looking meaningfully at Johnny.

Johnny leaned forward earnestly. "Men will generally act or react according to their character, right?" He was intent now. "I mean, a man who is a coward will eventually run away from a fight. Or a lazy man will eventually walk away from a job. Nobody can fake it all the time, right?"

Carter nodded. "I'd agree with that."

"Well, Sheriff, I've known Char Sixkiller for the better part of fifteen years. I've seen him broke and with money, healthy and hurt, tired and rested, drunk and sober. Mainly, though, I've seen him in the arena. I've seen him throw himself in front of a mad killer bull at times when another bullfighter would think twice, be careful or at least move a half second slower. And"—he pointed at the sheriff for emphasis—"I've seen him do it for redneck cowboys he knew damn well would just as soon spit on him as look at him if they were to meet in a bar someplace."

Johnny leaned back, surprised at himself for talking so much. "In all those years, I've never seen Char fake it. He's not a murderer, Sheriff. He's the exact opposite. It's like his whole purpose in life is to snatch people out of harm's way, to keep them alive."

Carter gave him a half-smile. "You've actually thought seriously about this, haven't you?"

Johnny shook his head. "Only recently, Sheriff. Before all this came up, Char was just another cowboy, as far as I was concerned."

Sheriff Carter leaned forward, his shoulders hunched, a troubled look on his face. "What about mental illness, though, John? I've seen good, brave, dependable men snap after enough horror, and I don't know that it had anything to do with their character. Couldn't

Sixkiller have had just too many years of sacrificing himself, living with the fear, and still being spit on for his trouble?"

Johnny's shoulders sagged. "Well, I have thought of that too. And I don't have a good answer. I'm not a psychologist. Maybe Char is one of those multiple personality characters . . . Dr. Jekyll and Mr. Hyde." He nodded. "Sure, all that fear and pain and racist crap would be enough to . . ." He waved his hand vaguely, letting the thought trail away.

"As a cop," he started a new thought, "I've met and dealt with some certifiable crazies and there's always something"—he pointed at his eyes—"missing. That's not the case with Char—never has been. And lately, since he did this AA thing and quit drinking, it's like something has been added." Johnny shrugged, giving the sheriff an embarrassed smile. "Maybe not the most scientific reason, but there it is. I don't believe Char's crazy."

Sheriff Carter sighed and toyed with the edge of some papers on his desk. "Maybe I am," he muttered. "The FBI wanted your head, John," he said quietly. "Conspiracy to commit murder, the whole nine yards. I couldn't go along with that. I've got the same problem you do, I suppose. When I think I've judged a man rightly, I can't shake it." He shook his head. "So this is the deal, and I'm not too happy about it either. You will not be charged in this, but, you've got to walk away. Just leave it alone. No more investigation, no more contact with Sixkiller, no comments to the press and"—he sighed again—"no more badge. You are no longer a Kiowa County deputy sheriff. You're free to go cowboy or whatever, but your lawman days are over. I'm sorry, but that's the best deal I could make for you."

Johnny sat in stunned silence. Since his days as an army MP in Vietnam, he'd always been at least a part-time lawman. Never a particularly serious one, perhaps. Until this minute, he'd thought of it only as a pay check to support the family while he rodeoed. But now, he felt a loss like a death in the family. "Well," he cleared his throat. "I guess it beats hell out of going to jail for the rest of my life." He nodded at Carter. "Thanks, Sheriff. I'm grateful."

"Me?" Carter growled. "I'm angry . . . at them and at you. It's such a waste."

Both men sat wrapped in their own thoughts for a long time.

"Go home, John," Sheriff Carter said quietly. "Do some serious thinking. Keep out of the way and we'll see what happens once this Sixkiller thing is over."

"Over?" Johnny asked.

Carter pushed back from his desk and stood up. "Arrest, trial, jail, whatever it takes."

Johnny winced as if physically hurt. He nodded and stood. "See you, sir." He extended his hand. "Thanks."

Carter nodded. He shook Johnny's hand, then waved him angrily toward the door. "Get out of here."

CHAPTER

11

ᴧᴧᴧ

"Well, the house and barn are still standing," Mr. Cross grumbled from the back seat.

Sandy, seated in the front seat next to Agent DiRosa, said nothing. She stared gloomily out the window as if she were alone in the car.

DiRosa was sorry he'd offered to drive the Crosses home from the hospital. It had been a tense, silent drive. "Here we are," he announced with forced cheerfulness, as he pulled the vehicle to a stop in front of the house.

The morning was perfect. After a chilly night, the still air was just beginning to warm comfortably. Bird song and stillness greeted them as they climbed out of the government sedan.

Plywood had been nailed over the shattered front door and Sandy's bedroom window. Yellow plastic tape reading "Police Crime Scene—Do Not Enter" hung limply from the doorpost.

"Helluva thing!" Mr. Cross muttered, his jaw muscles twitching with anger. "Helluva thing!"

"It's not as bad as it looks."

All three turned, surprised to see Johnny walking toward them from the barn.

"I went in through the kitchen," Johnny continued. "The two doors, that window, and some cleanup work in the bedroom is about all the damage I saw."

Mr. Cross stared hard at Johnny. "So lawmen are breakin' into folks' empty houses as well as beatin' down the door while they sleep?"

Sandy laid a calming hand on her grandfather's arm. "It's all right, Grandpa. You can't break into a broken house." Her voice was flat and weary.

Johnny tugged on his ear with an embarrassed grin. "Not to put too fine an edge on it, but I'm not a lawman anymore, either."

"Yeah, I heard," DiRosa said, his arms crossed. "I'd say you got off pretty easy."

Johnny lifted his hat and scratched his scalp. "Well, I guess you would say that."

Sandy waved her hand in annoyance at both men and walked away. She disappeared around the side of the house toward the kitchen door.

Mr. Cross turned to DiRosa and said, "Thanks for the ride. Now get the hell off my land." He then walked with slow, painful steps in the same path that his granddaughter had followed.

"You gotta love a crusty old coot like that, don't ya?" Johnny said.

DiRosa laughed and shook his head. "Can't say that I blame him. We did make a mess out here, in more ways than one."

Johnny laughed now. "That was nice of you, giving them a ride and all. I'm pretty sure Sutton didn't assign that job to anybody."

"No," DiRosa agreed. "I volunteered. I've had more fun at the dentist, though." He took the few steps to his car, opened the door, and paused. "Tell me something, Hart. What was Sixkiller doing in the barn? I mean, I thought he and the lady"—he pointed with his chin toward the house—"had something going."

Johnny smiled and shoved his hands into his pockets. "Did you ever trap varmints, Mr. G-man?"

DiRosa shook his head. "No. Where I grew up, 'wildlife' means something totally different."

Johnny nodded. "Well, it's like this. You aren't going to catch a thing standing on top of your own trap."

DiRosa frowned. "Sixkiller was the one being hunted. You mean to tell me he was also setting a trap for somebody else? Who? The FBI?"

Johnny's lip curled in scorn. "Of course not. You mean to tell me after all that time tapping my phone, the name Ross Lee never landed in your file?"

DiRosa shut the car's door and walked slowly back to where Johnny stood. "You think there really is a Ross Lee?" he asked, incredulous.

Johnny frowned. "Of course there's a Ross Lee! We're talking about a serial killer, not Santa Claus!"

DiRosa held up his hand to dampen Johnny's indignation. "Sutton figured a Navajo named Lee was just something Sixkiller and that counselor, Little Crow, dreamed up to send us off chasing shadows."

"Well, Sutton's got a problem. He's either too stuck on Char or . . ." Johnny let the sentence hang, his brow furrowed in perplexity. "Or something else is going on."

"Like what?" DiRosa demanded. "What are you talking about?"

Johnny shook his head. "I don't know. I just never figured Sutton for being stupid. Racist, maybe. Mean, for sure. But not too dumb to follow a lead." He shook his head again. "Never mind. But, if I were you, and I had all those government computers sitting around the office, I think I'd do a little checking up on Ross Lee of Tuba City, Arizona, and Provo, Utah. Shoot, you could catch a killer, be a hero, maybe get a damn medal from the president. That's, of course, if I were you."

"And if I were you," DiRosa said, "I'd lie awake nights, thinking how stupid I was to let a beautiful woman like Barbara slip away." He turned and walked back to his car, opened the door, and climbed in.

"How do you know I don't?" Johnny commented, too softly for DiRosa to hear.

DiRosa started the car, then leaned out the window. "I've got one for you to think about, Hart. Ever hear of two FBI agents named Colter and Willis?"

Johnny shook his head. "Sounds familiar, but I can't place them. Why? Is it important?"

"Seems to be important to Sutton. I thought I'd ask around and find out why. You might do the same, even if you don't have a badge anymore." Putting the car in gear, he started forward. "Later, cowboy."

Johnny touched the brim of his hat. "Later, G-man."

When the car was out of sight over the ridge, Johnny turned and walked to the kitchen door. Every other time he'd been there, Lady had been nearby keeping an eye on him. Not today, though. Not anymore.

Sandy and Mr. Cross sat gloomily at the kitchen table. Johnny came in, shoved his hat back on his head, and leaned against the counter. "It's really not that bad, you know. I was just out in the barn. I'm not as handy as Char, but I think I'll have that front door fixed before too long. A little paint, and no one will ever know what happened."

"It ain't the damage to the house," Mr. Cross said. "It's the whole idea of the government comin' in here like that, breakin' down doors, throwin' bombs into my grandbaby's bedroom . . ." His voice rose in anger. "It's just such a helluva thing!"

"I'm okay, Grandpa," Sandy soothed. "I've got a concussion and a busted eardrum, but, shoot, I could get hurt worse than that shoeing a horse." She shook her head. "No, it's just . . . we had plans. We were going to cull down the herd this fall, try to start a few buffalo to breeding come spring. And now . . ." She let her hands rise and fall weakly into her lap.

Johnny cleared his throat. "Well, I realize I'm only a rodeo cowboy, but I do know the difference between the north and south ends of a horse, and I'm fresh out of a job right now."

"Well, that's mighty neighborly of ya, Hart," Mr. Cross nodded. "But we can't afford no kind of wages, even for a green hand."

Johnny smiled. "I wasn't looking for wages, right off. Same deal you had with Char is fine with me. I can't afford rent anymore anyway. So if I had to choose between sleeping in the barn and sleeping in my truck, well, the barn sounds like home to me."

"You don't have to sleep in the barn," Sandy said. "Char didn't either but, for some reason, he seemed to prefer it." She barely got the words out. She stifled a sob, but a tear escaped anyway.

Johnny cleared his throat. "I don't think he preferred it. It was just . . . better."

Sandy shook her head. "What's better about it? People might talk? What people? Used to be neighbors would come by to visit or help out but lately, half of our neighbors have given up, sold out to corporations or city folks and moved away."

Johnny seated himself at the table. "Char probably never talked about it much, but keep in mind, that he was in the Army Special Forces and he was very good at what he did."

"You mean fighting?" Mr. Cross asked.

"Well, sure, he was good at that, but that's only part of it. He was a hunter, too—a manhunter. When the trap is set, you have to back away enough to keep out of sight of the prey."

"And I was the bait?" Sandy gasped.

"He didn't plan it or like it, but there it is. This killer is out there after blonde women and here you are, less than a mile from the Sand

Creek Massacre site. I think Char thought he could protect you better at a little distance than up close."

She lowered her head. "No, he didn't let himself get too close," she whispered.

ᴧᴧᴧ

The Indian Center was packed with people. The excited shrieking of children, the smell of fry bread, and the throb of a drum greeted Johnny as he came in the front door. While he waited for the receptionist to find Jimmy Little Crow, he sat next to a round-faced baby in a cradleboard who stared at him solemnly. The infant's babysitter, a beautiful little girl of eight or nine, studied him shyly, her hand hiding a bright smile that had recently lost a tooth.

Shortly after the drumming stopped, Little Crow appeared, breathless and smiling. "Johnny Hart," he greeted, shaking Johnny's hand. "I'm one of the singers," he indicated with his thumb in the direction of the drumming.

"Lots of people here tonight," Johnny remarked.

"It's the change of season, summer into fall," Little Crow nodded. "We like to get the community together two or three times a year. We sing, we dance, we eat, and shake a little concrete off our moccasins." He grinned, enjoying the friendly crowd that eddied and flowed around them.

"I hate to pull you out of the party," Johnny said, "but I wanted to ask you about a couple of things."

"Sure." The drumming and singing started again. "Probably outside is quieter than anyplace in the building," Little Crow said, cupping his hands into a megaphone.

Outside, they sat on the tailgate of Johnny's pickup.

"So what's up, Deputy?"

"Well, one thing, I'm not a deputy anymore. Strictly civilian, so there's nothing official about this visit at all," Johnny said.

"You quit?"

Johnny shook his head. "Fired."

"For helping Sixkiller?"

Johnny nodded. "That's one of the reasons I'm here. Also, because I can't trust the phone lines anymore." He looked at the counselor. "Have you heard anything from Char?"

Little Crow shook his head. "Not for a couple of weeks, since right after that FBI raid in Kiowa County."

"Did he say where he was heading?"

"Nope."

Johnny scratched his ear. "Any idea where he was going?"

Little Crow nodded. "Yup."

"Would you like to tell me?"

He shook his head. "Nope." He laughed and punched Johnny lightly on the shoulder. "Not because I don't trust you, Johnny. It's just that I happen to know that the FBI has listening devices that can hear every word we say."

Johnny looked around. The street was dark and filled with parked cars and trucks that, he realized, could contain eavesdropping FBI agents. "Are they keeping an eye on you or me?"

"Maybe both," Little Crow's eyes twinkled, amused. "I'm obviously more used to them than you are."

Johnny nodded. "I did have another question for you."

"We'll see if I have a better answer for you."

"Have you ever heard of two FBI agents named Colter and Willis?" Johnny asked.

Little Crow stiffened and his expression went blank. "No. Never heard of 'em."

Johnny frowned, certain that Little Crow was lying, but with no idea why. He shrugged. "No matter. Somebody just mentioned the names to me like they might be important."

Little Crow stood up and waved toward the door of the Center. "I'd better get back inside."

Johnny stood also, stretching and wincing slightly in pain. "I appreciate your time." He shook hands.

Little Crow pointed. "You look pretty stiff. That old injury from last year?"

Johnny shook his head. "Nah. I got a new job now, cowboying for real and, I tell you what, my butt is killing me."

The counselor laughed, more relaxed again. "You want to come in, have some coffee, something to eat?"

"No thanks. It's a long drive back. I'd better get on down the road."

Little Crow nodded. "Well, keep in touch."

"I sure will," Johnny said, touching the brim of his hat as he walked to the driver's door of his truck.

It was nearly eleven when he pulled to a stop in front of the Smithland Avenue home in La Junta. The only light he saw spilled from the kitchen window into the narrow side yard.

Barbara answered the door. "Johnny! What are you doing here?"

"You're up late, Barb," he noted, smiling. "Are you busy, or can I come in?"

She waved a thick report in her left hand. "I'm studying up for a trial tomorrow. The arresting officer is a bonehead, but I need his testimony."

"Anybody I know?" Johnny grinned.

Barbara nodded, smiling. "Yes, but I'm not telling." She gestured for him to follow. "Come in for a little while. I'm tired, I need a break."

Johnny closed the door and followed her into the kitchen. The table was strewn with documents. A yellow legal pad containing pages of her notes was on top of the pile in front of her chair.

"There's coffee," she said, waving toward the pot.

Johnny poured a cup. Turning the chair around backward, he straddled the seat, resting the cup on the chair's back.

"You look good, Johnny," Barbara noted, pushing her papers away. He laughed. "I haven't heard you say that in years."

"No, seriously," she stood up and walked halfway around his chair, studying him. "You look healthy. Are you feeling all right?"

He sipped his coffee and nodded. "I still want a drink at least once every hour of every day, but clean living is the only option out at the Cross place. They may work me to death, but I'll die healthy."

"What do they have you doing?"

He stretched his back and neck. "We're rounding up every animal on their range to try to sell before the cold and snow hits. So I'm just a regular roping, riding fool."

"Are they going to sell off the ranch?" she asked.

"No. Sandy and Char dreamed up a notion to raise buffalo instead of cows. Forward into the past," he smiled.

Barbara cocked her head, nodding. "It could work. *Quien sabe?*"

"How are the kids?" he asked.

"Good. They're both asleep. School tomorrow."

Johnny nodded, frowning into his cup. "I miss them," he said quietly. "I miss you all."

She pursed her lips tightly. "What brings you here, Johnny? It's late."

He sighed. "I had a talk with a friend of yours a couple of weeks ago. Special Agent DiRosa?" He watched to see her reaction, but she only blinked. "Anyway, he suggested I ask around about two FBI agents named Willis and Colter. He said they were important to Sutton, the guy in charge of their investigation. I asked Char's friend, Jimmy Little Crow, the counselor, about them and he acted like I'd stuck him with a cattle prod. But"—he stood up, finished his coffee and put the cup in the sink—"he lied and said he'd never heard of them. Now I have to figure out why."

"All you have to do is stay sober and healthy, Johnny," Barbara urged. "Keep out of it, please."

"You know I can't do that, Barb. But I need a favor from you. DiRosa doesn't much like me but, I get the feeling, he really likes you." He looked out the window at the night. "I don't have the right to say how I feel about that, Barb, but I am going to ask you to talk to him. See if he's found out anything about Willis and Colter. And see if he can find a connection between them and Little Crow."

"Johnny!" Barbara exclaimed in annoyance. "If I don't want you involved in this, what makes you think I want to get involved?"

Johnny pulled at his hat brim. "I know you don't, honey, but I can't help it. Something is going on here that just feels wrong, and I need your help to make it right."

She shook her head. "And here I was bragging about what a good cop you were. Let the evidence speak for itself! And all you can tell me is you have a feeling." She pressed the palms of her hands to her forehead. "Okay, I'll talk to Joe—Agent DiRosa. But if he makes the slightest peep, forget it. I won't jeopardize my job or the kids' futures to help you get arrested for conspiracy."

Johnny bent forward and kissed her lightly on the cheek. "Thanks, Barb."

"*Ay, Dios mio*, why do I let you talk me into such foolishness?"

Johnny put his hat on. "Well, according to Sandy Cross, it's because you're still my wife. Always will be."

"Oh, is that so?" Barbara said indignantly, following him to the front door. "Well, I have some court-approved divorce papers that say otherwise."

"No matter," Johnny said, opening the door. "Sandy goes to a higher court. The Bible says you are bone of my bone and flesh of my flesh." He smiled. "Don't fight it."

She shook her head. "*Todavía estás loco, Juanito.*" She laughed.

"Just for you, baby." He touched the brim of his hat. "Just for you."

∧∧∧

The evening breeze was chilly as it rippled through the brown grass. Johnny, Sandy, and Mr. Cross rode silently back to the house. Although they didn't mention it, the Crosses were very aware of the absence of Lady. It made the work of handling cattle harder and the homecoming lonelier.

They unsaddled their horses at the barn. Noticing how tired and stiff he was Johnny took the halter of Mr. Cross's horse. "I'll curry and feed her, Mr. Cross. Maybe you could light a fire under the beans. I'm plenty hungry."

Mr. Cross nodded, his face tired and drawn. Without a word, he limped stiffly away toward the house.

"Thanks, Johnny," Sandy said. "He shouldn't even be working anymore, but the fact is, we need him in the saddle. He knows it, too. That's why he doesn't complain."

"How much longer do you think it'll be till we've got all these cows shipped?" Johnny asked, hanging the saddle blankets over the edge of the stalls.

"Maybe another week," Sandy answered. "We're almost done. It's not that we had so many cattle, either. Just too much space for them to hide in, and too few of us to drive them out." She poured a bucket of grain into the trough where the horses were tied. "You've actually turned into a pretty fair hand, Johnny. You don't have what we call cow sense yet, but you're a pretty good horseman for a rhinestone cowboy and you've got a real talent for roping."

Johnny laughed. "That kind of surprised me, too. I really enjoy roping."

"Char was pretty good at roping, too," Sandy said, her voice turning wistful, as well as tired.

Johnny paused in grooming the horses, the brushes in his hand. "It's not like Char died or something, Sandy."

"I know," she sighed. "It's just that I know the FBI is going to get him sooner or later." She leaned forlornly against the barn door.

"I don't know that I'd bet on that," Johnny said. "Actually, I had an idea for something. Once we're through shipping beeves, I thought I'd play lawman again and maybe make a trip down to Texas."

Sandy turned around, her eyes bright. "If you think it will help Char, you can leave tomorrow, Johnny. Shoot! Leave tonight!"

Johnny straightened up. "But we've got to get these cows in. I may not be a big help, but you and your grandpa can't do it alone. What if the weather turns?"

Sandy grabbed him by the arm. "I'll just pray that it won't," she declared.

Johnny nodded. "You're the only person I know who really means it when they say that."

"Grandpa and I will do what we can, and when you get back we'll finish," Sandy said, decisively. "How long will you be gone?"

"Well, if it works, I should be just a day or two." He shook his head. "'Course, if it doesn't work, I may not be back for a lot of years, unless I make parole."

"Oh, Johnny, thank you!" Sandy seemed more animated than she had in weeks. "I just know you'll solve this and get Char cleared. Char always knew you would."

"Yeah, well, I always suspected Char believed in the tooth fairy, too," Johnny cautioned. "But I'll give it my best shot."

⋀⋀⋀

"No, really, it's true!" DiRosa nodded his head, smiling at the others' laughter. "My cousin, Carmine, was not what you'd call real swift."

"Are you sure you're not Mexican?" Barbara asked, laughing. "Every time I see you, you've got another story about yet another cousin. How big is your family?"

"I'm not sure," he frowned, considering the question seriously. "But then I've only told you about my father's side of the family. Someday

I'll tell you about my mother's side. Now, those people are really strange, completely crazy."

Gloria was laughing so hard that tears were leaking from her tightly closed eyes. Even Jack was laughing, his long legs stretched out under the dining room table.

Outside, a car horn honked. Jack glanced at the clock. "Whoops! Gotta go," he announced. "That's Eddie."

"Where are you off to?" DiRosa asked.

"We've got an evening basketball practice. Our first game is only a couple of weeks away," Jack explained, rising from the table.

"Well, heh," DiRosa rose, extending his hand. "It's good to see you again, Jack. Let me know the date of that game. I'd like to see it."

"You would?" Jack asked, surprised, as he shook the agent's hand.

"Sure," DiRosa nodded. "I was a forward on my high school team. Not a great shooter, but I could rebound with the best of them." He tapped his elbow, winking. "The secret is in the elbows, if you catch my meaning."

"Ouch!" Jack smiled, touching his ribs in mock pain. "I do know what you mean."

"See you, Jack," DiRosa waved as the boy grabbed his jacket and headed for the door.

"Home right after practice," Barbara called. "*Me oistes?*"

"I hear you. Bye, Mom. Bye Joe. Later, Gordy." The door closed and the screen door slammed.

"I always thought it would be real scary, growing up in a big city like New York," Gloria said. "But you make it sound like fun."

DiRosa nodded. "I had a pretty good time. I always thought it would be cool to live in a small town in the Wild West, too." He smiled. "Wherever you grow up, the good comes from the people around you. I had good parents, a good family. So do you."

Gloria leaned forward eagerly. "Did you used to ride the subway and everything?" she asked.

"*Ya, mija,* that's enough," Barbara cautioned, gently. "You've got dishes to do and homework. Joe will be back. Save some of your questions."

"Oh, all right," Gloria said, disappointed, as she stood.

"Why don't you bring your coffee into the living room," Barbara invited, leading the way.

DiRosa sighed contentedly as he settled into the chair. "That was a good, good meal, Barbara."

She sipped her coffee. "The kids really like you, Joe. You seem to like young people. I'm surprised you haven't gotten married and started a family."

"You sound like my mother, now," he said. "I've been pretty busy the last several years,—working, law school—you know, the whole routine. But, yeah, lately I've actually been giving some thought to the subject of family." He sipped his coffee, looking intently at Barbara over the rim of the cup.

She pretended not to notice, concentrating instead on plucking an invisible thread from the arm of the couch. "I haven't seen much in the news lately about the Sixkiller investigation. Anything happening, or has Char just vanished?"

"No, the investigation is back to basic police work again. We get leads and follow them up. The problem is that not too many people in Indian country want to talk to us. We've got a few contacts . . . criminals mainly, though. And, aside from a tendency to murder people, Sixkiller doesn't really fit the usual pattern for criminals. He's not hanging out in bars, or dealing drugs, or fencing stolen property, so that kind of leaves us at a loss."

"So you have no idea where he went?"

"Well," he explained, "it looks like he hitched a ride out of Colorado with a long haul trucker who let him out somewhere east of Oklahoma City. We thought he was heading for relatives in Cherokee or Adair County, Oklahoma, but nobody's seen him." He cocked his head. "Or at least nobody's told us they've seen him."

"I was talking to Johnny a while back," Barbara began tentatively. "He mentioned that you were curious about two FBI agents named Colter and Willis. Did you find out anything?"

DiRosa drained his coffee cup. "Yeah, I did, but I don't really see a connection to Sixkiller . . . not a direct one anyway. Fifteen years ago, those two agents were killed by some Indian radicals on the Pine Ridge Reservation, up in South Dakota. Sutton talks about Sixkiller and his friend Little Crow and calls them 'AIM-types.' That's the American Indian Movement. According to some old timers I talked to in the Denver office, they were the people that killed Colter and Willis . . . guy named Larry Pelham was convicted for it. But I recall from his file that Sixkiller was still lost in the jungle somewhere in Vietnam when that happened."

"Lost in the jungle?" Barbara laughed. "What are you talking about?"

"You didn't know?" DiRosa seemed surprised. "Yeah, Sixkiller was in the army in Vietnam. Special Forces—Green Beret and all that. Well, most of our troops came home in '73, but not the spooks like Sixkiller. A group of them stayed on for another two years, supposedly giving training and support to the South Vietnamese Army. In fact, what they were doing was roaming through the jungle raising hell. Cambodia, Laos, Vietnam, north, south, it didn't matter. Their job was to do whatever they could to disrupt the Viet Cong and North Vietnamese Army. They traveled in small groups of two, three, four. Except for Sixkiller."

DiRosa leaned forward, warming to his topic. "Sixkiller worked alone. He was like the Vietnamese version of the bogeyman. He could pop up anywhere, kill somebody, blow something up and—pow— just disappear again. For two years, he was in the country on his own with only occasional contact even with his own command.

"Then comes April '75," DiRosa leaned back. "The call goes out to evacuate Saigon. So everybody comes back to the embassy to be choppered out to the ships off shore. There must be a thousand guys who claim to have been on the last helicopter out of the U.S. Embassy. But Sixkiller," he laughed, "is the only guy I've heard of who actually gave up his seat on that last chopper.

"Yeah," he nodded at Barbara's confused look. "He gave his seat to some Vietnamese clerk whose family had already been evacuated. Then he just slips off the roof, out of the compound and disappears. Six months later he surfaces in a refugee camp in Thailand, about forty pounds lighter, with no explanation to anyone. He just taps a missionary on the shoulder and says, 'I'm an American. I want to go home now.'"

"That's incredible!" Barbara exclaimed. "I had no idea."

DiRosa shook his head. "Yeah, well, that's how I know he didn't have anything to do with the killing of Colter and Willis. He was out somewhere the hell on the other side of the world."

They both sat in silence, thinking about it.

Quietly, Barbara noted, "For a while there, you sounded like you admired Char."

DiRosa looked at her seriously. "Who wouldn't? But this is almost twenty years later and our hero has maybe been a little warped by his time in purgatory. Correction—very warped! There's no denying that this was a pretty amazing guy back then, but being a good killer in a war is one thing. The same behavior just doesn't make it, though, back home in peace."

"Still," Barbara said, "what about giving up his seat? That wasn't just a polite gesture on a bus. That was a life-and-death decision . . . possibly his death for somebody else's life. That doesn't sound like a monster or a psychopath."

"No," DiRosa sighed, rubbing his temples, "no, it doesn't, does it?"

"So you have your doubts?"

He stood up and began to pace. "Of course I do! There's too many inconsistencies. But I'm not in charge of the investigation. I can't just go off on my own. If I'm not using Sutton's playbook, I'm off the team, like your ex, there, Hart."

Barbara cleared her throat. "Maybe you could use Johnny to do a little investigating for you, on the side?"

DiRosa looked doubtful. "No offense, Barbara, but I'm not sure Deputy Hop-along is really up to that. He's got kind of an elbow problem, I understand." He pantomimed bending his elbow to take a drink. "Besides, he doesn't have the authority to really dig into things."

She leaned forward. "Actually, Johnny and I talked about that the other day. Remember when you first met him?"

He nodded. "Yeah, down in Texas."

"Right," she continued. "He was delivering a prisoner. Well, he thinks there may be some connection between that prisoner and Ross Lee. The sheriff down there knew Johnny from the rodeo. He'd remember him."

Barbara sipped her coffee. "Johnny figured if you would call and tell the sheriff that Johnny was going down to talk to the prisoner on FBI-related business, he could bluff the rest and try to get some leads on this Lee person."

"That's great," DiRosa frowned. "So if John-boy screws up, they've got my name and my butt? I don't think so!"

"He won't screw up," Barbara said, letting a little annoyance show. "I keep telling you, he's got problems, although he quit drinking. True, he wasn't a model father or husband, but he's a good cop." She repeated, "He won't screw up. Besides," she added, leaning back, "you can always deny you made the call, if you're really afraid it will come back on you."

"I'm not afraid," he asserted, defensively. He drummed his fingers, thinking. "All right," he decided. "Give me the name of that prisoner. I'll call tomorrow. But I sure hope you're right about Hart."

∧∧∧

"You're looking pretty fit," Sheriff Craig noted. "You gonna be back on the bulls pretty soon?"

They were standing in the interview room of the jail in Amarillo. With them was the public defender assigned to the prisoner.

Johnny nodded. "I've been thinking about it, but my doctor keeps telling me to forget it."

"That's right, it's only been a year now, hasn't it?"

The door opened with a loud clang as a deputy escorted the prisoner in. He looked slightly uncertain as his eyes checked out the three waiting men. Seeing Johnny, he smirked, "Well, well, if it ain't Deputy Hart! How's the dog bite?"

Johnny smiled affably. "Just fine. How's the gunshot?"

"I'll live longer than you, Deputy," he said unpleasantly.

"Wouldn't surprise me a bit," Johnny nodded.

"I want it to go on the record, Sheriff, that my client is cooperating fully with this investigation, so I expect you to put in a word with the prosecutor for him," the public defender declared.

"Shoot, Teddy, we're not keeping a record of this," the sheriff said. "But, yeah, if Billy tells us anything useful, we'll see he gets some Brownie points."

The public defender persisted. "Now he's not going to be asking him anything about Billy's case," he emphasized, pointing at Johnny. "If he does, I'll just have to object."

"You just go ahead and do that," the sheriff nodded, amused. Squinting at the attorney, he asked, "How long you been out of law school now, Teddy?"

"A little over a year, why?" Teddy asked, defensively.

"Just asking." Craig smiled. "Go ahead on, Deputy," he added to Johnny.

Johnny sat down at the metal table and waved the prisoner into the chair across from him. Pulling his note pad out of his shirt pocket, he asked, "Do you remember a few months back, up in Colorado, you gave a ride to a feller who was driving an old red Ford truck and ran out of gas? Looked like he could've been an Indian?"

"His momma was probably a whole lot more certain he was," Billy said sarcastically. "Yeah, I remember. It was the first time I laid eyes on your sorry ass, Deputy."

"Heh!" Sheriff Craig pointed his finger at the prisoner. "Play nice, now, Billy! You hear?"

"So you knew the man?" Johnny persisted, unmoved by Billy's animosity.

Billy nodded. "He worked for my Daddy, off and on, driving a cattle truck."

"He never did any driving for you?" Johnny asked, matter-of-factly, although he knew he shouldn't have.

"Now don't you answer that, Billy," the public defender sputtered. "That's not a right question, Deputy," he scolded Johnny. "He's not supposed to be asking about anything to do with the charges against my client," he protested to the sheriff.

"Now don't get your jockeys all in a jumble," the prisoner said. "I never used Lee for nothing. He just worked for my daddy."

"Lee?" Johnny asked, masking his excitement. "Would that be Ross Lee?"

"Yeah," Billy nodded. "Ross Lee."

Johnny wrote it on his pad. "If he wasn't working for you, did he say what he was doing up there in Colorado?"

Billy shrugged. "Just said he was passing through and ran out of gas. The gas gauge didn't work on that old truck."

"How long ago did he work for your father?"

"Oh, let's see," Billy leaned back in the wooden chair, considering. "Must've been more than a year, year and a half now."

"You're not sure?" Johnny asked.

Billy smiled. "I had my own business, so I didn't pay a whole lot of attention to my daddy's drivers."

"Now, let's just drop the whole subject of 'your own business,' Billy," the public defender cautioned.

"He was a truck driver?" Johnny continued.

"Yep. He hauled them cows all over Texas, New Mexico, Oklahoma . . . anyplace my daddy did business."

"Do you know if he came with references? Had he worked someplace you know of before he started with your father?"

Billy frowned slightly as he thought about it, then shrugged. "I can't recall nothing specific, but I think it was over in Utah, Arizona, that country."

Johnny paused in his questioning as he made notes. "Why'd he quit? Or was he fired?" he asked.

"Oh, he was fired all right!" Billy laughed. "Couldn't hold his firewater, that Indian. Though it wasn't from lack of practice."

"Did he ever talk about himself? Where he was from, what tribe? That sort of thing?"

"Navajo, I think, but we weren't what you'd call real close," Billy said. "Fact is, Lee could be a real pain in the ass, drunk or sober. When he was drunk he could be mean. When he was sober, he could get all preachy-like."

"What do you mean, preachy?"

"Well, he was a Jack Mormon, if you can believe that." Billy shook his head at the thought. "He'd go on about Lamanites, Jesus and Satan being brothers, Holy murder . . . crazy shit like that. Nobody paid much attention."

Teddy asked, "What's a Jack Mormon?"

"Well, what a jackrabbit is to a little cottontail, a Jack Mormon is to all the good praying Mormons. Kind of a wild, no-count relative you don't want to claim," Billy explained.

"Sounds like you, Billy-boy," Sheriff Craig chuckled.

"Fuck you, Sheriff," Billy snarled.

"When you say he was mean," Johnny interrupted, "did he get into fights with the other employees?"

"Nah," Billy gave the sheriff another hard look before answering. "Lee was just bad on the bitches."

"He'd beat up women?" Johnny frowned.

"Damn straight," Billy nodded. "Lee's a pretty good-looking guy, I guess, if you like Indians. You know, cheekbones, long hair, and all that. Well, it seemed like the whiter the woman, the more she liked him. You'd always see him with these blonde babes hanging off of him. But, I don't know, maybe it was the drinking, but when things got down to business, so to speak, he'd turn mean like and start beating on them."

"Did he ever say why?" Johnny asked.

"Not to me, he didn't," Billy replied. "Waste of good woman flesh, if you ask me." He shook his head.

"Was there any particular incident that caused your father to fire him?" Johnny continued.

Billy gave a nasty smile. "Old Lee tried to mix business with pleasure. He was driving one of Daddy's trucks one time when he picked up a woman. She ran off screaming to the cops. My Daddy thought that might be bad for business having women beat up in the cab-over of a truck with his name on the door."

"When did that happen?"

"Oh," Billy considered, "probably about a year ago, now."

"Did Lee ever mention the name Sixkiller?" Johnny asked.

"Not that I can recall," Billy replied.

"How about the names Willis or Colter?"

Billy frowned, thoughtful. "Nah, don't recall them neither." He shook his head.

Johnny tapped the pen distractedly against his chin, looking at his notes. "Do you know if this Ross Lee ever carried a weapon? Gun? Knife?"

"He may have, but I never saw it. Lots of truckers do, you know. It can get pretty dangerous hauling valuable stuff. Lot of hijacking goes on. But, then again, some truckers don't carry weapons 'cause they got a record and the cops are always pulling them over."

"Do you know if Lee had a record?" Johnny asked.

Billy shrugged. "Could be. He mentioned getting in trouble with the law when he was a kid. 'Big time trouble' he called it, but that's all he said."

Johnny crossed his arms, his brow furrowed as he studied his notes. "One last question, Billy. Do you have any idea where Lee was heading after he was fired? Family, friends, anything?"

"I think his family was dead. But, no, I don't know where he was heading, except most likely for the nearest bar."

"Okay." Johnny stood. "I don't have any other questions."

"Did I help any?" Billy asked.

Johnny nodded. "Yeah, I think so. I'm gonna have to chew on it a bit to get the flavor, but, yeah, I think you gave us some."

"Good." Billy turned to Sheriff Craig. "You heard him now, Sheriff. I expect ya'll to cut me some slack now, hear?"

"I heard him," Sheriff Craig nodded. He simply nodded to his deputy who tapped Billy on the shoulder and escorted him out of the room. Teddy also left.

When he was gone, the Sheriff asked Johnny, "Did that really help any? This Lee feller didn't seem to have any connection to Sixkiller at all."

"The connection came later, after he left Texas," Johnny explained. "Last winter."

"That part about beating on white women might be worth something. You think he's working with Sixkiller?" the sheriff asked.

"What I really think, personally," Johnny said with a sad smile, "is that this Ross Lee is the real killer and Char Sixkiller is taking the rap for it."

"Well, then, I guess ya'll are gonna start looking for this Lee then, huh?"

Johnny shrugged. "It's not my investigation. I'm just . . . helping. But, yeah, I think we need to start searching real seriously for this Ross Lee."

CHAPTER 12

S o what? So the guy used to drink too much!" DiRosa said. "Lots of people do, for whatever reason. That doesn't make him a killer."

Johnny was uncomfortably aware of the fact that Agent DiRosa was comfortably seated in what used to be his armchair. "No, of course not," Johnny snapped, annoyed, and not just at DiRosa's obstinacy. "This is the same guy that used to get his jollies beating up blonde women . . . our victims are blonde women, you remember?" He let some sarcasm seep into his tone. "This is also the same guy that was driving Char's pickup truck . . . the same truck that was found in New Mexico with traces of the victim's blood in the box. The same guy that Jimmy Little Crow said was tapped in to a pretty dark and twisted higher power. And the same guy who even looks a little bit like Char Sixkiller—at least to white folks who think all Indians look alike, and all Chinese look alike and all blacks look alike."

"Don't forget us Mexicans, *gringo*," Barbara added with an exaggerated Mexican accent, trying to defuse some of Johnny's irritation. She stood in the doorway to the kitchen with her arms folded, watching the two men in the living room.

Johnny waved her comment away. "Well, anyway, you get my point."

DiRosa drummed his fingers on the arm of the chair, frowning. "Yeah," he conceded, "I get your point."

"But . . . what?" Johnny prodded.

"But what am I supposed to do? Announce that I've had a revelation? A dream? A burning bush told me to start a nationwide manhunt for a Navajo named Ross Lee? Or, better yet, an alcoholic, broken-down rodeo cowboy, fired from the smallest sheriff's department in the country, gave me a hot tip?!"

"That was uncalled for, Joe," Barbara chided.

"Okay, sorry, cheap shot," DiRosa held up his hands. "But you get my point. I'm already pretty marginal to Sutton's team. He doesn't really trust me anymore because of . . . you know . . . the fact that I'm seeing you." He nodded toward Barbara. "I'd have a certain credibility problem popping up with a hot lead out of thin air."

"Well," Johnny said, "why don't you tell him it's your lead? You found a reference in my reports to the rustler letting off an Indian who drove off in Sixkiller's truck."

"You kept detailed reports like that?" DiRosa asked, surprised.

"No, of course not," Johnny scoffed, "but Sutton isn't going to waste time checking on that. He'll just think you did some good, honest cop work, sifting through the details. Then you can call up Sheriff Craig in Texas as if to clarify something I said, and honestly report that you investigated the lead with him."

"Actually," Barbara interjected, "maybe you should just start a records search on this guy, Ross Lee, and save that story," she pointed at Johnny, "in case any one asks what you're doing."

"Even better," Johnny agreed.

"Yeah, maybe so," DiRosa nodded, still somewhat skeptical. "My turn, I guess, to report." He cleared his throat. "I did a little more

checking on Willis and Colter, the two agents killed up in South
Dakota sixteen years ago. It seems that, even though they convicted
that Larry Pelham guy, most of the other defendants walked. And,
from the looks of it, our case against Pelham wasn't real solid either.
But"—he leaned forward toward the couch where Johnny sat—"it
seems that a certain agent named Adam Sutton was very involved in
the investigation. Willis, in particular, was a friend of his, kind of a
mentor. Sutton took it real hard. Hard enough that he was given a
medical leave of absence after Pelham's conviction, to kind of get it
together again."

Johnny snapped his fingers. "I just know there has to be a connection to this."

"Well, I'll do some more looking," DiRosa said, standing.

"Wait a minute," Johnny said, waving the agent back to his chair.
"What about this latest killing? The one down in Oklahoma they're
saying Char did?"

Barbara came over and sat on the couch with Johnny. "Is there
anything new that would really seem to link Char?" she asked.

DiRosa shook his head. "No, not really. He didn't leave a business
card or anything. Just the same pattern as the others. It was near the
site of another battle along the Washita River. Cheyenne Indians
again, under a chief named Black Kettle. He was killed. The murderer
left a little black pot behind as a souvenir."

"You know," Johnny leaned back, slouching into the worn couch, "I
have never seen Char with a weapon. Not so much as a pocketknife.
What is the killer's MO?"

DiRosa paced a couple of steps before answering. "Now this is
really the nitty-gritty of the investigation, and I'll only tell you because
I trust Barbara."

"Aw, now you've gone and hurt my feelings, G-man," Johnny said,
sarcastically.

"Hey," DiRosa shrugged. "You tried to tip Sixkiller before. I can't be a hundred percent certain you're not in touch with him now."

"Smoke signals!" Johnny grinned. "You're on to me! Since you tapped all the phones in southeast Colorado, I'm using smoke signals to communicate with the suspect. I confess!"

"Ya, Johnny, that's enough," Barbara cautioned gently. "Put yourself in Joe's place."

Johnny grunted. "Don't I wish I could!" He looked unhappily at DiRosa and his ex-wife.

"All right," DiRosa sat back down. "Apparently Sixkiller, or whoever the killer is, picks his victims up at random. We can't find any connection between any of them other than being in their twenties or thirties, and blonde."

"Who are . . . were they?" Barbara asked.

DiRosa sighed. "Some we know. A couple, we haven't been able to identify yet."

Johnny frowned. "They were that badly cut up?"

"I'm afraid so. Whoever is doing this just has an incredible rage, once he gets going."

"*Santo Dios!*" Barbara whispered, leaning back in the couch as if to distance herself from the information.

"The South Dakota victim seems to have been a Minnesota woman who had recently left an abusive husband. I interviewed him. The guy's a jerk of truly epic proportions, I want to tell you." DiRosa shook his head. "He was more upset that his wife had been with another man, than he was that she was dead."

"Did she take anything with her when she left?" Johnny asked. "I mean, like, did she have a car?"

"No. She just walked out the door after a fight with Prince Charming. All she took was her purse, no luggage or anything."

"Did you find the purse?" Johnny asked.

"Yeah," DiRosa nodded. "We got lucky. It was in a ditch not too far from the body. That's actually how we identified her."

"Was there anything in the purse?" Johnny persisted. "Like a bus ticket or anything?"

"We didn't find one," DiRosa said.

"She leaves home in Minnesota walking and winds up in western South Dakota," Johnny said. "Kind of a long walk, don't you think?"

DiRosa shrugged. "She hitched a ride, I guess."

"Was she killed at the scene where the body was found, or was she just dumped there later?"

DiRosa gave a slight smile. "Pretty good cop question, cowboy." Glancing at Barbara, he added, "Maybe you were right about him." To Johnny, he replied, "There were no signs of struggle and not much blood around the body, considering how cut up she was. But it looked like it had been quite a while before the body was found. It wasn't until the snow melted this spring."

"How about the other victims?"

"The one in Silver City we haven't identified yet. The Arizona victim seems to have been a prostitute out of Tucson. The victim at Fort Sumner was a waitress at a truck stop in Albuquerque. The Texas victim seems to have been a college student from Lubbock. We found her car broken down outside of Boise City, Oklahoma. Same with all of them, though, not much blood."

"And how about this latest victim in Oklahoma?" Barbara asked.

DiRosa shook his head. "No ID yet."

"How did you make the others?" Johnny asked. "More purses?"

"I wish," DiRosa said. "Dental records for a couple. The college girl had been reported missing by her family when she was overdue coming home. They identified a birthmark on the body."

"I know I'm going to be sorry I asked this," Johnny shook his head, "but how come there were no fingerprints?"

"No fingers," DiRosa said simply.

"I was afraid of that," Johnny said.

Barbara closed her eyes, making no comment.

Johnny took a deep breath. "Do you think the no fingers thing is deliberate, to obscure the identification, or just incidental to his method of killing?"

"Another good question, Hart," DiRosa admitted. "I don't know, though. There's so much other damage, it's hard to tell."

"Still," Johnny pressed, "are there any other body parts missing?" At a groan from Barbara, Johnny added, "I'm sorry, honey."

DiRosa leaned forward, elbows on knees. "No, I don't think so. That's a good point, too. It does sound like he's consciously trying to louse up any investigation, doesn't it?"

"In that case, he should probably take the heads too, though," Johnny mused.

"I'm going to make some coffee," Barbara gasped, lurching up from the couch.

Johnny watched her leave. "Now that she's gone, let me ask the really hard stuff. Does the wacko do all this mutilation before or after they're dead?"

"Pathologists say afterward," DiRosa explained. "The wounds don't appear to bleed all that much."

"Last question," Johnny said, also leaning forward. "Is there anything sexual going on? Either before or after?"

DiRosa hung his head. "That's what we've really been trying to keep from the media. The answer is, yes, but we don't know if it's before or after."

"That's great!" Johnny exclaimed. Seeing the horrified look on the agent's face, he quickly explained. "I mean, 'great,' because you'll have some solid DNA evidence that can be used to clear Char and nail the real killer."

"I'm glad you explained yourself, Hart," DiRosa said with a nervous laugh. "That's true. Of course, right now we don't have any samples from Sixkiller, or anyone else, to compare with."

Barbara returned to the kitchen door. "Coffee's about ready. Why don't you come in here, I have some *pan dulce*, too."

"Sweetbread, all right!" Johnny stood and led the way to the kitchen. "Did you get those little *maranitos*, Barb?"

She laughed. "*Si, Juanito*, I got your *maranitos*." She patted his arm as he passed. "I know they're your favorites."

Johnny stood at the counter while DiRosa and Barbara sat at the table. "What I'm thinking," he said, his mouth half filled with sweet-bread, "is that this Lee feller is a trucker, right? So far it looks like all the victims were either on the road or had some reason to be where a truck driver could logically happen along."

"Did anybody see a truck near any of the locations where the victims were found?" Barbara asked, looking at DiRosa over the rim of her cup.

DiRosa shrugged his shoulders. "I don't think anybody volunteered that information. I know nobody asked."

"Maybe somebody could still ask on this latest Oklahoma one," Johnny suggested. "Is it too late for you to get back in the game?" he asked.

DiRosa made a face. "Probably, but I've got a friend who's still on the investigation. I'll see if he can ask around. It won't be too illogical. The killer has to transport the body somehow." He sipped his coffee. "Speaking of getting in the game, Barbara, what time is Jack's basketball game this Friday?"

"7:30," she replied, glancing nervously at Johnny.

"Jack has a game this week, huh?" he noted with forced casualness. "First one of the season?"

"Yeah," DiRosa explained. "He and I were talking about it the other day. I used to play basketball in high school, so I thought it might be kind of fun to see him play. I understand he's pretty good."

"Yeah, he's good all right." Johnny said. "I guess U.C. is even talking about a scholarship for him."

"Is that right?" DiRosa smiled at Barbara. "Hey, that's great." Turning again to Johnny, he asked, "So are you gonna be there this Friday? I suppose you taught him everything he knows. Isn't that what every father says?"

Johnny put his coffee cup in the sink. Without looking at either Barbara or DiRosa, he said, "No, I never taught him much that was useful." To Barbara, he said, "I'd better get on down the road. It's getting late and the cows get up early."

"Sure, Johnny," she gave him a sad smile. "Drive carefully, okay?"

"Sure thing," he said. Putting his hat on, he shook hands with DiRosa. "Let me know what you find out, G-man."

"I'll do that, cowboy. You take care." When the front door had closed, DiRosa said to Barbara, "You know, you were right. Hart really is a pretty good cop. He thinks . . . hey, are you okay? Are you crying?"

Barbara dabbed her eyes with her sleeve. "No, I'm all right. It's just too much talk about murder and ugly things. I'm all right."

⌃⌃⌃

The sound of angry voices woke Sandy. From habit, she looked first to see if Lady was lying beside her bed before putting her feet down. She shuffled down the hall in her slippers, tying her robe as she moved toward the light in the kitchen.

"I may be old and stove up, but this is still my house, by God!" Mr. Cross spluttered at Johnny. His face was red with anger as he stood gripping the back of a kitchen chair. Johnny was also flushed in the face, but not just from temper.

"What is it, Grandpa?" Sandy asked. "What's wrong?"

Mr. Cross pointed at Johnny. "This here no-count, brush-hand rodeo bum comes walkin' into my house reelin' and reekin' like a skid row bum. I ain't gonna stand for it! No, sir! I wouldn't allow my own son to do it, and I ain't gonna allow him to do it, neither!"

"I'm not your son," Johnny snapped. "My father's dead!"

"No, you ain't my son. My boy is dead!"

The two men stood silently glaring at each other. Johnny was the first to look away.

Quietly, Sandy said, "It's all right, Grandpa, I'll talk to Johnny. It won't happen again." She laid a soothing hand on his gnarled fingers. "It's not worth giving yourself another heart attack over, Grandpa. Why don't you just go on back to bed. I'll talk to him."

"Nope, nope!" Mr. Cross's chin trembled slightly. "He sure ain't worth it." He looked Johnny up and down in disgust, then turned and walked slowly and stiffly off into the darkness of the hallway.

"It's hot in here," Johnny muttered. "Maybe I'll sleep in the barn." Clumsily, he opened the back door and stumbled outside.

"Wait a minute, Johnny," Sandy called. "This is October. It's freezing out there. Are you nuts?" She followed him outside, catching him by the sleeve at the bottom of the kitchen steps. "You're sweating!" she noted in surprise. Laying her hand on his forehead, she said, "You're burning up. Come back inside. You'll catch your death out here."

Johnny shook his head. "No, it's too hot." He swayed slightly, steadying himself with a hand on Sandy's shoulder. "Let me just set for a while." He half sat, half collapsed onto the steps, his head hanging, his eyes closed.

Sandy sat beside him. "What have you done to yourself, Johnny? You were doing fine for weeks and weeks. Why'd you go and do this to yourself?"

"Oh, it seemed like a good idea at the time," he sighed, giving a crooked smile. "You have no idea how many minutes and hours and days went into those weeks and weeks. And tonight, I just said to myself, here I am all clean and dry, and for what? My life doesn't look any better when I can focus on it than it did when I was drunk. So, what the hell, why torture myself? And that, little girl, is that." He hunched forward, hugging his stomach and rocking slightly.

Overhead a bright full moon was visible in the bare branches of the tree. Gusts of wind rustled the fallen leaves and caused the limbs to wave at the eastward sailing clouds.

Sandy pulled her robe tighter under her chin. "So what in particular set you off on this pity party tonight?"

"Oh, it's not self-pity," he said, lightly. "It's just that I used to really enjoy drinking, and I can't say that I've enjoyed much else lately." He gave a slight grunt of pain. "Course, drinking didn't used to do this to me." He hugged himself tighter. "Barb has a new boyfriend." He nodded, glancing sideways at Sandy. "Yup. Looks like my son may have a new dad, too," he added under his breath. "Sheriff Carter must have a new deputy by now. The PRCA has plenty of new bull riders everyday. I'd say that you could stand to have a new ranch hand who knows what the hell he's doing and God knows, between me and Ross Lee, Char could sure use some new friends." He closed his eyes again, rocking.

"Not self-pity, huh?" Sandy snorted. "You're not exactly the first person to ever be divorced, you know. Or lose a job, or be an alcoholic, for that matter."

"It's a helluva resume so far, isn't it?" Johnny interrupted.

Sandy laughed. "My point is that the Bible says that God doesn't allow more to come on us than we can bear and it also says that he disciplines those he loves."

Johnny gave a brief cough of laughter. "Well, it appears that he just loves me to death, now, doesn't it?"

"As a matter of fact, yes," Sandy nodded. "Only it was his death. On the cross at Calvary."

"Whew!" Johnny whistled, laughing. "You're good, lady! You just turned that whole thing into a little sermon, didn't you?" He shook his head.

"Well, but it's true, Johnny!" Sandy insisted. "God's not the one that trashed your life. No offense, but that seems to have been your particular mission in life these last several years. God's just waiting for you to pick up the broken pieces and give them over to him so he can fix it. He's the higher power that Char found."

Johnny didn't respond. He sat rocking himself on the step, his eyes closed.

Sandy was cold and had just stood up to go back inside when he spoke.

"What are you doing here, Sandy? You're smart, you're decent, you're a hell of a good-looking woman, and here you are, a million miles from anybody, working yourself to death pushing cows around." He opened his eyes and looked at her seriously. "Your marriage went south, so you're going to hide away out here forever? Forgive me, but now that's a waste!"

"Is that what you think?" she asked, sitting down again. "I'm not hiding out. I'm home! Those people scrambling like ants to make money, have lots of things, make their mark on the world, they're the ones hiding out. They're hiding from their own humanity."

Johnny held up his hand as if to ward off a blow. "You're not gonna get all heavy and philosophical now, are you?" he winced.

Sandy laughed. "You know I could, but no. You're in no condition for another lecture."

Johnny got unsteadily to his feet. "Well, I'm feeling a little better, now. Believe me, it wasn't something you said. But anyway, I think I will go in and go to sleep." He stopped with his hand on the door. "I'll apologize to your grandpa tomorrow. He's right, it is his house."

Sandy stood up also. "You have to understand where he's coming from. My mom and dad were killed in a car accident. My father was driving drunk at the time."

Johnny lowered his head. "I didn't know."

Sandy placed her hand on his shoulder. "It happens."

Johnny nodded and held the door open for Sandy to enter first.

CHAPTER 13

DiRosa had just hung up the phone when Sutton appeared at the door of his office. He quickly exited from the program he was in before the senior agent could see what was on his screen.

"Late nights again, eh, Joey?" Sutton sat down in the chair across from DiRosa and stretched his legs. "What are you working on?"

DiRosa rolled his chair back from his desk to get more comfortable. "That stolen car thing. You know, the one where the chopped parts wind up in Mexico then come back into the States in the parts aftermarket?"

"Oh, yeah," Sutton nodded. "Having any luck?"

"Some," DiRosa shrugged. "We've got a snitch who can dish us a couple of chop shops, but we'd like to play him a bit and see if he can't lead us across the border to some bigger fish."

Sutton studied the tips of his shoes as he spoke. "I understand you've been fishing around in the old Pine Ridge file—the Willis and Colter murders. Any particular reason why?"

"No," DiRosa tried to sound nonchalant. "You had mentioned it a couple of months ago and it just kind of got my curiosity, that's all."

"That was one of the first cases I worked on when I came out here," Sutton said. "Ugly, very ugly. Two good men, executed in cold blood after they were wounded and down."

"From the reports, it looked like things were pretty crazy on the reservation for quite a while even before the murders." DiRosa was surprised at Sutton's apparent willingness to talk.

"Crazy doesn't begin to describe it," Sutton shook his head. "It was nothing but a damn civil war between the AIM people and Dick Wilson's goon squad. We should have just stayed out of it and let them kill each other off. Good riddance, I say. With those guys out of the way, the decent people up there could have gotten on with normal lives again. But no, everybody was paranoid and armed to the teeth. And Ron and Jack rode right into the middle of it and somebody—some scumbag—offed them."

"Somebody?" DiRosa prompted. "I thought you were sure it was Pelham. He's still doing time behind it."

"Oh, yeah," Sutton nodded. "We had a good case against Pelham, but any one of those bastards would have loved to smoke an FBI agent. That's the way it was back then. The cavalry versus the Indians like some stupid John Wayne movie." He sounded tired and slightly sad.

"How's the Sixkiller investigation going?" DiRosa interrupted Sutton's reverie.

"It's tough." Sutton sat up in the chair and stretched his neck. "Still no sign of Sixkiller, and very little physical evidence to link him since it all happens outdoors."

"Did you ID the last victim?"

"Looks like another truck stop waitress. This one from Oklahoma City. Not much to go on. We asked her co-workers if they'd seen her with anybody matching Sixkiller's description, and the answer is yes, two or three customers were tall Indians with long hair. What the hell, it's Oklahoma, right? . . . Indian Country, for Christ's sake!" He shook his head.

"Well, Joey, I'm going to head home," Sutton stood up. "I hope there's no hard feelings from me taking you off that investigation. It's just with you dating the ex-wife of a suspected conspirator in the case, you know, it just doesn't look good."

"Sure, I understand," DiRosa nodded affably.

"Oh," Sutton paused in the doorway. "And why don't you leave the Willis and Colter stuff alone? There's no point stirring up bad memories. If you have any questions about what happened, just ask me. I was there. I know."

When Sutton's footsteps could no longer be heard, DiRosa picked up the phone and dialed. "Barbara? Joe. Listen, can you get our friend over to the house tomorrow night? I've got something I think we really need to talk about."

⋀⋀⋀

Jack opened the door to Johnny's knock. His friendly expression faded to a stone face when he recognized his father.

"Hey, Jack," Johnny greeted his son with a forced smile and an aching heart. "How's it going?"

Jack grunted, signifying nothing as he walked away from his father to the kitchen door. "Dad's here," he announced flatly. "I'm out of here." He grabbed his coat and his basketball from beside the door and brushed past Johnny without a word.

"Home right after practice, okay?" Barbara called.

"I hear," Jack waved over his head, shutting the front door without looking back.

Johnny stood looking sadly at the closed door, unaware that Barbara had come to stand beside him. "Hi, Johnny," she said softly, breaking into his thoughts.

"Oh," he turned to look at her. "Hey, Barb," he gave a weak smile. "How did his game go?"

"They won."

"Good," he nodded. "Did Joe make it to the game?"

"Yes, he did," she said simply, not wishing to elaborate.

"Is he here yet?"

"No, not yet." Barbara turned back into the kitchen. "Come on in. Did you eat?"

"I grabbed a chili dog at the Dairy Queen in Las Animas on the way over," he said.

She wrinkled her nose in distaste. "How can you eat those things?" She pointed at the stove. "There's some *calabacitas con queso* left from dinner. Help yourself. You need vegetables." She poured a cup of coffee and sat at the table while Johnny served himself a plate. "What do you eat out there at the ranch?" she asked.

"Beans, mostly," Johnny said. "The Crosses have been pretty strapped for cash lately, so we've been eating pretty basic stuff."

"I thought they just sold most of their cows. How come they're so poor, still?"

"Well," Johnny paused in his eating. "That money is all earmarked for buying buffalo stock."

"Couldn't they spend a little of it, to eat right, then get a loan for the buffalo?" Barbara asked. "I mean it's a business expense, isn't it?"

Johnny shook his head, smiling. "Nope. That's not the way they see it. Mr. Cross is stubborn and old fashioned and Sandy is stubborn and biblical. Either way, they do not believe in borrowing. They're determined they're not going to lose that ranch to any creditors, even if they have to live on beans forever."

"They're probably right," Barbara nodded. "I remember how ugly things got back in the '80s when banks started foreclosing on people around here."

"Hi, Daddy!" Gloria squealed into the kitchen and hugged Johnny's neck.

"Hey, little girl," Johnny beamed with pleasure. "Where've you been hiding?"

"Mom said I had to finish my homework first thing," Gloria said over her shoulder as she rummaged through the refrigerator.

"What are you looking for, Gordy?" Barbara asked.

"I don't know," Gloria replied, still searching. "Something sweet, I guess."

"*Ay, muchachita!* You and your sweets!" Barbara shook her head. "You don't get enough exercise to be eating so much candy."

"I'm going out for softball this spring," Gloria asserted defensively. "Maybe I'll just have some cereal as a snack, okay?"

"Okay," Barbara conceded, "but not too much sugar." To Johnny, she asked, "What are you smiling at?"

Johnny just shook his head. "Me? I'm just a happy man." He stood and took his plate to the sink. "That was good, Barb. Thanks."

The doorbell rang.

"That must be Joe," Barbara said, rising. "For some reason, he always rings the bell and you always knock."

When she had left the room, Johnny said to Gloria as casually as he could, "So, how do you like Joe?"

"Oh," Gloria smiled, "he's real nice. He's got all these cool stories about New York and stuff."

"Hmm," Johnny tried not to look disappointed by her positive reaction. "Cool, huh?"

"Say, what's going on, Deputy?" DiRosa greeted Johnny as he entered the kitchen. "Yo, Gloria, what's up, girlfriend?" he saluted Gloria, his fist clenched.

Gloria smiled, her mouth full of cereal. Swallowing, she said brightly, "Hi, Joe."

"Gordy, why don't you take your snack into your room?" Barbara suggested. "We've got some serious things we have to talk about."

DiRosa draped his overcoat on the back of the chair Gloria had just vacated and helped himself to the coffee.

"Barb made it sound like you had some hot news," Johnny prompted. He suddenly felt like a visitor in the house and was anxious to leave.

"I think so," DiRosa nodded, taking a seat at the table.

"Coffee, Johnny?"

"Yeah, thanks, honey." He noticed DiRosa's eyebrows rise slightly at the endearment. Barbara placed the cup before him and he smiled, pleased at having gotten a small emotional jab at the other man.

"Remember the Willis and Colter murders back in the seventies?" DiRosa began. "Well, you were right Hart. There is a connection to this thing. Among the dozen or so Indians at the Jumping Elk ranch where this shootout took place, was a young Navajo kid, about thirteen years old, by the name of Lee Begay.

"When the others were bugging out after the shooting, Begay decided to surrender, so he walked out with his hands up. The BIA police took him in, then turned him over to the FBI."

DiRosa sipped his coffee, then hunched forward and tapped his finger on the tabletop for emphasis. "A certain agent, Adam Sutton, was assigned to keep an eye on Begay and get him ready for trial . . . as a witness against the other defendants. Well, as a witness he didn't do too well. A lot of his testimony at trial was directly contrary to what his initial statements were when he was taken into custody. But, I don't know if the defense attorneys ever saw those earlier statements. It was Lee Begay who supposedly placed Pelham down near the agents when the fatal shots were fired.

"I'll tell you what I think, after reading the transcripts," he addressed himself to Barbara. "I think he was coached all the way, and probably it was Sutton who force-fed him the line. He was one scared kid when he was first taken in. They probably told him he'd get the death penalty himself unless he testified against the others."

"So he perjured himself in order to make a deal." Barbara shook her head.

"Was he ever charged with anything?" Johnny asked.

"Not as far as I can tell," DiRosa shook his head. "But that's only part of it. And this is where I hope I didn't leave any fingerprints behind, if you know what I mean. I was digging even deeper into some files I had no clearance to look at." Unconsciously, he lowered his voice as if someone in Denver might be listening. "They didn't put Lee into Witness Protection or anything, but Sutton did kind of rig up a new identity for the kid—new birth certificate, a phony school transcript, driver's license, that sort of thing. He used the ID a little later to get into a truck driving school in Salt Lake City . . ." he leaned back and smiled triumphantly, "under the name Ross Lee."

Johnny leaned back, nodding. "Damn fine work, Joe. Real good!"

"I hate to be negative," Barbara frowned. "But simply showing an old connection between Sutton and Lee doesn't really amount to proof that Lee's the killer. I mean, speaking as a prosecutor, that's not anything I could take to court."

"That's true," Johnny agreed. "But cases are like brick walls, you build them one brick at a time, and Joe just delivered a wheelbarrow full." To DiRosa, he asked, "Can you keep searching for anything more recent under either Lee Begay or Ross Lee? I think Char said Lee was married. Maybe there's a marriage license issued in Utah or Arizona or someplace."

DiRosa was making notes on a small spiral notebook, similar to the one Johnny always carried. "That's a good idea," he agreed. "Almost everything is on computers now. I'll just surf the law enforcement web and see what I can find."

"That's great," Johnny said. "If you can, you might be able to pull a whole paper trail together on this guy, everything from drunk driving convictions to overdue library books."

DiRosa laughed. "That's a scary thought, but I'll bet I could do it on almost anybody."

Barbara leaned back in her chair. "That is scary," she nodded somberly.

"So you think Sutton is covering for Lee?" Johnny asked.

"Could be," DiRosa shrugged. "Either he's protecting Lee, or protecting himself. If he really did force a teenage kid into giving perjured testimony, he probably doesn't want that to come up now that he's closing in on retirement. He may be afraid Lee will talk if he thinks it would help him cut a deal on a murder charge. I know I would."

"Is there anything new on Char?" Barbara asked.

"No," DiRosa shook his head. "But that reminds me." He pointed at Johnny. "I asked my friend on the investigation to check on trucks in the area around the time of the murder. There was an Indian trucker at a self-service car wash in Sayre the day after we think the girl was killed. Somebody remembered because she thought it was odd that he was hosing out the inside of the cab as well as the outside."

"Just the tractor? No trailer?" Johnny asked.

"Just the tractor." DiRosa nodded.

Johnny whistled softly. "So if the bodies are dumped after the damage is done, maybe the murder scene just drives off with the murderer."

"That's what I was thinking," DiRosa said.

"Joe, you've got to find a driver's license and truck registration in Lee's name," Barbara said. "Either of his names. If that truck can be found and searched, I'll bet there's still some forensic evidence that would link him to one or more of the killings. He can't clean it that well."

"Did you get a description of the truck?" Johnny asked. "It wasn't a rental, was it?"

"I don't know," DiRosa said, jotting more notes in his notepad. "But I'll check on it."

"Course, even if you identify the truck and find Lee," Johnny frowned, "you'll probably have to go over Sutton's head to get a warrant."

"That could be a problem," DiRosa agreed, "but I'll worry about it when the time comes. In the meantime, I've got plenty to keep me busy." He tapped his notepad. "I've got to find Lee first."

ᴧᴧᴧ

A light dusting of early November snow had fallen overnight. Johnny entered the kitchen to find Sandy standing at the sink, looking out the window.

"Morning," he greeted, heading for the coffee pot.

"Morning, Johnny," Sandy said. She turned to give him a brief smile. "It snowed some overnight. I'm glad we got the last of the cattle shipped."

"Is this just a taste, you think, or are we in for a real storm?" he asked. "Have you heard any weather reports?"

Sandy shook her head. "I haven't turned on the radio. Grandpa's not up yet. I didn't want to wake him. I thought it might do him good to sleep late."

Johnny looked at the kitchen clock. "It's 8:00 o'clock. Has he ever slept this late before?"

"Not that I can recall," she replied. "I heard him cough earlier, so he's still alive, if that's what you're worried about."

Johnny gave an embarrassed laugh. "I'm afraid that did cross my mind."

"Well, he's probably awake, just not up yet." Sandy went to the coffee pot and poured a cup. "Why don't you take him a cup of coffee and check in on him. You can say I sent you."

"That's a good idea," Johnny agreed, reaching for the cup.

Sandy didn't immediately release the cup. "You got home pretty late last night," she noted, studying his face. "How did it go?"

Johnny smiled. "You mean did I tie one on and drive home drunk?"

"That's what I mean," she admitted.

He shook his head. "Two cups of coffee and a cold drive back . . . the heater's not working so well on my truck. That was it and straight to bed."

She let go of the cup. "You'll have to tell me later what's going on with the investigation."

He nodded. "I'll do that. It's getting kind of interesting."

As he walked down the hallway he heard a click, and country music drifted quietly after him from the kitchen. He knocked on Mr. Cross's bedroom door.

"It ain't locked," came the response.

Johnny entered the room and entered another time. The room appeared to have been furnished and decorated at least fifty years ago. There were at least as many photographs of horses and cattle as there were of family and friends.

"Sandy sent some coffee, Mr. Cross," Johnny announced approaching the bed.

Mr. Cross struggled to sit up, scowling. "I ain't no J. P. Morgan or Al Capone to be drinkin' coffee in bed," he growled. "She gonna have you spoon feedin' me next?"

"I think she thought you'd like to rest a little, now that the cattle are all shipped," Johnny explained, slightly annoyed.

"I got all eternity to rest in after I'm dead. Right now, I got a ranch to run," he rasped.

"Suit yourself," Johnny shrugged. "I'll pour it back in the pot to stay warm." He reached for the doorknob.

"Hold on a minute!" Mr. Cross ordered.

When Johnny turned to look, Mr. Cross frowned angrily at him for several seconds before speaking. "Close the door, John."

When the door was closed, Mr. Cross directed, "Come on over here and set for a spell."

Johnny placed the coffee on the bedside table and sat in the old oak rocker that was beside the bed. "Are you all right, Mr. Cross?" he asked, puzzled.

"No, I'm not all right," Mr. Cross snapped. He exhaled angrily. "Fact is, I'm so knotted up with the damned arthritis right now, I can't get out of this bed." His swollen hands rose and fell in frustration on the blankets. "Helluva thing!"

"Do you have some medication I can get for you?" Johnny asked in concern.

"There's some muscle relaxers and pain pills in the medicine cabinet over the bathroom sink," Mr. Cross explained wearily. "Don't let Sandy see ya, though."

Johnny slipped carefully from the room and across the hall. Finding the prescription bottles, he filled a glass with water and returned to the room.

"Did she see ya?" Mr. Cross asked.

Johnny shook his head. "She's got bacon sizzling and the radio on." He read the bottles and handed the pills to Mr. Cross. When the old man couldn't grip the water glass, Johnny held it to his lips. "You're in a pretty bad way, Mr. Cross. Maybe we should call the doctor."

"No need for that," Mr. Cross said. "It's just so danged cold, it gets to my joints, ya see. I'll be fine in a little bit." He closed his eyes, breathing heavily against the pain. "Helluva thing, after seventy plus years of good hard work, and I can't even get out of my bed." He shook his head. "But don't go and tell Sandy now. She's got worries enough."

Johnny sat down again in the rocker. "She's bound to notice sooner or later, Mr. Cross. It's November. I don't imagine we can expect too many more warm days for a few months now."

Mr. Cross closed his eyes and nodded. "I know, I know," he muttered. "Helluva thing." Turning to look at Johnny, he asked bluntly, "Can Sandy count on you, mister?"

Johnny cocked his boot on his knee, looking uncomfortable at the question. "To do what?"

"To be here and carry some of the load," he stated. "It's for dang sure I'm no more use to her now than a tick is to a dog. But this ranch is too much for one person to keep up all by themselves."

He tried to flex his fingers and grimaced in pain. "I trusted Char. He had some grit and gumption to him. He had heart and he sure had a way with animals. But he's on the run now and, before long the government's gonna lock him up just like they done to Satanta and Geronimo.

"But I ain't made up my mind about you yet, Mr. Deputy Hart. You can ride and rope passable well, but I don't know if you really got the heart for the long ride." He looked directly at Johnny, "No offense meant, you understand. It's just that I'm in a helluva fret right now. Come spring, I don't know if I'll even be above ground let alone in the saddle. And, 'sides, I'm a cowman. I don't know buffaloes from jackalopes. But my point is, a man with heart, it don't matter what he knows or don't know, or what might come ridin' over the ridge. He'll stand and fight or stand and take it, but he'll stand."

Johnny nodded, saying nothing. As a clock ticked loudly, he let his eyes rest on a photograph of a much younger William Cross, seated tall on a chestnut horse. A smiling boy of four or five sat in the saddle in front of him, happily clutching the pommel. "Was that your boy?" He pointed at the picture. "Sandy's dad?"

Considering the picture, Mr. Cross nodded. "That was Billy." He sighed heavily. "I loved that boy, but I have to admit he lacked heart. He was always lookin' for fun and excitement out of life. If it wasn't rodeo, it was whiskey. If it wasn't whiskey, it was women. Plain old real-life work, wear, and worry he just couldn't abide." He looked sadly at Johnny. "I think I'd like you better, John, if you didn't remind me so danged much of Billy. But there it is."

Johnny sighed. "I can't answer your question, Mr. Cross. I can't point at one thing I've ever really succeeded at in life. But, unlike your son, I'm still here. Maybe Sandy's right. Maybe there is a reason. I guess I'll stick around long enough to find out."

Mr. Cross nodded. "Help me see if I can't get out of this here bed now. That medicine should be doin' something."

Johnny carefully pulled him out of bed and helped him into his pants and boots. He buttoned the old man's shirt, to Mr. Cross's embarrassment. Stiffly, Mr. Cross shuffled down the hallway. Johnny followed.

At the kitchen door, Mr. Cross addressed Sandy. "That bacon sure smells good on a cold morning. I reckon . . . what is it, girl?"

Entering the kitchen, Johnny saw Sandy standing at the stove, wide-eyed with shock, the spatula suspended, forgotten over the bacon as it popped and spit.

"Sandy?" Johnny asked. "Are you okay?"

Sandy blinked at him and swallowed. "The radio just said they caught him twenty miles southwest of La Junta. They just arrested Char!"

ᴀᴀᴀ

"Can I help you?" Barbara asked in surprise, looking up from the file. "What's wrong? Sit, sit!" She pointed at the seat across her desk.

Sandy sat tentatively on the edge of the seat, an emotional struggle obvious on her face. "He won't see me," she said in a controlled voice.

"They told me he doesn't want to see me." She hugged herself tightly, but the tears broke through anyway.

"Who won't see you?" Barbara asked in confusion. "And may I ask who you are?"

Sandy took a deep, shuddering breath and answered. "My name is Sandy Cross. I came over here to visit Char Sixkiller. They told me at the jail that he didn't want to see me." She took another breath and appeared more controlled. "I thought maybe you could help. Johnny said that you were a real nice person." She started to cry.

"Oh, Sandy," Barbara stood and rounded the desk to put her arms around the distraught woman. "I'm sure he has a reason. I know he talked to Johnny earlier."

"God, this is so ridiculous!" Sandy said angrily, wiping her face with both hands. "I have thought about Char almost constantly for seven months like some stupid schoolgirl. Now he doesn't want anything to do with me." She took a deep breath and shook her head. "Boy, I really set myself up for this. I, of all people, should have known better," she said wryly.

"What are you talking about?" Barbara frowned, moving back to her own chair again.

"I'm talking about letting myself get into this whole, dumb, romantic frame of mind again," Sandy said bitterly. "I've been down this road before. You know what I'm talking about. You've been there too, with Johnny."

Barbara leaned back as if to bring Sandy into better focus. "I guess love always carries with it the risk of hurt."

Sandy waved her hand dismissively. "Love is not the same as romance. Romance is all about emotions. Love is about sacrifice. The Bible says that God so loved the world that he gave his son, Jesus, as a sacrifice for sin."

Barbara gave a short, astonished laugh. "And you think that didn't hurt?" she asked, incredulous. "I'll be honest with you. I can only remember one scripture from the Bible, and not just because it's so short. It says, 'Jesus wept.'"

Sandy lowered her head, saying nothing.

Barbara stood up and paced a few steps. "I know I'm a fine one to talk. I divorced Johnny. But it's not because I don't . . . didn't love him." She put her hand to her mouth as if to guard her words and feelings. "I just got tired, and my children needed some peace to grow up in." She stopped, crossed her arms, and turned away.

Sandy looked up. "You're still trying to convince yourself you did the right thing, aren't you?"

Barbara didn't answer immediately. With a sigh, she turned back toward Sandy. "Yes." She returned to her chair. "I was taking a litera-ture course at the University in Pueblo a few years back. I remember reading an essay on love by Stendhal. At the time, I rejected it, but it stuck in my head anyway. He was talking about Americans back in the 1820s. He said, 'I can see no trace of the passions which make for deeper joy. It's as if the sources of sensibility have dried up among these people. They are just, they are rational, and they are not happy at all.'"

She gave Sandy a sad smile. "Just maybe that describes us a little too closely. I got rid of a lot of my old college books, but for some reason, I hung on to that one."

Sandy stood up and paced, her right hand playing unconsciously with a strand of her hair. "But what am I supposed to do? How do you love someone in a vacuum?"

"You're really asking the wrong person," Barbara shook her head. "But I've thought about it a lot lately. I didn't see Johnny for over a year. A very calm, peaceful year, I might add. Then, this year, he's more and more back in my life, in my house, in my office, on my phone, on my mind." She threw her hands wide. "No more calm, no more peace. I lie awake at night sometimes worrying about him. I'm afraid for him once again. But after a year of kind of numb existence, I'm very much alive again."

Sandy sat down again. "Do you think you can talk to Char? Find out what's going on?"

"I don't know," Barbara admitted. "I'm a prosecutor. I'm sure his public defender will object to it, but Char has the final word on jail visitors. I'll ask."

Sandy stood up again. "Thank you, Barbara." She smiled, gratefully. "Johnny's right. You really are something special."

Barbara laughed. "That Johnny," she shook her head. "He's something else."

"You'll call me?"

"I'll call."

CHAPTER 14

ᴧᴧᴧ

J ohnny Hart," Little Crow laughed. "You're spending more time here than some of the Indians I know."

Johnny shook hands with the counselor. "I saw Char Sixkiller this morning. Can we talk?"

"Sure." Little Crow led the way to the Center's meeting room, where they sat, side by side on folding chairs. "I heard that they arrested Char. Outside of La Junta, wasn't it?"

Johnny nodded. "He was with some other Indians, and their car broke down near Timpas, on Route 350."

"Ah, Indian cars!" Little Crow shook his head.

Johnny nodded.

"So how is Char?" Little Crow asked.

"He seems healthy enough. He sure hates being locked up, though." Johnny frowned. "Did you know he was down in Mexico the last few months?"

Little Crow smiled and nodded. "I was pretty sure that's where he was. The Kickapoo Indians at Eagle Pass?"

Johnny nodded.

"Char had some friends, Kickapoo people, over by Horton, Kansas," Little Crow explained. "I thought they might try to get him over the border."

"They did," Johnny said.

Little Crow frowned. "Why did he come back so soon?"

"Sand Creek," Johnny said, studying the counselor's face.

"What do you mean?" Little Crow's face was unreadable.

"Char thinks that Lee is going to kill again on the anniversary of the Sand Creek massacre."

"That's just about a week away," Little Crow said. "What was he going to do about it?"

"Be there to stop it." Johnny shrugged. "He heard about that last killing down in Oklahoma and realized that Lee was still at it and nobody but me even seemed to be looking for him."

"You haven't had any luck yet, huh?"

"I haven't had much help yet, Jimmy," Johnny snapped.

"What do you mean?"

Johnny stood up and took a couple of agitated steps before turning back to point at Little Crow. "I mean you knew a hell of a lot more about Ross Lee, also known as Lee Begay, than you ever told me."

Little Crow said nothing, just frowned at Johnny.

"Pine Ridge Reservation, 1975. There was a shootout at a ranch owned by some folks named Jumping Elk." Johnny stood in front of Little Crow, reciting the history. "One dead Indian, two dead FBI agents, and one very scared thirteen-year-old Navajo kid named Lee Begay. The FBI sweated him into testifying against some of the defendants in the murder trial of the agents. Most of the defendants walked. Larry Pelham went down. Now, a guy I know told me something interesting this morning." He crossed his arms on his chest. "He said that one of the defendants acquitted was none other than James

Little Crow. Now why do you suppose that never came up in any of our earlier conversations, Jimmy?"

Little Crow stood up and paced back and forth a few times, his hands shoved deep into the pockets of his jeans. Finally he stopped and faced Johnny. "It was Lee's testimony that got me off."

"What do you mean?"

He came closer and lowered his voice. "I mean, the government put him up there on the stand expecting him to hang me, but instead, he broke down and told the truth. He said I was nowhere near those agents when they were killed."

"Who did kill Willis and Colter?" Johnny asked.

"I honestly don't know." Little Crow held his hands wide, palms up. "I've got a pretty good idea, but I really didn't see it happen. Jesus!" He turned away, his hand to his forehead.

"It was just crazy that day! It started out as just another quiet, hot day, and all of a sudden, people were yelling and bullets were flying and those two white guys were down there shooting up at the house from behind their cars. It was like . . . it was like Vietnam all over again, man!" He took a deep breath to regain some composure.

"We could see cops coming from everywhere, so we just took off. We figured they were coming to kill us, so we split. Just as fast as we could." He fell silent, staring unhappily at the floor, seeing his memories.

"All except Lee," Johnny prompted.

"Yeah, except for Lee," Little Crow continued. "He'd seen Joe get killed—shot right in the head—and he was scared spitless. He was just a kid! So we told him to give himself up, to look for the BIA police—not the FBI or one of Wilson's goon squad—but to look for the Indian cops and then go out with his hands up. He'd be okay."

"What was he doing there, anyway?" Johnny asked. "He was pretty young to be that far from home."

Little Crow sat down again, wearily, his hands lying limply on his thighs. "He was a runaway. He'd been living with some white family in Utah and wasn't too happy about it. AIM had been in the news a lot for a couple of years, with the Trail of Broken Treaties and Wounded Knee and all. So when he got into some kind of trouble in Utah, he just took off. I guess he landed in Denver and hooked up with some Navajos who were going to come up to South Dakota for a while before heading back to Arizona." He shook his head and gave a humorless laugh. "Poor little guy, just wanted to go home. Things just didn't work out."

"So when he didn't testify the way he was supposed to against you," Johnny mused, "they must have really put the spurs to him to testify against Pelham."

Little Crow nodded. "They said they'd charge him as an accessory to murder—a co-conspirator."

"I've heard that one before," Johnny nodded. "So did you keep in touch with him or anything?"

Little Crow shook his head. "After I got out of jail—after the trial—I started my nosedive to the bottom of Whiskey River. So when Lee walked in here last year, I didn't even recognize him at first. I mean, besides being all messed up from the booze, he was all grown up now. He'd been coming in for about a week when he finally says to me, real quiet like, with a strange smile, 'Jimmy, don't you know me?'" Little Crow grabbed his chest in imitation of a heart attack. "Totally freaked me out, man! I could not believe it."

"So what did he tell you?" Johnny said, sitting down again and leaning toward Little Crow. "And don't give me the patient-counselor privilege bit again, okay? We are talking about a murder that could happen any day now. I did some research. The privilege doesn't hold under these circumstances."

Little Crow looked miserable. "I know. I know." He bit his lip. "I don't know what I can tell you that would help."

"Anything," Johnny urged. "Char thought he'd married a white girl. Do you know her name?"

Little Crow snapped his fingers. "Angela! Her name was Angela. She was from a Mormon family, too. I remember now. They wanted to name her after the angel Moroni or something. Lee laughed about it and said, 'Lucky for her, her parents hit on Angela instead of Morona or something.'"

Johnny had his pen and notepad out. "Were they separated, divorced, any idea?"

Little Crow leaned forward, elbows on his knees, head in hand, concentrating. "I think just separated. I don't think they were divorced. In fact, I kind of had the impression he still saw her quite a bit."

"Where was this? Where did they live?"

"Salt Lake City." Little Crow nodded. "He was with that white family in Provo. She might have been from there too, but he talked about Salt Lake like he'd lived there more recently."

"Can you think of anything else, Jimmy?"

The counselor shrugged apologetically. "I can't think of anything that would be useful."

"How about his boozing? Did he recover?"

He shook his head. "We never recover. We spend the rest of our lives recovering. But Lee dried out and seemed pretty determined about staying sober."

"And his higher power?"

Little Crow frowned. "I don't know what to tell you. I don't know if I saw anything really spiritual happening with him. But it's like he made a decision about something. Something made sense to him and he didn't feel like he needed the sauce."

"What made sense? I don't understand?"

"I don't either, Johnny. But after a while he'd come to the meetings and—he never did talk much—but when it was his turn, I'd ask him how he was doing. He'd give this little smile. 'Atonement,' he'd say, kind of nod, and that was it."

"Atonement?"

"Yeah, 'atonement.' I have no idea what he was talking about." Little Crow shrugged.

Johnny looked over his notes and shook his head. "You're sure there's nothing else you can think of?"

"Not a thing," Little Crow closed his eyes. "He gave me back my life." Opening his eyes, he looked pleadingly at Johnny. "Can you understand what it's like to be looking at life in prison? Lee Begay told the truth and he gave me back my life. If there's any way you can stop him and help him, please do it, John. He wasn't always a monster. At one time he was just a scared kid."

⌄⌃⌄

DiRosa parked the rental car at the curb and he and Johnny climbed out. The sky was leaden and threatening snow. Pulling their collars tighter against the cold, they stood on the sidewalk in front of the gray apartment building. The complex looked like several others in the neighborhood near the industrial side of Salt Lake City.

"So how do you want to play this, Hart?" DiRosa asked. "Good cop, bad cop?"

Johnny shook his head. "She may not feel all that good about the FBI, particularly if Lee told her anything about his past experiences with you folks." He chewed his lip as he thought. "Why don't you be from CBI instead, and we're looking for Lee because he may have information on Sixkiller."

DiRosa nodded. "Sounds like a plan. You lead or me?"

Johnny shrugged. "Why don't we just see who she smiles at first."

There was an iron fence around the building, but it didn't appear to have deterred any graffiti artists. A security intercom near the front door was now just a tangle of wires dangling from an open box. Entering through the unlocked front door, they walked down the dim hallway to the last door on the left. They could hear the muffled din of a television set behind each of the half-dozen closed doors they passed.

Johnny knocked on the door of apartment 17. It was cold in the hall and they could see their breath as they stood waiting. He was about to knock again when the door opened. A small, thin blonde woman in a motorized wheelchair studied the two men through thick glasses before smiling at Johnny.

Johnny touched the brim of his hat. "Angela Lee?"

"I'm Angela Lee," she acknowledged, pronouncing each syllable deliberately.

"I'm Deputy John Hart, Mrs. Lee." He opened his jacket enough to give the woman a glimpse of the badge he had pinned to his shirt a few minutes earlier on the way from the airport. "This is Agent DiRosa of the Colorado Bureau of Investigation." DiRosa nodded pleasantly without offering any credentials. "Could we ask you a few questions regarding an investigation we're involved in?"

"Me? I never leave my apartment. I don't know how I could be any help. But come in," she nodded. Her wheelchair whined as she turned and led the way to the small but tidy living room. When DiRosa and Johnny were seated on the lumpy couch, she said, "I will try to answer your questions. If you have trouble understanding me, just tell me. I have MS." Angela smiled and nodded.

Johnny smiled. "You sound just fine, ma'am." He took his pen and notepad from his pocket. "Actually, we were hoping to be able to talk to your husband." Casually, he added, "Is he around?"

"Lee?" Angela sounded surprised. Shaking her head, she said, "He doesn't spend much time here. He's a truck driver and spends most of his time on the road. Besides, we're not really married anymore." She looked embarrassed.

"Oh, I'm sorry," Johnny said.

"You see," she lowered her voice conspiratorially, "he was making too much money for me to qualify for services, but not enough so that we could afford to pay for them ourselves. So we got a divorce." She frowned at Johnny. "You're from Colorado, so you won't tell anybody here in Utah, will you?"

"Not me," Johnny assured her. "How about you, Joe?"

"My lips are sealed," DiRosa smiled.

Angela nodded, satisfied. "Why did you want to talk to Lee . . . I mean, Ross?"

"You've heard about Charles Sixkiller, the guy they say has been killing all those women?" Johnny asked.

"Oh," she grew wide-eyed. "Isn't that so terrible!"

"Well, we think your husband—Ross—may be able to help us. It seems he may have known Sixkiller in Denver last winter."

"Oh, my Lord!" she opened her mouth, astonished. "He never told me."

"When was the last time you spoke to Lee?" Johnny asked.

"He called me last Sunday." She smiled affectionately. "He calls me every Sunday, wherever he is."

"I guess he travels around a lot," Johnny noted, hoping to prompt more information.

"Oh, yes," she nodded. "He's worked all over the country." She pressed the control of her wheelchair and rolled to a bookshelf beside the small television. "He brings me things from all the places he's been." With difficulty, she picked up a small rock mounted on a polished wooden base. "This is real Black Hills gold. Lee said the Black Hills are just beautiful." She looked wistful. "I've never been there."

DiRosa stood up and walked to the bookshelf as well. "You've got quite a collection of things here, don't you Mrs. Lee?"

Proudly, she pointed out other souvenirs. "This little pot is from Silver City, New Mexico. It's like the ones they found in the cliff dwellings near there, Lee said. And this little doll is an Apache mountain spirit dancer. He brought me that from Safford, Arizona." She carefully touched each of the objects she pointed out. "That postcard is from Fort Sumner, New Mexico, where Billy the Kid got shot."

Johnny ran his hand over postcards from the Alamo and Amarillo. "And look at these," Angela said, picking up a pair of miniature beaded moccasins. "He just brought me these from Oklahoma. Aren't they cute? Lee said that they're Cheyenne."

Softly, Johnny said, "Your husband is very good to you, isn't he?"

Angela smiled happily. "Oh, yes. I just wish we could be together more. It used to be, when we were younger, that I could travel with him. He bought one of those trucks you can sleep in, you know, so that we both could go. But," with shaking hands, she pointed to her own body, "my MS got worse. And now I can't go anywhere. So he tries to bring everywhere he's been to me." Her eyes misted slightly behind the thick lenses of her glasses. Brightening, she said, "Oh, wait." Purposefully, she pushed the switch and her wheelchair hummed into the bedroom.

Without saying a word, DiRosa raised his eyebrows and Johnny simply nodded in reply.

In a moment, Angela rolled back into the room. "Lee brings me these, too." With difficulty she opened the lid on a wooden jewelry box that was resting in her lap. "Before my hands got so twisted, I used to love to wear rings and bracelets. I can't now, but he still brings me these presents. Aren't they beautiful?"

DiRosa and Johnny dutifully admired the jewelry.

"I've been talking too much, haven't I?" Angela asked, looking down in embarrassment. "I don't get to see many people—just Lee and the visiting nurse. I thought it was her, when you knocked."

"You don't have any family nearby?" Johnny asked.

She shook her head sadly. "They're all down in Provo. But they won't see me anymore since I married Lee."

"That's a shame," Johnny said, and meant it. "One more question, Mrs. Lee. Do you know where your husband is now? We'd still like to talk to him."

"He called me from Pueblo in Colorado last Sunday. He was working for a livestock company, shipping cattle now, I think." She sighed. "I wish he weren't so far away all the time. But," she smiled bravely, "like they say, 'If wishes were horses, beggars would ride.'" She paused and added. "I used to ride horses when I was a little girl."

"Well, we sure thank you for your time, Mrs. Lee." Johnny stood up, putting his note pad back in his pocket. "Oh, has your husband sent you anymore postcards lately?"

Angela nodded. "This one came just yesterday." She pointed to a postcard propped up on the bookshelf. Even from across the room, Johnny recognized the picture of Bent's Old Fort, in La Junta, Colorado.

Back in the car, DiRosa gripped the steering wheel tightly and took a deep breath. "He's the one, all right." He shook his head. "That poor lady. What in the world could have flipped a devoted husband into a serial killer?"

"I don't know," Johnny said. "But we've got to move fast. Not only is the anniversary of the Sand Creek Massacre coming up next week, but Angela is bound to tell Lee that we were here."

"Did you see those rings?" DiRosa asked, starting the car. "There was a sorority ring in there that I'll just bet came from that dead college girl in Texas." Pulling away from the curb, he added, "Now I guess we know why he cuts the victims' hands off."

Johnny just nodded grimly. Turning toward DiRosa, he said, "You know it's your move now, Joe, don't you? I mean, you're going to have to go over Sutton's head in order to get a tap on Angela's phone. And then a search warrant for those jewelry items and a serious search through employees of livestock haulers in Pueblo."

DiRosa didn't answer immediately. He frowned more deeply as he drove. It wasn't until they had pulled off onto the airport exit ramp that he finally said, more to himself than to Johnny, "Yeah, I know what I have to do."

ᴧᴧᴧ

Barbara stood in the gray-green concrete hallway of the jail, waiting for permission to enter the interview room with Sixkiller. The door to the sheriff's department administrative offices opened, and Sheriff Tom Franklin walked into the hall.

"Well, well, well," he drawled, pushing his hat back on his head. "If it isn't Assistant District Attorney Gutierrez. So you've come to visit our famous prisoner, Injun Charlie, have you?"

Barbara sighed and leaned a shoulder wearily against the hard wall. "Hello, Tom. You look very pleased with yourself."

"And why not?" he asked grinning. He came to a stop, standing uncomfortably close to Barbara. "I'd say reelection is a pretty sure thing for the sheriff who captured the most wanted man in six states."

The interview room door swung open and a deputy stepped out. Nodding to the sheriff, he said, "You can come in now, Mrs. Hart."

"Thank you, Jerry," Barbara said, starting forward.

"Now, hold on, Missy!" Franklin said. "I'm gonna have to insist that my deputy be present with you during your visit."

"Why?" Barbara asked, annoyed. "Char's own attorney said it was all right for me to see him. And you've got a camera and a microphone in the room to monitor everything."

"This man's a vicious killer," Franklin said. "So far he's only killed white women, but we can't be too careful. It's almost Thanksgiving.

He may have developed a taste for dark meat, too." Franklin guffawed loudly.

Jerry, the deputy, looked away, embarrassed.

Barbara gave the sheriff a withering look of disgust. "Thank you, Tom. You've just settled an old argument Johnny and I used to have. It turns out I was right all along. You really are a world-class jerk." With that, she walked into the interview room, slamming the door shut behind her.

Jerry looked at the closed door. Then, with eyebrows arched in inquiry, he looked at the sheriff.

"Ah!" Franklin waved his hand dismissively. "Just wait there. If she screams, take your time going in." He then turned and walked back down the hallway.

The room was small and very quiet. The buzzing of the fluorescent light sounded unnaturally loud.

"Hello, Barbara. Excuse me if I don't stand up."

Char was seated on the other side of a small metal table. The table and the chair were bolted to the floor. There were chains on Char's wrists and ankles, which were attached to a thicker chain at his waist. That chain was then secured to the chair by a padlock.

"Hello, Char," Barbara answered softly, moving to the wooden chair on her side of the table. "I won't say it's nice to see you—not like this. But how are you?"

Char gave a weak flicker of a smile. "Oh, I've been better." He took a deep, shuddering breath, forcing a brighter expression. "I haven't seen you in a long time. You're looking well."

"Thanks. I guess it's been seven or eight years since you came by the house." Barbara found that she was embarrassed to be there, seeing him chained like an animal. She felt as if she shouldn't be looking at him in that condition, but she finally made herself concentrate on his eyes. "I'm so sorry, Char. I believe you're innocent. I really do."

"Thanks," Char nodded, lowering his head. "Is Johnny having any luck?" he asked flatly.

"Well, yes, kind of," she said. "You know, Char, they're listening to us." She pointed at the camera, high up in the corner of the room. "I'm not your attorney, so they have a right to tape us. Keep that in mind when you're talking."

Char just shrugged. "Doesn't matter. The more people that hear me, the better."

"Okay," Barbara nodded. "Johnny called me a little while ago. He's on his way back from Denver. He's managed to convince an FBI agent that you're innocent and he thinks that Ross Lee is working as a trucker in Pueblo right now. He sounded pretty sure that the official investigation will finally get going on the right track." She frowned. "Did you know that Ross Lee's real name was Lee Begay?"

Char shook his head, his brow wrinkled with concern. "No, I didn't know that. He's in Pueblo, you say?" His chains rattled as he moved his arms in agitation.

Barbara studied her hands. "Sandy asked me to find out why you won't see her."

Char exhaled wearily like a tire losing air. "She should just forget about me. No offense to Johnny, but I don't know that he's right. I'm not so sure the FBI is going to admit it's been wrong and just dust me off and turn me loose. I may be going down for some jail time just so they can save face." He shook his head. "Sandy's wasted enough time on losers. She needs to forget about me and get on with her life. I can't help her." He lowered his head again, repeating in a low voice, "I can't help her."

Barbara drummed her fingers on the table in frustration. "I've learned a few things about you in the last few months, Char. What you've been through." She shook her head. "Aren't you sick and tired of them? I know I am."

Char lifted his head. Frowning, he asked, "What are you talking about?"

Barbara stood up and walked a couple of steps away from the table, her fingers combed into her hair. "I'm talking about white people, Char. All my life—all your life, too—it's just one battle after another as they try to take everything—dignity, pride, language, culture, you name it. Tell me the truth, Char. Deep down, don't you just hate them?"

Char looked intently at Barbara for a long time before answering. "No, Barb. I get angry. I get sad and frustrated, but I don't hate them. They don't do it because they're white, they do it because they're human."

"But just look around, Char. It's their world. They call all the shots. Life is hard enough. Why do they have to lay all this extra, racist crap on us?" With trembling lips, she sat down again, hunched forward, her hands clutched in her lap.

Char leaned forward as if to confide in her. "You know, when I first went to Vietnam, I hated everybody. I hated whites for what they'd done to Indians. I hated Indians for letting them do it. I hated the army for getting my brother killed. I hated the Vietnamese because it was their country where he died. And I hated myself for letting it happen. I was just consumed with hate. So I killed." His voice grew quiet and intense. "I was good at it too, and, I have to admit, I almost enjoyed it at first.

"But, in early 1975, right before South Vietnam fell, I was hiding out from a Viet Cong patrol in a Buddhist monastery. One of the old monks made the comment that the destruction of Vietnam was karma—sort of like payback—for past sins. I asked him what he meant. He told me that there was another civilization—Indrapura, he called it—in Vietnam before the Vietnamese moved down from the north. It was an ancient culture that had been there for centuries.

Then, in the fifteenth century, even before Columbus took off from Spain, the Vietnamese invaded and completely annihilated the Champa, the people of Indrapura. And now, he said, the Vietnamese would be destroyed to atone for that sin."

He leaned back in the chair. "That just blew my mind. All along, I guess I thought the world was a wonderful, peaceful place until the whites came along. And there I was, in Vietnam, supposedly the latest example of white racist imperialism, and this monk was telling me the Vietnamese were doing the same thing before Columbus even set foot in the Americas.

"When I was trying to get out of Vietnam and over to Thailand, I had a lot of time to think about it. I realized that racism and war, hatred and conquest . . . it's wrong, it's evil, it's sin, I guess you'd call it, but it's also human. It's the human race that's the problem, not the white race."

He smiled. "I suppose if we were the majority, we'd be doing the same thing to them.

"Anyway, when I got back to the States, I decided I had a lot of atoning to do myself. I killed a lot of people, Barb. Not battlefield stuff, but up close and personal, like a hit man." He struggled with a strong emotion before continuing. "So I spent years trying to protect people, defend them, keep them from harm. And I suppose I did a little good, here and there. But it never gave life to a single one of those people I killed so, really, the scales never did balance out. I know that. Their faces would still come to me in my dreams. Maybe that's why I let myself slide more and more into drinking. Finally, I slipped and fell, and I couldn't pick myself up. I was just another drunken Indian who couldn't help himself, let alone anyone else."

He lifted his arms as far as his chains would allow. "It's not just booze. I think our own human nature is like these chains. It binds us and weighs us down." He shook his head. "But I don't think we humans can ever do justice. We're all just broken in too many places."

"So you think you're here, in chains, as some kind of karmic retribution for the people you killed in Vietnam?" Barbara asked.

Char shrugged. "Maybe. I don't know. I guess even my own death wouldn't bring those others back to life. If only life were like a movie, and you could run it backward to before I went to war, the dead would get up out of their graves, and I'd have stayed in jail at Leavenworth rather than go to Vietnam."

Barbara shook her head. "That doesn't mean they'd still be alive, Char. Maybe it just means someone else would have killed them. You'd have to roll that film all the way back to Adam and Eve to get it right."

There was a knock on the metal door. "Just a couple more minutes, Mrs. Hart." The heavy door muffled Jerry's voice.

"All right," Barbara called back. "What do you want me to tell Sandy, Char? She's in love with you, you know."

Char closed his eyes. "She's good people, Barbara, she really is. Tell her I'm praying for her. And if she's going to remember me at all, let it be when she prays. But, more important," he leaned forward, his features tight and intense, "tell her to leave the ranch right now. Go to Denver, go to Albuquerque, go someplace away from there, right away. Lee is going to try to kill her. If he waits for the actual date of the Sand Creek Massacre, he's going after her in three days. But he may not wait, and there's nobody there to protect her as long as the FBI still thinks I'm the killer."

"Johnny knows that, Char," Barbara assured him. "He told me he was heading straight back to the ranch and would stay there."

Char shook his head. "Johnny's a good man, but he's not a killer. Lee is. He's got the killer instinct and Johnny doesn't, which means that Lee has the advantage."

"But I think they're going to start looking for Lee now, Char. You'll be out of here pretty soon," Barbara said.

The door clicked and swung open. "It's time now, ma'am," Jerry said.

"Thanks for coming to see me, Barb," Char said.

She smiled. "I never got a chance to thank you for saving Johnny's life last year in Arizona."

"That's what friends are for," Char shrugged. "Johnny still loves you very much, you know."

"I know," Barbara said quietly. "And I still love him. I just couldn't live with him."

Jerry cleared his throat.

"You and Johnny have known each other for a long time, Barb," Char continued. "What is it, twenty—twenty-five years or more? You know, you can never find new old friends."

"It really is time, Mrs. Hart," Jerry repeated.

Impulsively, Barbara leaned across the table and kissed Char on the cheek. "Take care, Char." There were tears in her eyes as she turned toward the door.

"Barb," Char called. "Tell Johnny to hurry. They're transferring me to the maximum security prison in Florence the day after tomorrow."

CHAPTER

"We need to talk, Adam."

Special Agent Sutton frowned. Very few people felt familiar enough to address him by his first name. He liked it that way. "Sure, Joey, come on in." He pointed at the chair across his desk.

DiRosa closed the office door before sitting. "I've been doing some investigating on my own and I've discovered some things that I think you, in particular, will find interesting."

"Oh?" Sutton pushed his chair away from his desk and leaned back. "I'm listening." Resting his elbows on the arms of his chair, he laced his fingers together and waited.

DiRosa shifted slightly in his chair. "Ross Lee," he began. "Turns out he's not a figment of Deputy Hart's imagination. In fact, he's a truck driver with a disabled ex-wife in Salt Lake City. And, sweet guy that he is, he sends his wife postcards from all the place's he's been."

He wrinkled his brow in seriousness and waggled his finger pedantically. "Coincidentally, those postcards come from the same places where bodies have been found in the Sixkiller investigation and they're postmarked around the same time that the murders occurred. Ross Lee is a Navajo Indian, just like Hart said, and it seems he kind of looks like Sixkiller. I believe I mentioned he's a truck driver? Well, a witness saw an Indian trucker hosing out the inside of his truck the day after, and about ten miles from where that waitress's body was found in Oklahoma."

DiRosa appeared to be enjoying himself. "Now, all the victims were missing their hands, you'll recall. That struck us as kind of odd. We thought the killer was just trying to make identification harder. Well, I went through some of the statements of the friends and relatives of the victims when they were trying to help us identify the bodies. On all the victims, there should have been rings or bracelets, according to the statements. But we never found any. I'll be darned if old Ross Lee hasn't been sending the little woman back home rings and bracelets. Even a sorority ring, of all things." DiRosa paused to look at Sutton. "Am I boring you?"

"Not at all," Sutton said in a bored tone. "I'm breathless with interest."

DiRosa smiled. "That's good, because now we get to the really interesting part. It seems that Ross Lee is not his real name. He's actually named Lee Begay. And, I'll be darned, if he's not the same Lee Begay that was a teenaged prosecution witness in the Willis and Colter murder trial back in the seventies. You remember that, now, don't you, Adam? The same Lee Begay who perjured himself on the stand and just happened to be in the protective custody of a certain FBI agent named Adam Sutton." DiRosa grinned broadly. "Ain't life a bitch?"

Sutton didn't respond at first. He sighed, sat up, and rolled his chair up to the desk again. "So why are you telling me this? If you think you've got proof that I'm covering up, why not just blow the whistle? Go to the media, go over my head, be a hero!"

"Oh, I thought about it," DiRosa responded. "But maybe it's my warm-hearted Mediterranean nature. You know, here you are a couple of years from retirement after a long and distinguished career. A good agent. Got the job done! Why should I shoot down your pension because of a couple of mistakes in the past?" He lifted his hands as if seeking an answer to his rhetorical question.

"On the other hand," he continued. "I know what happens to whistleblowers. I mean, come on, I came up through the NYPD! We're talking about Code Blue here! Whistleblowers are heroes to the public for about two days, but to their fellow cops, they're roadkill for life. I don't suppose the Bureau's any different. A whistleblower's career is going nowhere."

Sutton nodded. "And you want to go somewhere, am I right?"

"You are so right," DiRosa agreed, smiling affably.

"So what do you suggest?" Sutton asked.

"I'm glad you asked," DiRosa said, leaning forward. "I know you gave me kind of a poor performance report when you took me off the Sixkiller investigation. It would be nice if that could be lost from my file, you know what I mean? I'd like to be back on the investigation and get my fair share of credit for breaking the case—not a lot, it's your investigation, after all. But, when it's over, I'd like a commendation and a recommendation for reassignment out of here. Someplace back in civilization like San Francisco or Miami, maybe even Washington if you really want to show your gratitude."

"And in return for all this, what do I get?" Sutton asked.

"You get my silence and my help in making sure the investigation is confined to these murders, with no mention of Willis and Colter. And you get to retire with honors."

Sutton was quiet for a long time. "I misjudged you, Joey. Here I thought you were a romantic little goody two shoes." He shook his head. "Just for the record, I did what I did because my friend, Ron Willis, was murdered and I wanted some justice. It wasn't a career move. The defense had all these grandstanding, radical lawyers swinging from the courthouse chandeliers and everybody seemed to lose sight of the fact that two good men were dead for just doing their jobs. The kid, Begay, turned out to be too unstable, that's all."

"So do we have a deal?" DiRosa pressed.

Sutton sighed. "Yeah, we have a deal. Give me what you have on Lee's whereabouts. I'll get somebody on it right away."

"What about Sixkiller?" DiRosa asked.

"Well, what about him?" Sutton replied. "There is a past connection between Sixkiller and Begay. We don't know for a fact that Sixkiller isn't a partner in these murders."

DiRosa nodded. "Fair enough." He stood to leave. "Do you want local sheriff's department people to stake out the Cross ranch, in case we don't locate Begay?"

Sutton didn't answer right away. "No. The local yahoos might be too high profile and scare off Begay. We want to draw him in and arrest him, get this thing over with. Why don't you go out there yourself. That way you can be in on the arrest and really put a spit shine on that medal you want."

DiRosa grinned. "Good thinking. Thanks."

"Oh, Joey," Sutton asked, as an afterthought. "Who else knows about my connection to Begay?"

"Just that cowboy, Hart, and his ex-wife," DiRosa replied. "Hart's a joke. Nobody would take him seriously. And the ex-wife?" He smiled. "I have a little influence there. She's a smart lady who I think is ready to go places herself. Don't worry."

"Oh, I never worry," Sutton said. "I just get the job done."

⋏⋏⋏

"Damn, it's cold today!" Deputy Bob Evans stomped his feet as he waited beside the back door of the jail. Fifty feet away, beyond the yellow police tape and painted wooden barriers, the demonstrators were gathering again as they had every day since Char was arrested. "These jokers are the reason we have to transfer Sixkiller," Bob said to the La Junta City Policeman who stood beside him. "Too much of a security risk for our little old county jail. Now I've got to drive a couple of hours when it sure as hell looks like it's getting ready to snow."

Someone started to beat on the drum and a single Indian voice rose in song among the demonstrators. Because of the drum, Bob didn't hear the rap on the metal door warning him that the prisoner was exiting. He was nearly struck as the door swung open. Char, shuffling in chains, was hurried toward the waiting police car, an armed federal marshal at his elbow. As soon as he appeared, most of the demonstrators began to chant "Free-Six-Killer! Free-Six-Killer!" while other sticks and voices joined the drum and singers. A half-dozen television crews moved as one, like a flock of sheep, to get a better angle on the prisoner.

Bob hurried to the patrol car and opened the rear door. The marshal shoved Char into the back seat. Slamming the door, he hurried around to the front passenger door and jumped inside. Bob slid behind the wheel and fastened his seat belt.

Grim faced, his eyes scanning the crowd, the marshal ordered, "Let's roll! There might be snipers."

That was incentive enough for Bob. Stomping on the accelerator, the car fishtailed slightly as it squealed away, bounced into the street, and sped toward the highway.

"Damn weather," the marshal complained. "Supposed to be a blizzard coming in. They grounded all small aircraft. Otherwise we'd just use a chopper and fly this sucker to Florence."

Once they were beyond Rocky Ford and rolling at seventy miles an hour on open road, both the marshal and Bob relaxed. Smiling for the first time, the marshal offered his hand. "I'm Tony Rojas."

"Bob Evans." He shook the marshal's hand, glancing away from the road to nod a greeting, before again tightly gripping the wheel with both hands. He looked in the rear view mirror at Char's tired, drawn face. Char looked absently through the side window, not aware that Bob was studying him.

"Not much traffic out today," Rojas noted.

"Nope," Bob agreed. "They all heard the weatherman talking about that norther coming down on us. Folks out here have learned to respect Mother Nature. More than a few folks have frozen to death driving in a blizzard."

"You sound worried," Rojas smiled.

"Some," Bob nodded, seriously.

They drove for several minutes in silence. The sky continued to darken and a few small flakes of snow skidded off the windshield. Bob turned his headlights on.

"Sure is a lot of nothing out here," Rojas said, looking around. "Miles and miles of nothing but miles and miles." He shook his head.

"We like it," Bob said agreeably, as if accepting a compliment.

Looking at his watch, Rojas said, "It's been about half an hour. You'd better radio in."

Bob picked up the microphone. "Unit Five to base, come in."

"This is base," the dispatcher's voice crackled. "What's your twenty, Unit Five?"

"We're about two, three miles west of Fowler now. Over."

"Any problems, Bob?"

"Not so far." Bob studied the sky. "Say, have you heard any weather reports lately? It's starting to look pretty bad off to the north. Over."

"Stand by, Unit Five." There was a pause. "Base to Unit Five. Radio says that blizzard is moving pretty fast in our direction. You might want to stomp it some and see if you can't get in the shelter of the mountains as quick as you can."

"That's a ten-four," Bob said, immediately pressing harder on the accelerator. "Unit Five, out."

"You guys really take this weather thing pretty seriously, don't you," the marshal said.

"Yes, sir, we do," Bob agreed, concentrating on the road, his speedometer topping eighty.

There was a noise from the back seat. Bob could see Char bent forward, his head down, loose hair streaming forward to cover his face.

"Did you say something?" Rojas turned in his seat to look back at Sixkiller through the wire screen.

"I'm sick," came Char's muffled voice. His head lolled and his face looked slack-jawed.

"Oh, hell!" Rojas said. "You'd better pull over."

"We've got to get off this open country, pronto," Bob protested. Gagging sounds were coming from the back seat.

Rojas frowned. "Look, unless you want him to launch all over the back of your head, you'd better pull over," he snapped.

Bob grumbled. "Joe's damn cooking! It's not the first time he's poisoned a prisoner." Slowing down, he pulled onto the gravel shoulder.

Rojas got out. Pulling his gun from its holster, he opened the rear passenger door, signaling with the gun barrel for Char to get out. "All right, if you're going to toss breakfast, you've got the whole state of Colorado to do it in. It doesn't have to be in the back seat."

Char struggled with his chains to shift along the bench seat. "Uh, oh," he said, starting to retch and lean forward toward the floor of the car.

"No, man!" Rojas exclaimed. "Give me a break!" Leaning into the car, he grabbed the back of Char's jacket with his free hand. "Get out of there!"

When the marshal's head was within a foot of the prisoner's, Char quickly and forcefully snapped his head up. He caught Rojas in the nose, driving it up between his eyes. As blood gushed from the broken nose, the eyes became glassy. With a slight grunt, Rojas melted backward out of the car and onto his back on the roadside pebbles.

Bob heard the thud of the marshal's body falling. As he turned to look at the back seat, he found himself staring into the barrel of a .44 caliber Smith and Wesson pistol that had been issued to Marshall Tony Rojas but was now in Charles Sixkiller's manacled hands.

Leaning in at the open front passenger door, Char said, "Now, Bob, I want you to relax and not even think about being a hero. I can't go to Florence with you today. I've got some business to attend to. I want you to unstrap your weapon and use just two fingers to pull it, real slowly, out of your holster. That's it. Just lay it real easy on the floor over here."

Wide eyed, Bob complied. "What happened to the marshal?" he croaked through a throat as dry as sand.

"Well," Char nudged Rojas's body with the toe of his boot, "he appears to be breathing, so I'd guess he's just out cold. He'll come to pretty soon, but he'll have a whopper of a headache, two black eyes, and a new profile, I'm afraid." He pointed the gun at Bob's pocket. "Now, fish out the keys to this jewelry and unlock it."

Bob, again, quickly did as he was told. "What are you going to do with me?" he whispered.

"Out of the car," Char ordered. As Bob got slowly from the driver's side, Char leveled the pistol across the roof of the vehicle. "Come on around and get the rest of these chains off."

More snow was falling, stinging against the men's faces.

When Char was completely unrestrained, he said, "I'm going to borrow your car, Bob."

"But we'll freeze!" Bob protested.

"No." Char pointed back the way they had come. "I saw an abandoned store back there about a quarter of a mile. You and the marshal should be all right in there. Unless, of course, you want to wait and try to flag down a car. But I haven't seen another car in a long time. If I were you, I'd get in out of this weather."

Char walked around the car to the driver's side. "I'm real sorry about this, Bob. Tell Tony, there, I'm sorry, too." On the ground, Rojas groaned and stirred slightly.

Char climbed in and slammed the door. Through the open passenger door, he called, "Come here, Bob."

Bob stepped over to the car and looked in.

"Here's a book of matches I found in the seat," Char said, proffering the matches with "Capri" printed on the cover. "These should help you stay warm. Now, close the door on your way out."

"Thanks," Bob said, indicating the matches.

As soon as the door was closed, the patrol car screeched away in a sharp U-turn. There was a sound like ripping paper as it sped away toward the east.

"Why do these things always happen to me?" Bob muttered as he buttoned his jacket and turned up the collar. Bending over Rojas, he said, "I gotta find another line of work."

⋀⋀⋀

Johnny stood at the window studying the gray sky, a cup of coffee in one hand.

"Morning, Johnny," Sandy said as she came into the kitchen. "You're up early."

"I made coffee." He pointed toward the pot. "It sure looks like it's gonna snow out there."

"What's the forecast say?" Sandy asked, walking to the radio atop the refrigerator. She clicked it on, but nothing happened. "Huh!"

Opening the refrigerator, she saw that the light did not come on. "Power's off. Must be the wind from that storm that's coming. It happens all the time in the winter out here."

Johnny frowned. "I didn't hear all that much wind last night."

"Well, top of the morning to you both," DiRosa said cheerfully as he came into the kitchen. "So what's for breakfast? This country life really gives you an appetite, doesn't it?"

"Morning, Joe," Sandy smiled. "I'll get some bacon and pancakes going pretty quick. There's coffee."

When he'd poured himself a cup, DiRosa came to stand beside Johnny at the window. In a low voice, he said, "Well, Hart, if our theory is right, this is the day Lee will make his play." He sipped his coffee.

Johnny nodded. "The electricity's off. Sandy thinks it's this storm coming in, but I'll check it out in a couple of minutes. I don't want to spook her."

"You two can quit whispering," Sandy said above the sizzle of bacon grease. "I know what day this is. With all of us here, though, what can he do? Right?"

"You're right," Johnny smiled reassuringly as he turned around and leaned against the counter. "It's part of the job, though. We get paid to worry about things. Well, I used to get paid for it. Now, it's just a bad habit."

"Keep an eye on my bacon," Sandy directed. "I'm going to see if Grandpa's awake yet."

After she left, Johnny shook his head. "You know, I really don't like this, Joe. We should have taken her out of here."

"You can't set a trap without bait," DiRosa shrugged. "So how do you think Begay is going to approach it? Just walk up to the front door and ask if Sandy can come out and play?"

"I kind of doubt that," Johnny said. "He may assume we don't know he's coming and just plan to make a move on her at some point as she goes about her regular chores. The three of us often go off in different directions."

"Johnny!" Sandy screamed from down the hall.

DiRosa and Johnny nearly collided as they both rushed through the door. Johnny was quicker though, and arrived at the door to Mr. Cross's bedroom first. "What is it?" he asked, entering.

"He's not breathing," Sandy gasped, barely breathing herself.

The old man lay very still, his eyes closed. Johnny laid his ear against the old man's chest. "It's his heart. It's beating but it's real weak."

"I know CPR," DiRosa announced, stepping up to the bed.

The two men quickly flung back the blankets and sheet. As DiRosa began the process, Johnny said to Sandy, "Call the Sheriff's Department and tell them to send a car and an ambulance."

Sandy rushed down the hallway to the phone in the kitchen. In a moment, though, she was back, her face pinched with anxiety. "The phone's out, too."

"He's breathing," DiRosa announced straightening up.

"Shoot!" Johnny fretted. "Look, I'm gonna have to take Mr. Cross in to the hospital. We can't send Sandy alone. Begay might catch her out on the road. Maybe she should come with me. It'd be safer."

"No," DiRosa protested. "This is our best chance to grab Begay. If he sees her leaving and thinks he's lost his shot at her, who knows where he'll disappear to. This is an FBI operation now, Hart, so it's my call."

"It's all right, Johnny," Sandy patted his arm. "Joe's here and I've got my varmint rifle in the bedroom. You've got to get Grandpa to the hospital, though."

"I don't like it," Johnny bit his lip.

"Well, you don't have any choice," DiRosa pointed out.

"He's right," Sandy agreed.

"Damn," Johnny frowned. "Let me go start the truck."

Together, the two men carried Mr. Cross to the truck where they laid him on the seat, his head resting on Johnny's right leg. "Now keep your eyes open, you hear?" he cautioned them both. "I'll be back as quick as I can."

"Yes, Daddy," DiRosa mocked. "Get moving, cowboy. We know what we're doing."

Sandy merely waved, her face clouded with worry, as Johnny put the truck in gear and drove away. After he had cleared the ridge, she pulled her jacket tighter, turned and headed back to the house. DiRosa followed.

"So," DiRosa said, cheerily, "what would be the usual routine for a home on the range?"

"Well," Sandy said, still distracted, "I guess we'd better eat breakfast. Usually, I'd be out riding to make sure the cattle were okay before a big storm. Maybe hauling some bales of hay out for them. That sort of thing. But," she took a deep breath, trying to get her thoughts off the old man struggling for life in Johnny's truck, "since we sold off the herd, that's not a problem this year. Otherwise, I guess I could do some work in the barn, mending tack, tending to the horses."

"All right," DiRosa said, carefully looking out the window. "I'd better keep out of sight, but if you go out there, stay near the entrance where I can see you."

"That'll make it a little hard to get any work done," Sandy protested.

"Humor me," DiRosa responded dryly. "You can get caught up after we nail the suspect."

They ate breakfast in near silence. Sandy barely responded to DiRosa's attempts at conversation. After the dishes were washed, she took a long time to get ready. Finally, standing at the door with her jacket on, she suggested, "Maybe we should wait until Johnny gets back before I go out."

"I'm sure Hart would be real choked up at your confidence in him," DiRosa sneered, "but I'm the one that's an FBI agent. He's your hired hand."

"I just kind of feel like a worm on a hook," she smiled feebly.

"It'll be fine. I'll be watching you the whole time. And, who knows, Begay may be a late sleeper. You'll get your work done, you'll come in, we'll have lunch, and Hart will be back." He tried to sound cheerful. "Besides, the sooner we get this guy, the sooner your boyfriend gets out of jail, right?"

Sandy just nodded. With a deep breath, she opened the door and stepped outside. The wind was picking up and it snatched at her jacket as she walked across the yard. A few flakes of snow were starting to fall.

She entered the barn and looked carefully around. All she saw, though, were the horses looking back at her from their stalls. In a short time, Sandy began to feel better, soothed by the familiarity of the work. After only fifteen minutes, though, the cold had her shivering. The wind was picking up, moaning through the cracks in the dry wooden walls and gusts of snow were sweeping into the open barn every few seconds.

Ordinarily, she'd have closed the barn door and continued her work, but this was not an ordinary day. The horses were becoming restless. Their eyes widened and their nostrils flared as they listened to the hissing sound of snow being driven against the sides of the barn.

Sandy shook her head. Stowing the tack back in the closet, she pulled the heavy barn door closed and headed across the yard to the house. The wind caught the kitchen's storm door and banged it shut behind her. It was very quiet in the house.

"Joe?" Sandy wasn't surprised that he wasn't in the kitchen. In order to see her in the barn, he'd have to be able to look out the living room window.

As the storm increased, the light in the house grew dimmer. Sandy went to the door of the living room. A tall man, long black hair flowing halfway down his back, stood looking out the window toward the barn.

Sandy's heart lurched. "Char?" she gasped, stepping forward. Abruptly, she stopped. Beside the couch, a small pool of blood spreading from beneath his body, lay DiRosa.

The man at the window turned and smiled. "Hello, Sandy," he said, in a soft, deep voice. "We've waited a long time for this, haven't we?" He lowered the barrel of his gun to point directly at her.

ᴧᴧᴧ

Johnny drove as fast as he could, his right hand resting on Mr. Cross's chest to make sure he was still breathing. Small dry flakes of snow were beginning to fly across the hood of his truck. The dry, brown grasses were bristling and waving as the wind gusted and swirled.

Coming in to Brandon, he noticed the neon "Open" sign glowing in the convenience store window. "They still got power," he muttered, jerking the wheel over and skidding into the parking lot. Leaving the engine running on the truck, he hurried to the pay phone, fishing a quarter from his pocket as he went.

"Sheriff's Department."

"Kate, this is Johnny. I've got an emergency."

"What's going on, cowboy?" Kate asked.

"I'm in Brandon. I've got Mr. Cross in the truck and he's having a heart attack. Get an ambulance rolling as quick as you can."

"I'm on it, Johnny." He silently blessed Kate. For all her teasing ways, she was a professional.

"Kate, is the sheriff there?"

"Well, yeah." She sounded surprised. "Stand by."

In a moment, a crisp, military voice came on the line. "This is Carter."

"Sheriff. I got pulled away from the Cross place. The old man's having a heart attack. The phones seem to be down, and Agent DiRosa is by himself out there with Sandy Cross. You'd better tell the agents standing by."

"What are you talking about, Hart?" Sheriff Carter sounded perplexed and annoyed. "There's no agents here. I haven't been briefed on any operation in this county. What's going on?"

That old, familiar, icy cavern began to form in Johnny's stomach. "There are no backup FBI agents there?"

"Is something happening, Hart?"

"I think the serial killer is going to try to get Sandy Cross today."

"Have you been drinking again, Hart? Sixkiller is on his way to prison in Florence today. It's all over the news."

Johnny slammed the phone down. He felt sick to his stomach. Rushing back to his truck, he checked to be sure Mr. Cross was still breathing. Should he go back to the ranch? His hand tapped nervously on the steering wheel. The neon Coors sign in the store window seemed especially bright to him. Slamming the truck into gear, he sped away heading west.

The snow was growing thicker now, forming shifting patterns as it writhed across the highway. "Come on! Come on!" he muttered, straining to search the opposite lane for the approaching ambulance. No other vehicle seemed to be on the road. Finally, after an interminable ten minutes he saw a Kiowa County Sheriff's Department patrol car coming, lights on.

Johnny flashed his lights and pulled to the side. The patrol car did a sliding U-turn, coming to a stop behind the truck.

Jumping out, Johnny yelled at the deputy climbing out of the car, "Where the hell's the ambulance, Lyle?"

"It isn't coming, Johnny," the deputy answered, hurrying forward. Pointing to the black clouds approaching from the north, he said, "This storm's already torn things up pretty bad north of here. And it's coming down on us like a freight train. The nearest ambulance is in Lamar, so the sheriff sent me to see what's going on."

Johnny grabbed Lyle by the arm and hustled him over to the passenger door of his truck. "Give me a hand here."

Together, they carried Mr. Cross to the patrol car and laid him carefully in the back seat. Lyle took a blanket from the trunk and spread it over the unconscious man.

"It's his heart, Lyle," Johnny explained. "He's in a bad way. Now you're gonna have to drive like you did in high school, and I mean fast!"

Lyle climbed into the driver's side.

"Once you're rolling," Johnny said, holding the door open, "call in and tell the sheriff I'm sober and something is going down at the Cross ranch. He needs to send as many cars as he can spare. We may have an attempted murder." He slammed the door shut. Through the closed window, he yelled, "Now I want you to hit the ground, just in the high places, you hear?"

The deputy grinned, giving Johnny a thumbs-up before spraying gravel and fishtailing off toward the west.

Johnny sprinted back to his truck. There was no traffic to interfere with the hard U-turn he made. The wind moaned through the telephone wires bouncing and swaying overhead, muffling the roar of his truck's engine.

⋀⋀⋀

Sandy was as angry as she was afraid. The combination of emotions allowed her to ignore the icy snow that stung her face and whipped her hair. She stumbled across the rough and frozen ground, her hands tied tightly behind her back.

Prodding her occasionally with the gun, the longhaired man had been talking steadily since backhanding Sandy to the floor of the living room. "You see, Sandy," he shouted over the wind, "there are some sins for which the blood of Christ is not sufficient. Only the sinner's own blood can atone for the wrong and save their soul. There has been so much injustice, so much sin, this very earth we're walking on is stained, soaked, saturated with innocent blood that cries out, like Abel's, for atonement. Can't you hear it?" His face was alight with wonder as he listened to the wind, sobbing in the barren branches of the cottonwoods. They were almost to the creek by now.

The creekbed was dry. Snow was beginning to drift along the streambed where it curved toward the east. Sandy slipped and fell to her knees on the sloping ground.

Without breaking stride, the man grabbed her by her hair and jerked her to her feet again. "Such blonde hair," he noted. "Such blonde, blonde hair." He shook his head, marveling. "It was black hair here that day. Women, children, old men, it didn't matter to the soldiers. They all wanted a trophy, a souvenir, a nice, shiny, black-haired scalp to remind them of the day they set Colorado free from the Indian plague." His eyes glowed with a strange inner light.

"These terrible people," he continued, sarcasm dripping from every word, "these people who came seeking peace, shelter from the war, whose only crime was that they wanted to live and see their children live in their own land. If they'd been white, it would've been called patriotism. But they weren't. They were redskins, Lamanites, evil incarnate." His face was nearly hidden by his windblown hair, but he didn't seem to notice. He was looking at something only he could see.

"And what is my sin?" Sandy demanded, shouting against the wind.

"Why, Sandy," he smiled gently. "Surely you know that 'All have sinned and fallen short of the glory of God.'" He nodded. "You who have fattened your cattle on the grass watered by the blood and tears of the innocent? What is your sin? You who have lusted after a man not your husband?"

"What are you talking about?"

"Oh, please, Sandy," he laughed harshly. "I'm not blind. I can see how much you want me. You should thank me. You should rejoice and be exceeding glad, that I have come, like an angel of God, that your sins may be washed away."

Smiling kindly, he leveled the rifle at Sandy. "You have every reason to love me. Today is the day of your salvation."

"Lee!"

Lee Begay turned to face the man approaching out of the swirling snow like a developing photograph coming into focus. He held a Smith and Wesson revolver.

"My brother!" Begay greeted Char, smiling delightedly. "This is wonderful! The power of this moment has set you free from the white man's bondage."

"Lee, listen to me," Char said, moving slowly until he could stand between Sandy and the killer. "This is not the way, Lee. This is not our way, brother. You don't have the right to do this." Char was within a few feet of Sandy. Quietly, he said, "Help me out Sandy! Give me some Bible stuff."

"Most of what he's saying isn't in the Bible, Char! I don't know what he's talking about!" she hissed.

"Justice must be done, Char. Those who died here require it of us. There's no other way," Begay said.

Char listened to Sandy's whisper, then repeated, "Let he who is without sin, cast the first stone, Lee. Isn't that the way, brother?"

Begay shook his head, piteously. "There is none so blind as he who will not see. Can't you see, Char? I am the Lord's anointed come to do justice throughout the land!"

"And what does the Lord require of thee," Char replied, "but to do justly and to love mercy and to walk humbly with thy God?"

"Mercy!?" Begay scoffed. "The time for mercy is passed. This is the day of judgment! The great and terrible day of the Lord!" He closed his eyes and lifted his face toward the sky, savoring both the occasion and the storm.

Char continued to hold Begay in the pistol's sights. "There's something more important than justice, Lee. There's forgiveness."

Begay's face clouded with anger. "How can you stand there, the blood of your own grandfathers and grandmothers washing about your feet and speak of forgiveness?" He raised his rifle, pointing it at Char. "Have you betrayed your own people, Char? There can be no forgiveness. Now there is only atonement."

"Then you'll have to kill me too, brother. Because I need forgiveness as much as anyone," Char said.

"This woman must be sacrificed, Char. Step aside," Begay commanded.

"I can't do that, Lee."

"Why not?"

"Because I love her."

"Then you should want to see her cleansed," Begay shook his head, perplexed at Char's lack of understanding. "There can be no forgiveness without atonement."

"Then kill me, Lee. Let my death be a substitute."

The three people stood as if frozen by the cold, screaming winds.

"You guys have got to be kidding!" From the west, Special Agent Adam Sutton came walking down the slope, an assault rifle held comfortably in both hands. "I really should just let you two shoot each other." He turned the rifle toward Begay and called to Char. "Okay, Sixkiller, come on over here and give me your gun. I'm Sutton, FBI. Come on, it's all right. The cavalry has arrived."

"I'm an Indian, Sutton. Is that supposed to make me feel better?" Char continued to stand in front of Sandy, the pistol aimed at Begay.

"Quit screwing around," Sutton barked. "I'm freezing my ass off! Get over here!"

Slowly, Char moved toward the agent. "Come on, Sandy. Stay behind me."

"Ah, Sutton." Begay's lip curled in distaste at the name. "How appropriate that you should be here on judgment day."

"So you still remember me, Lee? I'm flattered." Sutton stuck out his left hand to receive the pistol from Char. As soon as Char released the weapon, Sutton swung the barrel of his rifle over hard, striking Char against the temple.

"Char!" Sandy gasped, as he crumpled to the ground.

Begay shook his head and smiled. "You haven't changed, Sutton. I see you're still a snake."

"And you haven't changed either, Lee," Sutton replied. "You still talk too much." He squeezed the trigger.

Begay, an astonished look on his face, staggered backward three steps before toppling onto his back. He lay with his arms flung wide, his eyes open, unblinking, as the snow fell, melted, and ran down his face like cold tears.

Sandy, her hands still tied behind her back, kneeled beside Char and sobbed. The snow was blowing so thickly that visibility was down to a few feet. "What are you doing?" she screamed at Sutton.

"Taking out the garbage," he explained calmly.

He walked over to the rifle that Begay had dropped and picked it up in his gloved hands. Carefully, he put his own weapon down. Walking back to where Char lay, he cocked a bullet into the rifle's chamber. "I spend my whole life taking out this country's garbage, and then Chief Talking Bull over there and your AIM buddy Sixkiller here are going to pull the plug on my pension? I don't think so." He aimed the rifle at the unconscious Char. "This way, Begay kills Sixkiller and you, and I kill Begay. Neat, clean, and righteous. One of these guys was even nice enough to cap DiRosa for me."

"No!" Sandy screamed, falling forward to cover Char's body.

Sutton was suddenly jerked backward off his feet, the rifle clattering to the ground.

Sandy struggled to her knees again in time to see Sutton sliding up the hill, a rope tightly closed around his arms, pinning them to the sides of his body. The rope stretched in a thin line that went to the ridge twenty feet away where Feather stood, the rope secured to her saddle. She shifted and backed and shifted again to keep the rope taut.

Johnny slid down the slope toward Sandy and Char. "Is he still alive?" he asked, kneeling beside Char and checking his throat for a pulse.

"I think he's just out cold," Sandy said through a combination of tears and laughter.

"Cold is right!" Johnny said, rubbing his hands together.

"Hart! Hart, you asshole! You don't know what you're doing!" Sutton shouted. "Cut me loose! You're screwing with a federal agent, cowboy! You're in some deep shit!"

Johnny ignored him, struggling to untie the wet ropes at Sandy's wrists.

"Why didn't you just shoot him?" Sandy asked rubbing her raw wrists.

"I couldn't find my gun," Johnny explained. "I know it's in the truck someplace, but when I couldn't find it, I didn't think I ought to take the time to really look for it." Rubbing Sixkiller's hands and wrists, Johnny urged, "Come on, Char. You're too big for me to carry, hoss! Come on, wake up!"

Char's eyelids fluttered and his right arm jerked up before his face, nearly punching Johnny.

"Easy, there, partner," Johnny said. "You're about five minutes late with that reaction, I'd say. I told you we were getting old."

"Johnny! Sandy! What . . .?" Char lurched to a sitting position, and immediately regretted it as he grabbed his throbbing head.

Sutton had quit threatening and sat quietly, his arms pinned to his side, his head lowered on his chest.

Johnny untied Sandy and they both helped Char to his feet and supported him as they struggled up the hill. Carefully, Char swung into the saddle. Johnny went down the slope again and collected all the fallen weapons.

Prodding Sutton with the toe of his boot, he said, "You'd better get up on your feet and walk, G-man. It's a long way to be drug."

From the ridge, it was clear that Begay's body was cooling as the snow was settling on his legs and starting to drift against his face. At that distance, it appeared that he was melting into the ground.

"What about Lee?" Char asked.

"We'll have to come back for him after the storm," Johnny said. Quietly, he added, "I don't think he'd mind. He's in pretty good company out here."

Sandy took the halter and led Feather while Johnny followed behind the stumbling Sutton. They hadn't been gone long before the snow covered the creekbed, completely hiding Begay's body. Soon, it was as if no one had ever been there.

ᴧᴧᴧ

"Johnny, you made it." Barbara smiled as she closed the door behind him. "It's cold out there tonight," she said as Johnny hung his coat and hat on the pegs beside the door.

"Mmm. It smells good in here," he commented. "Chicken enchiladas?" he asked.

Barbara nodded. "It's Jack's birthday. So, for dinner, it's Jack's favorites."

Johnny held a gift-wrapped package awkwardly in his hands. "I didn't know what to get."

"Don't worry about it," Barbara assured him. "Last year you didn't get him anything, remember?"

He nodded. "You just had to remind me, huh?"

She smiled. "Oh, don't be nervous. Come on in. Everybody's in the kitchen."

"Hey, Cuz!" Char waved from where he stood at the counter, his arm around Sandy's shoulder.

"How's your grandpa doing?" Johnny asked.

Sandy nodded. "Not too bad. Course, he spends most of his time in bed fretting and fuming, but the doctors say he should be feeling better come spring."

"And how are you feeling, G-man?" Johnny moved over to shake DiRosa's hand. The agent sat at the kitchen table looking pale and weak, his left arm in a sling.

"It hurt my pride more than my shoulder and head," DiRosa said with a wan smile. "I can't believe I let him slip up on me like that."

"Have you heard anything about Angela Lee?" Johnny asked.

DiRosa nodded sadly. "Poor lady. She took the news hard. She's really all alone now. The social worker thinks she probably won't be able to continue with independent living much longer. She'll have to wind up in a county hospital."

"Hi, Daddy!" Gloria bounded in from the back porch, a gift-wrapped package in her hands. She hugged her father, then shook the package, a worried look on her face. "I hid it out on the porch. I hope it didn't freeze."

"What is it?" Johnny asked.

"Aftershave," she explained.

"Nah, too much alcohol, it won't freeze," he assured her. Quietly, he asked Barbara, "Is Jack shaving already?"

She laughed. "Yes, Johnny. He's seventeen now."

Johnny shook his head.

"He's coming!" Gloria called. "Everybody be quiet."

Barbara clicked the switch and silence and darkness fell together on the kitchen.

The front door opened. "Later, dude!" Jack called to his friend outside. They could hear a car honk as it pulled away.

Footsteps approached the kitchen. The light switch clicked. "Surprise!"

Jack stood, his hand still on the light switch, wide-eyed and shaken before the group of smiling faces. "Shoot!" he exclaimed.

"Happy birthday, Jack!" Gloria was the first to come forward, shoving her gift into his stomach. "It's aftershave, so you won't smell like the locker room all the time."

"Gimme a break, Gordy," Jack smiled. "Thanks."

"Happy birthday, *mijo*," Barbara hugged her son. "Chicken enchiladas, just for you." She pointed toward the oven.

"All right! Thanks, Mom."

Johnny stepped forward, more nervous than he'd ever been in the rodeo. He cleared his throat. Sticking out his hand, he said, "Happy birthday, Jack."

Everyone in the room was silent, waiting.

After a moment of hesitation, Jack shook his father's hand. "Thanks, Dad. And thanks for being here."

Johnny didn't release Jack's hand. With steady pressure, he pulled his son into his embrace, awkwardly at first, but more naturally when Jack lay his head on Johnny's shoulder.

Pulling back, Johnny said, "I used to be able to kiss the top of your head but, shoot, I can't even see it anymore, you're so tall." He handed Jack his gift. "It's a videotape. Some guy named Jordan. They tell me he plays basketball."

Everyone laughed.

As Jack greeted the other guests, Johnny stood beside Barbara. "What do you suppose made him change his mind about me?"

"Oh, I don't know that he has," Barbara said. She passed her arm through Johnny's, giving it an affectionate squeeze as she looked contentedly at her house full of friends. "Just maybe, with enough time, everybody learns to forgive."